OUR OWN KIND

OUR OWN KIND

A Novel of Small-Town America
During World War II

ANNE DE LA VERGNE WEISS

To order additional copies of this book, contact:
Xlibris Corporation
1-888-795-4274
www.Xlibris.com
Orders@Xlibris.com
23833

CONTENTS

PART ONE

PART TWO

PART THREE

PART IV

PART V

PART VI

PART VII

PART ONE

1

The Van Leuvens

Mr. and Mrs. John Alton Sanford
request the honor of your presence
at the marriage of their daughter
Genevieve Lester
to
Mr. William Otis Sloane
at
St. Andrew's Episcopal Church
at
three o'clock in the afternoon
on
Saturday, the twenty-sixth of June
One thousand nine hundred and forty-three

The Sanfords had sent out two hundred invitations, engraved by Tiffany, most of them to people in Westerveldt but a few dozen to relatives and friends as far away as California. A hundred were accompanied by smaller cards in their own separate envelopes—invitations to "A Reception immediately following the ceremony at the home of Mr. and Mrs. Benjamin Chandler Swinton III, 742 Brunswick Road." Mrs. Swinton, Genevieve, was the bride's aunt. Since she had no children of her own and was devoted to her niece and namesake, she had insisted on offering her house and garden for the reception so she could, as she said, help give the bride away.

When the sun chose to shine in a cloudless sky on the morning of the twenty-sixth, after several days of rain and despite predictions of overcast skies and afternoon thunderstorms, the guests put aside the raincoats and umbrellas they had assembled to protect their finery and interpreted the sun as an auspicious omen—"Happy the bride the sun shines on today." Many of them were being charitable, for in their hearts they considered the Sanford-Sloane union a misalliance.

Jack Sanford was vice-president of the Westerveldt National Bank. Jacqueline Sanford (everybody called the couple "the Jacks Sanford" or "the two Jacks") and her sister, Genevieve Swinton, were the daughters of a much-respected attorney whose funeral in 1939, also at St. Andrew's Episcopal Church, had been attended by the Chief Justice of the State Supreme Court. Ben Swinton owned an insurance brokerage. Genevieve, the bride, was twenty-one and had graduated from Smith in 1942, in the spring after Pearl Harbor. She had been living at home with her parents ever since, watching one young man of her acquaintance after another go off to war. Bill Sloane was a salesman at the Chevrolet dealership; his father was a carpenter.

No one, in conscience, blamed Bill. He was good-looking, personable, mild and unassuming, not pushy or on the make, friendly, cheerful, and courteous. Katherine Osterhoudt said it should be a relief to buy a car from someone like Bill, if one were in the market for a Chevrolet and not a Cadillac or a Packard. No one could blame Bill's parents. Charley Sloane was the master carpenter affluent Westerveldtians hired from time to time to remodel their older family houses. He had never shown an ambition to marry his son to any of their daughters; few of his clients knew he had one.

The blame, since it had to be assigned, lay with Genevieve for being so off-handed in her choice; perhaps, more accurately, the blame lay with her parents. Either they should have brought her up properly or they should have nipped the romance before it flowered.

Gus Van Leuven, for example. No bond of friendship restrained him in his outspoken criticism of the Sanfords. The three-hundred-year history of Westerveldt could furnish him with any documentation he needed for his argument. Gus owned the Old Dutch Lumber Company which his great-grandfather had founded and his grandfather had expanded when the first railroad line connected Westerveldt to the City. His grandfather's generation had made Westerveldt what it was from the Civil War to the Crash of 1929, a thriving county seat for the surrounding towns. Select descendants of that generation survived the Depression since they owned nearly every enterprise in town that made any money: the banks, the shops, light manufacture, the river docks, the professions. They formed a self-protective clique that understood the importance, far beyond the value of the dollar, of pedigrees and connections, the rules of correct behavior, and, above all, "standards."

It was on "standards" that Gus Van Leuven was lecturing his family at the luncheon table on the day of the wedding. He could not understand, he said, how Jack Sanford had so neglected his duty.

"We were boys together." Gus had a healthy, hearty, bluff expression that never left his face no matter how lugubrious the tone of his voice might become. He looked, even when most miserable, like the energetic golfer he was. "Jack Sanford and I were boys together. We skated together. We swam together. We went to Miss Hollawell's dance classes together. We went to the same house parties. I was best man at his wedding. He would have been best man at mine if he hadn't broken his leg hiking down by the old Canfield quarry. So I asked Ted Osterhoudt. It was a toss-up, anyway, Jack or Ted. The three of us, we've been friends all our lives. I don't understand Jack. It's a father's duty to keep up standards. It's his duty—not just to his children—but to those who went before him and paved the way and to those who will come after him. It's his duty to see to it that his children marry suitably."

Gus' family—his wife Isobel, his son Peter, home on leave from the navy, and his daughter Mary D. who would enter Wellesley in the fall—had known for some time of his life-long friendship with Jack Sanford. They also knew only too well how Gus felt about his duty, so they spooned their soup in silence.

"Let there be no mistake about it," Gus continued. "A girl can have her head turned. For that matter, so can a young man. We can't always prevent such things. But that's why parents are here, to set matters straight. Children must not be permitted to marry just anyone they please. Just anyone off the streets. You have to draw the line somewhere. All right, so Westerveldt doesn't have as many young men as it should have. Jack has a daughter. The Osterhoudts have two daughters. I've got one, but at least I have a son. Horace Callendar has two daughters . . ."

"Daddy," Mary D. interrupted, "you don't have to tell me that all your friends have daughters, except for the Whittiers and the Van Vorsts and the . . ."

"Which is why," Gus ignored her, "we have to be prepared to look elsewhere. Which is why we send you to a good boarding school, so you can go to a good college. Once you're there, you can look around. You'll meet young men. There'll be more to choose from."

Isobel raised her soup spoon so that her lips barely touched the side of its bowl. Peter buttered a piece of bread. Mary D., her soup plate and bread plate empty, stared at her father, her sandy-colored eyebrows arched over the frames of her spectacles, until she was sure he had finished his paragraph.

"How do you go about choosing a mate for breeding purposes?" she asked. "If you'd followed the rules they use for horses and dogs, I mightn't have been stuck with these." She fingered the spectacles, thick-lenses to compensate for her nearsightedness.

Gus had been ready for Mary D. since she day she was born, anticipating and "dealing promptly with" an infant's mid-night cries, a two-year-old's temper tantrums, a twelve-year-old's gum chewing, or a fifteen-year-old's lipstick and pancake makeup.

"I said nothing about breeding," he answered, flexing his chest muscles inside the shell of his jacket. No man sat down to a meal in the Van Leuven house without his jacket on. No woman came to the table in trousers of any length. Such dishabille was for outdoor picnics. "I'm talking about choosing a life's partner. That is not the same thing. Certainly you wouldn't choose for a life's partner someone who is unhealthy or someone who has unfortunate physical characteristics. You would choose for your partner in life someone of your own kind, someone from the same background, with the same values, attitudes, tastes, standards."

"I guess you mean I have to marry a Republican." Mary D. was not always ready for her father, but she was gaining on him.

"Exactly," Gus said. "How could any daughter of mine marry anyone but a Republican? You wouldn't want to marry a New Dealer."

The colored maid who had voted three times for Franklin Roosevelt was now setting before each of the Van Leuvens a plate of lamb chop and baked potato sprigged with parsley.

"May I have some more butter, please, Essie?" Mary D. asked.

"In just a minute." Essie had known Mary D. since she was eight.

"There aren't that many Republican left, Daddy. You don't want me to be an old maid, do you?"

"There are plenty of Republicans left if you know where to look for them. And that's what you should be putting your mind on—meeting suitable young men. Unless you want to end up like Genevieve Sanford, which I will not allow in any case. So don't bring home any used-car salesmen."

Isobel Van Leuven was gentle in voice and manner, infinitely patient and pacific; she drew her attitudes, values, and standards from another source. "Now, Gus," she said, "he's not a used-car salesman. You know that."

"Used cars, new cars. No difference. He's a car salesman."

"He isn't any more," Isobel reminded him. "He's been working at Jack's bank ever since the engagement was announced. Don't be unfair."

"I'm not being unfair. I'm facing facts. Before he was a bank teller, he was a car salesman, and, if he weren't marrying Genevieve, he'd still be a car salesman. Once a car salesman, always a car salesman." Gus carved his lamb chop so neatly from the bone that no visible ribbon of meat or gristle remained attached. He never picked up bones in his hands to clean them off with his teeth. Neither did Isobel. Peter and Mary D., young yet, hoped he would be distracted momentarily so they could sneak a few chomps of the meat they were not skillful enough to cut away, but Gus kept his eyes on all of them.

"Maybe it's because their parents passed away," he thought aloud once he'd finished chewing. "Jack's parents died when Genevieve was a baby, and Mrs. Lester right after the Crash. Judge Lester was the last to go. He was a gentleman of the old school. He knew what was what. He would have put his foot down. He even made a fuss when Jackie wanted to marry Jack. Said he'd never be able to provide for her properly. Not enough get up and go. I think he wanted me for a son-in-law."

No one spoke. When it came to get up and go, Gus had few rivals. He continued to ruminate on the police powers of grandparents.

"The elder Osterhoudts, thank God, are still around to keep an eye on things. I doubt if old Ted overhears much these days—he's as deaf as a doorpost—but Nelly has her wits about her. I imagine the day will come when young Ted will be glad they live next door to keep an eye on the comings and goings. With two daughters he needs all the help he can get. Especially since Katherine always seems to find something to laugh at even in the most serious situations. I know I'm grateful Mother is nearby to lend her moral support."

The silence became eloquent. The dowager Mrs. Van Leuven lived fifty yards away.

"Car salesman!" Gus exclaimed. "Take the matter of the suits. Would anyone who was not a car salesman want to appear at his own wedding in a white suit?"

"Not again," Isobel pleaded. "The wedding is only a few hours away. It can't matter all that much."

"It can matter and it does matter. No daughter of mine is going to stand up with a man in a white suit."

"I can see it now," Mary D. eyed her chop as she spoke. "A Republican in a cutaway and me in virginal white."

As Gus slammed his hand down on the table and glared in her direction, Peter hastily picked up his chop and ripped off the meat with his incisors.

"There will be none of that kind of talk," Gus intoned, separating his words to give each one its own emphasis.

"Oh," Mary D. answered quickly, "so virgin is a dirty word now?"

Isobel gasped. "Mary D., please, don't annoy your father." She turned to her husband. "You know she's only trying to get your goat, dear."

"I don't care what she thinks she's doing. But if I hear such language again, young lady, at this table, in front of your mother and your brother, and in front of the servants, I will keep you home from the wedding."

"I'd like to see you explain that one away." His daughter wouldn't give up. "Mary Dwight couldn't come. I sent her to bed without her supper at twelve-thirty in the afternoon because she said virgin at lunch."

"That is enough." Gus rose from the table. "I don't want any dessert. And speak to Mary D., Isobel. Perhaps you can make her understand. He strode athletically from the room, head up, shoulders back. Mary D. devoured every edible morsel on her chopbone.

"Why do you do it?" her mother asked. "Ever since you've been home, you've set out to argue with your father. Do you think we enjoy sitting here meal after meal wondering what you'll say next?"

"I don't do it on purpose," Mary D. said. purpose," Mary D. said as she licked her fingers. "I can't help it. I see him planning my life for me, and the lower orders rise up against the absolute monarch. I suppose he wants me to marry some drip like Tommy Van Vorst so I can have two Vans in my name and three V's in my monogram. M D V L V V. One thousand five hundred five fifty five five. I will not marry a man who walks around with his mouth hanging open and talks with a drawl because he goes to the University of Virginia. I suppose he'll be at the wedding."

"No. He left several weeks ago for the army."

"You're kidding. You mean he passed the physical? With those sinuses? And the army IQ test? Talk about standards! Hitler, watch out! Tommy Van Vorst is coming to get you!" Mary D. started to laugh; Peter joined in. Even Isobel managed a prim smile.

There was a pause while Essie removed the luncheon plates and then served each of them a dessert dish holding half a canned peach, a mint leaf in the carved-out center, and two ginger snaps.

"You owe me, brother," Mary D. said between mouthfuls. "When I get him riled, he forgets to plan your life for you."

The smile instantly left Isobel's face, and Peter, seeing the sadness in her eyes, reached over to pat her hand.

"Don't worry, Mother. There's plenty of time yet. The war won't be over for years and years," he said comfortingly.

"Then we won't talk about your plans for the future while you're home. I want you to enjoy your leave. Perhaps you can renew some of your old acquaintances at the wedding, although not many of the boys you know will be there."

"Emily Osterhoudt will be there," Mary D. said. "Wait till she gets a look at you in your summer whites."

"Emily Osterhoudt! She's your age! Now if Genevieve Sanford hadn't been so anxious to get married. If she could have waited until the war was over. But it's too late for that now."

"It may be too late for Genevieve Sanford," his mother answered, "but you'll see. It's not too late for somebody else."

"Now, Mother," Peter said firmly, "let's not go into that again. I've made up my mind. I'm sorry it upsets you." Then he apologized. "I shouldn't have mentioned Genevieve Sanford."

"Not to change this unpleasant topic," Mary D. put in, "but when should we start getting ready for the wedding?"

"Soon," Isobel sighed. "There will probably be another argument with your father about the suits, and then we have to pick up your grandmother. We should be at the church well before two-thirty if we want to sit up front."

2

Nelly

The midday sun blazed on the lawn. Nelly Osterhoudt came out onto the back porch after a light lunch and sat down on a fan-backed wicker chair, prepared to enjoy the serenity of her garden until it was time to dress for the Sanford wedding. The chair was now her favorite piece of furniture, inherited from Lizzie Van Slyke. Every time she sat in it, she thought of Lizzie, her dearest friend, her maid of honor forty-nine years ago come August. They'd often talked of the party they'd give in the garden for the golden wedding anniversary. But poor Lizzie had been gone now for two years. Nelly's friends were leaving her, one by one, but still she planned the party for the handful that remained.

The lilac bush had completed its fortieth season of bloom and been carefully pruned and fertilized. The old pear tree now yielded only small sickly fruit, but it still sheltered the birdhouse Teddy had built the year he learned how to use tools. A pair of wrens on their annual visit swooped down from the home to flirt with the water in the birdbath. The border of the perennial bed was doing nicely; Crosby, the ten-hour-a-week gardener, had weeded around the ageratum, candytuft, and Rosy Morn petunias the night before. This year the selection at the nursery had been very poor. The Rosy Morns, in particular, had been pathetic straggling plants, but they had been coaxed into shape, and Nelly had not been forced to make any substitutions in the red, white, and blue motif she had designed in 1917, the year her elder boy had gone off to war and never come back.

As the bell in the Dutch Church tower struck one, all sounds ceased, except for the buzzing of invisible insects among the ferns. Crosby had finished mowing the front lawn and was undoubtedly trimming the edges; no cars or trucks rumbled past the houses under the canopy of elms that lined both sides of Franklin Avenue. In the warmth and stillness of that summer day, time stood still for Nelly Osterhoudt. It could have been any other June Saturday in any of her forty-nine married years; she was free to choose from her memories the happiest to relive.

Just as Nelly had exchanged thinning white hair for her original chestnut curls, topped them with a smart boater, and slipped mentally into a pale blue shirtwaist and flaring navy skirt, a voice called through the screen door.

"I'll see you at two, Mother." For a moment it had been 1912 and she was waiting for the Catsbys to whisk her and Ted and the two boys off to the lake for an afternoon picnic. The voice called her back to the present.

"Wait, Teddie, don't go. Come out here a minute."

Ted Jr. came out and sat down on the steps, very much as he had when he was six, or sixteen (the year of that wonderful picnic), or twenty-six, or thirty-six, or, as now, forty-six.

"I've just left Dad," he said. "He's all set. All you have to worry about is getting yourself ready."

"Your father has everything he needs? There won't be any fusses at the last minute?" Nelly had always disliked last-minute fusses. Now she dreaded them.

"Everything's fine," he reassured her and, as he stood up to go, he repeated, "I'll see you at two."

"Don't go just yet."

"Is there something on your mind?"

"It's about the wedding, Teddie."

"What about it, Mother? Have you forgotten something?"

"Sarah and Jeff."

Sarah and Jeff Catsby lived down the block in a four-room apartment which ten years earlier they had carved out of a twenty-room mansion; there were two other four-room apartments in the building and two smaller ones. It had been the most elegant house on Franklin Avenue with three acres of grounds bordering the Wester Kill. Jeff had lost everything in the Crash; he and Sarah now lived very simply on the rents from the apartments.

"What about them?"

"I promised you'd drive them to the wedding."

Ted didn't like to be impatient with his mother, but sometimes it was hard not to be. "Mother, you know there won't be enough room in the car. There's just enough room for you and Dad and Katherine and the girls. Can't Aunt Sarah and Uncle Jeff take a taxi?"

"I won't let them." Nelly pursed her lips. "It's not right for them to arrive at the church in a taxi. Besides, it's hard to get a taxi these days. Sarah tells me you have to call ahead of time and explain why you need it. Can you imagine explaining to the taxi company why you want a taxi?"

"The taxi company has its gas rationed just like the rest of us, Mother. They have to save it for emergency calls. Why didn't Sarah think of this several weeks ago and find someone to take them?"

"Because I told her all along not to worry. If we have a car, we can use it to make our friends' lives comfortable." (Ted was being reminded that his parents had paid half the cost of the Buick since he would be driving them to parties, weddings, and funerals). "When they were rich, they always shared with us." The picnic, one of the most glorious of outings.

Ted looked across the wire fence that separated his mother's garden from the one next door. "Then there's not much sense talking about it, if it's all settled. I can drive you and the Catsbys and come back for Katherine and the girls. Or," he hesitated, "they could walk. They walk to church anyway, whenever they go."

"But not to a wedding! I can't have that. What would the Sanfords think? Or Augusta Van Leuven? Run them over first and then come back for us. How could you even think of such a thing?" How could Ted think of such a thing? Nelly knew. Katherine. Katherine was an excellent woman, Nelly had said so many times. She was an exemplary wife and mother, a good manager, an efficient housekeeper, but her tastes were, well, modern or somehow not quite right. Probably because she was not from Westerveldt, like Jacqueline Sanford or Genevieve Swinton or Isobel Van Leuven. She had been brought up in Pennsylvania and in more than one town; the family had not, in Nelly's words, stayed put. Walk indeed, parading through the streets.

"We'll work it out, Mother."

As he started to leave, his mother said, "I hope Katherine won't be cross with me."

Ted said a quick goodbye. He could have gone down the back steps toward the gate to the right, let himself in his own backyard and then his own backdoor, but instead he went through the house to the front door and out across the newly-mowed lawn that served both houses. He always used the front door; so did Katherine. His daughters always used the back door.

Now that the problem had been disposed of, Nelly again surveyed the garden. Crosby was pushing the inverted mower toward the barn next to the fern bed. He, too, was getting old, his hearing was failing, he couldn't kneel to clip the edges properly, and more than once his dimmed eyes had mistaken a garden upstart for some new plant. As he came toward her, limping stiffly, his ragged workcoat over his arm, Nelly saw that he had forgotten to trim the collar of grass around the base of the pear tree.

"All done, Mr. Crosby?" she asked brightly. "It looks very nice." She averted her eyes from the pear tree. She knew if she offended him, he might quit and she could never replace him.

"You've got a fine garden this year, Mrs. Osterhoudt."

"I think it's never been nicer, Mr. Crosby," she smiled. She and Crosby might have their little ups and downs, their little arguments about how close the blades of the mower should be set or how often the irises should be divided, but they shared the memories of many summers and many gardens. He was one of the few familiars left, and, as he lingered in the shade of the back porch, holding the bills of his ten-hours' wages, they debated the extension of the rose arbor. Nelly was impatient to start in the fall. Crosby insisted on early spring. He didn't care what the books or the Garden Club might say.

"We'll have to think about it, won't we, Mr. Crosby?" Nelly said ambiguously. After he'd gone, she sat back in her chair and tried not to look at the pear tree. Perhaps after the sun went down she could do it herself if she weren't too tired after the wedding. Or perhaps one of the girls. It would only take ten minutes, and she didn't want to bother Teddie.

The kitchen door in basement slammed, and Martha, who had been with the Osterhoudts for thirty-eight years, climbed the basement steps to the back lawn. In her small clawed hand she held a pepper container.

"We're all out, Mrs. Osterhoudt," she announced in her childish voice, a trace of brogue.

"Oh, Martha." Nelly stamped her foot lightly. "Not again. Why didn't you tell me sooner?"

"I didn't notice until now. If I hadn't had to bake the pies for dinner, I would have seen it." Martha always took refuge in a grievance so she could wrench new privileges. Early dinner so she could attend the novena at St. Peter's every other Sunday off. The last, most shocking, request was for ten dollars more a month. Nelly could not understand why. Didn't she have a free room in the basement and all her meals? What did she need money for?

"Well, you'll have to run around the corner and get some, I guess," Nelly decided. She wouldn't have time.

"I can't, Mrs. Osterhoudt. My pie's in the oven."

"Oh bother." Nelly pulled herself up from her chair and walked heavily into the house. In the pantry near the dumbwaiter which pulled the meals up from the kitchen was a table with a telephone. She sat down, took the receiver off the hook with one hand and held the long upright speaker in the other, an inch or two away from her lips.

When she heard, "Number, please," she answered, "Operator, will you please get me six-nine-oh-three." She heard the ring in her ear and simultaneously heard the echo of the ring through the open kitchen window next door.

"Hello," said a young voice.

"Emily, is that you?"

"Yes."

"This is Grandmamma." Accent on the last syllable. "Emily, dear, would you do your Grandmamma a favor."

"Yes, certainly, Grandmamma."

"Would you go over town and buy me a box of black pepper?"

"Can't it wait until after the wedding, Grandmamma?"

"Martha needs it to make dinner while we're out. Aunt Sarah and Uncle Jeff are coming back with us."

This sort of last-minute errand-running didn't go on every day, but nearly every day. The younger Osterhoudts tried to coordinate the errands of the two households, but when the elder Osterhoudts realized that they needed something, they needed it right away. Nelly did not approve of borrowing. Luckily it was only a two-block walk to Main Street, and it was quicker to trot "over town" than it was to discuss the purchase.

"All right, Grandmamma, what kind of pepper do you want?"

"I'll call Mancuso's and tell them you're coming. And, lambie, while you're there, would you pick up a box of Holland Rusk? Tell Mrs. Mancuso to charge it to my account."

After she'd phoned Mancuso's, Nelly went back to the porch to wait for Emily. She was pleased to have solved the problem but equally annoyed that one problem should follow so closely on the heels of another. As usual, she resigned herself. Martha was forgetful and petulant and not a little hard of hearing, but she was loyal and familiar with their ways. Nelly had a prayer that she said to herself several times a day.

"If only I can keep things as they are. For as long as possible. That's all I ask for."

3

Genevieve

Genevieve Sanford, her coiffure protected by a plastic cap, was soaking in the bathtub for the last time as an unmarried woman. Her mother was waiting, indulgently, in the master bedroom and trying not to check the time on the silver traveling clock her sister had given her on her own wedding day twenty-four years earlier. Thank God for the downstairs powder room, and Thank God the aunties had been lodged at the Westerveldt Arms! She was studying the list, the last and most accurate of the dozen she had prepared during the week, when there was a discreet knock at the door and her husband poked his head in.

"She's not out of the tub yet."

"I know. I'll call her." Genevieve always spent an inordinate amount of time on her toilette, but the results were worth it. "I promise you I'll only be a few minutes myself. I've laid out your clothes on the guest room bed, except for the cufflinks." She moved toward the dresser. "Which pair do you want?" "The ones I wore to our wedding. It's going to be a sentimental day."

"Don't," Jacqueline exclaimed. "If I weren't so nervous, I'd be crying. You must be calm so we can lean on you."

Jack chuckled. "After today, I'll only have you leaning on me. Genevieve will be leaning on Bill. I hope those thin shoulders of his can support the burden."

"He's a nice boy."

"Nice, yes. But being nice isn't going to get him very far in the business world. Being nice at the teller's window may work half the time, but he's got to learn to be clever too. And tough."

"For the time being, I'm glad he's nice. You can always teach him how to be practical once they get back from their honeymoon."

Jack shut the door behind him, no longer ready to chuckle.

"Did you speak to her again, as I told you to? You promised me you would."

"Of course I spoke to her. It's all taken care of. You know she's been to Dr. Hansen, and I've explained as much as I dare. I trust Dr. Hansen has taken care of the technical matters."

Jack paced up and down on the Oriental rug at the foot of the bed. "You can't trust to luck. Are you sure she understands? She may be a beautiful girl and capable of appreciating what you keep calling the finer things in life, but she's too dreamy to put her mind on what I'm going to call the coarser things in life. What is she comes back from Canada pregnant? And, then, what if Bill is called up? We could be right back where we started, only worse."

Jacqueline stepped into her husband's path. "Don't go over all that again now. Please. Why do you come in here, an hour and a half before the wedding?" She glanced at the clock. "It's too late to do anything more than I've done already, and there's no guarantee anyway. What time will the limousine be here?

"Twenty of three. And they have gas. Ben and Genevieve will be here for you at the same time, and we'll give you ten minutes head start. Ben has half a tank of gas so he can get you to the church and then to the house with no trouble."

"Is Ben driving them to the station or are you? You never told me what you decided." Jacqueline was about to add another item to her list.

"Taken care of. Bill's father is driving them. He has a full tank. Where he got it, he didn't say, and, given the occasion, I didn't ask."

"Not in that dirty old car! The day begins in style and ends in style. I thought we had agreed . . ."

"Washed and waxed. Bill told me. Now, will you get her out of the tub or shall I?"

Jacqueline led her husband out of their bedroom and motioned him into the guest room. "Shut the door," she whispered. Then she knocked on the bathroom door. "Genevieve, hurry. dear. There isn't much time."

When she was able to get in for a quick rinse, Jacqueline found the bathroom temperature close to a hundred humid degrees; outdoors it was only a warm eighty-five. The window and the mirror were misted with steam, the odors of bubble-bath, after-bath powder, and eau de cologne mingled cloyingly. The floor was sprinkled with powder, the bathmat was sopping, and all the towels on the rack were wet. The tub, however, had been wiped clean. She quickly opened the windows to let the steam and perfumes escape and began tidying up as she ran water for her own bath, sighing with resignation at these final maternal chores and repressing the concern that it might be some time before Genevieve learned how to run her own household. Within fifteen minutes, true to her word, she relinquished to her husband a neat, neutrally scented bathroom with fresh, dry towels on display. She found Genevieve at the dressing table inspecting her complexion in the mirror.

"Take off that plastic cap," she said sharply. "Let your hair breathe. You won't have a curl left after an hour in that steam."

Genevieve very slowly removed the cap. "I never thought about my hair. I'm more worried about this." She turned to her mother and held out her palms.

"You knew very well they'd get wrinkled if you stayed in the water that long. They'll be back to normal in time."

"I have to pluck my eyebrows, and I think I'm getting a pimple over here." She pointed to the skin over her left jawbone.

Jacqueline peered into her daughter's face. "Leave your eyebrows alone. You should have plucked them yesterday. If you start plucking now, you'll irritate the skin. Ugly red blotches. That little dot is nothing. The foundation will cover it."

Both women had the same striking dark eyes and wide dark brows. Jacqueline's face was narrower and her lips thinner. Genevieve had inherited her father's fuller face and lips.

"Now, Genevieve." Jacqueline bent over her daughter and put her hands affectionately but firmly on her shoulders. "Starting this minute you have got to put your mind on what you have to do. First of all, put on your underthings, including your stockings, and then start on your face."

"But I have to do my nails." This time she held out her hands palms down.

"They were manicured at the beauty shop. They're fine."

"Colorless nail polish! I bought this." She showed a small vial to her mother.

"Magenta! Never!" Jacqueline snatched the vial and put it on the dresser at the other side of the room. "When you take off your gloves, you can't have that dark red gleaming against your gown and your bouquet."

"I was thinking about later, with the blue silk."

"Genevieve, that's after the ceremony. You'll have to wait until you get to Montreal to do your nails. Now get up, I'm going to work on my face while you get dressed." Jacqueline worked swiftly and professionally with foundation, face powder, the faintest touch of rouge and a whisper of mascara to darken the lashes and draw even more attention to her magnificent eyes. When Genevieve had adjusted the last garter, she motioned for her to sit at the dressing table, and, after shaking out a bedsheet, she covered her daughter's body with it and pinned it at the back of her neck.

"Now, be careful. Work slowly, and don't use too much of anything. It's a warm day."

Genevieve pulled her hands from beneath the sheet and looked again at her pale, glossy nails. "Did the flowers come?"

"They're in the refrigerator." Jacqueline put on her underclothes and slipped back into her dressing gown. The nile-green chiffon lawn dress and matching cartwheel hat lay on the bed next to the bridal gown and veil, ready to be put on at the last minute. There was a knock at the door—Jack.

"The limousine isn't here yet?" Jacqueline gave a startled look at the clock.

"You have half an hour" He glanced across the room at the sheeted figure. "Will she be ready on time?"

"Yes. If you don't bother us."

"I need help with my cufflinks."

"I'll come in there."

Left alone, Genevieve smiled at herself in the mirror. "Oh Bill," she breathed aloud, "I hope you'll be proud of me. I love you. I love you so much. Soon we'll be together forever and ever, in our own house, with our own furniture and our own china, and our own silver." Her mind traveled to the wedding presents she had viewed on display in her aunt's parlor. While she was ohing and ahing, her mother had entered in a notebook a description of each item with the name of its donor at the same time she committed to her extraordinary memory a good calculated guess of its cost.

Among the gifts were three large silver service trays, a dozen pieces of table serviceware—covered vegetable dishes, uncovered Revere bowls, meat and fish platters, a tea service, a coffee service, a water pitcher. Crystal glasses of every size for every sort of beverage, some monogrammed with her new initials, a beautiful set of amber water glasses, china, extra sets of dessert plates and salad plates, a set of ramekins—everything a young woman could ask for as she prepared to set up housekeeping in the depths of World War II.

The bed and table linens were stored in a chest in the hall until she and Bill returned from Montreal and moved into the house. As she powdered her neck and delicately behind her ears, Genevieve thought about the house. Her father had taken out a mortgage on the Van Slyke house. When elderly Lizzie Van Slyke had died, her only son, who lived in California, had put it on the market. Daddy had worked out some complicated arrangement whereby Bill would begin paying him back only after they were settled and accustomed to living on their income. There was to be a year of grace so they could accumulate furniture beyond what they had been able to buy out of Bill's savings. And Bill's father had been an angel too, taking care of the carpentry and painting, at cost, and, again, on a loan. He had spent many days of the spring months with his crew on the remodeling, listening patiently to Jacqueline who stopped by every day to choose colors and hold up samples of wallpaper.

If only there hadn't been all that fuss about the suits. Genevieve was glad, now, that she hadn't mentioned it to Bill. If he knew about the discussion, it was not from her, or from her parents. It was the only secret she'd kept from him since they'd announced their engagement. What would have been the sense in telling him? Bill's parents were very decent. They couldn't help it if they weren't top-drawer and didn't understand about such things as cutaways. They treated her with respect and affection. If Bill's mother insisted on sewing gaudy little aprons for her, the least she could do was to wear them cheerfully, for everyday in the kitchen. Genevieve smiled at the self in the mirror that was radiant with happiness.

4

The Osterhoudts

Nelly Osterhoudt wavered anxiously on the back porch; it was time to get dressed. As she stood up, the garden gate opened.

"I've got the pepper and the rusks, Grandmamma. Shall I take them to Martha or bring them up to you?

"Just a minute, child. Let me look at you. Did you go over town like that?" Emily was eighteen, a college student home for the summer, working improbably as a shipping clerk in a sweater factory so she could in her Mother's words "find out what the world was all about." At that moment she was wearing knee-length shorts (called clam diggers), one of her father's discarded shirts, tails out flapping, sneakers without socks, and, if that weren't bad enough, a flimsy scarf that failed to cover several rows of bobby-pin curls.

"I had to, Grandmamma. There was no time to change. I was doing my nails when you called and I had to stop in the middle." The hand that held the groceries had red-enameled nails; the other did not.

"And your mother let you go out like that?"

"She doesn't know I went."

Nelly sighed. For order in her own domain, she had created disorder in another equally important to her. "Thank you very much, dear. If you could give the package to Martha, I'll go in now and get ready. Oh Emily, one more thing. Do you think you or Beatrice could come over tomorrow and trim the grass by the pear tree? Crosby forgot and I can't let it go another week. It will be six inches tall by then. And," she added, "I hate to ask your father."

"Don't worry about it, Grandmamma. See you later." Emily ran past the back steps, through the gate and into the house next door. As she banged the kitchen door, her mother asked,

"Did she see you?"

"Yes, damn it. I went around back, but she was waiting on the porch."

"What did she say?

"She wanted to know if you let me go out like this, but I told her you didn't know I'd gone."

"Quick thinking. You were doing your nails. You'd better finish."

"How do you stand it, Mother?"

"It's hard, believe me. You should thank God you're away most of the time." Katherine lowered her voice. "It's hardest on your father. He hates seeing them get old. We try to be patient and help as much as we can. I'm used to the inconvenience; it's the constant complaining I can't stand. If you knew how many times a week I explain slowly and carefully that there's a war on."

Just then the most god-awful din assaulted their ears. An explosion? A series of explosions?

"What's that?" Emily ran to the kitchen window.

Katherine calmly checked the time. "It seems early. Unless, yes, it's Saturday. It must be a double-header. They were rained out last Saturday."

"I can hardly hear you," Emily shouted. The sound was reduced several levels, still very loud but not deafening.

"You haven't been back long enough, and you're not here weekdays. Your grandfather has become a Dodger fan."

"It's the radio! His radio! It's hard to believe. Does he have to play it so loud? Doesn't he use his hearing aid?"

"He doesn't like the battery aid your father bought him, so he puts on those little amplifiers—remember?—we called them bats' ears."

"Even so. Does this go on all the time?"

"It's not so bad in the spring because the window's shut, but with the warm weather, it's become impossible."

"I should think the neighbors would complain."

"They have. Mrs. Wood stopped your father the other day as he went by her porch. She and her husband nap in the afternoon—that is, they try to."

"Does he listen to night games too?"

"To all games that are broadcast, and I should warn you. He also likes Jessica Dragonette."

"It can't go on like this. The whole neighborhood will be up in arms. We may have to be patient, but they don't."

"I'm surprised at how patient they've been. Your father is looking into some of the newer hearing aids, but it's hard to get anything these days."

"A hearing aid for Granddaddy deserves first priority. This could be a national emergency. Listen to it—low and on the outside. Ball Two. I'm going to finish my nails."

Katherine put the last glasses in the cupboard and was about to go upstairs when her husband came into the room. "It looks like we can't even get dressed in peace. Goddamnit. I hoped he'd forget today."

The radio noise stopped abruptly. Instead they heard a bass-baritone voice raised in angry protest. Then they heard Nelly explain in her everyday voice that it was time to get ready, and then explain, over again, more loudly, and then a third time, very loudly, slowly, and deliberately.

"Wedding. Shave. Dress."

"I can shave with the radio on," her husband answered. The next second the radio emitted a roar of mixed cheers and groans.

"I missed a home run," the bass-baritone boomed through the noise.

"Tarnation, woman, I missed it. Leave me in peace."

"Emily says a new hearing aid is a national priority," Katherine commented.

"I'll be ready to go straight to the President after another week of this. But, you know, I don't think his hearing is as bad as he claims. I had no trouble making him understand a little while ago."

"When you were talking about the suits?"

"Yes. I think he was delighted he didn't have to wear his cutaway. He doesn't seem to enjoy dressing up any more. The white suit looks fine. I put out his shirt and tie. He's all set."

For a few blessed minutes in the tub, Katherine was spared the excitement carried from Ebbets Field in the middle of Brooklyn through the air to their quiet, elm-shaded neighborhood. But back in the bedroom, as she began dressing, the game entered the top of the third inning. Her window was no more than ten feet from her father-in-law's so she pulled down the shade. The old man's eyesight gave him no trouble. Ted was tying his tie when he heard his name thundered.

He pulled up the shade and saw his father leaning through the window.

"Yes, Dad?' he asked, keeping his voice audible and low at the same time.

The old man tried to whisper, but the sound carried fifty feet. "My zipper's stuck. I can't fix it."

"I'll be right there, Dad." Ted motioned exaggeratedly to make himself understood. As he left to go next door, he could hear the radio turned off and the windows of the bedroom shut emphatically, one by one, but through the glass and the shades and the curtains, even as he hurried down the stairs, he could hear his parents quarreling.

Emily rushed into her parents' bedroom, followed by her sixteen-year-old sister. "What's wrong?"

Katherine drolly shook her head. "Make sure MY zipper's right, will you? Did I catch the hook? Your grandfather's having trouble with his zipper."

The girls started to laugh.

"Shh," said their mother. "I'm afraid that's not all. Your grandmother has probably found out that he's not wearing his cutaway, and she'll see your father isn't wearing his either. There could be a battle royal."

"Were they supposed to wear their cutaways?" Emily asked. "I haven't seen Dad in his for several years. Not since Tommy Van Vorst's sister got married."

"Jacqueline Sanford spoke to me a month ago. It seems Bill's relatives will be wearing white suits, and she thought it would be more tactful if everyone went along. It IS wartime and no time to be emphasizing class differences."

"But Grandmamma doesn't know?"

Beatrice cackled. "They decided not to tell her. You know how she gets when everything isn't just so. Aunt Sarah knows, but she promised Mom she wouldn't say anything. She dropped by here every morning on her way to see Grandmamma to keep the conspiracy going. And she wasn't the only one. The phone rang all the time. 'Is Ted going to wear morning clothes?'

'Is Ted going to wear morning clothes?' You should have heard Mom. 'Oh, no-o-o, he will be respecting the Sanfords' wishes.' 'It's a wartime wedding, Isobel.' 'It's a wartime wedding, Evelyn.' 'I think we should respect the Sanfords' wishes, don't you?' 'There'll be enough time for pomp and circumstance when the war's over, don't you think?' They talked more about the dumb suits than they did about anything else, including the war. You'd think, to listen to Mom, that wearing a white suit was a patriotic duty."

"That's enough, Beatrice," Katherine chided. "But I do feel strongly about it. The Sanfords are doing things properly, as if Genevieve were marrying Peter Van Leuven or Tommy Van Vorst. The least we can do is accept Bill Sloane as one of our own kind and wish the bride and groom well."

"At Barnard," Emily commented, "this all seems very far away."

"Girls, I've been thinking. I hate to leave your father alone to cope with all four of them. There's room for one more in the car. Perhaps one of you should stay behind and go with them."

"Not on your life, Mom," Emily answered. "If you feel guilty, you stay. I'd walk through a hurricane before I'd go through that."

"Besides," Beatrice added, "by now Grandmamma may have thought of another old biddy to take up the extra seat and I'd end up walking anyway."

"Don't talk like that. We'll all be old some day."

"They're not very efficient about it." Emily was studying sociology.

"I'm forced to agree. Martha is almost as old as they are and just as decrepit. Your father has tried to persuade them to find someone younger and more vigorous, someone who could solve all those nagging little problems. For a while last winter when your grandfather was ill, they had a practical nurse, and the peace was delicious. Hat, gloves, don't forget your gloves."

"In this weather? Mother!"

"In this weather. This is a proper society wedding, morning clothes or no morning clothes. We must look our best. And it may be the only one you'll ever see."

"If this damn war keeps up, there won't be any men left to marry," Emily said testily.

"I mean," her mother came back, "that no one will be able to afford all that show. With the war on, it seems wicked to waste."

"I guess we should be grateful for any excitement," Beatrice said. "There's nothing doing in this town any more. I can't wait to get out of here. One more year!"

*   *   *

"You can't." "I can." "You mustn't." "I must." "Please, Gus, don't. I beg you. Wear the white suit." "Not to a wedding." "Gus, everybody is wearing white." "Not to a wedding."

Gus replaced the white suit in the closet and rummaged through its farther reaches to find the clothes bag that held his tails, his tuxedo, and his morning suit. All three were thrown on the bed, and he now began to search the bottom drawer of his dresser for the appropriate shirt. There would be an eruption if he couldn't find the appropriate tie or discovered that his shoes needed to be shined.

"You'll hurt Jack's feelings."

"What about my feelings? I've been asked to appear at an afternoon wedding in a white suit!"

"Peter is wearing white." A futile argument.

"He has to. It's his uniform. This," he buttoned the fly of the striped trousers that still fit him, albeit a bit snugly, after fifteen years, "is mine."

"Gus, what if the moths have gotten at it? I didn't take it out to look at it. What if it needs pressing? Your white suit is ready for you."

"Essie will press it."

"I gave her the afternoon off to visit her sister. We're not eating in."

"Then you'll have to do it."

"I won't," Isobel said bravely. "I won't. If it's rumpled, you'll wear it rumpled, or you'll put on your white suit."

"Never. I'll wear it rumpled. Somebody has to stand up for what's right." He ripped off the paper ribbon that held his shirt folded. "There'll always be an England, and England shall be free," he sang as he shook out the shirt.

"Gus, why must you be contrary?" Isobel almost pleaded.

"I'm not being contrary." Gus flung the ties off the rack until he found the right one. "I'm doing my duty."

"But I promised Jacqueline."

"I didn't. Jack didn't speak to me, and, even if he had, I would have told him what I thought. He should see to it that the groom is properly dressed."

Isobel knew she was not likely to win, but she tried again. "It's not Bill. I've told you it's not Bill. He could have bought a morning suit. It's his father. They couldn't ask him to buy one."

'And why not? He's coming to our church and to the reception at the Swintons'. Let him wear the proper clothes."

"He thinks his white duck is proper. He bought it last summer when his niece got married in Hempstead or some such place."

"Westerveldt is not Hempstead, and Genevieve is not his niece. She's a Sanford."

"It's not just Mr. Sloane. His relatives and friends. They'll all be wearing white suits."

"Only the bride wears white. They'll look like hospital attendants." One last time. "They won't stand out like sore thumbs, Gus, you will."

"Good, Everyone will know where I stand. I know what's right. I do my duty. I'm not afraid of ridicule. Augustus Van Leuven will not let down his side."

5

The Church

St. Andrew's Episcopal Church stood on Brunswick, the Avenue which ran northeast from Franklin (the Westerveldt Arms was located at the junction) and continued for several miles, wide and elm-lined, before it became State Route 7 on its way to the State Capitol. On its right side were comfortable substantial houses, spaced far enough apart to permit landscaping and gardens on both sides, but on its left, the one that overlooked the Wester Kill, were the mansions, some sprawling three-storied Italianate villas with verandahs on three sides and a porte-cochere on the fourth, others three-storied stone castles with neo-medieval turrets or neo-Tudor bay windows, strong self-contained bastions of the wealth acquired during the 1890s. (Earlier wealth had built the clapboard Federal dwellings at the far end of Franklin, two blocks from what was now the business district.) An occasional overgrown hedge, neglected garden, or peeling house paint testified that not all of Brunswick had survived the Depression, but for every residence that showed signs of wear and tear, there were two that gallantly kept up appearances. Brunswick was still very much an Avenue.

St. Andrew's with its native blue-slate facade was an unpretentious structure, but the ancient Dutch elms on either side of its entrance were among the finest in town. The parishioners viewed their church with casual pride and opened their pocketbooks accordingly. Gus Van Leuven, Jack Sanford, and Ted Osterhoudt were among the vestrymen who oversaw the finances and pledged their "tithes" (in none of their cases anywhere near ten percent of

income either before or after taxes) to correspond to whatever
contributions could be wrenched from the most wealthy
communicants.

Bosworth Giles, the pastor, responded to his parishioners' brand
of generosity with an anxiety that he kept under prayerful control,
except on his birthday or when the treasurer's report was read at
vestry meetings. He had just turned sixty-five and wanted very
much to retire to the cottage in Connecticut his wife had inherited
from her father. Her modest income in dividends had been dissolved
in the Crash, and the Gileses would now be dependent on a pension
and very meager savings. Mr. Giles placed his hope in his age—
sooner or later the parish would want a younger man, and, even if
frugal, economical, tight-pursed, or cheap, it would not send an
aging pastor away without a pension after thirty-five years of service.
This year he was gambling on his summer replacement. Not Father
Wadsworth from the Anglican Monastery who would preach during
July. Although spiritual and very uplifting, especially to the young,
his sermons struck the older members of the congregation as too
other-worldly for year-round Sunday fare. For August Mr. Giles
had found a young divinity student, not yet ordained but newly
married, with a pretty and pregnant wife. Perhaps as he was
gardening in Connecticut and praying for release from St. Andrew's,
the parish would take a liking to the young man, think ahead to
his ordination, and, when Mr. Giles again brought up the possibility
of his retirement, they would buy him off with a pension he could
live on. If not, of course, he was prepared to die in the saddle.

Mr. Giles enjoyed officiating at weddings almost as much as
he did at funerals. As he grew older he labored with little
enthusiasm over his weekly sermon, fine-honing a Biblical text to
slice lessons for daily living. Only at funerals did the meaning of
life—"he that believeth in me, though he were dead, yet shall he
live"—spark his imagination and prompt profound and comforting
thoughts. At weddings he was not required to say from the altar
anything more than what was written in the service. Later, at the
reception, he would accept as much champagne as he dared,
remembering with the first glass the Marriage Feast at Cana and

with the second, Timothy I, 5:23—"Drink no longer water, but use a little wine for thy stomach's sake and thine often infirmities."

When he arrived at the parish house at two-fifteen, Mr. Giles found the six ushers waiting perspiringly in their white suits. He rehearsed their instructions with them and sent them out to wait for the guests. Then he greeted the organist and they both donned their vestments. White-haired and over seventy, the organist had already retired from his job as bookkeeper at the Old Dutch Lumber Company and intended to continue pumping out the familiar weekly hymns, Christmas carols, Easter Alleluias, dirges, and wedding marches until stilled by a last Amen. When an usher came back to announce that the first guests were arriving, the organist went to his instrument to execute the neutral, semi-ecclesiastical, solemn but joyous compositions that serve as mood music for such occasions.

At two-thirty the groom arrived with his best man. Bill Sloane was five-eleven, quick on his feet, a high-school basketball star, now twenty-three, still sporting an expression of delighted bewilderment on his open, cheerful face. Such a nice boy—did he ever lose his temper, snap, think the worst of someone (even a clever car buyer), fall into a depression, doubt himself, wonder if he were good enough for Genevieve? He accepted his good fortune but never asked himself if he deserved it. He loved Genevieve; she loved him. He was prepared to work hard, to be a good husband, to get along with his in-laws who had been so generous to him. There seemed to be no drama in Bill Sloane—no conflicting passions, no dark calculations, no hesitations, even when his knee bothered him, even as he prepared to enter into the new life that would surely be strange at times. In his own masculine way, he was just as "sweet" as Genevieve. He'd manage, one day at a time; that was how his mother said she coped with life.

The day's drama, or its theatricality, was taking place in the churchyard or in the conversational buzz among the early arrivals in the pews. Everyone seemed to be coming ahead of time to get a front row seat or at least two on the aisle for a good look at the bride as she passed by. Pews were no longer rented at St. Andrew's as they had been once upon a time, but the Van Leuvens, for example, always sat in the tenth row on the right side, coming in; the Osterhoudts in the fourth row to the left. Today any such long-standing if informal arrangements were canceled.

As the guests approached the church portals, an usher stepped up and discreetly inquired if they were friends of the bride or friends of the groom. The former were led to the left, the lady on the arm of the usher, and seated on a first-come, first-served basis. The first rows on each side had been left vacant for close relatives. The bride's side filled rapidly, the groom's much more slowly.

Katherine Osterhoudt and her daughters, brisk walkers all, were waiting outside under the elms when Ted drove up with parents and the Catsbys. He would let them out and then drive as far down Brunswick as necessary to find a place to park the Buick. (He estimated that if his passengers had not been elderly, he could have parked most efficiently in his own driveway, and they could all have "paraded" through the streets.) Katherine moved forward to help her mother-in-law and Sarah Catsby from the backseat where Jeff had been wedged between them puffing unsatisfiedly on an unlit, moist cigar. He had tried twice to light it on the drive over and been scolded each time, in no uncertain terms, by his wife. ("You'll smell up the car. You'll get ashes on our frocks. You'll start a fire in the ashtray. Ted won't be able to see for all the smoke.") Nelly had mentioned, wistfully, that although the men looked handsome in their white suits, it still didn't seem right, somehow, that they were attending an important wedding in such informal attire. Ted Sr., up front next to his son, was not wearing any hearing aid at all and therefore did not contribute to the conversation as he relived in his imagination the Giant-Dodger game he had been forced to leave at home. Once he glanced to see if Ted Jr. could be persuaded to drive to the Polo Grounds the next time the two teams were matched. An exciting day off without the women. Why not? He'd taken his son mountain climbing, swimming, to the circus in the old days.

The Van Leuven Packard pulled up at almost the same time, and Peter helped his Grandmother out of the front seat. Augusta

Van Leuven was the most magnificent dowager in Westerveldt. Her white hair had not thinned but rose like a lion's mane, even under the pastel peacock-colored garden hat. Her chiffon dress of the same shade was daringly décolleté between softening frills and ruffles. At the triangle of the V-neck, at the separation of her aged breasts, was emblazoned the diamond brooch her husband had given her on their thirtieth wedding anniversary. The diamond earrings from the twenty-fifth dangled from her ears and on her wrist was the matching bracelet from the thirty-fifth. Around her neck was a gold choker; she leaned on the gold-handled cane she could poke at dogs or small children who got in her way.

"Sarah! Eleanora!" she called to her contemporaries. "Over here!" Ted Jr. and Gus Van Leuven waved to each other as they re-entered their cars. Ted Sr. and Jeff Catsby (he had just thrown his useless cigar into the privet hedge of the churchyard and was fingering his breast pocket to see if he had brought enough fresh smokes for the reception) walked behind their wives. Katherine and Isobel greeted each other affectionately, as did Emily and Mary D. Peter and Beatrice didn't even notice each other—the seven-year gulf in age rendered them invisible. Each looked around hopelessly for someone familiar.

At the portals the ushers asked the magic question and escorted Augusta, Sarah, and Nelly, husbands trailing, to the fifth pew from the rear, to the left. As Katherine and Isobel entered the church ("Are you sure we shouldn't wait for Ted and Gus?" "No, it's better to get seats; they'll find us."), Katherine's quixotic streak came to the fore. She wasn't, after all, a native Westerveldtian but from "somewhere" in Pennsylvania. She saw the crowded left side and half-full right side and quickly said to the usher, "We'll sit over there—to the right." Was she generously leaving room for those who would come after her? Was she identifying with the lower middle-class associates of the groom? Was she saying to herself, "He's one of us now"? Or was she saying to herself, "These things don't matter to me. Let those who stand up for their privileges have my rightful seat"? Isobel gasped as they were separated and Emily and Beatrice followed their mother to the coveted aisle seats.

Mary D. moved to join her friend, but her mother pulled her back. "What about your father?" she whispered telegraphically.

The organist continued to play as the guests chatted, pointed to people they recognized, waved if someone they knew turned around, commented on each other's clothes, identified guests from out of town ("That must be Jack's cousin from Detroit and his wife. It looks as if they didn't bring the children.") and wondered just who the occupants of the right side of the aisle were. "My God," thought Isobel, as a man in the sixth row turned around, "that's Mr. Wiley, the plumber. He looks so clean, and I suppose that enormous woman in the flowered print is his wife." The electrician was there and the mason, as well as several Masons from the lodge Charley Sloane belonged to.

The altar was decorated to the heavens with ornamental white flowers of the sort cultivated only for weddings, the odors perceptible only to occupants of the first few rows before they were mingled with aromas of eau de cologne, after-shave, and other scents of animal, not floral, origin. People began to look at their watches and back toward the church portals through which the bride would pass on her father's arm, preceded by her maid of honor and her bridesmaids. But, of course, she wouldn't be coming yet. The organist hadn't struck up the Wedding March, and, besides, the first-row seats were vacant on the left side. The wedding party had not arrived yet. "Oh, wait. That must be the groom's mother and father. They're sitting in the first row on the right. Yes, that's Charley Sloane. So that's his wife! You know, I've never met her. Charley's been at the house several times. He put a closet in the foyer. He made a morning room out of that ugly sun porch, but I'll never forget the summer we had the kitchen done over. He made all new cabinets, but it took forever. Sawdust all over everything. We ate out for days. So that's Mrs. Sloane."

Mrs. Sloane was a comfortable-looking matron in her late forties, plump but not fat, well-corseted, with a pneumatic bosom, her figure smoothly draped in mauve chiffon. The hat on her freshly marcelled coiffure (the style unchanged in the twenty-six years since her own wedding) was the same color and trimmed with pale pink velvet roses. Her brother, a painter who worked with her husband, was beside her with his wife, and next to them her sister with her husband, the butcher. There was still no sign of the Sanfords. "Maybe they thought better of it at the last minute," Gus Van Leuven whispered to his wife. He had come back with Ted, found his wife, asked loudly why Katherine was sitting on the other side, albeit next to the aisle, and why Ted didn't get her and bring her back. There were no longer any seats on the left side.

"Oh-h-h" Isobel had said, mortified. "You're conspicuous enough already. You're the only one here." And indeed he was. All the other men wore white.

Then, suddenly, a bustling and rustling as hundreds of bodies turned around. Jacqueline Sanford, regal in carriage, head held high, dark eyes expressing the most noble of maternal emotions under those dark brows, a sweet half-smile on her face, walked down the aisle on Ben Swinton's arm, her sister behind her on the arm of an usher. More than one guest observed how beautiful she was. "Better looking than her daughter," someone said, but he had not yet seen Genevieve.

The moment of excitement passed into the restlessness of more waiting. It was two minutes of three, three o'clock, three after. Necks craned, the organist continued to play his background music, five after, ten after, and, then abruptly, the organist brought his hands down on the keyboard to blare out a resounding chord as if the gates of Paradise were about to open. An instant of silence and then the strains of Wagner's Wedding March, "Here Comes the Bride."

An acolyte first, bearing aloft the large cross, his face as expressionless as a guard's at Buckingham Palace ("the Hodges boy. I do declare. He's grown. All that puppy fat gone.") The six bridesmaids in pink, retarding their steps to keep time with the music, to prolong their advance, to heighten anticipation. The maid of honor, Caroline, "I forget her last name. She was Genevieve's best friend from Smith. She's engaged herself, to a pilot, an Amherst graduate." Caroline in blue cast down her eyes before all those strangers. And then, and then—Genevieve, on her father's arm, the two of them in white, Jack, straight as an arrow, proud, nervous but stalwart. Genevieve was veiled, but her dark hair and eyes were visible even through the netting. "Oohs" and "Ahs" greeted her as she walked slowly down the aisle to the rail where Bill and his best man were waiting.

Onward they went, step by step, the majestic music saturating the atmosphere, imposing its grandeur, until, as Genevieve and her father stood beside Bill and in front of Mr. Giles, the organist improvised a few notes of transition and relinquished the air to the human voice.

> Dearly beloved, we are gathered together here in the sight of God, and the face of this company, to join together this man and this woman in Holy Matrimony; which is an honourable estate, instituted by God, signifying unto us the mystical union that is betwixt Christ and his Church: which holy estate Christ adorned and beautified with his presence and first miracle that he wrought in Cana of Galilee, and is commended of Saint Paul to be honourable among all men: and therefore is not by any to be entered into unadvisedly or lightly, but reverently, discreetly, advisedly, soberly and in the fear of God. Into this holy estate these two people come now to be joined. If any man can show just cause, why they may not lawfully be joined together, let him now speak, or else hereafter for ever hold his peace.

There was silence. No one spoke, although there was the sound of a throat being cleared. Only Isobel Van Leuven knew if it were her husband's, and she would never tell.

"William Otis, wilt thou have this Woman . . . ?"

"Genevieve Lester, wilt thou have this Man . . . ?"

"I will. I will."

"Who giveth this Woman to be married to this Man?"

Jack Sanford placed his daughter's hand in Bill's and stepped backward skillfully and self-effacingly; then he turned, his face cast down, and joined his wife in the first row. He wanted to take her hand now but thought better of it and clasped instead both his own hands, one to another. Jacqueline gave him a sweet, sad, wistful smile which he returned, almost in kind.

The bride and groom exchanged rings. Mr. Giles exhorted no man to put them asunder and then pronounced them Man and Wife.

Before the organist could play the first note of the Mendelssohn march as a recessional, before the bride and groom could turn around to begin their triumphal sweep back down the aisle, there was heard a sob. Mrs. Charley Sloane had controlled herself throughout the ceremony, but as her son's health, welfare, well-being, and happiness were forever consigned to the manicured and glovèd hands of Genevieve Sanford, now Sloane, a wave of trepidation overwhelmed her. She knew there would be money, security, a beautifully decorated and well-equipped house; she knew he was in love and she was not jealous (except, maybe, a little), but her warm maternal heart was worried. As she swallowed the second sob that was struggling to escape her lips and as Charley whispered, "Now, Mother," she consoled herself with the anticipatory thought, "I can always make them a nice little chicken or a roast beef." Her brother-in-law, the butcher, was standing only a few feet away.

Genevieve, now unveiled, on Bill's arm, smiling as she was wished well, as beautiful as any bride could ever be and as happy, brushed past the spectators and out into the limousine for the two-block ride to her aunt's house. The church emptied slowly; the guests clogged the aisles to exchange comments. As Gus and Ted moved quickly to retrieve their vehicles and transport their aged parents, Katherine couldn't resist.

"You look magnificent, Gus," she said. "Truly magnificent." She wanted to say, "You never looked lovelier," but she remembered in time that she was not a native Westerveldtian.

6

The Reception

The Swintons' garden, the pride of Westerveldt and three-time Northeastern regional prizewinner of the Garden Club Federation, was ready for the guests who began to arrive after passing through the parlor to "wish the bride every happiness" and to "congratulate the groom" and to shake the hands of other principals on the receiving line. The uncle of the bride, (Benjamin Chandler Swinton III), was in charge of shepherding the guests toward one of the two tables at opposite ends of the lawn. He couldn't, as the ushers had done at the church, ask each newcomer to identify himself as a friend of the bride or of the groom, so he had to rely on his memory of his large acquaintance and assume that an unfamiliar face belonged to the groom's guest list. The second table was a concession, grudgingly made, to the rather militant teetotaling beliefs of the groom's mother who, in all other respects, had seemed to be a sensible woman.

Both tables were laid with identical white linen cloths, both held large crystal punch bowls, one monogrammed with Genevieve Swinton's initials, the other with her sister Jacqueline's. The punch bowl to the left held a mixture Ben had experimented with for several weeks; a rich infusion of tea was the base to which he had added different fruit juices, adjusting the proportions until he decided that the blend no long tasted like a breakfast drink but a reasonable alcohol-free equivalent of real punch. In the punchbowl to the right was his recipe for champagne punch which he knew by heart how to concoct to perfection. Graciously he led the first arrivals, quite unmistakably from the groom's side, to the left and consigned them to a negro butler, hired from the Westerveldt Arms for the afternoon, who took up the silver ladle in his white-gloved hand, filled a fluted crystal punch-glass an accurate 7/8ths full and bowed slightly as he offered it to the guest.

Another negro butler, double expense but there would be a saving on champagne, served to the right. A third butler, hired for the entire day, and the Swintons' maid were waiting in the pantry for the signal to bring out the trays with tiny, crustless finger-sandwiches they had spent the morning preparing, carving loaves of white bread into thin slices and daubing them with one or another of a dozen delicate spreads. The sandwiches, numbering about a thousand, had been arranged in intricate patterns on silver platters, covered with damp cloths, and stored in the refrigerator.

The women exclaimed at the beauty of the garden, even if they had seen in a hundred times. It never ceased to amaze. On the sides of the spacious lawn were tiers of green and color, shaded by ancient trees. The garden had three cycles of bloom: spring, summer, and autumn, with some intermediate or transitional plantings so that even as the total appearance of the garden changed, it remained always prodigiously productive. Genevieve Swinton had worked for two decades with charts, books, and magazines, using her sharp eyes and excellent memory when she visited her competitors or the formal gardens now found only on the richest estates.

Ben Swinton had said, "Delighted to see you" several dozen times, introducing himself to those he didn't recognize and then guiding them firmly to the left, when Horace Callendar appeared on the terrace. Here was an old friend. Ben clapped him on the back. "Horace, old man, it's really good to see you."

"Well, Ben, quite a day," Horace said as they shook hands vigorously. "You look very well organized."

"I am. I am. Practically professional. I'm thinking of hiring myself out."

"You may have to. They passed that pay-as-you-go income tax and that bastard signed it, and now come July first, they'll be bleeding us white. I told Clara this morning, we'd better marry off Marianne before we're completely wiped out."

"You're not going to let a little thing like that tax stand in your path, are you, Horace? Get yourself a good accountant, and make sure you've got a good lawyer."

"Accountants and lawyers cost money."

"They save you money in the long run. Remember, sometimes you have to spend money to make money. Think ahead, old man, think ahead. Or the parade will pass you by. Come, have a drink," but as Horace turned to the left, he steered him to the right and said in a low voice, "the Episcopalian punch is over here."

"What is that?" Horace pointed to the table and punch bowl to the left.

"I call it ambrosia. It's my own invention, and I'm sure it would be a great thirst-quencher after eighteen holes in the sun, but what you want is over here." He nodded over his shoulder. "My niece has married into the WCTU."

"And Jack let her?"

"The boy's all right. Go, have Calvert fix you up," and he called out, "Calvert, do your best by Mr. Callendar here."

"Yes, sir, Mr. Swinton." Calvert smiled, bowed, and faced the challenge. Ceremoniously, he swirled the ladle around the bowl twice to run the punch over the cake of ice; he found a pocket of fluid on one side that would just fit the ladle in one scoop, and, with a flourish, he poured a cupful.

"There you are, Mr. Callendar, now tell me if that suits you."

Horace took a sip. "Perfect," he said as he walked off to mingle with the guests. He turned back. "Thank you, Calvert."

As the number of guests in the garden increased, the groups standing in front of the two tables began to merge. Ben realized that soon someone going back for a refill might head unsuspectingly toward the wrong table so he moved quickly to avoid confusion or embarrassment.

He whispered to Dunham, the negro butler at the left table, "If someone comes up for punch who hasn't been to you before, tell them, before you pour, that this is fruit punch. If they look like one of our friends, tell them the champagne punch is over there." He crossed the lawn and spoke to Calvert. "My new

nephew's relatives don't drink. If any of them come to you, you'll
have to tell them that this is champagne punch and send them
over to Dunham for the fruit stuff." Calvert nodded, wise in the
ways of the world. He was ageless; no one could remember when
he hadn't been the best waiter in the Westerveldt Arms dining
room and most in demand as extra help when there was a large
party off the premises. The hotel management acquiesced in these
arrangements without demurral; the hotel's mortgage was held by
Jack Sanford's bank.

Emily found Mary D. and after they had each received a glass
of punch from Calvert and greeted "Uncle Ben" who kissed them
both, while pinching Mary D.'s waist, they walked off toward the
edge of the garden near the rose arbor to share confidences.

"Did you notice?" Mary D. asked as she fished in her bag for
cigarettes, "there's scarcely a man here. Christ! How long is this
damned war going to last?"

"Your brother's here."

"A lot of good that does me," Mary D. answered. "And he didn't
even bring a buddy home with him. What else are brothers for?"

"He looks handsome in his uniform." Emily looked across at
the tall naval lieutenant in his summer whites.

"A lot of good it'll do you or anyone else." Mary D. was
disgusted.

"Guess what his postwar plans are? You'd never guess. Mummy's
in a first-class snit and Daddy keeps arguing with him."

"Tell me. Is it something exciting like climbing mountains in
Tibet or exploring jungles?" Peter, she remembered, had once
constructed a very authentic teepee in the woods and lived in it for
a week.

"No such luck. But solitary enough. He wants to go to a
seminary and be ordained."

"What's so terrible about that?"

"When he first told us, the only objection Mummy had was
that he'd be poor. Daddy was furious because he wants him to
work at the Yard. Why else have a son, he says, if he can't plan to
retire some day and hand over the business. But before they could

proceed to argue him out on those grounds, he dropped the second bomb."

"What was that? I can't imagine."

"He's got religion in a big way. Mummy blames the navy."

"For giving him religion?"

"No. For driving him to religion. Now he doesn't want to be just a minister. He wants to be an Anglican priest and, get this, if you can imagine this for a peaceful dinner table conversation, he intends to take celibate vows."

Emily was dumbfounded. She looked over again at the tall figure in white she'd known all her life. "I can see why they're upset," she said. "Where did he ever get such an idea?"

"God knows—and no joke intended. He says he has a calling, and if he didn't have his duty to his country, he'd start at the seminary right now. You can't imagine how serious he is. He doesn't laugh any more or tease me or Mummy. I've never seen such a change in anyone."

"Maybe it's just a phase, as my mother would say." Emily commented. "Maybe he'll meet some girl who'll make him change his mind."

"You're welcome to try, if you dare, and good luck to you. You're likely to get a sermon on the vanity of the things of this world. They never taught us that in Sunday School."

"Oh, yes they did. You just didn't listen. Wait until Father Wadsworth gets here next month. He's full of that kind of talk. People are getting more spiritual now, since the war started. If you paid attention, you'd know. Come to think of it, I didn't see you in church last Sunday."

"I can't go, alas. Sunday's the day I have airplane spotting duty."

"What are you talking about? Airplane spotting, here, in Westerveldt?"

"You may not have noticed," Mary D. said acidly, "that no matter what Westerveldt may or may not have here on the ground, it does have air over it. Civilian Defense need people to spot the planes, identify them—I had to take a course in identification— and log everything that flies by. Every plane has to be accounted for. You never know what might try to slip through."

Emily looked up at the blue sky, planeless and cloudless. "I can't picture a Nazi plane flying over us."

"They're keeping track of all planes. They worry about spies, black marketeers, illegal flights of all kinds, and they're training us in case the Nazis do try something." She looked at Emily. "Why don't you try it? It's something to do."

"You forget. I've got this nasty job my mother made me take. I'm so tired when I get home, I wouldn't do a good deed even at gun point."

Mary D. stared at her. "You've got it all wrong. Okay, so I stand up on the roof of the Westerveldt Arms and play with the binoculars, but that's not all there is to it."

"I don't get you."

"The hotel has other attractions. In the first place, we work in teams. To verify the information. You never know what you might draw, although I nearly flipped my lid when I was paired with Uncle Ben last week. Now he thinks he can pinch my waist every time he sees me. But, be that as it may, you obviously don't know that WWST has its studios on the fourth floor."

"So what? So what if WWST is in the hotel?"

"So what? Emily, you don't know what goes on around you."

"How can I? I have to be at work at eight ayem."

"You poor thing! Luckily, I'm safe. Mummy is still trying to protect me from the real world, especially after what it's done to Peter. I get stuck helping her with her volunteer projects—that's how I got involved with Civilian Defense—but she doesn't see me solving the manpower shortage in some factory."

"Hooray for you, but what's at the station?"

"Disk jockeys, silly. Who do you think runs the station? I met this divine guy. He works the weekend shift and other off hours. So, whenever I have a break and after my stint on the roof, we sneak some time together."

"You actually found somebody in Westerveldt who's worth going after?" Emily shook her head in amazement. "Boy, I have to hand it to you. What's he like?"

"Too short." Mary D. clapped her shoulder blade. "But I decided not to be fussy. These days you take what you can get."

"Do I know him? How come he's not in the service?"

"You don't know him. Nobody knows him. And he's the sole support of an invalid mother. How long this will keep him out is anybody's guess, but we're making hay while the sun shines."

"How do you know nobody knows him? What's his name?"

"I'll tell you," Mary D. looked around. Her father was at the punch bowl. Her mother was chatting with Katherine Osterhoudt. Her grandmother was sitting in the shade with the other octogenarians. "But only if you swear you won't tell a living soul. This is going to be a long vacation, and I'll be bored out of my skull if I don't have some excitement."

"I swear."

"Willard Cranston."

"Cranston." Emily thought for a minute. "I knew a Henry Cranston."

"You did? Where did you know him?"

"When I used to go to Flossy Vinson's to play, there was a Henry Cranston in the neighborhood. That was a great neighborhood, full of kids."

"You don't know anything about him?"

"He was just in the neighborhood, and you know that neighborhood. The Vinson house is the last old-time house. I don't even know what his father did, if he had one."

"That's the same one," Mary D. deduced. "His father died when he was little. He uses his middle name now that he's working, but his first name is Henry. Now it's H. Willard Cranston."

"You're lucky. I haven't met a man since I've been home. Everybody's gone."

"Nobody where you work?"

Emily shook her head. "Kids. Married men. Some of the kids are fun, but there's nobody I can bring home. They're all Italians."

"If the war lasts another five years, we'll not only be old maids, we'll be crazy as well. There's a time salesman with a punctured eardrum at the station, but he's not around much on weekends. No sense bitching, I guess, but when they started building training bases, couldn't they have built one near here? We could have a nice little USO and entertain our brave boys in the evening. I wonder if the guys feel as crazy as I do."

"Don't think that if they had a base near here you'd meet anybody. Can you picture our parents letting us out at night to dance with soldiers? Unless it was an Officers' Candidates School, and even then."

Ben Swinton came up at that moment and asked them if they were enjoying themselves. He hit a sore spot as he said, with some malice aforethought, "Slim pickings for you girls these days, right? Leaves the field open for old codgers like me" He put an arm around Mary D.'s waist feeling for a fingerful of soft flesh.

Emily seriously and tactlessly replied, "When will this war be over?"

Ben was insulted. "It can't last forever. We've got them on the run. But I'm no military expert. Go talk to Gus Van Leuven. He follows the campaigns on all fronts. You leave me to Mary D. here. Mary, Mary, sweet as any name can be."

Emily moved off to get another cup of punch and was interrupted by her father. "One is enough," he said.

"I'm over eighteen, and this is nothing," she answered.

"Champagne sneaks up on you. If you're going to have more, at least eat something." He picked two sandwiches off a passing tray and handed them to her. "They'll be cutting the cake soon, I think. Beautiful wedding."

Emily agreed between the four bites it took to finish both sandwiches.

"We probably won't see another like it for years to come, if ever," he shook his head sadly, and said to Mr. Giles, "Good afternoon, Reverend. Beautiful service. Beautiful wedding. Here, have a little wine for your stomach's sake."

Peter Van Leuven seemed to be exercising the mastery of self he had learned on the parade grounds. He stood almost at attention with an impassive, impersonal smile on his face but didn't move to strike up a conversation or get himself a cup of punch or light a cigarette. He murmured, "No, thank you" every time a sandwich tray was passed and "How do you do?" every time someone caught his eye. He didn't look unhappy, just removed and patient. Emily watched him for several minutes from the punch bowl and then, well aware what he thought of her as a pal of his sister's, decided that his resolve, however it defeated her own purposes, at least made him an interesting person. She approached him deferentially, as if he were already an ordained priest.

"Hello, Peter. Mary D. tells me you're home on leave."

Peter acknowledged that it was true.

"Are you enjoying the peace and quiet of Westerveldt in wartime?" She tried to cock her head coyly.

"It's unreal," he said. "It's even too good to be true. But I know it will end soon enough. That thought keeps me from enjoying it."

"Where do you go next?"

"Who knows? I'm to be assigned to a new ship, and I can get my orders at any time. I'm living from day to day."

"Do you have any idea where they'll send you?"

"None. But given my training, I suspect it'll be the Pacific."

"What kind of training?"

"You don't really want to know." Peter looked over her head at the view of the Wester Kill on the other side of the garden.

"Oh I wouldn't, wouldn't I," Emily teased. "Try me. You're not the first naval officer I've met, you know. You're just the first who thinks I won't understand. If you translate your technicalities into English, I'll understand."

Peter smiled, such a superior smile. "Maybe you would," he said, "but if you don't mind, I'd just as soon talk about something else. I'd like to forget the war while I'm home."

Emily was stung but determined to make an impression. "You should have no trouble forgetting the war here. I don't think anybody pays much attention to it except to gripe about rationing. Although Uncle Ben says your father is an armchair strategist."

Peter glanced around the garden to see where the cutaway was standing—over near the peony bed, hands behind the back, under the tails, talking heatedly about something with Horace Callendar.

"Dad's only interested in the land war in Europe since he was there in the army in the last war. He doesn't pay attention to the navy, except as transportation for land units. He has no picture in his mind of the war in the Pacific, which is the navy's war."

"Doesn't he ask any questions?"

"Only about my postwar plans. He's not interested in the inconveniences of the present. He's concerned about postwar expansion, as he calls it. He says the housing industry will boom, and he wants me to help him plan for it."

Emily hesitated. Should she mention what Mary D. had told her? Not yet.

"What do you think about his plans?" she ventured.

"They have nothing to do with me," Peter answered. His eyes took on a gleam of purpose. "Except that I wish him success. I've decided to enter the ministry."

Emily was relieved. "Oh, how fascinating," she said as sincerely as she could. "You know, Reinhold Niebuhr gave a series of lectures at college during the spring semester. He made Protestant theology much more absorbing than poor Mr. Giles ever could. Are you going to enter a seminary when the war's over?"

"Definitely. I've made up my mind. It's all settled." Peter changed his tone from defiant to curious. "Did you really attend those lectures? You were only a freshman."

Emily tossed her head. "Even a freshman is ready to learn. As a matter of fact, Peter, believe it or not, the reason Niebuhr gave those lectures was because the war has shaken people's beliefs. The standard answers don't work any more, especially not with people our age who are mostly directly affected by it all."

"Our age?" The indulgent smile again. "How are you affected by the war?"

Emily forgot that she was trying to flirt by making herself as attractive as possible.

"You think we're not affected by the war?" she snapped. "We may not be called upon to fight, but the war affects everything we do. Every man or boy I know is in the service or wondering if he will be. Or he feels like an outcast because no one will take him. It's impossible to have normal friendships or dates or contacts with men any more. They come and go. Their minds are on what they have to do. Here am I in college, studying, and writing letters to guys I know all over the world. And," she couldn't stop herself in time, "some of the letters come back." She looked away, embarrassed and almost tearful as she realized what she'd said.

Peter was also embarrassed so he said calmly, "You'll get used to it. You'll have to get used to it."

Emily flared at him, "I'll never get used to it. I don't want to get used to it. Stan Morrissey, Mark Crellin, Walter Franklin—you're asking me to get used to the fact that they were killed? They were my friends, and I loved Walter Franklin. Get used to it! Like rheumatism!" She stomped off toward the champagne-punch table where her father encountered her.

"Not a third one," he said sternly, "and this time I mean it."

Gus' voice could be heard above the ordinary conversational hum. "Sits in that wheelchair and decides our fates. He's never had to work to build up a business or a profession. He never had to meet a payroll. It was all handed to him on a silver platter. He can afford to give it all away. What about the rest of us? He's a traitor to his class." Isobel had moved at the first syllable to quiet him.

"I notice," Emily said to her father, "that he wore it anyway. He's the only one."

"Gus doesn't give in. He's a rockbound Republican, a rockbound Westerveldtian, and a rockbound member of his class."

"He'll be wiped out as things change. And they're changing fast."

"Not Gus. The rest of us, maybe. Gus is ready for anything. All over town the workers in the plants and factories are organizing. They want to join unions and get contracts with wage increases. They want their share. Gus got the jump on everybody. He's organized his own shop union with a contract that runs for the duration. He gave out a modest raise, but he won't have to hand over an extra penny till the war's over. And he's bidding now on two government contracts. He talks a lot of bombast, but he's smart."

At that moment Genevieve Swinton told her husband it was time to cut the cake; the two of them mingled with the guests to urge them back into the parlor, and none too soon. The maid had told her five minutes before that they were "down to the last tray" of sandwiches. Ben saw the groom's uncle (Mrs. Sloane's brother) stroll toward Calvert's table for a last sip of punch on the hot afternoon. Ben thought of stopping him, shrugged off the responsibility, and went inside.

The three-tiered cake, even when cut up and served on the dessert plates Genevieve had collected throughout her marriage—she had five sets of twelve each and a miscellaneous assortment of unmatched gems she had picked up in antique stores or discovered while traveling—didn't go far toward satisfying the appetites of Bill's relatives. Most of them had put in a hard morning's work, taken the afternoon off and eaten a light lunch to save room for what they assumed would be a groaning board of a feast in such a rich and elegant home. As soon as they had finished the last crumb of the two-by-four inch slab of cake and known without asking that there would be no more to eat, they moved to collect their wives. There were several impassioned *sotto voce* conferences. As soon as the bride and groom had left, they paid their respects and began to walk to their cars. Bill's Uncle Rich, who had just had a taste of champagne and who was not known for his self-control although he had an excellent reputation as a master house-painter and paper-hanger, could be heard sounding off,

"This is one time when Molly's dry ideas are going to have to take a back seat. I move we all meet at the Wops' on Washington Avenue and have ourselves some spaghetti and some veal parmajohn and a couple of pitchers of beer to wash it down. Molly and Charley can join us there after they drop the kids at the station, and we can celebrate the way we know how."

7

The Swintons

As soon as they had acknowledged the last thank-you, accepted the last congratulation, and said the last goodby, the Swintons and the Sanfords repaired to the garden. Calvert, Dunham, and Marvin from the hotel had already, invisibly, removed the punchbowls, collected all the punch glasses and the napkins, folded the tablecloths, and carried the tables to the terrace. There seemed not to be a trace of the party—only the cigarette butts, two of Jeff Catsby's splatted cigars, and the blades of grass, exhausted from so many milling shoes, struggling to right themselves.

Ben brought out an ice bucket, four highball glasses, and a bottle of scotch.

"Alone at last," he said as he put the tray down on a white-painted wrought-iron garden table. They sat down on the chairs the elderly guests had just vacated.

"Not for me," Jacqueline warned. "Today I feel like Bill's mother. I don't want another drop."

"I never asked you," her sister said, surprised at herself for the oversight. "What do you call her?"

"We're very proper. I decided it was the only way." Jacqueline explained carefully. "Jack and I talked about it. I didn't want to get carried away by intimacy too soon. We'll be seeing a lot of each other over the next twenty years. It's better to keep a certain distance. I call her Mrs. Sloane and she calls me Mrs. Sanford. Jack and Mr. Sloane are on a first-name basis, but they run into each other now and then. Business. Of course, Jack calls her Mrs. Sloane and I call him Mr. Sloane."

"That's very sensible," Genevieve agreed after brief consideration. "You can always switch to first names, but I can't imagine how you could switch back. Not easily. At least you couldn't. You wouldn't know how to pull rank if you thought you were unkind."

"You're the one who's kind, Genny," Jacqueline reached for her sister's hand. "I can't thank you enough. I couldn't have managed without you. The wedding took all my strength. If I'd had to put on the reception as well, by now I'd be lying down with a headache instead of relaxing. You did a marvelous job. Everything was perfect."

"I'm glad you're pleased, dear. I think it went well, if I do say so myself. It was a day for all of us to remember, seeing Genevieve married. I think we did ourselves proud."

"Genevieve looked lovely, didn't she?" Jacqueline felt herself becoming tearful.

"There never was a more beautiful bride, unless it was you," her sister answered generously.

"Do you think she'll be happy, Genny?" Jacqueline asked as the men moved to the edge of the garden with their highballs.

"Why shouldn't they be? He's a nice boy, and they love each other. You've done everything you can for them. The rest is up to them."

"You know what I'm referring to, Genny," Jacqueline said meaningfully. "How can you tell ahead of time?"

There was no immediate answer. That subject, taboo, was a secret the sisters shared only with each other. Jacqueline had never mentioned it to Jack. She had never, until now, been the first to bring it up with Genevieve. In their early married years, Genevieve had often cried. Jacqueline could offer comfort but not advice. They were not sure they understood what the problem was. There was a name for Ben's "condition"; Jacqueline had read about it in the marriage manual. The book offered hope of a cure *if* the patient would face his situation "squarely and frankly," submit to counseling and be willing to learn about "sound sexual practices." Instead of frankness, there was shame and embarrassment, and sound sexual practices remained mysteries known by mythical counselors found probably only in those cosmopolitan centers where everyone didn't know everyone else.

Jacqueline quickly apologized. "I didn't mean to upset you, Genny. It was a tactless remark. I'm thinking of Genevieve, and I had to ask someone."

"It's all right. I don't get upset about it any more. Not very often, anyway. At the beginning, I was upset all the time, but if I'd gone on that way, I'd have gone crazy. Ben's a good man. I have a beautiful home, everything I want." Genevieve seemed to mean what she said as she smiled contentedly at her garden. "I count my blessings."

"But what do you think about Genevieve?" Jacqueline persisted.

"As you say, who can tell? They seem very much in love, very romantic. Maybe they'll figure it all out. I don't know why," her tone became dry, "if this was worrying you, knowing what kind of misery she could be in for, you didn't advise her to find out ahead of time."

"I thought of it," Jacqueline admitted with relief. Only to her sister could she voice such thoughts. "God knows I thought about it. But how can a mother tell her daughter to do such a thing? Especially after the way we've brought her up. She's beautiful, and she's an only child, and everybody thinks we're rich. Young men have been swarming around her ever since she started college. I couldn't suggest she experiment after telling her for years to keep men at arm's length,"

"Once she became engaged to Bill you could have."

"How can you say such a thing? What if 'it' hadn't turned out? The engagement was announced. The machinery put in motion. How could we have backed down? What could we have said?"

Genevieve smiled as she pictured such a chain of events. "True. But if you want her to be happy, you have to take some chances. Didn't you talk to her at all?"

"Of course I talked to her, as best I could. Jack was after me for weeks to see that she got to a doctor."

"Then you had every opportunity for a thorough discussion,

especially after she'd been to the doctor," was Genny's practical assessment. "Who did you take her to? Dr. Hansen? I hope you didn't take her to Dr. Forrest."

"Dr. Hansen. Everybody says he's the most modern. He gave her some things to read. I've always liked old Dr. Forrest myself. He's kind, but he doesn't discuss birth control. For that I had to go to Katherine's man in New York. But, Genny, you shock me. You think I should have warned her of the-um-problems of marriage in advance? How could I do that? Have her on the lookout for trouble when there might not be any? Make her self-conscious. No." She shook her head. "Besides, I would never have put her in the position of having to make the first move. Bill never would have. He's too respectful. He would never have betrayed our trust."

"So you decided to trust to luck, instead."

"And nature."

"It's hard, I guess. I don't know what I would have done if I'd been in your shoes. If it weren't for the war, you could have taken her on a trip to Paris after she got out of college. Remember that summer they wouldn't let me get engaged to Barney Comstock, and Mother whisked me off to Paris to forget? That opened my eyes."

"I remember. I ran the house while you were gone."

"The French have a different attitude. They protect their girls as much as we do. Chaperones, watchful eyes, never leave them alone with a young man, but the girls know what they're being protected from. I don't think our girls do. They have only a dim idea. In France it's in the air, in the way men and women talk to each other. They're not prudish when they use the word pleasure. I think Americans are terrible prudes."

"The French are immoral, Genny. We all know that. That's all they think about. Besides," Jacqueline added after mulling over some idea of Frenchness for a moment, "we're not French."

"The French also have more fun. If Mother hadn't been at my side every minute . . ." Genny's eyes gleamed at the memory. "But never mind. You sound as if Westerveldt itself weren't teeming with infidelities, unwanted babies, and fooling around. Why, before she died, there were even rumors about old Lizzie Van Slyke and her chauffeur. We're just as human as anyone else."

"But you know as well as I do that nobody talks about it."

"That's not true." Genny flatly disagreed. "They talk about nothing else, but not in plain English. Innuendoes, hints, jokes, or such vague terms you need an education in life to understand what they're talking about. Come to think of it, Jackie, Genevieve spent four years at a good woman's college. She must have picked up some knowledge."

"I've been counting on that. But I wouldn't be surprised to find out that Smith is like Westerveldt. The girls who do won't talk about it to the girls who don't."

"It's a miracle the race continues. Perhaps she took biology courses. She does know about reproduction."

"Not really," Jacqueline sighed. "She had to take some science, but she chose geology. There was a course in health: nutrition, physical fitness, a film on the birth of a baby which she remembered because two girls fainted. Probably enough to scare them off sex for life."

The men came back for a refill, and Ben suggested, "Let's go to the Arms for dinner. The aunties will have left by the time we get there."

"Won't everybody be going there?" Genevieve asked.

"I don't think so," Ben answered. "I overheard people making plans. Most of them are going to the Sea Rover or the Riverboat or the Villa Florentina."

"I wonder if I could eat a full dinner," Jacqueline said. "I ate so much this afternoon." (Six sandwiches and a slice of wedding cake.)

"Just an appetizer and salad then," Genevieve suggested. "It would do you good. Let's go in and freshen up."

"Jacqueline seems low," Ben commented to his brother-in-law. "Sad to lose her little girl?"

"We're both sad, but I don't think we've lost her." Jack tried to put his emotions in perspective. "They'll be back in two weeks, and they'll be just down the street. I assume Jacqueline will be over there every day to help them settle in. And there's going to be the little matter of teaching Genevieve how to dust and make beds, not to mention cooking."

"They won't have help? How much are you paying that poor boy, Jack?" Ben needled.

"As much as I dare," Jack said firmly. "I can't overpay him too much at first or he'll lose his ambition and think he can get something for nothing. I've got to turn him into a businessman somehow. If they manage carefully, they'll be able to afford someone to come in and clean. If not, Jacqueline will slip her a dollar here and there. I don't want her doing any heavy cleaning. There's no reason she should suffer. Believe me, however, the young shouldn't get too much too soon."

"I would have liked a son," Ben said unexpectedly. "What's going to happen to my business when I'm gone?"

"These are hard to days to be a young man," Jack observed by way of comfort.

"Any danger of Bill's being called up?"

"I hope not. He's got a game knee from playing basketball. It will all depend on how desperate the war gets. If they lower the standards, if this damned war doesn't end, he may have to go."

"The only other problem I foresee," Ben mused, remembering his duties that afternoon, "is your new relatives. What are you going to do about them?"

"Nothing," Jack answered impatiently. He and he wife had accepted the discrepancy; did their friends have to keep pointing it out to them? "What can I do? They're Bill's parents."

"Are you planning to include them in our circle?"

"There's no need to. We'll invite them for informal family dinner with the children once or twice a year to show good will. If we give a big party, we'll invite them out of courtesy. As for the rest of it, Charley and I have dealings with each other."

"You get along with him?" Ben asked in genuine surprise.

"Of course I get along with him. He's a first-rate carpenter, none better. I can't always see my way clear to float loans for all his schemes, but he's a solid citizen."

"Still, it must be awkward to see them socially." The Swintons never entertained outsiders. Ben would pass on new people in town at the Van Vorsts or the Callendars or the Osterhoudts or the Van Leuvens before he would have them in his house. An invitation to the Swintons' was the accolade—the newcomers had arrived.

"Needn't be. Just common sense. You can't make a silk purse out of a sow's ear. I wouldn't try. They're decent people." Jack emphasized "decent."

"I'm wondering what you'll do when they invite *you* for an informal family dinner and serve you corned beef and cabbage and god knows what to drink with it."

"I can always have something before I go."

"It won't be the same. In our circle, with our own kind, our hosts know what we want and see that we get it."

"It'll never be the same, Ben."

"Let's have another, Fortify yourself against your first family dinner with the Sloanes'."

*   *   *

At Dante's (pronounced "Dandy's") over on Washington Avenue, the ladies of the Sloane-Otis clan studied the menu and discussed the wedding. Uncle Rich was out in the bar describing the afternoon to Vince the bartender.

"Some affair. St. Andrew's. Reception down the street at the Swinton place—set up in the garden. White tablecloths, negro butlers, silver trays. But get this. They got two tables, see, one on each side of the lawn. I come in, Swinton takes me over to one of the tables for a glass of punch. Not bad, kinda sweet, no kick to it. When I go back for more, I go to the other table, and this time I get real punch. But did he tell me I had a choice? It's a wedding, for Chrissake. I figure he made the fruit stuff for Molly, okay, but the sonovabitch made us all drink it. Let me have another."

As the other husbands appeared, one by one, Vince set up a row of shot glasses and poured an ounce of Vat 69 into each one.

"And a Bud all around," Rich gestured magnanimously as he continued his story. "So we stand there drinking lemonade and whaddya think they give us to eat! Sandwiches this size!" He spread his thumb and forefinger a quarter-inch apart. "Hundreds of 'em, but how many can you eat? I say to myself, well, this is what they give us before the real food. They'll bring out the heavy stuff later on, but no, all of a sudden, they cut the cake and it's all over."

"You mean," Vince asked as he poured the beers, "that was all you had to eat? Don't make sense. Swinton's got a bundle. It's not like he didn't have it. So, Charley, your boy's new in-laws going to starve you all out? Is that the picture?"

"Food ain't everything," Charley answered.

"Oh yeah?" Rich jeered. "You think you're gonna get fat on loans from the Westerveldt Bank?"

"I don't ask favors. I never have and I never will. Sanford's okay, and he's been good to my boy."

"I can see it now." Rich crooked his little finger off the side of his beer glass. "You get invited to la-di-dah dinners where they give you one slice of roast beef and some frozen peas. And since Molly will be there, you won't even get to wet your whistle. Why didn't you make Bill stick with his own kind?"

PART TWO

1

On the Porch

After dinner the elder Osterhoudts and the Catsbys adjourned to the back porch to catch the evening breezes and watch the fireflies dart about in the gloaming near the fern bed. Peace was harder and harder to achieve even in that carefully tended haven. Jeff and Ted started talking politics as they sat down. Sarah and Nelly exchanged comments on the wedding, but it was difficult to complete any intelligible paragraph over the raised voices of the men. Jeff had to talk loudly so Ted could hear him, but Jeff wasn't deaf so there was no excuse for Ted's bellowing. They agreed—why did they have to shout so? They both hated Roosevelt, they both resented government interference in business affairs, they both hated the war and felt the United States should not have entered it. They saw no reason for taxation, rationing, allocations, priorities, paper work—"A man's word is enough"—but as they went down their list of complaints, they released their fury in yelling at each other. Every time Nelly said something quietly like "I understand Lizzie Van Slyke's son is here from California," Sarah's reply, "I wonder what Lizzie would have said to the striped wallpaper Jacqueline Sanford put in her foyer," was drowned out by a "Goddamnit" which Nelly would try to shush.

Several times she suggested they go inside and start a hand of bridge. Once she rose from her chair and approached them, but they put her off with, "We haven't finished." The litany of grievances grew as either Jeff or Ted remembered another government encroachment. That man could do nothing right. He was gobbling up the country. They continued to sit outside until it was quite dark and they could no longer see each other except as shapeless forms. Nelly was thinking such desperate thoughts as "this is the last time I invite anyone over for a pleasant evening if this is what comes of it," when the air raid siren sounded from the firehouse three blocks away.

"Oh, drat." Nelly disliked strong language but what else was there to say? She got up to turn off the lights in the parlor where the bridge table had been set up and the light in the pantry where the cakes had been laid out on trays. "Turn off all your lights, Martha," she called down the cellar stairs to the kitchen where Martha was finishing the dishes. Then, on her way back to the porch, stumbling a little in the darkness, she noticed a light from upstairs shining down the stairwell. "Drat," she said again and turned on the nearby hall light to guide her return passage.

When she was on her way back downstairs, there was a loud knock at the door. Who could it be? In an air raid? It couldn't be Teddie. He was a warden and over at the firehouse by now. The girls? They wouldn't knock. Nelly knew better than to hurry. Two of her friends were nursing broken hips from their carelessness. There was another knock and then another. No one from the porch moved, perhaps they hadn't heard, so Nelly proceeded down the front hall toward the front door, not alarmed or afraid, but faintly apprehensive.

She opened the door to find a young man who was wearing a helmet and carrying a flashlight.

"You got lights on," he said, with no preliminary good evening. "This is an air raid. Get your lights off. We got sixty more seconds," and he ran down the steps, beaming his flashlight ahead of him.

Nelly went back down the hall, turned off the hall light, and made her way slowly out to the porch. It was completely dark now—no street lights, no house lights, but the men were still arguing as if nothing had happened other than to add "confounded air raid alerts" to their list of complaints. Sarah was rocking. "Who was that at the front door?"

"Some boy in a helmet. I didn't recognize him, but he must be somebody from the neighborhood. He didn't seem to know my name. He didn't say 'Mrs. Osterhoudt.' He told me to turn off the lights. Not please or would you. Just 'put your lights out.' I was doing my best. Ted left a light on upstairs. There goes our bridge game, I guess. How long will this last, do you think?"

Sarah's chair rocked soothingly as she said, "If it's just a drill, it might be over in fifteen minutes."

"If it's just a drill. What do you mean if it's just a drill?" Nelly felt her heart flutter.

"It could be a real air raid," Sarah said imperturbably.

"Oh." Then a pause. "Why would the Germans want to bomb Westerveldt?" Nelly asked her impatiently. Before Sarah could think up an answer to lead her best friend into fresh harmless distress, they were both startled to see a figure rustle over Teddie's fence near the lilac bush. It streaked across the grass, through the fern bed, and scrambled over the fence that separated the Osterhoudts' garden from the Woods's. Sarah and Nelly gasped in unison as that figure was followed by another and then another.

"My ferns!" Nelly cried. "The men don't seem to have noticed anything. Sarah, who could that have been?"

"Who knows?" Sarah was no longer inclined to tease. "Nelly, did you lock the front door after you answered it?" Had she locked her own door, she wondered.

"Lock the door? No, of course not. I never lock the door."

"I'll go with you. Do you have a flashlight?"

"Yes, but I don't know where it is. Teddie tells me I should keep one on the hall table, but I forget."

Sarah switched on the hall light.

"Sarah, what are you doing?"

"Dammit, Nelly, I'm not going to risk my neck for the war effort. Now we can see to lock the door and get back to the porch."

"Don't swear, Sarah. It's not becoming."

"I hate to tell you, Nelly," Sarah answered wickedly, "but when I saw those figures, I couldn't help thinking of *Gone With the Wind*."

They reached the door and turned the lock before Nelly could ask her what she meant.

"Reconstruction. Scalawags. Marauders. When it's dark like this, who knows who goes out to commit mischief or worse. You should start keeping your doors locked."

"Sarah Catsby, I haven't locked the doors in this house in my whole life. What if Teddie wanted to get in or the girls? What are you talking about?"

A voice hollered from the street, "Lights out. Lights out. Lights," and they hurried to turn off the hall light.

"Give them keys. I'm only telling you for your own good. You'll feel safer. You and Ted sleep upstairs, and he' s stone deaf. Martha sleeps in the cellar and she's hard of hearing herself."

Nelly put her hand to her heart. "I have never, never, never been afraid in this house. Oh this awful war."

2

The Van Leuvens

Just before the first siren sounded, Augusta Van Leuven had risen from the sofa and said she would be on her way. Gus and Isobel made sure she had her gold-handled cane, her shawl, her handbag, and her hat. She was adjusting the peacock straw over her wonderful white hair when they were all startled by the alarm.

"There's nothing to do but come back and sit down," Gus said. "I'll get you some sherry while you wait. When the all clear sounds, I'll walk you home." Home was the Victorian mansion where Gus had been born, a hundred yards off Brunswick on the other side of the duckpond.

Isobel hurried from the room checking the lights and called upstairs to her son.

"What's all the confusion about?" Peter asked sleepily from the head of the stairs. Isobel was pleased to see him in an undershirt and old trousers rather than any part of his uniform. Handsome as he looked in his dress whites, she was always a little uneasy when she saw him wear them.

"An air raid drill. There's nothing to do but sit in the dark until it's over. You can come downstairs and sit with us, if you like, But turn off your lights and please check the other rooms upstairs for me."

"Why don't you get dark curtains? Then you could go on with whatever you're doing."

"Too much trouble. It doesn't happen often enough to bother about."

"Why do they bother at all, if they don't make you do it right?"

"I don't know, dear. I think they do it to remind us there's a war on, if case we might forget."

"I'll take a nap till it's over. Have fun."

Gus had brought sherry for Isobel and his mother, something else for himself, and a flashlight that he beamed at his mother every time she reached for a sip.

"Where is Mary D.?" Augusta asked. "She shouldn't be out in a dark city."

"She's spending the evening with Emily Osterhoudt," Isobel answered.

"Is that where she is? You just said a friend." Gus thought for a minute. "That's impossible. I'm going to call to see if she's there."

Isobel stopped him. "You can't use the phone until the all clear sounds. Why are you so worried? She can take care of herself. Ted will see she gets home safely."

"I'm not worried about her."

"I don't understand, Gus."

Her mother-in-law tapped her cane on the rug to some unknown rhythm. "I do," she said slyly. "The chickens have come home to roost."

In the darkness Isobel could see neither of their faces, but she heard Gus snort. "Will someone please tell me?"

"Your Mary Dwight takes after her father," her mother-in-law answered and added maliciously, "I should have thought you'd have noticed by now, Isobel. A mother has to keep track of her children, especially her daughters. Gus was a great one for leaving the house with the best possible excuses and coming in at all hours. In those days, not everyone had a phone. Sometimes I wouldn't find out the truth for a week. And there were two escapades I never did find out about."

"You mean you don't think she's with Emily?" Isobel couldn't believe it.

"Of course she's not with Emily. I saw Ted drive off with his parents and the Catsbys. Mary D. wasn't in the car. And I also saw Katherine walking up Brunswick with Emily and the younger girl. Mary D. wasn't with them either. Besides, if Katherine and Ted planned to take her home, they would have spoken to you or me. They know how to do things properly—most of the time." He was thinking of the white suits. "As soon as she asked you, you should have gone immediately to Katherine."

"Gus, she's nearly eighteen. I did that sort of thing when she was little."

"You shouldn't have relaxed your vigilance. Now, the question is, where is she? I'm sure you have no idea. She's out there somewhere in the dark."

"She didn't know there would be a drill."

"You can be sure she's taking advantage of it."

"How can you talk that way about your own daughter?"

Augusta cackled. "Guilty conscience. His past is coming back to haunt him. And a daughter can give you a lot more to worry about, Isobel." She delighted in needling her daughter-in-law. "It's your duty to find out her secrets. How else will you know what she does?"

"I can't find out anything she doesn't want to tell me," Isobel answered loftily.

"Doesn't she keep a diary or leave letters around? There are two phones in the house. My dear, you're not very clever."

"My own daughter! She's not a Nazi agent."

"She smokes. I've seen her. She goes out to the duckpond every hour or so to smoke a cigarette and I saw her smoking at the wedding. She likes champagne punch. She had several cups. Who knows what other habits she picked up in boarding school. The other vices are only steps away, you know that. If she were mine, I wouldn't let her out of my sight. She's a wild girl, as wild as her father was."

"If some people are to be believed, Mother," Gus answered her, "you led as flaming a youth as was possible in the gay eighties and nineties."

"I never got caught at my little adventures, which were harmless enough. Young ladies knew how to behave in my day. Besides, they had no choice. You give her too much freedom, sending her off to school where she meets people you know nothing about and picks up their bad habits. The only cure for that girl is an early marriage."

"Now, Mother," Isobel set the record straight, "you can't expect young woman in the 1940s to stay home and embroider. She wants to be busy, to be useful. She spends a lot of time with Bundles for Britain and Civilian Defense. She's an airplane spotter at the hotel."

"Aha." Gus leapt to his feet in the dark. "That's where she is. I should have thought of that. She's met someone over there at the hotel."

"Gus, where are you going? What do you mean? They spot airplanes on the roof."

"She has to go through the lobby to get to the roof. I hope it isn't a bellhop or a clerk." He thought a minute. The clerks were elderly, the bellhops underage, except for two negro porters. There were several shops on the ground floor of the hotel, a florist's, a gift shop, but they would be shut in the evening. He thought harder.

"There's only one way to find out," he said at last.

"Gus, you can't go out in the drill."

"I'd like to see someone try to stop me. If my daughter is out in the drill or sneaking around the hotel, I have to find her and I'll take my belt to her when I do. You see that Mother gets home." The front door slammed behind him.

"Mary Dwight is in for a surprise," her grandmother said gleefully. "I think I'll stay and see what happens."

"You need your rest, Mother," Isobel choked. "I'll see you get home as soon as the all-clear sounds. Or better yet, I'll ask Peter to walk you home."

"You know what the trouble with you is, Isobel? You always look for the good in people. That may be noble, but it's a lot safer to look for the bad and be on your guard."

"Mary Dwight is not a bad girl."

"High spirits. No sense. She needs a firm hand. She gets around you."

"She knows I trust her."

"Exactly. Your trust gives her the freedom to do as she pleases. Is there nothing she can find to do? The devil finds work for idle hands. Doesn't she garden?"

"I don't think gardening would use up all her energies."

"What do girls do nowadays? We were always kept busy. French lessons, dancing lessons, music lessons, riding lessons. Perhaps she should ride."

"It's hard with the war on."

"The war, the war, the war!" The old lady suddenly became querulous. "It's always the war. The inconveniences. You can't get things. Do you know what I had for luncheon Tuesday? Spam! Unspeakable. And I've had to give up my Saturday morning appointment at the hairdresser's. The women from the defense plants come in then. After all these years and Mr. David gives me a Thursday morning appointment." As she continued to recite the interruptions of her ordinary life, she remembered something else. "I spoke to Dr. McCullough about the Spam. He's writing a letter to the ration board so I can get extra meat, for my health."

"Oh, Mother, how could you? You're as strong as an ox. How could you ask Dr. McCullough to do such a thing when we're all asked to sacrifice?"

"I've sacrificed enough for my country. I gave my boy."

Isobel wanted to say: young Roger was killed twenty-five years ago. What about your grandson, the only Van Leuven left to carry on the name? Don't you know that the extra meat you cheat to get might some day save his life? But she knew better than to voice such thoughts. They sat in silence listening for an all clear but heard nothing in the summer stillness but far-off sounds of official vehicles patrolling the streets.

"Would you like to sit outside?" Isobel asked finally.

"Too many mosquitoes."

Another sore spot. Old Mrs. Van Leuven's duckpond was a breeding ground that irritated both households, but it could not be discussed. Isobel sighed. It was all right to discuss the way she brought up her children, to find the failings in her character, to criticize the way she managed her household or the people she chose as her friends, but it was not all right to discuss the duckpond, even if the ducks had died long ago and no one could enjoy the evenings out of doors.

"Tomorrow my Roger will have been dead six years," Augusta droned mournfully.

"Tomorrow's the twenty-seventh, I'd forgotten." Isobel was sympathetic.

"I'll never forget it," her mother-in-law rebuked her. "As long as I live, I'll never forget the sight of him lying there on the floor, one arm through his dinner jacket, the most dreadful expression on his face." She began to reconstruct the scene for the hundredth time. "I was ready and waiting downstairs. I may be nothing else, but I am punctual. Roger was always slow. He liked to take his time, always careful, every little detail. Young Roger was just like that. There was no sense hurrying either one of them. It never did any good. He wouldn't listen, he'd take his own sweet time as if he didn't have a care in the world. Penrose had brought the car around and was waiting outside. I had my wrap on, all ready to go—the Gibsons were giving an evening party for some friends of theirs from Saratoga Springs. I waited and waited and he didn't come. It was getting late and I called upstairs. To think, I was cross with him for keeping me waiting. Poor Roger—all that time he was lying there on the floor. I went up and when I opened the door I found him. I don't remember to this day what happened next, whether I went to him or whether I screamed first. I did not faint." She banged her cane firmly on the carpet. "Penrose came and Maggie. They said he was gone for sure, but we called Dr. McCullough anyway. It was too late. A stroke the doctor said. Poor Roger. He looked so thin in his coffin. Nothing has been the same since. That day was the beginning of the end. We had been married for nearly fifty years. I always used to say to Roger, if we can only last fifty years, have our golden anniversary together. But," she sighed, "it was not to be." Then she banged her cane again. "I must not dwell on the past," she said sternly. "He's gone. Some day I'll be gone too. And what has it all been for? Answer me that, Isobel, you're a good churchgoer. What has it all been for?"

"No one has that answer, Mother," Isobel said softly.

"They must say something."

"That we must have faith in God's love for us."

"Faith! And Hope! And Charity! I'll tell you what life is all about, Isobel." She pointed her cane in the dark in Isobel's direction.

"Life is what you make it. You decide what you want, then you figure out how you can get it. What is it you want, Isobel?"

Isobel was spared having to answer as the all clear sounded. The old lady was in one of her dangerous moods which were more frequent the older she got. She seemed to enjoy witnessing the family disagreements so she could take sides, usually Gus'. And she wouldn't always wait for them to find their own issues. She knew or could divine potential areas of conflict which, if they had not yet ripened, she could hurry along. She relished above all testing Isobel's tolerance and patience. Behind her back she called her son's wife a candidate for sainthood; she waited to see if Isobel would lose her temper, say something wounding or uncharitable, but she didn't want to see her cry. That would be no fun—not part of the game. Isobel was, after all, a good woman, if dull, no spirit, no fight. She never stood up to Gus. "Yes, dear, perhaps, dear, I'll see, dear." In her mind Augusta mimicked the patient voice. Why had Gus married her anyway? What did he see in her? It was easy to see what any woman saw in Gus—energy, decisiveness, self-assurance, no-nonsense, a real man.

3

The Osterhoudts

When the all clear sounded and lights began to appear again in the neighborhood, Nelly insisted they have at least one rubber of bridge so she could forget her fears of the marauders. They had no sooner become engrossed in the first hand when they heard someone fumbling with the knob of the front door. Sarah moved quickly. She picked up a shovel from the fireplace and handed it to Nelly and then grabbed the poker for herself.

"I'll go with you." At the front door the fumbling was louder.

"Who is it?" Nelly asked bravely.

"It's me, Mother. Ted."

He was wearing an air raid warden's helmet. There were a few confused moments of explanation—that door had not been locked in all of his forty-six years except when his parents had taken a vacation. Nelly blamed Sarah, and Sarah offered in her own defense the three figures in the garden.

"Who were they? What did they look like? By the lilac bush? Through the ferns? Come on inside and sit down." He comforted them with his authority as district warden. "I'll have it investigated. You're not to worry or be frightened. Remember Katherine and the girls are next door."

"But Teddie, we were all in the dark."

"That's why I dropped by, Mother. Lights were reported from the house during the alert."

"Yes, dear, I know. A young man came by. I turned them off as fast as I could."

"I'm responsible for the first ward, Mother," he explained very slowly and carefully. "When I get the reports at headquarters that all lights in the ward are out, I call City Hall and tell them. In the last three alerts, our ward had been the first to call in. We have the record as the best run and most efficient district in the city. My boys are on the streets the second the siren sounds."

Sarah broke in, "How can that be, Ted? They could be busy doing something."

"I get a call from Headquarters twenty minutes before the alert. I call my boys and tell them to get ready and stand by."

Sarah chuckled. "That's cheating. If it were a real air raid, you'd be as caught short as your mother was."

"That's the way it's done, Aunt Sarah. Now, Mother, tonight we were sixth, and when I checked to see whose lights were on, it turned out to be 295. My own mother and next door to me."

Nelly was ready to cry. "Teddie, don't scold. I did what I could, but I had to call Martha and your father left a light on upstairs."

Ted nodded compassionately. "It's a big house, I know. We'll have to work out a system. You need flashlights. Didn't I give you two flashlights? I don't want you falling. But I have to have a dark ward—that's my job."

"Teddie, you'll find out about those people in my garden, won't you? They went through your garden too, you know, and probably Sarah's as well. Over the fences. Up to no good, I tell you."

"I'll take care of it. Don't worry. Monday, I'll see about flashlights. And extra house keys. We'd better start locking the doors, at night anyway. There won't be another air raid for several weeks. The chief warden is going on vacation. You get a good night's sleep." He kissed her and brushed Sarah's cheek. "Say goodnight to Dad and Uncle Jeff for me." Left alone, the two old men had taken up their argument again.

Back in his own house, Ted put away his helmet and sat down in the living room with Katherine and Emily to describe the drill. He observed, after a minute or so, that Beatrice wasn't with them. "Is she upstairs?"

"She's out," Emily answered innocently.

"Out?!"

"As soon as the siren sounded, she put on her sneakers and went out on the terrace while Mother and I turned off the lights."

"Where did she go? Is she out there now?"

Katherine looked uncomfortable. The front door opened softly and Beatrice came in in her jeans and shirt, breathless, flopped down on a chair, and took off her sneakers.

"Wow," she said, "that was a long one."

"Where have you been?" her father thundered.

"What are you yelling at? I was out."

"You're supposed to be in. Here, in the house, with your mother. Only wardens and official personnel are allowed in the streets. Where have you been? The all clear sounded a half hour ago."

"We got caught over on Greene Street when the all clear sounded. It took us a while to get back. We couldn't just walk through the streets."

"What in God's name is going on?" Ted demanded.

"That's what I want to know," Beatrice answered. "Why the third degree? What's up?"

"First of all," said her father, "Who is we? You said us. That means you weren't alone."

"Bert and Billy were with me. What are you carrying on for?"

"Was that Bert and Billy whistling when the raid started?" Emily asked. "Jesus, what kid stuff."

"There's nothing else to do in this damned town," Beatrice said huffily. "I'm going to take a bath."

"You just wait a minute, young lady." Ted stood up. "Do you mean to tell me that every time there's an alert, you and Bert and Billy take off in the dark to roam the streets?"

"We never go near the streets. We don't want to get caught."

"Aha. That means you stay in backyards. It was you! Do you know you frightened your grandmother half to death going over the fences! Through her ferns!"

"She didn't see us."

"Oh yes she did. She was on the porch with Granddaddy and the Catsbys. What am I going to tell her? That her own granddaughter was the one who frightened her? I'll have to tell her the truth, or she'll be even more frightened," He walked to stand over Beatrice. "You are never to do this again." He turned to Katherine. "You knew she did this."

"I didn't see any harm at the time," Katherine said. "I didn't realize they might frighten people."

"That's not the point." Ted began to pace up and down. "In the first place, she's supposed to be in the house. I'm responsible for everyone in the ward. We can't have hoodlums taking advantage of the darkness."

"I'm not a hoodlum," Beatrice cried.

"Anybody who is out during an alert is a hoodlum in my book. Well, I know how to put an end to this nonsense. I'll see Bert and Billy tomorrow and make them scouts. Then there'll be no more fence-climbing and running around in the dark."

"That's not fair." Beatrice jumped up. "Make me a scout then too. If they can be out legally, so can I."

"Not on your life. No daughter of mine, no young woman, is going to be out alone in the dark. Something might happen to you."

"Nothing happens to me when I'm with Bert and Billy."

"Scouts patrol alone. I won't have it."

"Then let me patrol with Bert and Billy. What are you afraid of? That I'll be raped? I'd rather be raped than sit in here and be bored to death."

"Stop that talk. Nobody said anything about," he lowered his voice, "rape, as you call it."

Emily laughed. "What do you call it, Dad?"

"None of your smart-aleck college talk. What is the matter with these girls anyway?" He looked at Katherine. "Don't they know there's a war on?" "I'll say," cried both girls in unison, and Emily added, "That's all that's on."

Katherine thought quickly. "Women are joining the service every day, Ted. In England women have to do the men's jobs. That may be the solution. Make Beatrice a scout and let her patrol with one of the boys, just to be on the safe side."

"It's against regulations."

"Make an exception."

"I can't. When they find out, all the girls in the ward will want to be scouts, and, instead of a team, I'll have pairs of scouts smooching in the dark when they should be rounding up violators." He twinged as he remembered his mother as the major violator that night.

"I give up." Beatrice flung herself out of the room.

Her father thundered again. "Your sneakers!" He turned to Katherine. "Aren't you going to train her to pick up her sneakers?"

"Ted, it's been a long day. We all need a good night's sleep."

Emily sensed that her father's mood needed consoling and withdrew to leave them alone, if not to avoid being the target of his next outburst.

"Can't you do something about those girls?" he began as soon as she left.

"You're probably right that Beatrice shouldn't be out in the dark like that."

"Probably?"

"But only," Katherine continued evenly, "because you're the warden. You aren't going to blow up at Bert and Billy, are you? No, you're going to make them scouts. You expect boys to get into mischief. Half the stories of your childhood are pranks of the same harmless sort."

"She frightened her grandmother, she really did, you know."

"They all three did. If she hadn't been with them, the boys would have frightened your mother anyway. Do you want me to remind you of the times you and your chums frightened the old ladies of your day?"

"Boys will be boys. My mother understands that. All boys' mothers understand that. You don't understand that. You didn't have any brothers and you don't have any sons."

"I had cousins. The trouble with you is that you never had any sisters. Boys may be boys, but girls can be tomboys, and, in case you haven't noticed, both your girls are tomboys. Maybe that's what comes of your wanting a son and treating them like boys. Hep, two, three, four, to the rear, march."

"I expect you to teach them to behave like ladies," Ted said stubbornly. "That's your job."

"I have news for you. I was a tomboy, too. I see no harm in the girls."

"Oh, and what about the sneakers on the floor?"

"That's not harm, that's just irritating. If Beatrice were a boy, she'd leave a lot more junk lying around."

"I never did. My mother wouldn't let me."

"There were also servants to pick up after you, if you did. As Emily would say, this is a dumb argument. They're both good girls, and they don't have much fun these days."

"How can anyone think of having fun at a time like this?" Ted turned sober, but Katherine laughed.

"You have fun. You love being an air raid warden and supervising the scouts and running around in the dark and calling up the mayor. You're just an overgrown boy yourself."

Ted had to join in the laughter. "Somebody has to do it, but I could have done without the alert tonight. I'll tell you a secret. I think the mayor called it on purpose. He knew the wedding was this afternoon. Naturally. Everybody in Westerveldt knew about the wedding. I think he wanted a little revenge on the upper crust."

4

The Van Leuvens

Isobel moved swiftly to turn on a light and to rouse Peter. She collected her mother-in-law's belongings again, in spite of the old lady's protests, and ushered them both out the door. She was surprised at her own forcefulness, but Peter's calm presence, promptly obeying her and not seeming to notice his grandmother's reluctance, gave her determination. She wandered about the living room, rearranging the pillows on the sofa, removing the glasses, emptying Gus' ashtray, as if changing the scenery after the first act and preparing for the one that would take place if Gus found Mary D.—and especially if he found her where she ought not to be.

She thought of calling Katherine to see if Mary D. were indeed at her house, and she was on her way to the telephone. She stopped; how could she bring up the subject without exposing her daughter and her own gullibility? If Katherine were a close friend, she could call just to chat trivially about the wedding and only incidentally mention her daughter, but, again, if she were a close friend, she could ask her outright. Katherine was an interesting woman to whom she enjoyed talking, but they were no longer close friends. They had been friends, and, Isobel remembered with irritation, tried to stay friends. They both liked to read—an activity which too many of their contemporaries considered strenuous. Not that Westerveldt's matrons were illiterate; they had, for example, all read *Gone With The Wind* and could be counted on not to miss other literary sensations, but they confined their reading to current books of general interest and wouldn't rummage through the past to discover a book omitted from their education. Reading *Anna*

Karenina, say, would be like going back to school, and for a woman to choose to read it, on a whim, unless she was marooned in the summer cottage on Cape Cod with nothing to do for a month, there would be no sense to it. There would be no one to share the experience with.

Isobel and Katherine read anyway, lending each other books and recommending titles, even if the conversation between them was sometimes limited merely to telling each other what they'd read. Temperamentally, they were too different to find common ground any longer. Katherine had taken to reading whatever semi-scholarly books came out that explained the events and historical trends leading up to the War. How the Nazis came to Power. Why France Fell. The Failures of Democracy. Other books which blueprinted the peace to come so that another war could be prevented (not like last time when the peace contained the seeds of the next war). Isobel was not averse to understanding these matters, but she balked at an underlying theme she encountered in the first few books of this genre she had tried. The western democracies, once they had finished off the Axis enemies (the alternative was unthinkable), would have to find some way of living in the same world with the Soviet Union. This was as unthinkable to Isobel as living in the world with Nazi Germany. She knew that if no accommodation were found, the alternative in that case might some day be another war, and, since that thought was more horrifying, she gave up thinking about it. Gus, a very practical man, did not look at the broad picture and its projected possibilities. He concentrated on condemning socialism in all forms as an attack on private property, his own in particular. Anything tainted, therefore, with socialist thinking, scientific or otherwise, was to be despised and eliminated from consideration.

Isobel had had a fierce argument with him over the ballet. She liked, once or twice a season, to go to New York, stay overnight at the Sherry-Netherland, shop on Fifth Avenue, and go to the ballet, which, at that time, was still strongly Russian in influence. She had explained to Gus that the Russians of the ballet were anti-Soviet Russians, White Russians as opposed to Red Russians, Good

Russians as opposed to Bad Russians. Gus was never at a loss. Any culture that could have produced a Red government was rotten to the core, therefore anything else it produced was another sign of its rottenness, decadence; it could only contaminate. Isobel had stood up to him that time. She couldn't condemn millions of unknown people categorically, especially since White Russia had been a Christian country, and she knew he was wrong. They compromised. She went by herself to the ballet, and he went to Radio City Music Hall.

As Isobel's mind wandered so far away from calling Katherine, Peter returned.

"Grandmother is safely tucked away, if not safely tucked in. She was in no hurry to go home and in no hurry to go to bed. What's up?"

"She wanted to wait until your father got back."

"She said something like that."

"Sit down, Peter. You'll probably be involved sooner or later. Mary D. isn't home."

"I know that. She's off somewhere with Emily Osterhoudt. They spent most of the afternoon together at the reception."

"Your father thinks she isn't with Emily."

"Then if she isn't with Emily?" He stopped. "Oh, oh. You mean she just said she was going to be with Emily. Then where could she be?"

"Your father suspects she's somewhere in the hotel—the Arms—that she's met someone when she's there airplane spotting and that she's been sneaking off to meet him whenever she can find an excuse."

"What do you think?"

"I don't know what to think. I don't like to think she would lie to me or that she would want to do anything disreputable, but both your father and your grandmother have accused me of being innocent. And," she added sadly, "of not keeping a proper eye on her. As if I were a policeman."

"Do you think she's likely to get into trouble?"

"If what they say is true, I don't know my own daughter. I've always found her easy to get along with. Cheerful, except when she gets bored. Then she's nervous and irritable."

"How has she been since she's been home?"

"The first few days very itchy. After that, no problems. Several arguments, unpleasant ones, with your father. She called him a fossil."

Peter laughed. "Dad's no fossil. If he's anything, he's a dinosaur rampaging through the swamps."

Isobel giggled. "You mustn't say that."

"I thought it was flattering. He is old-fashioned, a vanishing breed, but he has too much energy to be a fossil. I'd like to see anyone put him down."

"True. He said he was going to take off his belt to her."

"I think I'll go back upstairs." Peter got up.

"Don't leave. Please don't leave. I need you. Mary D. may need you. If the three of us stand up to him, maybe we can shame him, and he won't be too harsh."

Peter shook his head. "I'll try to remember all they taught us in boot camp, but I would prefer not to be involved. I thought this leave would be a vacation from war. Instead we've got one in our own house. I'm so tired of thinking in terms of conflict all the time. I'm not cut out for it."

"I know, dear. It must be hard for you."

The front door opened and then slammed shut.

"Up to your room. Right this minute. Upstairs. You'll have your orders in the morning."

"Goodnight, Daddy," they heard Mary D. say meekly.

Gus joined them in the living room. "I found her all right. What did you do with my glass? Peter, I want to talk to your mother alone." He went out to the pantry; Peter kissed his mother and hurried from the room. When Gus came back with his drink, Isobel was still standing. Evidently, the battle was not to be three-against-one but hand-to-hand combat.

"Sit down, Isobel. There's something we have to discuss." He took a long sip and looked very sternly at his wife. "I found her. And as I thought. She was at the hotel. In the radio station!" He said "radio station" as he might have said "speakeasy" or "whorehouse." "In the dark, of course, with some disk jockey, or whatever you call them. Some boy who puts records on the air and reads ads for hardware. She claims to have been caught there when the drill started. She claims she just looked in to see how the station worked. She claims she was on her way home. I do not believe her. She hangs around there. I know it. Around that boy, whoever he is."

"What's his name?" Isobel asked.

"How should I know? I didn't wait to be introduced. I didn't want to be introduced. As far as I'm concerned, he doesn't exist. No young man exists who doesn't present himself on my doorstep and ring my bell and come into my living room. I got her out of there in no time, I tell you."

"What took you so long to get home?"

"As we were leaving the station, the all clear sounded. We went into the Grill so we could straighten this mess out."

"Did you have something to eat?"

"I had a scotch."

"What did Mary D. have?"

"A daiquiri. What difference does it make what we had? There were more important things on our minds."

"Gus, she's underage. She won't be eighteen until next month."

"She was with her father. That's the way to learn how to drink. With your family. Not with some callow youth. I laid down the law. Monday morning she reports for work at the Yard. I'll keep her out of mischief if it's the last thing I do. There's a lot of paper work and filing in the office."

"When I suggested that at Easter time, you were dead set against it."

"That's because I thought you were bringing her up to be a lady. Now that I see that she does not know how to behave like a lady, I will at least keep her out of trouble. She'll get wages, like everyone else, and if she's smart and saves her money, she can get a car when the war's over."

"Gus!" Isobel was shocked. "Do you mean to say that after

what's she done, you dangled a car in front of her? Didn't you scold her for lying and deceiving us and for running after that young man?"

"I left that for you. You're her mother. You give the lectures. I solve the problems. She'll be too tired when I get through with her to run after anybody. Tomorrow, I want you to speak to her. Give her hell. What a night! Did Mother get home all right?"

"Peter took her."

"Poor Mother. She's getting on."

"Tomorrow's the anniversary of your father's death."

"Damn." Gus breathed softly, then said lugubriously, "that's right, the twenty-seventh, six years now. She must have been feeling low, remembering. I'm glad I wasn't here." Then suddenly he said, "Did she say anything about going to the cemetery?"

"She didn't mention it and I didn't either."

"Thank God. I'm not up to it. I get the willies every time I go there. It's hell, pure hell, She carries on so. She looks at Father's grave and starts in on him. Then she looks at Roger's grave and starts in on him. Then she shows me, again, where she's going to go, and then me." He looked up, "and you. Then she complains about the landscaping. More this, more that. Maybe Peter could take her this time."

Isobel flashed. "Absolutely not. You must not ask him. I put my foot down. He's home on leave. He needs the little rest and peace we can give him. It's your job. She's your mother."

"You're protecting him! He doesn't need protection. He's a sailor. He has to be tough. I don't see why . . ."

"I'm sure he's tough when he has to be. It's not easy for him. You can't ask him to take on your chores."

"Oh, can't I? I've carried the burden of this family on my shoulders and my shoulders alone. I don't know why my son can't give me a hand. I work hard; I handle the Yard, the men, the business. I do battle with the government and the rationing boards. I do battle every day of my life for my business, for my church, for the country club, and I solve the problems of my family. I have more than my share of battles and burdens."

Isobel decided not to answer him. Sometimes he talked himself
out of his tirades. If she disagreed, his position would harden.

"All I ask is a little consideration," he continued. "Wait! We're
going to the Lodge tomorrow. Excellent. A day in the mountains.
We'll get there in time for lunch."

"But Mary D. has air spot duty."

"Not any more she doesn't. She'll do as I say. I've given her a
job, haven't I? If Mother wants to take a quick look at the grave on
the way out of town, I can manage it. Five, ten minutes. And then
peace until Armistice Day. What about flowers?"

"I can make two arrangements of cut flowers from the garden,
if you like."

"Good. No sense wasting money at the florist's. Well, I'm going
to have a nightcap and get to bed."

Upstairs on the extension phone in his parents' bedroom, Peter
was asking the operator for six-nine-oh-three, forgetful of
Westerveldt telephone etiquette which decreed that no one should
place a call after nine o'clock at night or before nine o'clock in the
morning unless there were a genuine emergency.

As Katherine Osterhoudt answered, worried thoughts of her
mother in Pennsylvania, one sister in New York City, the other in
Buffalo, and even her in-laws next door flitted through her mind,
and she was tempted to give young Peter Van Leuven a piece of her
mind, but since he was "in the service," she confined her
remonstrations to a broad hint. It was, after all, only ten-thirty.

"I believe she's gone *upstairs*, Peter, but I'll call her."

When Emily came to the phone, unbelieving, Peter asked her,
as if nothing had happened between them at the wedding reception
more than had happened the day he took the ladder away when
she was still in the apple tree ten years earlier, if she would go
swimming with him the next afternoon. He couldn't get the car
because his parents were going to the Lodge, but they could walk,
or better yet bike, out to the swimming hole in the Wester Kill.

Emily tried to play hard to get. "Don't you have to go to the
Lodge with your parents?"

Peter laughed like his old self. "I don't want to go, and I'm not going to. I had enough of the older generation, both older generations, this afternoon and again this evening. I want to be with someone my own age."

"In that case," said Emily, "since you so kindly admit me to your age group, I'd love to go swimming with you. If you think weekdays around here are dull, Sundays are worse. What time will you be by? Shall we take something to eat?"

5

Emily and Peter

Peter and Emily lay on a blanket a few yards from the muddy bank of the Wester Kill, damp and a little muddy themselves from a swim. It was another beautiful sunny, warm day. There were no clouds in the sky; a hint of breeze moved the leaves on the trees to and fro, and in the silence they could hear crows cawing in the fields half a mile away.

"The Kill doesn't run as clean as it used to," Peter observed ruefully, looking at his ankles and thighs.

"It usually does," Emily answered. "Remember it rained a lot during the week, just before the wedding. The water is roiled and it hasn't had a chance to settle yet."

"I don't remember it this muddy. But then nothing in Westerveldt seems quite the same."

"You forget. This place used to get filthy in August. When I'd get home, I'd have to scrub for an hour to get clean. You didn't notice in those days. You were younger then and you probably liked being dirty."

"Maybe you're right. Maybe I'm letting my state of mind color everything. Looking back, those seemed like such carefree days."

"They were fun. No doubt about that. This town is a great place to grow up in. Swimming and hiking in the summertime. Camping out sometimes. Skiing and making snowmen in the winter, and skating nearly every day. Remember? I don't want to depress you, but do you know they're going to build a parking lot for the tool factory over the skating rink?"

"What!" Peter sat up, fingered around in the grass until he

found a pebble, and in his anger heaved it into the Kill. "Why? That rink has been there for fifty years. My father used to skate there. Yours too. Why do they want to build a parking lot?"

"The tool factory makes parts vital to the war effort, that's what they say. The workers have to park up on the hill and walk down to the plant, and the trucks can't get in easily to load or unload. Our old rink is just in the right place for a parking lot. They're filling it in now."

"How has traffic been managing up to now?"

"Parking on the hill was a mess. No room to turn around. It tied up traffic coming off Route 7, and it got worse when the plant went on three shifts. They're producing so much more, they're loading more. No room for the trucks. And some of the workers began parking on Brunswick Avenue. You know we can't have that."

Peter closed his eyes. The sunny skies were too cheerful for his darkening mood. "And what do they make in there that's so vital to the war effort?" he sneered. "Nothing produced in this town has ever been 'vital' from the beaver furs to the present. You'd think they'd want a big plant for something vital."

Emily laughed. "Maybe you've seen too much of the world, Peter. You think everything is done big. One thing I've learned working at that rotten job this summer is how much our economy depends on little shops and factories. Now the tool factory, according to my father, is just the right size to produce several small parts for an aircraft. We're not allowed to know which parts or what they're used for, but they're small and the government needs a lot of them. But a big factory would make too many."

"And after the war, what will happen? Will they go back to making tools? Will they tear up the parking lot and give us back our skating rink?"

"Who knows what they'll make after the war? But they certainly won't give us back our skating rink. The kids will have to find a new place to skate. And you know kids, they will."

"What made that place a great skating rink is going to make it a terrible parking lot. No matter how much they fill it in, it's still a marsh. I hope it sinks." He pulled furiously at a few clumps of grass and then turned to Emily. "It doesn't seem to bother you, all this change."

"Sure it bothers me." When she felt his eyes on her, she turned to face him. "I don't like it any more than you do. But I don't skate here any more. I feel sorry for Beatrice. She loves to skate. My mother says we have to be prepared for the war to make all kinds of changes. She says nothing will ever be the same again. It wasn't after the last war, she says. War changes everything, and we can't stop it."

"I suppose not. They tell us we're fighting to keep our life the way it was."

"They mean Hitler and fascism. They don't mean skating rinks."

"I know, I know," Peter sighed. "I guess I'm not cut out for a war."

"Sure you are. They wouldn't have made you a lieutenant if you weren't."

"Oh, I passed everything easily, and I'm a good officer. I know how to do my duty, and I can think on my feet. I'm smarter than I thought I was. It's the meaning of it all I can't stand. There I am with all the others, torn from the life I'm used to, just as they are, going out to fight and kill other men like ourselves because they're the enemy." He gave a bitter twist to the last word.

Emily laughed again. "You're not supposed to think that way. You say you're going to the Pacific. You're supposed to think of 'them' as yellow-skinned, slant-eyed animals who stabbed us in the back. You can't kill anyone you feel sorry for."

Peter chuckled.

"Seriously, Peter, you won't really have to kill anyone yourself, will you?"

"Not at close range. We'll shell them from a distance. But I'll see it all later."

"You know, Pete." Emily ran her forefinger along his nose. "You think too much. You didn't used to be like that—a thinker. You used to be just as tough and nasty as all the other guys."

Peter closed his hand over hers and held it. "Oh I was, was I? What did you expect when you and Mary D. used to follow us around and threaten to tell on us?"

"We never did, you know. Never. We just wanted to be where

you were and do what you were doing. We only threatened to tell when you were mean and told us to go home."

"Really?" Peter moved their clasped hands from side to side. "And do you still like to be where I am?"

Emily hesitated. "I'm here, aren't I?"

"After the dressing down you gave me at the reception yesterday, I wasn't sure you'd come."

"As long as you're nice and not high and mighty."

"Nice!" Peter dropped her hand and sat us abruptly. "How can anyone be nice? War is Not Nice." He leapt up and jumped again into the muddy water.

Emily sat for a minute on the bank. There he was being moody and sorry for himself. She reminded herself of what Mary D. had told her of his post-war plans (including what Peter had not yet revealed), and, moved by a feeling of tenderness and pity for the young man who had been such a glamorous and tormenting bully in her childhood, she dove into the water to join him.

"That's the way to work off your rage," she called gaily. "Swim. You could always mow the lawn. And stop thinking so much."

Peter didn't answer but dove under the water to grab one of her legs. She shrieked and struggled to kick him away, and after she had kicked herself free, she thrashed in the water to swim away from him. But Peter was too quick. Suddenly, he bobbed up directly in front of her and took hold of both her wrists. She tried to pommel his chest, but he was too strong for her.

"Let go," she cried. "You're a rat. You're just as rotten as you always were. And this time I will tell on you."

He watched her face closely and smiled. "I'll let you go on one condition. I don't know how long I'll be here, but I'd like to see you as often as I can while I'm still here. You do me good."

"You need someone to bully, that's what." Emily was fishing for a compliment as she strenuously treaded water to keep afloat. "Why don't you bully Mary D.?"

"She's on to all my tricks. Besides, she's my sister. She's no fun."

"I'm practically your sister." Couldn't he think of anything flattering to say?

"Oh no, you're not. You could never be my sister. You're not even little Emily whose socks were always falling down around the ankles. You're a grownup college girl." That, apparently, was the best he could do.

"All right," Emily said breathlessly. "I promise, if you let me go right this minute."

Reluctantly he released her wrists, one at a time, and Emily swam off toward shore calling over her shoulder, "Extortionist!"

As they biked home, Peter suggested that they meet again for dinner after they'd washed off the mud from the Kill. Again, no car, they'd have to find some place they could walk to. There was the Arms . . .

"Okay," Emily said, "but let's be really wicked. Instead of going to the Arms, where my parents take me all the time, let's go some place they never take me. How about the Shanghai Gardens on Main Street? I don't know what's wrong with it—whether it's germs, or because it's foreign or it's just low—but I'd like to find out. Have you ever been there?"

"Are you kidding?" Peter said. "Not even with the guys. We went where we could get a beer. My family is just as fussy and choosy as yours, any day." He knew they were even fussier. "It's a deal. We'll walk to the Chinks."

The decor of the Shanghai Gardens, the food (chop suey, rice, tea, and fortune cookies), the clientele, nothing explained why the eating place was shunned. It was clean and crowded and served decent but pallid food, not as tasty as the dirty Chinese restaurant on Morningside Heights Emily had visited several times.

"Perhaps," Emily said to Peter as they wandered up and down Main Street looking in the shop windows as if they'd never seen them before, "our parents have never been in there themselves. Maybe they just think it's not a proper place. Or else there's something in their attitude I don't understand."

"Local tribal custom. We'll put it down to that. Westerveldt elite no eat food with sticks. Good God, look at that." Peter pointed to a mannequin in the window of the Vanderlyn Dress Shop. "That skirt is ridiculous."

"That's our contribution to the war effort," Emily explained. "To show our knees when we sit down. If each one of us gives up two inches of fabric on our skirts and dresses, the war will be over faster. You'll all fight harder so you won't have to look at our knees."

"Let's forget about the war for an hour," Peter said.

"Wouldn't it be wonderful if we could? What can we do? There isn't much open on a Sunday night except bars and movies. What's at the Colonial? Can you see the marquee from here?"

"*China.* Alan Ladd."

"Why not? After a Chinese meal?"

"That's no travelogue. It's a war movie. Sorry. Either we drink beer or we'll have to walk some more."

They walked. "What can we do tomorrow night?" Peter asked at last. "We've eaten at the Chinks' and we can't see the movie. What is there left we can walk to?"

"There's a new pizza place down near St. Peter's. I've never eaten there either, but I love pizza since it's supposed not to be good for me. Or we could try the greasy Greeks'. I mean the Parthenon. And after we eat, we can explore some of the streets we haven't taken a good look at in years."

"We could, couldn't we?" Peter agreed. "There's nothing to stop us, no matter how silly it is. If I could get the car, we could go to a decent restaurant out of town, but let's make do with what we've got."

So they did. Emily had to get up at seven every morning to be at work at eight. Home at five-thirty, she was fresh and ready for Peter when he called for her an hour later. Monday they ate pizza and afterwards walked along Elm until it emptied into Brunswick, then down spacious Brunswick past the Van Slyke house the newlyweds would soon be inhabiting, past the Sanford house (no lights on, they must be out), past St. Andrew's. In front of the church, Peter suggested they turn back; half a mile further down Brunswick stood his parents' house. Tuesday they ate at the Parthenon and decided that Greek food was even more deliciously greasy than Italian. That night Emily insisted on showing Peter where she worked: the dingy little brick building that housed the offices, next to the factory proper, two blocks from the railroad station.

By Wednesday morning Isobel had spoken to Gus several times. The third time he listened. When he realized that his son had been escorting the Osterhoudt girl to low-down dives in the business district where they could be seen by everyone, he volunteered his car.

"Take her to the Villa Florentina or the Sea Rover or the Riverboat, for God's sake, and give her a decent meal and a proper good time. You should have spoken up," Gus added, putting the blame where it belonged. "What must Ted Osterhoudt think of you—and of me, for that matter—letting you drag Emily to those places? You could invite her here, you know, to have dinner with the family. I'd like to get to know her better, now that you're seeing so much of each other. So would your mother."

"No need, Dad, no need. This is not a serious romance. It's not even a romance. Emily is just keeping me company while I'm home. We reminisce about old times and try to forget there's a war on."

"Sorry to hear that," Gus said. "I thought you'd come to your senses," and before Peter could answer him back, he pressed two ten dollar bills in his hand. "Even if it's not a romance, do whatever it is you do properly."

"He says it's not a romance," Gus told Isobel. "What's wrong with that boy? He could have had the car if he'd asked me. He lies around here all day reading and mooning. What does the Osterhoudt girl see in him?"

"You mustn't talk that way about your own son," Isobel answered. "He's handsome, he's intelligent, and he's sensitive. I'm sure Emily Osterhoudt enjoys being with him. And you should be glad it's not a romance. Emily is barely eighteen, and they couldn't think of marriage until after the war. It's nice he's seeing her. Maybe he'll carry away pleasant memories, and when he comes home to stay, they can pick up where they left off."

"You mean we should encourage them?"

"Just leave them alone. We both hope Peter will give up those plans he has for the future." Isobel couldn't bring herself to refer to them directly.

"True enough. True enough. Maybe nature will find a way. Somehow I doubt it. Young men are not what they once were, in my day, I'll tell you. I'd have thought he'd be looking for telephone operators or girls in the five-and-dime. No, he takes out a girl from his own set. sees her every night, and says it's not a romance. Do you think there's something wrong with him?"

"I wouldn't know about such things," Isobel said loftily. "You're his father. You ask him. I have my hands full with Mary D." For once the tables were turned.

The Osterhoudts were suffering from similar apprehension. Peter was a nice boy, but every night? Emily was wearing herself out, working all day and gallivanting at night. What would come of it? Peter would get his orders and be seen no more; there would be a let-down for Emily. Was it serious? What if? Unlikely. Not with a girl of his own kind. Why did Emily look so feverish. She said she felt fine.

"Thank God for a restaurant with a liquor license at last," Emily was saying to Peter as they waited in the gloom of the Riverboat for their Manhattans to arrive. "I haven't had a drink since the wedding. All I'm allowed at home is an occasional beer and my mother keeps track. She counts the beers in the refrigerator."

"It's hard to come home when you've been away," Peter agreed. "They expect you to be grownup and not to have changed, both at the same time. They don't try to get to know you all over again."

"My mother's not so bad in that respect," Emily said. "She understands me. Perhaps too well. She watches me like a hawk who isn't sure her fledgling can fly."

"And can she?" Peter asked provocatively.

"I can hold my liquor, if that's what you mean," Emily shot back.

"I think," Peter said, retreating, "that that was all I meant."

There was an awkward silence until the Manhattans were served and they began to read the menus.

"It's dumb to have meat when they have the best fish in town." Emily said finally. "The question is, which fish?"

"Do you like seafood? That's what I'm going to have."

"Me too. I love it. What do we have to live so far from the shore?"

"One advantage of being in the navy is being near the shore. Dammit," he exclaimed. "That was my fault. I brought it up. Sorry."

"We can't keep this up, Peter. Pretending there's no war. Why don't you complain about it or at least talk about it? Tell me about your training. Or your buddies. What it's like every day. You let me chatter on about college, as long as I'm careful and don't mention 'war-time conditions.' I keep telling you, the war is all around us. We can't close our eyes to it. Can't we enjoy what there is to enjoy without gritting our teeth?"

"You may be right," Peter answered slowly. "Maybe that's what I've been doing—just gritting my teeth and waiting for it to end. That's no way to live. I have to take each day as it comes and find something good in it."

They lingered long after dinner, dancing to juke-box music, playing "Brazil" several times so they could try to samba.

"It's ten-thirty," Peter said at last. "You have to go to work tomorrow, so unless I want your parents on my back, I suppose the only decent thing to do is to take you home so you can get a good night's sleep. But for me, I don't want the evening to end."

"One more dance, and then we'll go. Let's find something slow."

Peter held her a little more closely this time and even more closely at the last reprise of the melody, cheek-to-cheek during the final bars.

On the drive home he remarked that Westerveldt was, after all, not such a dull place, if there someone to enjoy it with.

"We're the in-betweens," he said. "As a boy, I had a wonderful time here. Now, whenever I can't sleep, I drift back to those days. The times I went camping and exploring, or the summer eight of us built an Indian village over in Lloyd's woods."

"I remember that summer," Emily laughed. "Mary D. and I came over to see the village. Each one of you had a separate tepee. When we got close, you started ughing and you shot at us with your homemade bows and arrows. No squaws allowed. You guys were rotten."

"We were, I grant you. You and Mary D. were nosy little brats to us. Mary D.'s pigtails were always coming undone."

"She's put the end of a pigtail in her mouth and suck it, and the rubber band would come off. When we tried to put it back on, we never got it right. But what did you mean, 'in-between generation'?"

"I guess I mean that kids have a marvelous time growing up here. And the grownups seem happy enough. They have endless activities to keep them occupied. And it's a safe and peaceful place to get old in. BUT there is very little to do if you're no longer a child and not ready to get married. Young people have to play at being children until they're old enough to start playing house."

"You're right. I can't wait until I get back to college. Here I feel as if I'm always waiting. Too old for one life, too young for another, and nothing in-between that exciting or challenging."

"But," Peter said, as he pulled the car up in front of the Osterhoudt house and turned off the ignition, "being with you has taken me out of limbo. We seem to find things to do."

"It is fun," Emily agreed. "We've been rediscovering Westerveldt."

"Where do you want to go tomorrow night?" Peter asked through the darkness.

"Again tomorrow? Aren't you afraid you'll get tired of my company?"

"No." His voice took on the sad note Emily found so very appealing and irritating at the same time. "I'm more afraid you'll get tired of me. You're always using words like exciting and challenging."

"Peter Van Leuven! Stop talking like that! Let's see, We want excitement? What can we do? Let's be reckless and go to the Antlers. I may have been discouraged from going to the Chinks' or the greasy Greeks', but I've been positively forbidden to go to the Antlers. That's where all the kids go. They serve great hamburgers and french fries so I'm told. I've always wanted to see the inside. And we can dance."

"What if your parents ask where you've been?"

"That's easy. I'll tell them you insisted, and I couldn't say no. You led me astray."

"If that's what you want to do," Peter demurred.

"You've got it all wrong. It's what you want to do. You have to take all the blame. Sophisticated and traveled naval lieutenant drags naive college sophomore to local dive."

"I guess I can handle it," Peter chuckled.

At the door of the Osterhoudt house, he took hold of her shoulders and very softly and tenderly kissed her for the first time.

"Tomorrow we paint the town red," he said as turned quickly to go. "Same time."

6

Ketherine and Isobel

On the last Thursday of each month in peacetime, the Westerveldt Women's Club, founded during the twenties by women who had outgrown the Junior League and perpetuated by successive waves of matrons as they graduated into middle age, had met to play bridge after a dainty luncheon and plan activities their teen-age offspring could look forward to—a Christmas ball, a spring dance during Easter vacation, and another gala in the summer at the Country Club. Reluctantly, but patriotically, they gave up bridge, reduced the dances to two, one summer, one winter, and then concentrated their formidable organizing abilities on wartime charities.

Katherine Osterhoudt suggested at the June meeting that the rummage sale in August be turned into a bazaar, that they find someone who could play the accordion, that they build a wooden platform; everyone, young and old, could square dance.

"But the sales are for war relief," Isobel Van Leuven protested. "We can't turn them into parties."

"We'll make more money if we do," Katherine defended her proposal. "People will give something for a good cause; they think it's their duty. But if they're having a good time, they'll spend even more. Life is dreary enough these days. A little gaiety would be a tonic for all of us."

The debate was brief. In no time, the suggestion had been phrased as a motion, seconded, and passed. Committees were formed to deal with the different activities, and Katherine—she should have expected the honor—found herself chosen as Co-ordinator.

When the meeting was adjourned, Isobel approached her and asked if they could walk home together.

"I hope you don't think I'm being callous, Isobel, by suggesting a party. I feel the sorrow of the war, too, but I think we need a little fun to keep up morale."

"Oh, I'm sure you're right," Isobel agreed. "It's very hard to maintain standards these days. It takes all my energy to see that we have pleasant meals, that the house is kept properly. There are so many things I can't get. And I live in the terror that Essie will decide to quit and go to work in one of the plants. They pay so well she just might."

Katherine had not had a servant for over seven years, except for a woman who came for a week in the spring and again in the fall for the strenuous seasonal cleaning. Nevertheless, she answered sympathetically, "I know what you mean. It's one shortage after another."

As they walked along the blue-slate sidewalk under the ancient elms, Isobel finally asked, "How do you feel about Emily's seeing so much of Peter?"

"It's hard to say." And indeed it was. If Katherine said she approved, Isobel might think the Osterhoudts had expectations. If she said she disapproved, Isobel might think she was critical of Peter. "If they were both living at home, I would probably be concerned. Night after night after night. But he's home on leave."

"Yes, and we don't know for how long. He could be called back any minute."

What was Isobel telling her? To discourage Emily from seeing Peter? To exercise over her daughter the restraint Isobel couldn't exercise over her son? She chose her words carefully. "I think, and Ted agrees, that it will be a letdown for her when he does go. But she has her job to keep her occupied and now I'm even more thankful I insisted she take it." She knew Emily's working in a factory was considered déclassé.

Isobel sensed Katherine stiffening. "Mary D. is working now, at the Yard. Gus paid you a compliment. He was quite critical of you at the beginning of the summer, you know, when he found out Emily was working at Custer's, even if it was in the office, but now he sees the wisdom of keeping Mary D. busy. He's also rather pleased with her, although he wouldn't tell her that. She's learned her duties quickly, and she's very good on the phone. But I want to talk about Emily. Surely you must have some feeling about her being with Peter?"

"He's a lovely boy, Isobel. And you and Gus are our friends. How could I object?"

"Do you think they're getting serious?"

"I have no way of knowing. Emily tells me where they went, what they had for dinner—they seem to enjoy eating things that aren't good for them in places we would never take then. But not much else. What does Peter say?"

"Even less, They're both so young. And this dreadful war."

Katherine wanted to day, "It's the war that forces these whirlwind romances." She herself had fallen madly in love with a flier during the spring of 1917, but she knew that Isobel dealt in particulars not generalities, except in matters of deportment or spiritual concerns. Instead she said, "Oh, I don't think they'll do anything rash. They're too sensible."

"This is very awkward for me, Katherine." Isobel stopped under a very large elm and in the shade sheltering them from the late afternoon heat, she continued, "Peter has been morose for several months. I could tell from his letters. When he showed up in person, I could tell he was unhappy from the moment he came in the house. Now, this may be only his mood talking, all may change, but he's told us that after the war, he intends to study for the ministry and to become an Anglican priest and," Isobel added in a hollow, miserable whisper, "to take celibate vows."

Katherine prided herself on the calm, studied manner she had cultivated ever since she'd moved to Westerveldt and had to feel her way among strangers. She avoided gossiping more than she felt necessary for general conversation, and she preferred always to speak positively of people so that no one could quote her as having passed an unkind judgment. She wanted to say, "Good God!". As thought after thought danced across her mind, she frivolously wanted to say, "Jesus Christ!" and she struggled to keep her features composed. She went to church only when her social position required it; she took religious belief as casually.

"I see," she said, although she was not sure what she saw. "Are you afraid that . . ."

"I don't know what I'm afraid of," Isobel stopped her. "But I wouldn't want Emily to get her hopes up if he's serious about this. On the other hand, it may be only a passing fancy—his way of escaping the war in his mind. Maybe being with Emily will straighten him out. But then what?" her voice trailed off. "Perhaps you should speak to Emily."

"Oh, I don't know." Katherine pictured Emily confronting Peter with the information. "Perhaps I should and perhaps I should let well enough alone. If I said anything to her, it might make it awkward between them.'

"True. As you think best, but I thought I should tell you."

Katherine seized a cliché. "We can protect out children only so far, you know. They have to learn to protect themselves."

Isobel wanted to tell Katherine of Mary D.'s escapade on the night of the wedding. Perhaps a shared and sympathetic concern for their daughters would make being a parent a little easier, but family loyalty prevailed. Both mothers went their separate ways, each with her private anxiety locked silently inside.

7

Antlers

The Antlers was two miles outside of town on Route 7, going south, literally a road house, off the road only twenty feet so that any motorist could see its gaudy neon outline of a stag's head and hear the sounds of juke box music gushing out of open windows on a summer's evening. It was a hangout for anyone old enough to drink or willing to settle for coke, and there were rarely more than a dozen customers over thirty—middle-aged men at the bar who seemed to get a lift from the youthful spirits or were more openly on the lookout for girls.

Emily had eyed the Antlers from afar for several years, ever since she'd been old enough to take an interest in boys, liquor, excitement, and being where everyone else was. Not quite everyone. The Van Leuvens, the Osterhoudts, the Sanfords, the Callendars, etc. etc. did not permit their daughters to go to the Antlers. "It's a roadhouse." "It's a dive." "It's a hangout." That was the strongest epithet. A hangout where young people went to look for each other, flirt, dance, intrigue, gossip. Some girls even went there without escorts, in pairs of course, in hopes of finding either the boys they had crushes on or those who had just broken up with their steady girl-friends. The upperclassmen at Westerveldt High met there regularly. Their parents seemed to see no harm in it. If they did object, they gave into the logic of "everybody goes there" and let it go at that. Ted decreed, "No daughter of mine," and Katherine chided, "I don't care what everyone else does." So if Emily had not been whisked off to boarding school her last year in high school ("to prepare you for college"), she would have spent her senior year on the outside looking in.

Now it didn't matter any more. Emily could not be accused of hanging around if she went with Peter Van Leuven who had spent his high school years at Deerfield. He hadn't seen the local boys since adolescence when they had constructed Indian villages together.

The Antlers was a noisy as Emily could have hoped. They found an empty booth in a corner, and she insisted on taking the seat that gave her the fullest view of the dance floor and the bar. So this was the forbidden paradise, this dingy hall lit by colored lights strung from the rafters and the illuminations of the juke box. Odors of beer, the fresh beer on the tables and the stale beer spilt on the floor yesterday or the week before, hamburger grease and the oil used over and over again for frying the potatoes, that odor, simultaneously rancid and sweet that repels and attracts at the same time. The odor of frying oil can be inhaled all over the world in one essence or another, but the odor of grilled hamburger is peculiarly American. The French short-order cook would never put so much fat in chopped meat.

"So this is it," Emily commented. "At college we go to dumps like this all the time. For the same reasons. Where else can you get beer and hamburgers and meet your pals?"

"Nowhere," Peter agreed. "I suppose they serve hamburgers in the Westerveldt Arms dining room, but you can be sure they call it Salisbury Steak and they don't give you raw onion."

"The pals we'd run into would be our parents. I don't want to feel old before my time. What'll we have? Shall we stick with beer and be part of the crowd?"

"Beer's fine. I have to stay in shape. I promised to mow the lawn. The gardener's sick, and my parents are having a dinner party tomorrow night."

"Good, I told you you should mow the lawn. I have to do it. My mother says there's no excuse for healthy kids to sit around doing nothing while she pays good money to have that kind of work done. Of course, if I had a brother, he'd have to do it."

They had taken no more than one bite from their hamburgers when they looked up to see Mary D. standing over them with the date she introduced as Willy Cranston.

"I hoped we'd run into you," she said as she sidled in next to Emily. Peter grudgingly made room for her escort. "I thought that was Daddy's car I saw in the parking lot. You can be my alibi. You took me along, and it was Peter's idea to come here. Right, big brother?"

"I'm not getting in the middle of one of your home-front battles." Peter said. "You're on your own."

"If you bring Emily here, it must be all right for me to be here, especially if I'm here with you. So, Willy, what'll it be? Let's get a big pitcher of beer for the four of us."

"You're underage," Peter snapped.

"Sh-h-h." Mary D. looked around. "Don't spoil my evening. It's my only night out all week. You're in loco parentis, as they say in school, so if I can drink with Daddy, I can certainly have beer with you."

"How did you manage to get out?" Emily asked her, not quite ready to say, "How did you manage to get out with Willard?"

"Mummy and Daddy are playing bridge at the Callendars. It was simple. I called Willy, and he didn't have to work, so here we are."

"You'd better be home before they are." Peter warned.

"I left them a note. I said I was with you."

"You've got some nerve," Emily said. "If I'd done something like that before I went to college, it would have been lectures for days."

"They won't make a fuss if darling Peter is involved."

Peter shook his head. Willard Cranston said nothing but looked at them all with a fatuous grin on his face. Did he understand what their conversation was really about? It was hard to tell.

The big pitcher of beer arrived at the table and two more hamburgers, but before the newcomers began to eat, Mary D. yoo-hooed at someone walking near the booth.

"Mikey!" she called. "I haven't seen you in a dog's age. How are you? How's tricks?"

The dark young man who approached the table Emily recognized as Mike Mancuso whose grandmother owned the grocery store on Main Street; for many years Mike had delivered her grandmother's groceries after school.

"How come you're not in uniform?" Mary D. asked as if it were the most natural question in the world which any young man would be pleased to answer.

"I'm working at a defense plant, but it won't last. They'll get me before the end of the year," he said, flicking his cigarette ash on the floor. "So-o-o, are you going to ask me to sit down?"

"Sure, Mikey." Mary D. moved over, pushing Emily farther into the booth. "So that's why you haven't been around." Around meant delivering groceries. Mary D.'s mother also shopped at Mancuso's, frequently by phone. For years, Mary D. had waited around for the groceries so she could tease Mike and giggle and, as she got older, flirt. He usually stayed half an hour before he got on his bike and back to work.

"That's it. They had my kid brother working for a while, but he's been sick. Now they have some old man making the rounds. You missed me, did you, Mary D.?"

"My heart has been breaking." Willard Cranston looked uncomfortable as he munched his hamburger and ate his fries with his fingers.

"Well, Hank," Mike addressed Willard. "How's business? You still at the station?"

"Yep. Hunky-dory."

"He likes to be called Willard now," Mary D. said.

"Will," Will put in quickly.

"Willard. Hmm. Don't go getting fancy on us. You'll always be Hank to me, old buddy."

"Now that's mean," Mary D. said. "Why can't people change their names if they want to? Why should he be stuck with a name he doesn't like if he has another name he does like?"

Will lied fast. "Our salesman is called Hank. We couldn't have two of us, so I was willing to change."

"Don't let them bully you," Mike cautioned. "You've finished your hamburger. How's about we dance?" he said to Mary D., "If Willard doesn't mind."

Will nodded, and Mike led Mary D. out to a slow dance during which he held her very close. Will watched them mournfully for a minute and then excused himself.

"This is a fine mess," Peter said. "How am I supposed to handle her? She's uncontrollable. It's bad enough she comes here with a guy my parents don't know, but now she takes off with the grocery boy. What she needs is a good spanking."

"No," Emily said. "What she needs is a little more freedom. Once she gets to college, she'll tame down. I was wild my first three months. I'd never known the bliss of doing as I pleased. By Christmas, the worm turned. I had three term papers and exams to study for."

"Mary D. won't change. She'll be worse in college. She'll get herself thrown out."

"She survived boarding school, and you can be sure she broke all the rules. She knows how not to get caught, and if she is caught, she talks her way out of it. She's a born winner."

"She has no conscience. Look what she did to poor Will. If my date did something like that . . ."

"Do you mean me?" Emily asked pertly. "Are you giving me orders? If you don't watch out, I'll dance with Mike Mancuso."

"Why doesn't he bring his own girl?" Peter wondered.

"He's probably between girls. He has a reputation for being fast."

"He's a letch, is that it?"

"So they say. It's his Italian blood."

"You're not going to tell me that all Italians . . ."

"How would I know?"

They watched Mary D. and Mike gliding to the slow, sweet, cloying music which ended as they bent into a long "dip."

"I'd ask you to dance," Peter said, "but I feel I have to wait until Will gets back and until Mike takes off. I want to keep an eye on them."

"Like baby-sitters?"

Another slow song. Mary D. and Mike, now quite comfortable in each other's arms, shuffled in time to the music.

"When you say you have to keep an eye on her," Emily said, "I didn't think you meant not taking your eyes off her."

"What if he suggests they go off together? I assume he has a car. If I turn my back for a second, they may disappear."

"Peter, you're crazy. She'd never do a thing like that. She's feeling wicked enough for one evening."

"Who knows? Maybe Mancuso is persuasive."

"Mike? No. He may be fast, but he doesn't like to get into trouble."

"You know him?"

"The same way Mary D. does. I run into him at my grandmother's every now and then, or in the store. He's your age. He was at Westerveldt High when I was there. But he doesn't bother with kids like Mary D. and me. It would be robbing the cradle. He was going with Marcy Horton just before he graduated."

"Not any more?"

"They broke up. She's now going with Matt Jorgenson. Only he was called up. I think they intend to get married. You remember him? He didn't live too far from you."

"Matt? Sure I remember Matt, but he's one of the few I would remember. I've been away since I was fourteen."

"You sure have. You show up for Christmas and Easter parties and occasionally in the summer. It's as if your parents wanted to keep both you and Mary D. away."

"I don't think they were trying to get rid of us," Peter answered thoughtfully. "They wanted us to have good educations with people of our own kind, and there aren't any private schools in Westerveldt."

"I know. That's why my parents sent me away my last year in high school. I was having too good a time here. Sometimes I think that's what it's all about. We're not supposed to have too good a time. Not the same kind of good time everyone else in town has. We're in training for something. But I'd like to know what. Look at Genevieve Sanford. She's a real knockout, a Smith graduate, money in the family. Was all that training just to get married and settle in a house down the street from her mother? It's as if she never left home."

"I think her parents wished she'd made a better match. I dated Genevieve before I went in the Navy," Peter said a little wistfully.

Emily ignored the reference. If Peter had really wanted to marry Genevieve, he could have. "She still would have lived two doors from her mother no matter whom she married. Soon she and Bill will be just like her parents. Bridge, dinner parties. No real fun."

"Maybe that's all the fun they want," Peter answered impatiently.

Emily raised an eyebrow. "Not enough for me. What about you, Peter?" she was almost mocking him. "Is that enough fun for you?"

Peter drew himself up. "My future isn't mapped out for fun."

As they skated around the edge of what Peter had not yet told her, Emily pressed. "Are you talking about the war or after the war?"

"Both, The war certainly isn't fun, and I don't expect the ministry to be fun."

"Oh really?" Emily acted surprised. "But I assume you're not intending to torture yourself in your vocation. You must have made the choice because you want to."

"My mind is made up," Peter said in the same stubborn tone he used at the family dinner table.

"Then you should be cheerful about it. Right now you look very gloomy."

"I don't think I'm gloomy. The things of the world don't interest me." He sounded sanctimonious.

It was Emily's turn to be impatient. "Oh is that so? The things of the world don't interest you. How are you ever going to counsel your flock if that's all they're interested in?"

"I'll find a way," Peter answered with a enigmatic smile.

Emily looked out at Mary D, and Mike, still dancing. There was no sign of Will Cranston anywhere.

"Could we have some more worldly beer and another worldly hamburger? No, half a hamburger. I couldn't eat a whole one. Let's share one."

"Okay." A shared hamburger would bring peace between them. "But first let me look around for Mary D.'s date. I want to see if he's left. If he has, then I have to figure out what to do next. I'll be right back."

Emily sat alone in the booth, picking up the last three scraps of french fries on her plate, tapping her foot to the music, and watching the dozen couples on the floor. She still hadn't danced once. The song ended and was followed, as soon as the machine could change the record, by "Brazil." She saw Mike and Mary D., hand in hand, head toward the bar where Peter had gone to look for Will. As she tried to identify the other dancers, her hand was grasped, and Mike tried to pull her out on the floor.

"Can you samba?"

Emily resisted. "I'm waiting for Mary D. and Peter."

"They'll be back. They can't go far. Come on, lady, let's dance."

"Maybe later."

"If that's the way you want it," Mike shrugged, dropping her hand and sitting down opposite her. "So little Emily is all grown up."

Emily eyed him and said nothing.

"You're turning out all right." He appraised her coiffure, her make-up, her blouse, her arms, anything visible above the table. Emily took offense.

"Are you always on the prowl?"

"What can I do? All the girls want to get married. There's nobody left."

"Is that so? The town is full of girls and very empty of men these days."

"You noticed that?" Mike laughed. "I wish I could sit out the war on the home front and keep them all happy." He pretended to act very sad. "But it is not to be."

"You've been called up?"

"Not yet, but I'm going to enlist after the summer, much as I hate to leave you all. The way I see it, I can't afford to be the only healthy male left in Westerveldt. People will think there's something wrong with me, and I can't have that. What's your date's excuse? Weak heart? Flat feet? Ingrown toenail?"

Emily preened herself like a swan. "He's on leave. He's a lieutenant in the navy."

"That so." Mike was impressed. "J.g. or s.g.?"

"I don't know." Emily was surprised herself that she had never asked or noticed the insignia on his uniform at the wedding.

"Never mind. I'll ask him." Mike grinned.

Mary D. and Peter came back to the booth, Peter shepherding. Mary D. sat down next to Emily, but before Will could sit down next to Mike, Peter stepped forward.

"Okay, Mike. Nice to have seen you, but we want that seat."

Mike didn't move for a second, but then, grinning, he picked up his cigarettes and matches and moved off.

"Yes, Sir," he said solemnly. "Senior grade, at least, bucking for captain. Good night, admiral. Thank you, admiral."

They forgot about Mike over another pitcher of beer, especially when he didn't appear again on the dance floor. They passed the evening agreeably enough until it was time to go home. Mary D. wondered how it would work out.

"If I go home with Willy, they'll be on to me."

"Then you ride home with Emily and me," Peter decided.

"No," Mary D. said flatly. "There must be another way."

"What other way could there possibly be?" Peter asked.

"I've got it. You drop Emily off at her house. Then you meet us, in say twenty-five minutes, at the corner of Brunswick and Church. Then I'll get in your car—that is, Daddy's car," she giggled. "That way we get to say goodnight properly."

Peter didn't speak until they turned down Franklin. "We can't go back there tomorrow night. Mary D. will be sure to have some new scheme up her sleeve, especially since it's Friday. Where can we go?"

"Anywhere but the Westerveldt Arms."

"Right. I'll think of something. Out of town. Where Mary D. won't think of looking. She's on her own. I don't envy my mother. That girl's a handful."

When the car came to a stop in front of the Osterhoudt house, they noticed that the porch light had been put on, as it had not the previous nights.

"I guess your mother doesn't want us to say goodnight properly," Peter said, and before Emily could think of an answer, he had put his arms around her and kissed her, much less tenderly and much more passionately than he had the night before. Then he reached for the door handle to let himself out of the car.

"I have to pick up Mary D.," he said gruffly, as he went around the car to open her door.

Under the porch light, he kissed her very formally on the forehead, brushed his lips against her check, whispered "tomorrow," and hurried back to the car.

8

Emily

Emily was nervous as she dressed the next evening for her date with Peter. She couldn't understand what seemed to be such sudden changes in his moods. Withdrawn, melancholy, sorry for himself, fed up with the world, irritable with her; then, as they'd danced, cheerful, and, at the end of the evening, amorous. Passive, fretful about Mary D., and then downright forceful in getting rid of Mike Mancuso. He was two people in one. A split personality? Which was the real Peter? The one who wanted to take celibate vows or the one who kissed her? The one who fussed or the one who knew how to handle other men like an officer? What did these shifts in mood mean? Was he crazy? He wouldn't have lasted very long in the navy if he were crazy. Maybe he was on the verge of a breakdown. Would he crack up when he saw military action? Emily felt frightened for him, and a little frightened for herself. She no longer had any idea of what to expect of him. They were no longer just chums, but they weren't really anything else. They still didn't know each other very well.

They drove to the Villa Florentina, a country inn, far from the road, which served northern Italian food. They dined out on the terrace overlooking a garden and a lily pond, and, as the dusk slowly closed around them, the waiter lit a candle on their table and switched on a string of colored lights around the periphery of the terrace.

"So Mary D. got away with it," Emily said to Peter. "If she hadn't I guess you'd have told me."

"She got away with it. Mother and Dad were asleep when we

got home. Mother didn't say anything to me, so I guess she believed the story. Shall we have zabaglione for dessert?"

The proprietor's son strolled the terrace playing a jaunty tune on his accordion. When he came near their table, he stopped and started to sing a sweet song in Italian which neither Peter nor Emily could understand. Except for the word "amore" which ended each verse. When he'd finished, he beamed at them and bowed over his instrument while they applauded.

"This is a nice restaurant," Emily said. "Perhaps I've outgrown the Antlers, even though I've only been there once in my life."

Peter smiled at her through the candlelight. He was quieter this evening, but not moody, more controlled and at peace with himself.

"Tomorrow you don't have to go to work. My parents are going up to the Lodge, so I can't get hold of the car, but would you like to come along with us for the weekend? We can swim in clean lake water, canoe, take walks in the woods. They have tennis courts, badminton . . ."

"You sound like a brochure," Emily laughed. "Sure. Why not? I'll have to check with my mother. Is it all right with your mother? Did you ask your mother?"

"She suggested it. It's not going to rain so we can be outdoors as much as we like. We won't have much to do with anyone else except at meals."

"Won't Mary D. be there?"

"I forgot about Mary D. Damn. I'll have to bargain with her. I won't tell if she leaves us alone."

"Sounds like blackmail."

"Call it what you will. Maybe they have new waiters this season. Anything in pants from sixteen to sixty."

In the car, in the glow of the porch light, Emily thanked Peter for the evening. "It was beautiful," she said, "the nicest time we've had."

"It was," he agreed. "I'll remember it always." And he began to kiss her again as he had the night before, with interest and passion.

"I'll call you tomorrow morning early," he said at last, "to find out if you can come with us. We get an early start, so I'll have to call around eight-thirty."

Katherine was sipping a solitary cup of coffee in the living room at seven-thirty in the morning. It had been her habit ever since the children started school to rise as early as possible for a period of quiet before everyone else got up. Since it was Saturday, she intended to let them sleep late and grab an extra half-hour for herself. When Emily entered, hair in pincurls, her first words were, "Your juice is in the refrigerator. Would you like me to make you an egg?"

"Peter asked me to go with him and his parents to the Lodge for the weekend," Emily said matter-of-factly as she sat down in the wing-back chair. "What do you think?"

Not "is it okay with you?" Katherine caught the signal. "Oh, I don't know, dear. You've seen him every night all week. Don't you think two whole days together might be a bit much?"

"I'm not worried about being with him, Mother," she answered testily. "It's his parents. I don't want them to get the wrong idea."

"What sort of wrong idea?"

"That we're in love or engaged or something. I don't want to be on display. Have them looking me over or sounding me out."

"They'd do that anyway," Katherine said quickly. She wished she hadn't.

"I suppose." Emily seemed to understand. "But I don't want them treating me like Peter's girl."

"Well," Katherine reflected, "then maybe you'd better not go. Tell him we had plans for the weekend that you can't get out of. You could say you're driving to Pennsylvania to see your grandmother. Beatrice is going to be staying with her for a month."

"First I've heard of it. I can't make up a lie like that."

"It isn't a lie. I talked to your grandmother last night. She wants Beatrice to come. Your cousin Susan will be there."

"So you're going to Pennsylvania today?"

"Not actually today. Next weekend. But you could pretend it's today."

"They'll know if I don't go."

"We postponed at the last minute. Your grandmother had some sort of emergency—a minor emergency—and she called just as we were getting ready to leave."

"You brought me up not to lie." Emily laughed.

"Would you rather tell him the truth?"

"He wouldn't understand the truth even if I did tell him," Emily said mysteriously.

"I don't understand."

"Look. I'm not his girl. I'm not in love with him. He's not in love with me. But do his parents know that? You know grownups always jump to conclusions, and you can be sure he doesn't confide in them."

"He might talk to his mother. I can't see him confiding in Gus."

"There isn't anything to confide . . . that's the point."

Katherine paused. Should she tell or should she not? Emily seemed very adult and sensible this morning. The truth was better out.

"There's something you should know," she said finally. "Peter's mother spoke to me the other day after the meeting. She's worried about you."

"Me! She's worried about me?"

"She doesn't want you to get hurt. You see, Peter said that he wants to go into the ministry after the war. The Anglican priesthood, and he intends to take celibate vows. So if you were to think . . ."

"I know all about it," Emily interrupted. Nobody was going to tell her to watch our and not be hurt.

"Did Peter tell you?" Katherine was surprised.

"He told me about the ministry part. Mary D. told me about the celibate vows."

"Mary D. has her uses, I guess." Katherine was relieved. "How do you feel about this piece of information?"

"It doesn't matter. In the first place, I don't think Peter knows what he wants. He could always change his mind when the war's over. But if he really wants to be a monk, then let him."

"Then you're not . . . emotionally involved."

"I like him a lot."

"And?"

"I'm not emotionally involved. Not the way you think. I feel sort of sorry for him. He's so confused. When we have fun, he forgets to be depressed. I guess he's my contribution to the war effort."

Katherine raised an eyebrow. "Then why not go for the weekend?"

"I told you. His parents might get the wrong idea. They're anxious for him to reform and be a normal hot-blooded boy."

"Yes. I'm sure they are."

"They'll be looking at me to see if I can bring off the miracle. And they'll be leaving us alone a lot."

"Don't you want to be alone with Peter? You've been alone together all week."

"I don't mind Being alone with Peter. I don't want to be Left alone with Peter."

"I see your problem. What can I say? I've given you an alibi if you don't want to go. You wouldn't want me to 'forbid' you to go, would you?"

"No," Emily laughed. "Then my reputation would be completely ruined. And, besides, you'd have some explaining to do to Peter's mother. She's your friend."

"As a last resort, you can count on me."

"God. I don't know what to do. He'll be disappointed if I don't go. I'll get some breakfast. He won't be calling for another half hour." She kissed her mother's cheek on her way out of the room.

Katherine turned her attention to the morning paper. Emily seemed to know how to make up her mind, and either way it would work out. Ten minutes later the phone rang and was picked up before the second ring. Soon afterwards Emily came back into the living room, her face contorted.

"He's got his orders. He got them last night after he got home. He has to leave right away. I can't even see him to say goodbye.

Just like that. Here one minute, gone the next. I hate this war. I hate it. I hate it."

Katherine put her arm around her. "Now, now," she said. "You know how it is these days."

"I know, But I can't stand it." She shook herself free as she started to cry. "I'm going to my room before the others get up. Don't say anything."

"About Peter's getting his orders? How can I keep that a secret?"

"No. About my being upset. See you later." Emily ran up the stairs two at a time and closed her bedroom door behind her.

Katherine looked at the grandfather clock and decided to have another cup of coffee. Let Beatrice and Ted sleep a little longer. It was Saturday. Why was Emily so upset if she weren't emotionally involved? Had Peter said or done anything to hurt her? Her mind wandered back to the other war when she hadn't been much older than Emily. The excitement, the feverishness, the goodbyes, the letters, the unexpected leaves, the sudden departures, promises made and promises broken, emotions stimulated and then disappointed, plans and dreams desperately clung to, at least for a little while. Then the news. The loss of her cousins, her Aunt Ruth's older son and her Aunt Dorothy's younger son, both killed, those handsome good-hearted boys who had teased her when she was younger and taught her to dance once she put her hair up.

"It must be hard for her," Katherine said to herself, "but what can I say? That some day it will be over and we'll all pick up lives again? That she'll forget? That you can't count on anything in wartime? That you have to prepare yourself for the worst? No, never. I can't say that. That we must hope and pray. That we must be strong." Her cousin's fiancee had been so shaken by news of his death that she developed tuberculosis—the galloping kind—and died a year later. "Damn, I know what Emily means. I hate this war, too."

At one minute after nine, just as Katherine was about to call Ted and Beatrice, the phone rang again. It wa Jacqueline Sanford.

"Have you heard the news?" she asked. "About Peter Van Leuven."

"That he got his orders? Yes, he called here to say goodbye."

"Poor boy. Isobel is very upset. The Van Leuvens won't be going to the Lodge this weekend after all. Isobel asked us to call you. If you and your family would like to use their cabin to get away for two days, we'd love it if you'd come. There won't be many of us there, and we get lonesome for company."

Katherine thought fast. "That's very kind of Isobel, and of you, too, Jacqueline. We'd love a weekend in the mountains, but I'm waiting for a call from my mother. We're planning to drive to Pennsylvania later this morning if all is well there. It never rains but it pours, it seems. But thank you for thinking of us. What do you hear from the newlyweds?"

"Genevieve called last night. They're having a marvelous time. They'll be back next weekend, a week from today, so Bill will have Sunday to get organized before he goes to work Monday morning. I promised to set up the kitchen, put in groceries, all those little things. It will take them time to get settled."

"It will be nice to have them back."

"I've missed Genevieve. You can't believe, Katherine, how I've missed her. She's been away at school all these years, but I've never missed her as much as I do now. I realize that she'll never be home again."

"But she'll be nearby. You'll see her every day."

"I know, but," Jacqueline sounded a little tearful. "It will never be the same. Well, I won't keep you if you have that long trip ahead of you."

Katherine stood at the terrace door for a moment. "We couldn't possibly have gone to the Lodge," she thought. "Emily couldn't go in Peter's place. And the Sanfords would ask questions, and the Callendars and the Van Vorsts. Jacqueline, at least, is sympathetic. Hell, she's sentimental, but Horace Callendar and Ben Swinton can be very boorish. How do I explain all this to Ted?"

While she was serving Ted and Beatrice their eggs, the phone rang again. Martha's foot was acting up, Mancuso's had no one to deliver. Could one of the girls pick up the order before noon?

"I'll do it," Ted said. "I have to pick up a new basket for the lawn mower, anyway. Where's Emily?"

"I want her to sleep late. Peter Van Leuven called early this morning. He's got his orders and has to leave right away. Emily needs a good rest after being out every night this week."

"That better not mean that I have to mow the whole lawn," Beatrice said grumpily.

"I'll help," Katherine said. "We'll take turns."

"Yes," Ted agreed. "we'll take turns." Something in the brightness of her tone prompted him to acquiesce.

PART THREE

1

Emily Mowing the Lawn

Emily was mowing the lawn. Crosby had mowed her grandmother's side earlier in the morning, making a ragged line between cut and uncut grass, the joint Osterhoudt lawn divided for all to see between neat, precise, regular habits on one side, the other side running to catch up as soon as the good example had been set. It had rained hard all week, so Crosby's wobbly line pushed nearly two inches of uncut grass into high relief. The procedure was to cut the front lawn first, for appearances' sake. As soon as Emily had started trimming the edges by hand and raking up, Beatrice would have to start on the back lawn.

It was a hot August day. "You should have gotten an early start in weather like this," Katherine had said. "It has to be done today. If it's hot, that's just too bad."

There are two patterns to lawn mowing. Emily executed one on the left side of the entrance walk, cutting a rectangular border, erasing Crosby's line, and continuing in shrinking rectangles inside until there was only a foot of turf left. On the right side, she worked across and back between the walk and the driveway, running the mower smartly over the edges in the hope that she could avoid too much trimming. It had been a month since Peter had left so precipitously. She had heard from him twice, both letters mailed from an APO on the west coast. and the first probably written while he was still in the country. It described San Francisco. The second described nothing in particular, neither the sea nor the weather, neither his shipmates nor the "enemy." It possibly defined his state of mind.

Trying very hard to hope again. Perhaps I have concentrated too hard on other-worldly thoughts to take my mind off the things of this world that I find so depressing. I keep telling myself that I must live in *this* world and that it is not all bad. The evil will pass. Perhaps it is my fate—to have come of age at a time when we must all do battle against evil. I might have found it easier to face if I had been older, if my stake in the future were not so ephemeral. For over a year now, my only thought for the future has been to withdraw, to leave behind the contaminations of life that seem to me to have led the world to this sorry plight. Entering the priesthood is a way of contributing to the good in the world without partaking of the evil. But, now, as I sit here looking out at the ocean (I can't tell you which one, of course) on this peaceful morning, the war seems very far away. It is still hard for me to believe that violence, shelling, bombing could take place out here. We are tiny creatures in a small tub being tossed on an eternity of ocean.

I have not heard a female voice in several weeks. I suppose I'm used to such a phenomenon—a world totally without women, but it is even odder so far from land knowing that there is no woman around for miles, and, except for the record player and photographs, there is no reminder of a woman. Women exist only in the imagination. I think of you. I remember our "wild" evenings in Westerveldt walking up and down Main Street, looking in shop windows and eating greasy food. These memories make me smile every time they cross my mind. I don't think there's anything I want more than to see you again, on just such occasions, carefree, a little silly, making the best of things. I love you. I'm not sure what it means when I say that. I don't know what I can offer you. I don't know what the future holds, but, for now, loving you makes me smile, even as I write these words, with happiness.

As Emily re-read the second letter or remembered its phrases while, for example, mowing the lawn, she would also recapture the sense of their time together with the same mixed feelings she had found in her heart when she was with him. A deep tenderness that flowed into affection and, during their last two dates together, the beginnings of passion, and then, attacking that soft, warm, gently throbbing coziness were the stabs of irritation. Peter would never let well enough alone but articulate his sense of things in words—bitter words or defensive words. His disgust? His despair? Something unpleasant that shrouded the world in his vicinity. But he seemed to be trying. Perhaps he didn't really enjoy being miserable.

One side of the lawn done, now the other side. Even in the shade of the elms, the air was hot and humid, breezeless, and as Emily stopped at the end of a row to lift her shirttail and run it quickly across her face to sop up the perspiration, she heard someone say, "Hey, do that again. Higher!"

Mike Mancuso, carrying a carton of groceries, had apparently passed the fence just as she was lifting her shirt. No one else had gone by the house since she'd been outside.

"Hello, Mike," Emily said as calmly as she could. "It sure is hot."

"Is that." He put the carton down on an unmowed section of the lawn, evidently prepared to chat. "It's good to see you work."

Emily wanted to say, "Are those groceries for my grandmother?" but knew it was a nasty answer, calling attention to their difference in class and not to Mike's personal brand of offensiveness. Instead she said, "Almost finished."

"Your parents are right to keep you busy," Mike sneered. "You'll be too tired to get bored or lonely."

Emily decided to hit back. "There's always school to look forward to."

"Oh you college girls," Mike twittered. "I just got back from delivering to Van Leuvens, and guess who was waiting for me in the kitchen? Just like old times. I shouldn't stand here wasting time talking to you. I'm running late after my little conversation with Mary D."

"Don't let me keep you. You go right ahead. But I thought you weren't working for your father any more."

"I'm not. This is my day off, but I made a deal with the old man. If I help out for a couple of hours, I get his car tonight. He's getting generous in his old age. Time was when even the old bended-knee routine didn't work. I guess he wants me to think well of him when I'm far, far away."

"You're going to be leaving?"

"Sometime in September. They need me at the plant until all the summer vacations are over with. Then I sign away my life on the dotted line."

"That so? Army? Navy? Marines?"

"You know, I can't make up my mind. What's more important? Covering myself with glory? Getting a good deal? Saving my hide for the postwar world and all you beautiful girls?"

"Do you get seasick?" Emily asked.

"I never thought of that!" Mike exclaimed. "I don't know, but I'm not going to find out. Scratch the navy and the marines. We'll make it the good old regular army, even if the uniform won't show me off to advantage."

Emily reached for the handle of the lawn mower, and Mike added quickly, "But I shouldn't rush to make up my mind. Perhaps I could profit by your good advice. Since I've got the car tonight, not my old rattletrap but a real car, what do you say we go joy-riding? I'll pick you up around eight."

"I can't, Mike," Emily answered automatically.

"Can't, huh? Don't tell me there's another unattached male in Westerveldt! Are you being true to your admiral? What's his name? Mary D.' s brother. Give the army a chance. Here we are, ready to die for you. How can you refuse?"

Emily laughed in spite of herself. Before she could say another word, Mike had picked up the groceries and sauntered down the street.

"See you at eight," he called over his shoulder.

"When he comes out of Grandmamma's, I'll straighten it out," Emily decided. She refused to run after him, to chase him down the slate path that led to her Grandmother's basement kitchen. When she turned the mower around to keep a lookout for Mike, she instead saw her Grandmother slowly descending her front steps and coming toward her with Sarah Catsby. Emily mowed with energy and concentration.

"I wish," she could hear her Grandmother say, "that Katherine wouldn't make the girls mow the front lawn. Crosby would be happy to do it, and it would be an extra fifty cents for him. Look how she's dressed! Young girls shouldn't have to do such dirty work. Hello, Emily dear," Nelly said in a louder voice, "don't get overheated."

"Hello, Grandmamma. Hello, Aunt Sarah," Emily greeted them.

"I'm going over to Sarah's to pick up a book she said I could borrow. About Acadia. On these hot afternoons, there's not much else to do except read, especially if there's a ballgame on."

"The movie house is cooled, Nelly," Sarah interjected. "It's cool and it's dark. I go there several times a week. I might just as well nap there as in the house. Why don't you come with me this afternoon?"

Nelly gaped in amazement. "In the afternoon! Sarah Catsby! I don't believe you. You and Jeff go to the movies in the afternoon?"

"Who said anything about Jeff? I go by myself, but I'd enjoy the company."

"In the afternoon! I do declare. I feel wicked enough reading in the daytime."

As Emily listened to the two women discuss their afternoon, Mike appeared from around the side of the house, glanced in their direction, and came toward them.

"Good afternoon, Mrs. Osterhoudt," he said very politely as he stepped into the gutter to pass them. "Good afternoon, Mrs. Catsby. Good afternoon, ehhehuh, Emily," as if he weren't exactly sure what her name was.

"Good afternoon, Michael," the women said almost in unison, not noticing that Emily failed to greet him. She was blushing furiously. What a nerve!

Emily spent the rest of the day balancing two courses of action. She wouldn't dream of going out with Mike. She had to take a bath anyway after mowing the lawn. She set her hair without saying to herself, "just in case."

Should she call him at the store and tell him she had not agreed to go out? He might be delivering another order and she would have to leave a message. For the same reason she couldn't walk over town and see if he were at the store. He was only teasing her. She did nothing.

At seven the Osterhoudt phone rang. Jacqueline Sanford knew it was the last minute. It had been such a hot day she and Jack hadn't made any plans for the evening, but now they were feeling a little lonely. Genevieve and Bill were eating dinner with his parents. Would Ted and Katherine like a hand of bridge or an evening's chat?

When her parents left the house, Emily had still not figured out what she was doing, what she thought she was doing, or what she was going to do. She had said nothing to her parents about Mike's "invitation." She tried to picture a possible scene at the front door—"Oh, you weren't kidding!" "I thought I told you no," or an alternative scene if her mother or father answered his knock. She was glad they weren't home. If she were at college, there would be no problem. There was no harm in spending an evening with anyone who asked her out whether she liked him or not. She could always get out of a second invitation. At Barnard there was no shame or guilt attendant on one's choice of beaux unless one were seen with a succession of ugly, ill-dressed, or uncouth types. To have any date at all these days, to have a young man call for her at the dormitory, could only confer at least minimum prestige.

But home in Westerveldt, silly as it seemed after a year away, to live, even if only for the summer, on Franklin Avenue, was to be reminded of the rules, usually unspoken and deftly insinuated, that somehow some young men were not suitable. Mike Mancuso was not unsuitable because he delivered groceries for Grandmamma next door (although that reason would be enough for Grandmamma), and not just because he wasn't on a mythical list of eligible young men. He could never in a million years have had his name added to that list no matter how politely he said "Good afternoon." He was unredeemedly not only lower-middle class but brash, much too overtly sexy, and, above all, not prepared to reform, to adopt the proper demeanor and attitude. Bill Sloane, no matter how much some people carped, was acceptable. His manners, except for some lapses in the use of the nominative case after prepositions, were gracious and friendly. It might be fifteen years before he could earn the right to test the waters of familiarity, and such self-effacement recommended him. He tacitly acquiesced in his inferior role. Mike Mancuso acquiesced in nothing but the economic necessity of having to work in a factory, to obey his father more than he cared to, and to join the army. He may not have thought himself as good as anyone else, but no one was going to remind him of that fact and get away with it.

So, to go out with Mike Mancuso, although it might be perfectly all right in New York, was, in Westerveldt, on Franklin Avenue, to let him into the inner sanctum just because he dared knock at the door. At eight o'clock Emily was still playing it both ways. She had put on a pretty blouse that was nice enough to wear anywhere, but she was wearing clean clam diggers. He would think she was not expecting him. She had brushed out her hair. She could be ready in five minutes. By five of eight she was cross at herself for taking Mike seriously. Obviously he'd been toying with her, and here she was, half-ready to go with him. She picked up one of her mother's books and curled up in the wingback chair, forcing herself to concentrate. She thought she heard a car go slowly past the house, then another, and perhaps she now heard the sound to brakes. She continued to sit in the chair. "I will not be caught looking out of the window," she told herself. She opened the book, *An End to War?* by a political scientist at Harvard and turned to Part III, "The Failure of Nerve."

> If the average educated citizen of one of the Western democracies had been asked in 1919 the question, "Do you think there will be another war in your lifetime?", he would, in all likelihood, have thought the question obscene. Those who lived on the continent and had suffered most directly from the nearness of battle or the persistent . . .

Brakes screeched. A motor raced and then died. "privations or the loss of loved ones . . . property overrun by . . ." There was a loud knock at the door, and Emily slowly put down her book and uncurled herself from the chair.

It was Mike all right, grinning roguishly. He bowed low.

"Madame.' He was wearing a jacket and had probably just shaved. "The chariot awaits, but methinks the trousers on thy fair form are better suited to a pumpkin."

Emily had to laugh. "I'll change. I never know when you're serious."

"Never, fair damsel. Never. Life is a game. When it isn't a joke. And where do I wait for you? Here in the hall, standing?"

"Sorry. Come on in here." She led him into the living room and gestured toward the chair she had just vacated. "I won't be long."

She returned before Mike had finished inspecting the furniture, the pictures on the wall, the books in the bookcases, and the bric-a-brac on the end tables, estimating from little comparative knowledge how much it had all cost and how many generations had been necessary to accumulate it all.

"Very nice," he said coolly. "Nice, indeed, but not as fancy as your grandmother's living room. That's a museum piece." Emily didn't ask him under what circumstances he had seen her grandmother's antique and damask decorated parlor. Instead she said, "This room is more comfortable. You can't have both elegance and comfort."

"And you'll pass." He turned his appraising eye on Emily's flowered shirt and spectator pumps. "Shall we?" He bowed and crooked his arm to receive hers.

2

Ted and Katherine

Eight blocks away on Brunswick, Ted was looking up at the Corwin house.

"That northwest window should have been an inch or two to the left."

He put his hand up in front of his nose and squinted first on one side of it and then on the other. "Delta Corwin picked up some armoire in an antique shop, and she made me move the window over to have room for it. Inside it looks all right, but the outside line is spoiled."

Katherine stood at his side and now knew why he had suggested they walk to the Sanfords. Rarely did he ever consider walking with her after dark, no matter how low he was on gas. He might walk, himself, back to the office, to call on someone, but it was unseemly to permit one's wife to walk fifteen handsome blocks on a warm summer's night. Not done. One of his old-fashioned quirks in which Katherine acquiesced since debating, arguing, or teasing had never met with success. Sometimes she could convince him to walk in the evening if she adopted a sprightly tone and extolled the pleasures of fresh air. If she said it was more economical, more patriotic, or healthier to walk, some sort of sensible duty, Ted, in all likelihood, would get cross. Arriving at a destination in a car was the way it was done by people of his sort, no matter how things were done in Pennsylvania. His wife and daughters ostensibly gave in, but some of Katherine's alien spirit had rubbed off on her daughters. The night before, but Ted did not know it, Emily had walked home, instead of taking the bus, at eleven o'clock, after visiting an old high-school friend on Westerveldt Drive, four miles from Franklin, up Hamilton, from beginning to end, past the bus station, the high school, the YMCA, the railroad tracks, one bar and grill after another. She hadn't given a thought to being afraid. The streets of Westerveldt were like the streets of paradise, unlike those of New York City which she had roamed regularly during the school year.

"It's still a fine house," Ted said. "That's the best slate work in town, and it looks as good today as it did when we put it up. If I never do anything else, I'll have this to be proud of."

Katherine was about to utter words of encouragement—"things" had been slack at Ted's architectural office since the war started—but he continued, "Jacqueline didn't say there was anything on her mind, did she? Genevieve's house, the Van Slyke house, is done. Now, I'm not sorry I took that job. I couldn't have let just anyone remodel Lizzie's house; my mother would never have forgiven me. But I can't afford another like it. Even with Charley Sloane's boys working at cost, there was no margin, no room to move around. Price-fixing or no price-fixing, everything inches up or you can't get what you want in the first place."

"No. Jacqueline didn't say she wanted to talk about anything in particular. But, Ted, there's something on Your mind. I can tell."

Ted paced two feet to the left and sighted the roof angle. The Corwin house had been completed in 1936, one of his most lucrative commissions. (Jess Corwin was a mining engineer who'd cleaned up our West somewhere and decided to build a house in Westerveldt because his wife Delta had fallen in love with its history and its elm trees. They were rarely in town.)

"I've been thinking. I can't sit still and wait for the war to end. Emily's in college. Beatrice will be going in another year. We can't tighten our belts any more than we have already. I've got to branch out, take on something new. Domestic architecture is in limbo for the duration, and, as I said before, these remodeling jobs don't pay their own way."

Katherine waited for him to go on. Since she kept her husband's books, helped out at the office whenever necessary, and knew all phases of his work, so far he had not said anything surprising. (When she had suggested the year before that she go to work in Ben Swinton's office when his secretary quit to get married, Ted had had a fit. No walking after dark, no working in offices. He'd provide for his family somehow.)

"So, I've been thinking. H & B is going to convert to defense work, so rumor has it. I've looked at the building. It's sound structurally, good brick, good roof, but the inside hasn't been touched in twenty years. It'll have to be completely re-designed. I've never done an industrial building, it's out of my league, but I think I can learn how if I do my homework. Horace will get the commission to work out the retooling, that's his field, but he won't have time to do the whole job. Not now. He's overworked as it is, and his assistant just got drafted. I thought I might talk to him. He can explain what he wants, and I can do the plans and supervise the work." Ted now waited for her response.

"That's a good idea," Katherine answered. "There's certainly no harm trying. What have you got to lose?"

Ted flushed. "He could say no. Horace could say no, and he'd know I was looking for work."

After twenty years, Ted's flashes of pride still caught Katherine off guard. When her father heard someone had some extra money, he would ask them if they wanted a piano and his feeling weren't hurt if they'd rather buy a car. "Sometimes people have to look for work. Work doesn't come looking for them. Horace knows people aren't building houses these days. He knows they aren't remodeling houses. He knows he has more work than he can handle. You're his friend. Who else is there in town he knows as well as he knows you? Someone who can do the job and do it right."

"I'll be putting him on the spot. He'll be doing me a favor."

"You'll be doing him a favor as well. Why should he hire a stranger when here you are with your training?"

"I don't want him taking pity on me."

"Ted." Katherine tried not to sound impatient. "It is not your fault the United States is at war and people can't build houses."

"It's my fault I wanted to be an architect. I should have seen it all coming—the Depression, the war. I should have chosen a career that suited the times."

"Munitions manufacturer?" Katherine laughed at him. "Stop it. How can we possibly go to the Sanfords when you're in a mood like this? Now. Monday you march over to Horace's office. We'll think it through first. We'll be ready with ideas for the changes you'll have to make in the H & B building. You tell Horace what you have to offer and stop thinking he'll be doing you a favor. You're good. You know you're good. He knows you're good."

"My grandfather's bank lent his grandfather the money to get started in the coal business."

There were times when the web of obligations in Westerveldtian history seemed to Katherine like medieval arcana, but if the memory of past debts gave Ted a spurt of self-confidence, so much the better.

"Right. He owes you a favor."

As they walked on, Ted took one last look at the Corwin house, a monument to his past. "There'll never be another," he said. "Never. Not for me. If I get into industrial buildings, it'll be all over."

"The war will be over some day, too."

"We've nearly knocked Italy out of the war." Ted brightened. "Mussolini's resigned. Sicily ought to be ours any day now. But it's still going to be a long haul."

As they passed the Van Slyke (now Sloane) house, Ted stopped again to look at his handiwork. He didn't want to stay cheerful for long.

"It looks naked without the front porch. My mother says so every time she sees it, and she's right. Maybe once the garden and the shrubs take hold, it won't look so bare. Why they wanted a modern entrance, I'll never know. It would have cost the same to do the porch over."

Katherine kept silent. This was old ground.

"Genevieve is a lucky girl. Her parents could afford to buy up a good old house and have it done over for her. We won't be able to afford to. We couldn't have afforded our own house if I hadn't inherited it. And if Aunt Cranshaw's daughter had lived, I wouldn't have inherited it."

"Ted!" Katherine was sharp. "We're nearly there. Stop it. We'd have managed. People manage."

"Of course, if Emily married Peter Van Leuven, we won't need to worry. Gus'll see to it they're properly settled."

Peter was far away. Katherine had not told her husband of Peter's postwar plans, and this was not the moment. If Ted was thinking that Emily's future would be secure if she married Peter Van Leuven, if that thought made him feel less anxious about his own future, then it was an innocent fantasy. Peter was far away.

They agreed, the Sanfords and the Osterhoudts, without much discussion, that it was too warm an evening for bridge. It was good to see each other, to sit outside on the terrace and watch the sun set over the fields on the other side of the Wester Kill until they were driven inside by the mosquitoes. Perhaps then a round of parchesi just for something to do. After Jacqueline had swatted her stockinged leg twice, she said she'd set up the board, and Katherine followed her while their husbands, more of their bodies protected against the predations of insects, continued to sit over their drinks discussing the availability of mortgage money.

As Jacqueline listlessly placed the parchesi board on the card table and opened it out, Katherine quickly asked her if something was wrong.

"Aren't you feeling well? It's wretchedly hot. We don't have to stay, you know, if you'd rather rest."

"Oh, no. No, no, don't go." Jacqueline pleaded. "I wanted you to come. I need company."

"Then there's something on your mind. Something's bothering you. You're not yourself."

"I shouldn't talk about it. I promised myself I wouldn't. I haven't dared tell Jack until I'm sure, but I'm very worried."

"You aren't feeling well! What is it, Jacqueline?"

"I'm all right. There's nothing wrong with me but sleepless nights and fretting. It's Genevieve."

"Is it serious?"

Jacqueline thought for a second. "No, damn it. It isn't serious. She's not sick and she's not unhappy. But it is serious. Her whole life will change. Our lives."

"I think I'm beginning to see," Katherine said thoughtfully. "You mean, you're afraid she's . . ."

"Exactly. I'm not sure, mind you, but it's six weeks since the wedding, and there's been no sign. Two months were up yesterday. There's nothing to do but take her to Dr. Hansen early next week. But I know the answer before we go. She's pale, she feels queasy in the morning and her . . . there are other symptoms."

"Oh dear. So soon. I thought that happened only in novels."

"I warned her to be careful. I told her what could happen. Dr. Hansen gave her instructions. I did all I could." As Jacqueline outlined her defense, she walked toward the window to make sure the husbands couldn't hear. "It's a terrible problem. How can you teach two healthy young people who are very much in love to be careful, especially when they have no experience in the first place?"

Katherine thought fleetingly of the advice she'd received, of the equipment she'd tried, of her extremely good fortune in having to wait three months to conceive even after she and Ted had decided to start a family. She thought of her own daughters and what lay ahead for them, Emily, in particular, barely eighteen and away from home.

"They say those new diaphragms."

"That's what Dr. Hansen gave her," Jacqueline exclaimed impatiently.

"I knew we shouldn't put our faith in new-fangled devices. He said it was 99 percent safe if used properly. But you know how he is. He's never specific. He doesn't call a spade a spade. He acts as if you already know. Or he gets technical and uses big words or Latin. I'm sure Genevieve didn't understand him. But that's all water under the bridge by now, I'm afraid."

"I suppose it is," Katherine clucked sympathetically. "But trial and error doesn't seem like the best solution. Those poor children. They've hardly gotten to know each other. I can understand why you're upset, Jacqueline, but what I don't understand is why you're afraid to tell Jack. It's not as if he were Gus Van Leuven. Gus would blow his top if his daughter were pregnant on a schedule he didn't approve of, and, of course, he'd blame Isobel. I'm sure Jack will be as tender-hearted as he always is and helpful."

"Yes, he will be. But he'll brood until he gets used to the idea. I know he won't lose his temper and blame me the way Gus would." Jacqueline smiled at a distant memory. "Did you know that I was nearly engaged once to Gus Van Leuven?"

Katherine started to laugh. "No, I didn't. Really? I don't know what Ted's friends were like in their youth, except for some boyish pranks. So, once upon a time, you were in love with Gus?"

"It sounds unbelievable now when I see how we've all turned out. I didn't notice Jack much during those years. He was very quiet, almost shy. Very handsome, of course. But at dances, he'd stand on the sidelines most of the evening and dance once with each debutante as if he were trying us all out. Gus was the life of the party. Very dashing, always dressed to the nines, as you can imagine. He used to sport a cane some Sundays on his way to church. Always up to something. Sports, cars, hikes, trips. We'd hear he'd taken off for a weekend in New York or gone to Albany or Boston, one adventure after another. He seemed exciting and glamorous. A great dancer!" Jacqueline swayed as she remembered. "He still is, to give him credit, the best dancer in Westerveldt. Dancing with him is like floating on air. I think I fell in love with his dancing. How many men in town can waltz really well? Without thinking about it—just round and round and round over the entire dance floor."

"Yes, I agree heartily. He's a marvelous dancer," Katherine acknowledged with no difficulty, but she couldn't let her judgment of Gus stand unqualified. "His small talk, however, is disappointing. He never says anything flattering. I think he expects me to flatter him."

"That's it. That's the way he was, and still is. Because he was glamorous and exciting and such a good dancer, he wanted to be adored. Agreed with. Any opinion he had was the right one.

Everything he did was perfect and he wanted me to appreciate him. Now I adore Jack, but not because he's perfect but because he's so nice to me. I know he loves me. I never doubt it."

"When did you fall in love with Jack?" Katherine did not dare ask if Gus Van Leuven had willingly stepped aside, even for a boyhood friend.

"After I fell out of love with Gus." Jacqueline tried to remember. "I think it was my father. He never liked Gus much. He never said anything directly, but every time Gus came to the house, he'd start a conversation with him, something prickly, and in no time Gus would forget to be as polite as he should have been. Then my father would smile and leave the room, and Gus would be cross with me. It happened once too often. We were going to a picnic. Gus snarled at me all the way to the club, and when we got there he went off swimming and left me alone. Jack was there by himself, and so, well, one thing led to another."

"What happened with Gus?" Katherine had to know.

"What happened with Gus? What did happen with Gus? I see why you ask. Now I remember. I was lucky. He went out West on a camping trip and was gone six weeks. When he came back, it was too late. I was engaged to Jack. Oh, Katherine, what am I going to do? Jack is so good, so kind, so thoughtful, generous. I can't say enough good things about him. I know that when he finds out that Genevieve is—pregnant—he's going to be upset, and I can't bear it. I feel as if I've betrayed his goodness by letting this happen."

"But what could you have done, Jacqueline? I don't understand. You talked to her. You took her to Dr. Hansen."

"I," Jacqueline hesitated, "I could have done more. I was more worried about something else. When I talked to her, I emphasized the wrong things."

"Whatever do you mean?"

"I wanted her to be happy. I'm afraid I talked about the positive aspects of marriage. I didn't want her to be afraid or shocked or embarrassed. My greatest fear was that she'd be doomed to suffer like my . . . like someone I know. The thought that she was married and didn't enjoy that side of life was more than I could bear. Now what I should have done was frighten her about the possibility of pregnancy. I mentioned it certainly. I said to be careful, but I didn't put the fear of God in her. If Jack knew that, he'd never forgive me. I don't know which is worse—having a baby the first year you're married or being married to a man you don't truly love in that way."

"Put your mind at ease. If a woman has to choose, having a baby is certainly the more cheerful alternative."

Jacqueline brightened. "You're right, but it's a terrible problem. Wouldn't you think they'd find some solution? There must be some method that works, even for the inexperienced. It's not like the last century when women expected to be pregnant all the time. Nowadays it's considered improvident to have more children than you can educate properly. Or ignorant. Or vulgar. But what can we do? We can't always practice self-control. I wish there was something we could put in the food. Some substance. Some chemical."

3

Antlers

"If you'd dressed up, I'd have taken you some place fancier."
Mike Mancuso had just ordered two "Antler specials" (two
cheeseburgers on toasted rolls with side orders of french fries) and
a pitcher of beer. He surveyed the dance floor with an air of disgust;
he'd seen it a thousand times.

"If I'd known what your intentions were," Emily answered, perhaps
more coyly than she meant to, "I would have dressed accordingly."

"Black lace and high-heeled slippers," Mike leered. In his book,
"intentions" had only one meaning.

Emily moved to correct any false impression. "I didn't think
you meant it when you said you'd pick me up at eight. I thought
you were teasing or making fun of me."

Mike gasped in mock exasperation. "I never joke about
important things. But I have a confession to make. I wasn't sure I'd
find you home. How did I know the admiral wasn't in town? Where
is he, by the way?"

"Somewhere at sea. Probably in the Pacific. I don't hear from him
too often, at least not in answer to my letters. The mail takes forever."
Peter was evidently going to be the invisible piece in this chess game.

"Maybe he has a girl in every port. You know what they say
about sailors. Almost makes me want to join the navy. Seasickness
or no seasickness. But since I'm not officer material, I guess I'll
stick with the army. I wouldn't be caught dead, haha, in bell-
bottom trousers and coats of navy blue. Speaking of the Pacific,
did you see *Guadalcanal*? It was at the Colonial last week."

"No." Emily shuddered. "Not here. Maybe when I get back

to school, but not here in Westerveldt. I keep thinking I ought to see it—they say it's one of the best war movies made—so I'll know what the guys went through, but I think it would be easier to take if I were with my roommate than with anyone here. The war seems far away in Westerveldt." The image of Peter unwilling to see *China* (with Alan Ladd) flashed through her mind.

"That it does. That it does," Mike agreed. "The real war, anyway. It's some movie, I tell you. Scared the hell out of me. But I said to myself, if they can take it, I can take it. I came to one conclusion: I'd rather fight than watch a movie with fighting in it. I don't like feeling sorry for people."

"I'll bet you don't," Emily laughed at him

"So what's with the admiral?" Mike studied her facial expression for tell-tale signs. "You two serious? Did you promise to be faithful? Did you promise not to sit under the apple tree with anyone else but what's his name until he comes marching home?"

Emily eyed Mike warily. "If I had, I wouldn't be here now. I'm very fond of him, but we made no promises."

"You wouldn't keep such a promise even if you had made it," Mike said.

"How dare you?" Emily stood up. It was a good three-mile walk down Route 7 and through dark streets to Franklin Avenue, but she didn't think she could get away with a lofty "Would you be so good as to take me home?"

Mike stood up as well and grabbed her arm. "Sit down. Sit down. No insult intended. It was a compliment."

"I don't see how." Emily remained standing.

"I meant," Mike racked his brains for a plausible translation, "that you're just beginning to hit your stride. You're too young to settle down. But you might try sitting down. I don't see you walking home by yourself."

Reluctantly Emily took her seat. "Why are you always so nasty?" she asked finally.

Mike pretended to look hurt. "I'm not nasty. I'm kindness itself. Beneath this rough exterior there beats a heart of gold, beating with love for my fellow man, or woman at any rate."

Emily sniffed. "You'd never know it."

"I asked you out, didn't I? You can't deny that."

"And you call that kind?" Emily was ready to stand up again. Mike saw her hand on the table and put his over it to restrain her. He grinned.

"Relax. Relax. Okay, so it wasn't kind. I wasn't doing you a favor. I was doing myself a favor. Is that what you want to hear? I fling myself at your feet. Your humble servant. Your slave. How's that? Am I getting the hang of it? Is that the kind of line your admiral spins you?"

"Why can't you just act natural?" Emily was now exasperated. "There's no sense sitting here arguing. I'd rather be home."

"Natural! How can Mike Mancuso act natural with Emily Osterhoudt, the college girl from Franklin Avenue?"

"You could try. Why do you want to be with me if you can't act natural?"

"The challenge, my girl, the challenge. I wanted to see if you'd go out with me."

"And now I'm here, you want to be nasty. Are you punishing me for going out with you?"

"You're right, By God. You're right. I should be rewarding you. Let's dance. That'll be reward enough for now."

Emily felt helpless. "Only another hour," she thought to herself. "I'll say I have to be home by eleven." She let herself be led onto the floor where Mike immediately pulled her close to him, cheek to cheek, so she could smell the odor of his after-shave lotion.

"Hmm," he whispered in her ear, "you're a soft bundle, but not soft enough. Relax and let me lead."

As long as they danced, there was peace between them. Mike held her close but didn't let his encircling arm wander. Emily found the unfamiliar embrace if not pleasing, at any rate not displeasing. They moved around the floor to song after song, in tune with each other while they were touching, getting to know each other in a way that was beyond conversation. Two strange dogs meeting, sniffing, feeling, playing, or perhaps two beings keeping time to the same music on a celestial plane.

They started fencing with each other again the minute they sat down for another beer, and, as could be expected, Mike was the aggressor.

"Is that the way they dance in Noo York City?" he wanted to know.

Emily decided to give him a chance. "You dance very well."

"That I know. What I don't know is—is that the way they dance at that snooty college you go to? Or do those momma's boys hold you at arm's length?"

"Oh cut it out. There you go again. Everybody dances the same all over, and you know it. You go to the movies. You know how people dance."

"I want you to tell me."

"What can I tell you? You're a good dancer. I said so already. Are you fishing for more compliments? You're as good as Fred Astaire? I never danced with Fred Astaire."

"He's out of both our leagues. Okay, if you won't tell me about the college boys, then tell me how I stack up against the admiral. I know you've danced with him."

"He's a very good dancer, too." Emily told the truth.

"Does he hold you close? Can you hear his heart beating next to yours? Pitapat, pitapat, pitapat."

"Oh hell. Isn't there anything else we can talk about? I know." Emily made one last effort. "You can tell me about life in your factory, and I'll tell you about life in mine."

Mike must have sensed that she was trying to be nice. Instead of taking offense that factory life was all they had in common, he told her an anecdote, and they spent the rest of the evening pleasantly until the last minute.

In the car outside Emily's house, Mike fired his parting shot. "I suppose you think I'm going to kiss you goodnight." He put on an expression that fell between a leer and a roguish grin. "But I think I've done enough for you already. Maybe not, maybe a kiss is just what you need."

"Save it." Emily was beginning to get the hang of the banter. "I wouldn't want you to run out."

"Plenty more where this comes from," he said and he kissed her before she could move away. "But one's enough. All you deserve."

Emily let herself out of the car without waiting for him to open the door for her.

"'Night'," she called over her shoulder.

"Wee-oo. Great legs!" he guffawed after her.

4

Dr. Hansen

Jacqueline called Dr. Hansen's office on Monday and made an appointment for Tuesday morning, although she was forced to cancel her own appointment for a fitting at the dressmaker's. There was no question of Genevieve's going to the doctor's alone. Not only did Jacqueline want to protect her daughter from embarrassment and give her time to overcome her shyness, but she had a bone or two she wanted to pick with the doctor. When Genevieve flinched at appearing in public with the brown paper bag that concealed the required specimen, her mother uncomplainingly carried it for her.

They faced Dr. Hansen across the broad protection of his desk. Behind him on the wall was a reproduction of a Mary Cassatt painting of a mother bathing her child, the only softening touch in the otherwise forbiddingly functional room, metal and leather everywhere. Dr. Hansen studied the two women unblinkingly. His practiced eye had made the diagnosis from one look at Genevieve's face, but, as a professional skilled in the management of pregnancy, as well as of pregnant women and their mothers, he kept his counsel until he could produce scientific laboratory findings, irrefutable, factual evidence—"positive"—which could be typed on a form, signed by a technical expert.

"There is no need, Genevieve," he said carefully after he made little jottings in her file, "to examine you today. We will wait until Saturday when the lab lets me know the results of the test. The Aschheim-Zondek test it's called." He was prepared, if asked, to tell them exactly how the test was performed. College graduates sometimes insisted on knowing such details. He knew just how to say, "the ovaries of the mice are then examined" in such a way that the patient might not realize that they had first been removed from the animal. If questioned, he would answer truthfully, "Yes, the mouse must be killed." Sacrificed for science, for proof. "Well, my dear, you wanted to know if you were pregnant. Now you know."

Genevieve did not ask what the test entailed. Neither did Jacqueline. Instead she asked, to keep the conversation going, "You will know for sure by Friday?"

"Late Friday afternoon. I suggest you make a Saturday morning appointment with Mrs. Schaffer on your way out. As far as I can see, unless you have any questions," he rose to usher them out, "that will be all for today. On Saturday, we'll take up where we left off."

"Very well," Jacqueline said her to herself, "I'll tackle him on Saturday." She spent the week wondering what to say to her daughter. She knew as well as Dr. Hansen that Genevieve was most certainly pregnant. She had known, by instinct, from the moment Genevieve had told her she was "late" and then described other unusual sensations in her body. There hadn't been much discussion of what it all "meant" beyond the possibility of pregnancy— pregnancy being a condition to which women are occasionally subject. That it might mean the appearance on the scene, in the fullness of time, of a baby who would need to be cared for they had not mentioned to each other. Genevieve had said ruefully. "I suppose if I'm pregnant, I'll get fatter and fatter and have to wear those awful clothes," and, on another occasion, "Will I feel like this in the morning all nine months?"

Jacqueline knew there would be time; she hoped there would be enough. All the help, all the love in the world could not transform a sweet, dreamy girl into a competent mother. All she wanted, all she thought she had ever wanted, was her daughter's happiness. Not that happiness was enough; happiness was part luck. She and Jack were happy. She could have been the same sort of wife to another man—Gus Van Leuven, for example, (time out for counting blessings)—and not been happy. Dutifulness, efficiency, cheerfulness, appreciativeness, cooperativeness, all these very excellent qualities of hers would have been wasted on a husband like Gus. Isobel had all these qualities (both she and Jacqueline had been brought up to be good wives), but her husband, much as he recognized them, took gentle compliance as his due. Love, tenderness, sexual compatibility Jacqueline knew from grateful experience were what had made her a happy woman, her reward for being what she was.

Genevieve had love; Bill was unfailingly tender, and Jacqueline knew without asking that they found pleasure in each other, but there was something lacking. What was it? A sense of duty? Genevieve always did what she was told, sooner or later, without complaint or rebelliousness, an obedient, good-natured girl, but such a girl is not a real wife and certainly not a mother. Had Genevieve no image in her mind of what she had to be, to become? Had she no ideal to live up to, no determination to be a certain sort of person, no sense of inadequacies she should struggle against? The inadequacies were not glaring. Genevieve was a bit lazy, but not slothful. She dusted every day, but without energy or commitment. She made the bed every morning, but without snap or zest. She washed dishes carefully, but never quite lined them up in the rack in descending order of size as if she had a system. Her shopping lists were written in a neat, flowing hand, but the items were not classified by genre, such as vegetables, canned goods, or soaps. Only when cooking did she demonstrate nervousness or self-doubt. She followed directions from the cookbook assiduously. She understand what a level teaspoon meant or a scant cup. She peeled carrots and potatoes as neatly as she did her nails. It was when heat was applied to the ingredients that she became flustered. She could not remember to turn down the flame as soon as the broccoli water reboiled, and she would wonder if she had salted the water. If both potatoes and broccoli were cooking simultaneously, she would get their cooking times confused and not be sure when they should be done. Jacqueline often helped her plan a meal and write out the procedure. "You want everything to be ready at the same time. If you're going to mash the potatoes, don't start the broccoli until the potatoes are nearly cooked."

In brooding about her daughter, Jacqueline wondered how, as a mother, she had failed to instill in her that essential spark that would make her always want to try a little harder, to be less accepting of life as it was, no matter how comfortable. She quoted the Red Queen, "You have to run faster to stay in the same place."

Genevieve did not brood. She wondered if she were truly pregnant, she wondered what would happen next if she were, but secure in the love of her husband and her parents, affectionately treated by everyone she knew, for that matter, she did not know how to be troubled. Not that she had spent her twenty-two years totally without problems, without challenges to her self-regard. She still remembered with a shudder the summer when she was twelve years old and had experienced other physical changes including the wretched monthly pimples which blemished the complexion she had just learned to treat with interest and respect. Chemistry at Smith had been much harder than chemistry at boarding school, but she had studied hard, memorized conscientiously enough to pass with a C even if she would never think of atomic weights again. Two term papers in her senior year had seemed beyond her competence until she had sought guidance from her instructors. Nowadays it was learning to cook that sometimes made her sigh in despair, but her mother was at her elbow nearly every day to show her how or at the other end of the telephone if anything went wrong at the last minute. If she were pregnant, if it were really true, Genevieve knew she would live through the experience with the same patient, doting support that had always guided her through life. There was nothing to worry about.

Saturday morning, the pregnancy was confirmed. No doubt, no suspicion of a doubt, the baby would be born in Mid-March as far as Dr. Hansen could calculate from his calendrical chart. After he had given Genevieve instructions on watching her weight and taking her daily doses of vitamins, he re-assured her that the prospect was normal and healthy and were there any questions? He was about to rise from his chair.

"Yes," Jacqueline said. The time had come to pick that bone. "I want to know how this could have been avoided."

"It's a little late for that kind of talk, isn't it?" he answered gruffly. "Genevieve is a married woman, isn't she? Why should she not be pregnant?"

"But we came to you before she was married. We discussed preventing pregnancy. You examined her. You gave her a diaphragm. But, as you can see, it didn't work."

"Apparently not." Dr. Hansen was unperturbed.

"But I want to know, we want to know," Jacqueline persisted. "why it didn't work. It could happen again, and again, and again. Why use something if it doesn't work? I want to know why."

Dr. Hansen spread his pink obstetrician's hands on the desk blotter in front of him.

"Why don't we cross that bridge when we come to it?" he said slowly. "Why borrow trouble? After the baby comes, that will be time enough. We can have another little talk next spring."

"No, Dr. Hansen," Jacqueline said firmly. "I want to discuss the matter now. I want to know what went wrong. Why wasn't the diaphragm effective?"

Dr. Hansen shrugged. "How can anyone know? Conception takes place when a sperm penetrates an egg, usually shortly after ovulation, when the egg leaves the ovary and travels down the Fallopian tube to the uterus." He pointed to an ovary on the plaster model on the desk between them and traced a path with the eraser of his pencil. "Here. Now what is to prevent the sperm from fertilizing the egg? The diaphragm is designed to cover the cervix." He pointed again. "But sperm are determined little devils and very small. Microscopic. They can swim up over the rim of the diaphragm. That's why we recommend the spermicidal jelly, to kill," he emphasized the word, "the sperm before it can do any— er—damage. Now you ask me what went wrong. Perhaps the diaphragm was improperly inserted. How would we know? Perhaps it was not left in place long enough after intercourse. Perhaps the amount of spermicidal jelly employed was insufficient to kill all the sperm. Perhaps the diaphragm became dislodged during intercourse. Perhaps the patient let one application of spermicide do double duty. How do we know? Perhaps in douching, the sperm were forced up into the uterus. There is one way and only one way to prevent conception. The sperm must be kept from contact with the egg. Mechanically how the aim is accomplished is a problem each couple must solve for themselves. I can provide information and equipment. I cannot," he added sternly, "supervise its use."

Genevieve had been blushing ever since her mother's first question to the doctor. She was now scarlet, even her dark luminous eyes seemed to glow like coals. She tried to visualize her love making in these practical terms. She thought she had followed directions. Which error had she committed? All of them? How could she be sure? She looked at the plaster model of the female reproductive organs, the same on which several months earlier Dr. Hansen had also traced the path an egg traveled and the position of the uterus where it would come to rest. It rendered the same general scheme she had studied in her hygiene textbook. Nothing had changed. All the parts were still there and connected in the same way. She knew vaguely where each of them was located within her own body, but now, for the first time, as she was more consciously aware of their function, now that they were being used, she began to understand what before she had perceived as merely another required intellectual exercise, such as the electrolytic extraction of aluminum from bauxite. She shook her head at her own surprise at the discovery.

"Why are you shaking your head, young lady?" Dr. Hansen asked. If his sternness was paternal, he was much sterner than her father. "Don't you believe me? Or are you thinking you can run away from the truth?"

"I believe you," Genevieve answered. "How could I run away from the truth?"

"In that case," Dr. Hansen concluded, "what more can I say? Genevieve is a healthy young woman. By next spring she should be the mother of a healthy son—or perhaps a daughter—if she takes care of herself, eats properly, takes her vitamins, keeps a proper balance between rest and exercise. Walking is good for you, young lady. And, of course, refrain from intercourse as much as possible. You don't want to do damage to the fetus."

If it cannot be said that Genevieve matured into an adult young woman during her visit to Dr. Hansen, she certainly left his office much more sober and serious. On the walk home, she asked her mother,

"Do I have to do everything he says? First he says that the only way to prevent conception is to keep sperm and eggs apart. He sounds as if he means people shouldn't unless they want children. But then he says I shouldn't even though I'm already pregnant. If I'm already pregnant, what difference can it make? I can't get any more pregnant than I am, can I? I mean, I couldn't have twins, could I?"

"No, not that way," Jacqueline reassured her. "Some people say it works that way with dogs, but I wouldn't know about that. As far as I know, it's only toward the end of the pregnancy that you have to be careful. Just be sensible."

5

The Sanfords

Monday brought another hot Westerveldt evening. Humid, breezeless, sticky, enervating, and dampening to the spirit. As the Sanfords sat in their living room after dinner, Jacqueline embroidered. Jack smoked, as if smoking were a hobby in itself. He smoked in silence. There was much he could say. If given to ranting, he could have ranted without pause for half an hour. He had known about Genevieve's pregnancy for two days, ever since Saturday night after bridge at the Callendars'. In bed, the lights out, Jacqueline had said, "There's something you should know."

His reaction at the time had been, "Oh, hell," and he had not asked many questions. His daughter was pregnant. He had known all along that she would be, long before she and Bill had given thought to a family and a made a mature, sensible decision. With her vague, dreamy nature, an unwanted pregnancy was as inevitable as daybreak. If he wanted to rant, he would have to rant against her nature, her being, which no good advice, medical counsel, education, lecture, or good example could teach to study and adapt to changing circumstances. He knew why she was the way she was. An only child (when the Sanfords didn't want children, they didn't have children), beautiful and much admired, cuddled and coddled, given every advantage money and social position could procure, she had never had to learn to be clever or self-protective. Nothing unpleasant ever happened to her. She was without enemies. She didn't know how to plan ahead against adversities. Her upbringing was responsible. He and Jacqueline had made life too easy for her. If she weren't so sweet, so undemanding, so uncomplaining, he would say she was spoiled.

As he smoked he watched his wife carefully pull a thread up though the cloth to form a neat little stitch and then poke the needle back down again. How could he rant at her, bring tears to those beautiful eyes and nasty blotches to that creamy clear complexion? It wasn't her fault. She wanted to spare him pain as much as he wanted to spare her, as much as both of them had always wanted to spare Genevieve, the three of them victims of the tenderness they felt for each other which dissolved all rage. So, instead of goddamning, or railing against fate, or reliving their mistakes, and ruining a peaceful evening, as he snuffed out his cigarette, Jack spoke at last.

"I've been thinking about the cabin. You know, we've only used it three, or was it four, times this summer."

"Four," Jacqueline said. "It's a shame. But with the wedding," she hesitated, as if any mention of time spent on Genevieve's affairs might remind Jack of their indulgence, "we haven't felt free to go." It was not, in truth, the wedding that had kept them home on weekends; that had been two months earlier. Each Friday, Jacqueline would fret that Genevieve might not have bought enough groceries for the weekend or remembered to send out the laundry so that Bill would have clean shirts for the next work week.

Jack did not remind her of their regular Friday morning conversations. "There are two more weekends before the big Labor Day weekend. We should try to get away."

"No reason why we can't." Dr. Hansen had said Genevieve was in excellent health.

"Maybe you'd like to spend a week there by yourself—between two weekends." And let Genevieve plan her own menus.

"And leave you here all alone? No, I couldn't do that." A thought occurred to her. "Unless you want to be alone."

"No," Jack answered with conviction. "I don't want to be alone. I was thinking of you." Just uttering such a statement softened him. "You could take Genevieve with you, if you think it would be good for her."

"That's very unselfish, Jack, but I couldn't. I couldn't leave you and Bill to rattle around in two big houses."

"You're right. Son-in-law or no, I don't want to join forces and spend my evenings with him, or even eat dinner with him. He'd want to pester me about loans for his father's remodeling schemes."

"He could always eat dinner at his mother's."

"At a time like this, do you think that's such a good idea? You said they hadn't told her about the baby yet. I'm sure the Sloanes are going to be as distressed as we are. Who knows? They might blame us. We're the educated family. We're supposed to know how to manage our lives." His tone was self-mocking. He wondered to himself how the lower orders handled birth control when they couldn't afford the latest in medical advice.

Jacqueline's conscience pricked her again. "Weekends, then," she said flatly, "and a nice long weekend over Labor Day. Everybody will be there for sure."

"Tell me what you think," Jack ventured. "We didn't use the cabin much this summer, and with the war on and the baby coming, we probably won't use it much next summer, either, and who knows after that. How would you feel about selling it?"

"Oh, no," Jacqueline cried. Then she stopped, realizing what Jack meant. "I suppose we could use the money. It's been sitting there empty all summer, even though we've paid our share of the upkeep. But who would buy it?"

"That's the problem. Everyone in our set already has one, except someone like Ted Osterhoudt. He can't afford it now, not with two girls to educate." Even, he thought, if the education leads to This. "We'd have to look elsewhere for buyers."

"It won't be easy these days. I don't think the committee will be any more lenient about admission standards just because of the war."

The cabin was part of a rustic complex in the mountains, forty miles north of Westerveldt. Jacqueline's father, Judge Sanford, old Roger Van Leuven, and Horace Callender's father had formed a corporation to buy up five hundred acres of lakefront property deep in the woods. They had built a large lodge, and then, as the

years went by, family after family had bought into the cooperative
and built cabins.

"Not with Horace Callendar as president and Gus Van Leuven
as treasurer. Besides, it would be a shame to let it go forever. The
war will end some day. We'll never find another like it. But," he
stopped to light another cigarette, "I did have another idea. We
could rent next summer. On a monthly basis. We could leave spring
and fall for ourselves, but if we rent for June, July, and August—
one family or three separate families—we wouldn't be in the hole
for the upkeep, and we still wouldn't have lost it. It'll probably be
worth a lot more after the war anyway."

"That's very sensible, Jack," his wife agreed, "and there won't
be the same fuss over the suitability of tenants. Why I remember
the year old Roger Van Leuven died. Gus rented to some people
from Georgeport. Nice people, very quiet and polite, but Horace
was sure they were Jewish, that he was anyway. Remember them?
His name was Stone. They never came back."

"Faintly, That was some time ago. Six years. I guess they just
didn't fit in."

"Oh." Jacqueline had just finished threading a new color into
her needle. "I've thought of something. Wouldn't the cabin be the
perfect place for Genevieve and the baby next summer? Should we
rent?"

Jack measured his words. He knew Jacqueline would not easily
give up thinking of Genevieve above all other considerations. He
would have to force himself to be less generous, for her own good.

"I don't think so. The mosquitoes are worse up there than they
are down here, so the baby couldn't be outside much. Genevieve
would be stuck in the cabin, Bill around only on weekends. If
anything went wrong, she'd be miles from nowhere. They'll be
better off staying here. She has a back porch and a back yard. She's
near the doctors. She's near you."

A rosier picture. Jacqueline began to build on it. "You're right.
I wasn't thinking clearly. You know, I could fix up Genevieve's old
room as a nursery. Then, if they had somewhere to go, they could
leave the baby here overnight. Better than hiring a stranger."

"That's one economy I could do without, but I'm sure I'll have no say in the matter," Jack said dryly. Was there no way to put the brakes on maternal affection? "But I want you to promise me one thing. You won't begin redecorating until after the baby is born. Genevieve should spend at least a couple of weeks taking care of her own baby."

"Now, Jack," Jacqueline cocked her head reprovingly, "you don't want her to suffer unnecessarily. There's no reason why we can't help out."

"None in the world. But I want her to learn what life's all about." Firmly. "She doesn't realize. She's as much in the clouds as she was when they were courting. We have to help her grow up."

"She's coming down fast. She doesn't feel at all well in the morning."

"Is there anything wrong?" Jack asked quickly. Jacqueline had scored her point.

"Everything's perfectly normal, dear. Dr. Hansen says she's fine."

"As long as everything's fine, then, please, don't fuss over her too much. She has to learn to be practical. She could have a house full of children at this rate, and then where would we be?" He shuddered. "I'd still like to know how it happened, but I'm sure no one's going to tell me."

"No one knows. They did everything Dr. Hansen told them to do. At least they think they did. It just didn't work."

"I'll say. Why don't we sit outside? I know you won't be able to sew, but it's very sultry in here."

Jacqueline put down her embroidery. "I'd like a little walk."

*   *   *

Down the street, Genevieve and Bill were also sitting in their living room, side by side on the sofa, holding hands. After a simple dinner of lamb chop, baked potato, lettuce, and a cake purchased from the Woman's Exchange, Genevieve had stacked the dishes in the sink and come inside to be with her husband. The living room was neat, but when Genevieve had tidied that morning, she hadn't bothered to pick up the wedding portrait and dust behind it. The lamp above shone its reflection onto the shiny table surface and highlighted the square foot of fine telltale particles.

"Are you sure it's all right to leave the kitchen like that," Bill asked. "What if your mother found out?"

Genevieve reassured him. In her condition, she would be forgiven anything. "I miss you when you're out all day. This is the nicest part of the evening. Later, you'll be sleepy. Then I'll do the dishes, or tomorrow morning." She rested her head on his shoulder. "Do you want to look at the pictures we took of Montreal?"

"Not tonight," he said. "There's something I want to talk to you about."

She drew back from the warm soft cocoon. "Bill, you sound serious. Is there anything wrong?"

"No, no. Don't be worried." He pulled her back to nestle against him. "It's what's going on at the bank. I don't understand."

"The bank? Then you should ask Daddy, not me. I don't understand banking."

"You understand your father. Better than I do. I have asked him. I won't say we argued, but we had a difference of opinion."

"Bill, please don't argue with Daddy. After all he's done for us. Just do your job the way he wants you to do it."

"It's not that simple. I thought I was doing my job, but I don't understand the bank's policies. You'd think they'd be looking for new business. Instead of looking for it, they turn it away. I can't make head or tail of their reasoning. I thought I was helping, and making a spot for myself. I thought I was impressing them with my initiative. I thought in business you always tried to make more money. In banking it doesn't seem to be true."

"Did you ask Daddy to explain?" Genevieve couldn't picture her father not explaining patiently, more than once if necessary, anything that was important.

"Of course. All he says is 'This is the way we do business.' He wouldn't say why."

"Oh, Bill, what did you ask him to make him talk that way?"

"Here's the thing. The bank officers were all tied up in a meeting the other morning when a man comes in. I'm only a teller, but there wasn't anyone else around. He starts to tell me what he wants. He represents American Electric, that's a big electrical manufacturing company. It's looking for a site for its new plant. They like this area. We're not far from the City, we have good roads, good railroads. Three times now they've found a lot they think they can build on, and each time it turns out our bank holds a mortgage on part of the property. The bank refuses to sell. Flat out. Refuses. They don't want American Electric here, that's obvious."

Genevieve's smooth brow wrinkled in disbelief. It made no sense to her either. "Did Daddy say why?"

"No. That's why I'm asking you. Maybe you can think of some reason that doesn't have anything to do with business. Businesswise his attitude makes no sense."

Genevieve could think of only one. "Perhaps he's afraid the town will change too fast. I've heard him say that the chemical manufacturing plant ruined Newton. The schools got overcrowded, the traffic is terrible, and there aren't enough homes to go around."

"Could be. But the jobs! The number of men in this town and nearby who are looking for work. And when the war's over, the men coming back from the service, new kids getting out of high school. They'll need jobs. I don't understand. American Electric could give them all a leg up."

"I suppose," Genevieve murmured, seeing a certain justice on each side, but American Electric versus civic stability was not an issue she would be called upon to decide. No matter which way it was decided, her life would be unaffected.

"Please don't argue with Daddy, whatever you do."

"Of course not." The thought of arguing with his father-in-law was as unthinkable to Bill as it was to Genevieve, but he still had to fathom the meaning of it all. "I'm trying to learn the business. I keep my eyes and ears open, but I can't get it straight. Why is the bank so tight with its loans? When they lend money, they make money. For example, my father wants to buy up the old Terpenning house. It's been sitting there empty for five years, unpaid taxes, unpaid mortgage. My father says he can make four or five apartments out of it, for newlyweds or older people, but he can't finance it by himself."

"That sounds like a good idea."

"It is a good idea. Old houses like that deteriorate if no one lives in them and keeps them up. They're white elephants. No single family can afford to buy one of them these days. But my father can't get a loan. Your father was nice about it, but no loan. So my father wants me to talk to your father to see if I can get him to change his mind. Like I have influence—me, with only a couple of months on the job. I put in a good word anyway, but nothing comes of it."

"You mean Daddy said no? He refused to lend your father money?" How could Daddy have refused Mr. Sloane—American Electric was one thing, but Mr. Sloane?

"Not in so many words. He talked about eligibility. Now why isn't my father eligible? He's a good worker. He knows his craft. He's got good men working with him. Who could be a better risk? The house will be improved, the bank will make money, and my father will have an investment. I don't understand." Bill kept shaking his head.

Genevieve cuddled closer. "You will, darling. I'm sure you will. It takes a long time to learn business. I could never understand economics at Smith, and real life economics must be harder. You're smart; you'll learn." She yawned gently, a ladylike little yawn. "You work so hard. Just like Daddy. You need time off. Labor Day is coming up soon. What do you think, honey, if my mother invites us to go along to the Lodge for the long weekend? I'm pretty sure she will. Would it be all right with you?"

Bill didn't stop to think the question though but said the first thing that came to his mind. "My parents haven't said anything yet, but they usually have a weenie roast or a barbecue with the rest of the family on holidays like the Fourth of July or Labor Day. They'll probably want us to join them."

Genevieve was taken aback, surprised and confused. "Oh dear. I never thought of that. Is this going to happen every holiday? Your parents make plans and my parents make plans and they both want us?"

"Could be. My family likes get-togethers as much as yours. We'll have to work out a system. It'll probably be worse when the baby comes; they'll both want the baby."

"Have you told your mother anything yet? Does she suspect?"

"No hurry." Bill shook his head again. A habit he'd developed to give himself time to think, shaking his head from side to side to stir up his brain so it could see its way clear. "One thing to tell your mother—you need her advice. But I think I'll wait a week or two to tell my mother. And I'll let her tell my father."

"What do you think they'll say?"

"I don't know. My mother will worry, but she'll be happy for us. My father doesn't worry, he hollers. My mother will start sewing, and my father will bawl me out. What can I say? It's too late for recriminations. But I'd just as soon put it off."

DING DONG. The front doorbell chimed, a modern sound no one had yet gotten used to, not the heavy rap of a door knocker, as at the Van Leuven entrance, nor the bell on the Sanford house but two tinny notes that imitated a modulation on a real carillon.

"That must be Mummy and Daddy." Genevieve got up. When she noticed the evening paper strewn across an armchair, she collected it into a neat pile on the coffee table. Bill went to get his jacket. Hot as it was, there was no question of leaving it off.

"I bought some extra peaches today at Mancuso's," Jacqueline explained the package in her hand. "They were so beautiful I couldn't resist, but they're very ripe. I should put them in the refrigerator." A minute later in a tone that hovered between deep disappointment and total exasperation, she called to her daughter.

"Genevieve, I'd like to speak to you."

It was all Jacqueline could do to keep from crying in anger and sorrow. "How could you? What if your father had come out here? What if it had been Bill's parents at the door instead of us? How could you dream of such a thing? I can't believe it. Now, run the water this very instant, and we will get this kitchen cleaned up properly. Never, never, never do I want to see such slovenliness again. Never."

Genevieve blushed but did as she was told. She knew she had no case. A minor milestone.

6

Peter's Sermon

Every morning Isobel Van Leuven waited anxiously for the mailman. Punctually at nine-forty, unless it was raining heavily, he marched up the long slate walk and the porch steps and pushed letters and magazines through the brass-outlined slot in the front door. Then he rang the bell. In recent weeks, Isobel had taken to opening the door in his face, and, when he saw in her eyes the same expectant question, he didn't know whether to say, "Sorry, not today," or to make a diversionary comment on the weather. Isobel was not the only mother who lived for the mail; his own wife was following the Italian campaign as if their son were in all the battle zones at once. He also worried about his son, but he knew that an occasional letter was no cure for anxiety, perhaps because he saw pained disappointment on so many faces every day but also because more than once it had been his unavoidable duty to deliver a letter to a household deep in mourning after they had received a telegram from the War Department. He trudged along on his rounds day by day, trying to stay cheerful and appear cheerful, to keep up morale in his little community, a secular source of comfort.

On that Wednesday morning in mid-August, he was relieved to be able to hand Isobel a letter from an APO in San Francisco— it had been over ten days since the last one. She thanked him as if he had been personally responsible for writing and mailing it; then she gently reproached him for not having brought it sooner.

Peter wrote his mother once a week. The letters were addressed "Dear Mother and Dad," but it was of his mother that Peter thought when he composed them. He never gave her much news—

there didn't seem to be much to say. Warm sunshine, a nasty tropical storm three days ago, mild humorous complaints about the food aboard ship. He could have been at summer camp straining to think of some activity to describe, to reassure her that he was healthy, in good spirits, and not homesick. He was determined not to worry her, but he had to write a long enough letter so that she could feel she had spent a few minutes with him. It wasn't easy. He commented on the news from home, glad she was helping Katherine Osterhoudt organize a bazaar, delighted that the Shasta daisies were doing so well, amused that Mary D. was still working and staying out of trouble. Then, to fill up another page, he chose a passage from the Bible and expounded it, perhaps as he saw himself some day preaching, using it as a touchstone for ordering his thoughts.

> And should I not spare Nineveh, that great city, wherein are more than sixscore thousand persons that cannot discern between their right hand and their left hand; and also much cattle?

"So God spoke to Jonah." (Peter had written "spake" and then crossed it out, remembering that the Scriptures must be made accessible.) "Jonah has just told the Lord that he is angry, even unto death. He had been called by the Lord, as you remember, to preach in Nineveh, that great city, 'for their wickedness is come up before me.' Instead of obeying the Lord, Jonah tried to flee to Tarsish on board a boat from Joppa. But the Lord sent a great storm which threatened to swamp the boat, and the mariners were afraid. They cast lots among them in order to discover for whose cause this evil had come upon them, and the lot fell upon Jonah. He knew he had disobeyed the Lord, so he told them to cast him into the sea. They refused and rowed on. The storm continued. Whereupon they cried to the Lord and said, 'We beseech thee, O Lord, let us not perish for this man's life and lay not upon us innocent blood.' They were, you see, unwilling to kill Jonah just to save their own lives. But the storm persisted. So finally they cast

Jonah into the sea where he was swallowed by a great fish. Jonah was in the belly of the fish for three days and three nights, and he prayed unto the Lord, begging for mercy and promising to do as he had been commanded. The fish gave up Jonah and he traveled to Nineveh. He cried to the inhabitants of the city, 'Yet forty days and Nineveh shall be overthrown.'

"The people of Nineveh believed these words and turned from their evil ways. And God repented of the evil He had said He would do unto them, and He did it now. *He did it not.* He did not destroy Nineveh. BUT, it displeased Jonah exceedingly, and he was very angry. He sat down at the side of the city to see what would happen. God then prepared a gourd to grow and shelter him from the sun. And then God prepared a worm to smite the gourd and cause it to wither. Then, when the sun rose, God prepared a vehement east wind, and again Jonah wished himself to die. And then God said to Jonah, 'Doest thou well to be angry for the gourd?' And he said (that is, Jonah said), 'I do well to be angry, even unto death.' Then said the Lord, 'Thou hast had pity on the gourd, for the which thou hast not labored, neither madest it grow. And should I not spare Nineveh, that great city, wherein are more than six-score thousand persons that cannot discern between their right hand and their left hand; and also much cattle?'

"God shows his mercy. He spares sinners when they repent of their sins. It is Jonah who is vengeful. Jonah at first disobeys God and almost causes the death of innocent mariners. God spares him. The mariners, themselves, could have just thrown him overboard because he was a sinner who was threatening their lives, but they did not want his murder on their hands. But Jonah forgets. When he gets to Nineveh and tells its inhabitants to repent, he expects to see them punished. Instead they do repent, and God spares them. And Jonah, instead of rejoicing that the sinners have repented, is angry, even unto death, that they are not punished anyway. God tries to show him that only God can decide on punishment—that vengeance is His—Jonah has not made the gourd nor labored to make it grow. He has merely sat in its shelter, but still he is moved to wrath when it withers.

"The wrath in man—to what lengths does it lead him? He seeks vengeance when he is, shall we say, inconvenienced. When he is asked to take a long trip or when his shelter is taken away from him. He demands punishment and retribution. He wishes to destroy his enemy, even the young and the helpless who belong to the enemy, even the cattle of the enemy. In this way, even the righteous, the chosen of the Lord, can do evil and say that they do it in the name of the Lord.

'In these war-torn days, we have no choice but to destroy the enemy who comes against us and could destroy us if we did not fight back, if we did not drive him away from our shores and the shores of those he would enslave, back to his own shores where he must lay down his arms and pick up his plowshares. It is enough that we do this. But, if we will the destruction of the innocent, if we demand total punishment, we are un-Christian, unworthy of the blessings God has given us. We must not, of course, be foolish and moved to false pity before the threat of our enemy has receded, but we must keep vengeance out of our hearts. Vengeance belongs to the Lord."

Peter ended his "sermon" on this note. He did not spoil the effect he hoped his sentiments might provoke by explaining how he had come by them. The bloodthirsty remarks of the crew, some of them younger than himself, boys fresh from high school, upset and sometimes frightened him. Radio broadcasts from the States let no one forget what they were doing in the middle of the Pacific Ocean and what lay ahead of them. Peter dreaded the day when the ferocity would have to be turned off and, as an officer, he would be one of those called upon to tame it.

Isobel read the letter with pride. She pictured him standing in the pulpit, in his vestments, tall and handsome, commanding attention and then respect as he spoke with such conviction, such genuine feeling. The ministry *was* a calling, and those who answered the call could look on their lives as worthwhile and fulfilling. But why was it necessary to take celibate vows in order to be a true man of God? Peter could preach at a church like St. Andrew's, an American Broad church without the trappings of an aristocratic, secretly papish foreign church. Then, if he were merely an ordained minister, but not an Anglican priest, he could marry. There was time. They would have talks when he came home. Perhaps, Isobel thought, if she encouraged him (if Gus and Mary D. encouraged him) in his vocation, let him know they approved and were proud of him, they might be able to influence him not to draw away from the world so completely.

That night while they were waiting for dinner, Isobel read the letter aloud to Gus and Mary D. and to Augusta, who dined with them regularly mid-week. She, herself, was so impressed by Peter's maiden effort at Biblical exegesis that she accepted his observations at face value and expected her listeners would too. Mary D. was polite; she studied her nails. Augusta blinked and coughed twice through the story of Jonah. To her a Jonah was a person who brought bad luck to his fellows. The only object lesson she had ever learned from his adventures was that he had quite properly been tossed overboard. Gus stretched out his legs before Isobel had come to the first mention of the cattle. By the time Jonah had been swallowed by the great fish, he had poured himself a second scotch from the decanter on the coffee table and lit a cigarette. When Peter began to show even a qualified pity for any Japanese, he started tapping his foot and didn't stop until Isobel read, "and please give my love to Grandmother. Kiss Mary D. for me whether she's behaving or not. My best love to you both, Peter."

Isobel's eyes were full of happy tears as she folded the letter back into the envelope.

"He sounds wonderful," she said. "So calm and thoughtful."

"Thoughtful!" Gus snorted. "He's thinking too much. Don't they have anything to do on that boat to keep him so busy he doesn't think? Doesn't he have anything else to read except the goddamned Bible?"

"Gus! Don't swear like that and certainly not at the Bible!" The period of grace—the sense that all was well and would be well in God's world—that Isobel had been cherishing since first reading Peter's letter that morning had just been invaded by Gus' world of the here and now and no-nonsense.

"He seems in good spirits," Mary D. ventured to bridge the widening chasm between her mother's joy and her father's disgust. "You know Peter. That's the way he likes to talk. He's just practicing."

Augusta felt she had to say something, not to be left out of an emotional family discussion. She could see that Gus' irritation was temporary, easily focused elsewhere. "Does he write about deep matters to your friend, Emily Osterhoudt?" she asked Mary D.

"I don't know, Grandmother. She tells me when she hears from him, but she doesn't show me his letters. I don't think she gets that many. There isn't that much news out there in the ocean."

"Thank God for that. Thank God there's no real news," Isobel prayed silently. Aloud she asked, "You say he writes to Emily Osterhoudt?"

"Ever so often." Mary D. was cautious. Was her mother jealous that he was sharing his heart and thoughts with someone else? Or did her mother want someone else she could share her thoughts of Peter with?

Isobel blew her nose delicately, composed again. "We're still planning to go to the Lodge for Labor Day, aren't we, Gus?"

"Of course we're going to the Lodge. Big weekend. Everybody will be there."

"Then I think it would be nice if we invited Emily to come along. She'll be company for Mary D., and I'd like to get to know her better."

"Okay by me," Mary D. said, "but I don't know about Emily."

"You mean she wouldn't want to come, to spend a few days with you, to be out in the country? She's been cooped up in town all summer. She must be lonely with Peter so far away."

Mary D. blinked behind her glasses, almost as impatient with her mother as her father had been. Peter was her brother; Emily was her friend. So the two had dated for a week or two. Now her mother seemed to be adopting Emily as Peter's girl. Didn't she wonder if Emily had dates with other men? Didn't she wonder how serious Emily's feeling for Peter was? Pete was a great guy and a good catch, but one swallow doesn't make a summer. "At this

rate," she said to herself, "they'd have me married off to Willie
even before school started. But luckily they don't know I see him,
so he doesn't count. Memo to self: don't get involved with anyone
they could approve of or you'll be doomed before you hit your
prime."

"Invite 'em all," Gus suggested magnanimously. "That way
we'll be sure of enough hands at bridge. Liven things up. Fresh
faces."

"I'll do it. I'll call Katherine tomorrow." Isobel was delighted.
"Lovely. But Emily will take Peter's place at our table and have her
meals with us so I can talk to her. Is anyone else bringing guests
that you know of, Gus? Have you spoken to Horace lately? I want
to be sure there's room enough for all of them in the Guest House."

"I'll give him a call. They haven't had many guests this summer
at all. Even the young Sloanes." As always when he pronounced
the unfamiliar name, he smirked. "They haven't been up since the
wedding."

"The Jacks are going. I saw Jacqueline yesterday coming out of
Mancuso's. She said the newlyweds had other plans."

"What plans could they possibly have that couldn't include
the Lodge?" Augusta demanded to know. "There isn't anything
they can do here in town that they can't do at the Lodge. I'm
surprised her parents are letting her stay in town."

"I was surprised, too," Isobel agreed.

Mary D., startled, took another fresh look at her family. The
Lodge had been a glorious escape all these years from hot summers
in town. She had never thought of it as an obligation that took
precedence over other opportunities for pleasure. The newlyweds
had to go to the Lodge? She *had* to go to the Lodge, married or
unmarried, whenever her parents wanted to go? The Sanfords were
letting the Sloanes stay in town? Would it never stop?

Gus sniffed. "Maybe they feel the boy isn't ready for a weekend
at the Lodge. Wrong fork. Bank talk at table. Flowered shirt on the
verandah. Just as well they stay home until he learns. They've got
to get him shaped up before there are any children or they'll be
bringing up two generations at once."

"Now, Gus," Isobel said for the thousandth time, "he's a nice boy. Very personable. I always go to his window at the bank. He's so polite. And don't talk about children. They just got married. They're much too young, and they haven't got any money yet. How could you even think of such a thing? It'll be a while."

"I certainly hope so," Gus said. "They don't even have full-time help."

PART IV

1

The Lodge

Just as well, then, that Jacqueline had persuaded Genevieve to stay in town. She had pointed out that the pregnancy might not remain a secret over several days in such close quarters, and Genevieve agreed that she was not yet prepared to face even the friendliest of gibes, remarks, or whispers. And first Bill must tell his parents. Perhaps he'd tell them before the holiday as long as they promised not to tell any of their relatives, so long as they kept the secret until it could be a secret no longer. They would go to the Sloane barbecue only if his parents would protect them.

The embarrassment lay not so much in the pregnancy as in its unexpectedness. A century earlier conception on the wedding trip would have been considered a normal occurrence. Failure to conceive after several months might have spawned rumors that something was wrong—with the bride, with the groom, or, worse yet, between them. Now, in the enlightened 1940's, conception was preventable among those not bound by religious proscription. There was no excuse for an unwanted pregnancy, signaling unspeakable carelessness or the sin of ignorance. A nasty joke at which everyone, somehow, had to laugh either at the young couple who had been swept away by their passions beyond caution or calculation or, among kinder souls, at the tricks life can play on even the best-intentioned. Whatever, it was funny, never overtly belly-laugh funny—Genevieve was too fine and noble a girl to be guffawed at—but snickering, chuckling, giggling, never quite clear what the joke was about, but you know what I mean, funny.

A different sort of self-protective speculation was taking place at the Osterhoudts'.

"Did you have any idea when Isobel invited us that she intended to invite Mother and Dad as well?" Ted asked Katherine at dinner.

"None at all. She didn't even inquire about their health, as she usually does. She didn't mention them. She almost forgot to mention Beatrice. She said 'Emily' first and then you and me."

"I wish she had forgotten me," Beatrice put in. "I don't want to go."

"We have accepted," Ted said sternly. "You're going." Then back to his wife. "You mean she called Mother and Dad and invited them separately?"

"I don't know what happened. I suspect Augusta was behind it. She probably suggested inviting them when she found out Isobel had invited us. There aren't too many of the older generation left up there. I only found out they were invited this afternoon when Isobel called about the cars. Your mother never said anything to me. She never called me on the phone. We were both in the garden yesterday morning. We spoke for a few minutes over the fence, but the subject never came up."

"Mother says Isobel called her late yesterday morning. It must have been after you talked to her."

"Odd," thought Katherine, "that no one bothered to tell me."

"But what's this about the cars? You said Isobel called again today about the cars."

"I don't want to go," Beatrice said again.

"You have to go." This time her mother put her foot down.

"I may have to go, but I don't have to enjoy myself, no matter what anyone says."

"You can go swimming. You can go canoeing, you can play tennis. Why don't you want to go?" Katherine asked.

"There won't be anybody there for me to talk to. Everybody is older than me. I'll be bored. I don't know why I can't stay home and take care of the house. Of both houses. It'll give you more room in the car. I can see the ride up now. Emily will be in front between you two, and I'll be in the back between Them! Grandmamma will say something to Granddaddy and he won't hear, and I'll have to tell him what she said. Then he'll say, 'Tell her I'll let her know,' and she'll say, 'Tell him I want to know now,' and he'll say, 'Tell her I said later.' Damn. I don't want to go."

"Don't swear," Katherine said soothingly. "You won't have to sit in back with your grandparents. You'll sit up front with us. Or we'll let your grandfather sit up front and Grandmamma and you and I will sit in back together."

"What about me?" Emily hadn't been listening to the bickering, but her attention perked up when she heard the seating arrangements. "Or do I get to stay home?"

"I've been trying to tell you. Mrs. Van Leuven called again this afternoon and suggested that you drive up with them. That way there'll be five in each car instead of six in one and four in the other."

"Oh hell, and I suppose you said yes."

"I don't know what's the matter with you girls. Hell one minute, damn the next. Of course I said yes. Why should we be uncomfortable if we don't have to be? You'll be with Mary D.; I should think you'd like that."

"We'll be in the back seat on either side of Mrs. Van Leuven. One or the other of them, and I don't know which would be worse. That dragon or Peter's mother being friendly."

"You can always tell her you're going out with Mike Mancuso," Beatrice said. "She'll stop being friendly. She'll probably make you get out and walk."

"That's enough, Beatrice," Katherine said quickly.

"You can't pretend she isn't," Beatrice persisted. "People see them. It's no secret."

"When are you going to learn to keep your tongue to yourself?" Katherine said. "Of course it's not a secret. Emily has a right to see anyone she pleases while she's home, but we don't have to gossip about it."

"It's not gossip you're worried about, and you know it," Beatrice said. "It's not Mrs. Van Leuven either. You don't want Grandmamma to find out."

There was no denying that fact, and nobody did, although not denying it was an embarrassing burden.

"I see no reason," Katherine said at last, "to upset your Grandmother unnecessarily."

"Certainly not," Ted agreed. "Why are you acting like a troublemaker?"

"I'm not a troublemaker. I'm not going out with Mike Mancuso. I wouldn't be caught dead. But I don't see why Emily can do as she pleases and I can't. You made me go over and apologize for scaring her that night during the air raid, but you protect Emily. It's not fair."

"It's not the same thing," Emily said in her own defense.

"How come? Either way Grandmamma is upset, and we're not supposed to upset her. But you can upset her and I can't. I tell you it's not fair."

"Can't you make her understand?" Emily appealed to her mother.

"I'll try. Beatrice, that night you went through the yard with Bert and Billy, your Grandmother was frightened because she didn't know it was you. She thought there were burglars in the neighborhood. Now certainly you can understand why she was upset that night. The reason we wanted you to apologize was to make her feel better about the incident. To let her know that you didn't mean to frighten her. This business with Emily is quite different. There's no question of your Grandmother being frightened. She has some old-fashioned ideas about how young women should behave, whom they should see, etcetera, etcetera. If we can't abide by her way of looking at things, at least we don't have to flaunt our way of doing things. As you can see, these are two completely different cases."

"I don't see any difference at all. If you don't want Grandmamma upset, then you forbid me to climb the fence in her garden and you forbid Emily to go out with Mike Mancuso." Beatrice stabbed at her slice of meat loaf and sent juice spewing onto the place mat.

"Watch what you're doing," Katherine said sharply. "I'm going to try one more time. If Emily had gone through the back yard and frightened your Grandmother, I'd be scolding her just as we scolded you. And when you go to college and come home for vacation and want to go out with some young man, I can see no reason why you shouldn't go."

Ted ran his napkin quickly across his mouth before he snorted. "Why are you putting ideas in the child's head? It's bad enough that Emily is running around with that Mancuso, but are you trying to encourage Beatrice to do the same thing?"

"I suggest," Katherine said as calmly as she could, "that we cross that bridge or any bridge like it when we come to it. We really should be thinking about what clothes to take. We'll need knockabout clothes to go outside in, but I'm sure they dress for meals, at least for lunch and especially for dinner. I don't know if it will be warm enough for bathing suits, but we should bring them along just in case. I think I'll take my blue linen for one evening and my yellow with the white trim. And sweaters. It'll be chilly in the evenings. Beatrice, you don't have a nice sweater for the evening. Shall we go overtown tomorrow and see if we can find one? Something you can also wear when school starts?"

2

The Trip

Ted kept records of automobile trips, not each and every five-minute errand or half-hour spin (although he toted up the mileage every time he bought gas) but of all major outings, especially of those on which he transported his family. Katherine was deputized as recording assistant, sitting as she did up front near the notebook in the glove compartment. Once all the passengers were in the car, parked in front of his parents' house and presumably comfortable, and not earlier while the car was sitting empty in the driveway, he consulted the odometer and his wrist watch and dictated, "Mileage: 63,0997.6. Time: 10:33. Not bad. Only three minutes behind schedule."

He pulled away from the curb, proceeded down Franklin Avenue to the Westerveldt Arms, generally acknowledged to be the center of town, glanced again at his watch (one and half minutes) and turned onto Brunswick Avenue. "It's about an hour and a half to the Lodge," he announced. "You'll find the exact mileage back in early June, Katie. Remember, we went up for the day one Sunday before the Sanford wedding. Check and see if I'm right. 43 point something miles."

"We haven't been there since last summer," Nelly commented from the back seat. "The Fourth of July we were there. We all were. Abigail Callendar invited us and I guess it was the Sanfords who invited you. But the girls weren't invited as I remember. Is that right, Beechie, dear?" She patted the knee that had been consigned to the back seat at the last minute at Grandmamma's urgent request. "I never get to see much of Beechie now that she's such a big girl.

Let her sit back here next to me, and you'll have more room to drive, Teddie."

They passed the familiar houses on Brunswick, St. Andrew's, and then the Van Leuvens'.

"I wonder if they'll get to the Lodge before we do," Nelly said. "What time did they pick up Emily?"

"Ten o'clock, Mother," Katherine turned to say over her shoulder, "but Augusta wasn't in the car. They were going back for her, so there's no way of knowing if they've started out yet."

Once past the city limits, Brunswick Avenue became Route 62 as it ran north past factories and then fields, slowly gaining altitude as it rose through the mountain foothills. At the hamlet of Crystal Creek, a half a mile past the bridge at the intersection (a gas station and a general store which also housed the post office), Ted turned left on an unnumbered macadam road, and they ascended by twists and turns for a half-hour on the spurs of Blue Mountain. Then they turned off on a dirt and gravel road to the left just beyond a big plaque in the shape of an Indian arrowhead. The arrowhead was the insignia of the Lodge. Years ago, just before World War I, Horace Callender's mother, Abigail, had executed the design and it had been reproduced, over and over again, for road signs, for a large wood carving that hung over the door of the Main House, on Lodge stationery, and embroidered on the tablecloths and napkins in the Lodge dining hall.

"There's the arrow," Nelly exclaimed. "Have we come that far already?"

The road to the Lodge wound through the trees, branches here and there grazing the roof of the car, at an awkward incline with a steep embankment to the right which might give a motorist pause to consider what he would do if he met a car coming the other way. Mountain laurel bushes, their blooms withered, and wild rhododendron grew profusely in occasional treeless glens, and above, a bright blue gleaming sky. Just as the Osterhoudts had yawned for the third time to clear their ears, the road suddenly emptied into a large grassy and graveled parking area in front of the Lodge.

The Main Hall was tall, two-storied, shingled, with a four-gabled roof. The front entrance on the porch was an eight-foot double door, imposing if one were a stranger, a symbol of security if one were a member. As Ted parked the car, his father turned the handle of the door next to him and was ready to get out.

"Just a minute, Dad," Ted said authoritatively, but the old man didn't seem to hear him. "All right, all right," he muttered under his breath, "let him go. But the rest of you wait a minute. Katherine, put this down. Mileage: 64,022.3. Time: 11:55. Okay, now subtract them both and let me know how we did."

"Beechie, you go with Granddaddy. He's going to go in there all by himself," Nelly instructed. "Teddie, will you be long? Your father is up on the front porch all by himself. He shouldn't be there alone. He won't understand what anyone says to him."

"Go ahead, Ted," Katherine said briskly. "I'll come along with Mother. We'll check the mileage later once we're settled in."

If the Osterhoudts were somewhat intimidated by the Lodge and its occupants, in spite of having been guests of one member family or another over the years, it was for no other reason than that they had never felt they could afford to join. When her sons were young, before their educations began to consume any surplus monies, Nelly had approached her husband on more than one occasion, such as once or twice each spring when fair weather beckoned, with the thought of joining the Lodge and eventually building a cabin as so many of their contemporaries were doing.

When Ted Jr. married Katherine, Nelly again thought they should think again about a cottage, but the birth of the two little girls had been followed by the Depression, and there was never quite enough money in either generation to finance the venture. If they had combined forces, they could have managed it, if a cottage became an unquestioned good, which it was not. Ted Sr., for instance, although not exactly unsociable, had never been a particularly good listener, even before his deafness. He accepted passively whatever social obligations Nelly forced on him, but for pleasure he preferred long solitary walks in town or country to the company of his fellows. At second best, yelling at Jeff Catsby would do.

He could have been outvoted if Katherine had yearned for a cottage. Much as she like the Van Leuvens (Isobel anyway), the Sanfords (both of them), the Swintons, the Callendars, et al, as an outsider, a Pennsylvanian who had once lived in Philadelphia, in an apartment, and, it was whispered, by herself, she could only wonder how a lakeside cottage, comfortable and charming as it might be, could be the answer to the perennial family question, "What shall we do for a vacation this year?" To tie up all that money and spend weekend after weekend, year after year, with the same people was not Katherine's idea of either investment or pleasure. If the Osterhoudts had been really well off like, say, the Van Leuvens, they could have built a cottage and taken trips to the shore anyway.

Inside the double door, the desk in the vestibule was another reminder to all visitors that they were on private property, that they should wait before proceeding farther until someone in the room beyond should notice them and come to ask what could be done for them. It was Horace Callendar who found Ted Sr. poking his head around the vestibule into the lounge, and he was about to ask the old man, well as he knew him, much as he respected him, what he could do for him. Ted Jr. entered in time to save them both from a loud exchange.

"Morning, Horace. We're here as guests of the Van Leuvens. Should we wait for them here?" He glanced into the lounge.

"Why not?" Horace answered affably. "I haven't seen any of them. They may not be here yet. There must be somebody I can send down to tell them you're here. Come in and make yourselves comfortable." After he had dispatched someone's child down to the Van Leuven cottage, he came back to stand over the new arrivals, a little embarrassed.

"It shouldn't be long," he said. "You say they're expecting you. I assumed you'll be spending the night here in the Main House, but I can't show you to your rooms because, of course, I don't know which they are. But someone should be along soon so you can settle in. Your parents will probably have one of the rooms on the ground floor over on the west wing. Peace Pipe, maybe, or more likely Wampum; that's warmer on these cool nights. That's where we usually put parents, but as for the rest of you, I can't say. I don't even know how many guests there'll be this weekend. The secretary, that's Ronnie Harris, is supposed to give me a list of all guests in advance so I can post it out in the vestibule and we can all know what to expect, but Ronnie and Bess have gone south somewhere to visit their son in the navy, so this week there's no list. I'll bet they don't even know what to do in the kitchen—how many mouths to feed, but I guess we won't run out of food. The war interrupts one routine after another, but we'll muddle through somehow, as the Britons say." He laughed at his own mot.

The lounge was an enormous room with four long sofas, a dozen over-upholstered chairs, a mammoth table for games or writing letters, and miscellaneous tables and chairs arranged in conversational groupings. The only other door in that room led to the dining hall where all the members took their meals. No cooking was allowed in the cottages. Katherine smiled to herself as she saw Marianne Callendar setting the tables—aha, the servant problem must have stretched to the Lodge if the children were being pressed into service. She would soon see that the rigors of wartime had forced even more dramatic changes. Luncheon would be buffet, no longer served by the two waitresses who had gone to work in a defense plant.

Before Horace could begin again to put them at their ease, Isobel entered with Emily and Mary D.

"Forgive me," she cried as she hurried to Katherine and kissed her on the cheek. "I'm terribly, terribly sorry to keep you waiting. I meant to be here in the Lounge when you arrived, but we had a little trouble getting Mother settled. She says she saw a bat fly through her bedroom and she's giving Gus a hard time until he gets rid of it or convinces her it was never there. We only got here fifteen minutes ago, ourselves. Aunt Nelly, Uncle Ted, so good to see you. Teddie, Beatrice. Now let me see. Emily and Beatrice will be in Tepee, and I've put Mr. and Mrs. Osterhoudt in Wigwam. Be a lamb, Mary D., and show them all upstairs while I take Aunt Nelly and Uncle Ted to their room. They'll be in Wampum. We have about half an hour until luncheon. You'll all be at your own table, except for Emily, who'll be sitting with us."

The day proved warmer than expected, and the two younger generations spent the afternoon swimming, canoeing, or lying in the sun while their elders arrayed themselves comfortably on the rear verandah that overlooked the lake, dozing peacefully in rocking chairs, strolling up and down the length of the verandah for exercise, or disputing the quality of the meringue on the luncheon's lemon pie.

"We never use granulated sugar," Nelly said firmly. "I whip the egg whites myself to make sure that Martha doesn't use granulated sugar. That awful gritty texture on the teeth. Ugh."

"There you go again, Nelly," Augusta Van Leuven countered her, "bragging because you can eat pie with your own teeth. I don't mind the grit, and confectioner's sugar makes the meringue too sweet."

"I haven't been able to get sugar, granulated or confectioner's, for two weeks," Abigail Callendar whined. "Who's that swimming so far out alone? She has on a red bathing cap. Nelly, is that your granddaughter?"

It was indeed Beatrice, practicing her crawl, in no danger, certainly not as long as the grandmothers kept an eye on the red cap. By dinnertime, everyone was properly ravenous from the fresh air and, after the meal, properly sleepy from their exercise. They amused themselves at conversation or bridge in the lounge; the younger set played Monopoly or cards. By ten o'clock they began to say goodnight and retire.

*　　*　　*

The next morning as Emily came out of Tepee, Mary D. pounced on her.

"Boy, am I glad to see you. I've been waiting out here in the hall. I would have knocked but I didn't want to wake up your sister. I suppose you want breakfast, but I've got to talk to you. Can you give me five minutes outside where no one can hear us? Then I'll let you eat in peace."

"Okay, Mary D.," Emily acquiesced sleepily. "I'm awake enough, I guess. But what's so important it can't wait?"

"I'll tell you. I'll tell you." Mary D. led Emily down the stairs and out through the parking lot toward a grove of pine trees.

"You'll never guess who's here," she said at last in a breathless whisper.

"Not Peter!" Emily exclaimed. That was impossible. He was too far away.

"My brother? On, no, not Peter. I'm so mad I could have kittens. It's TOMMY VAN VORST. He's home on leave. His mother's been up here all summer, but he came up last night with his father. My mother just told me a few minutes ago. She knew he was coming, and she didn't tell me. Okay, so far, so good. It's their cottage. They're free to come and go as they please, but get this. My mother, and then my father, have told me that I have to be Nice to him."

"You're kidding! Tommy Van Vorst is here?"

"Not only that, kiddo, but as you can see for yourself, he's the only guy here. You can't be nice to him because my parents are saving you for Peter. Marianne Callendar is too young to be nice to him. That leaves me. I will not be nice to him. He could get some crazy idea in his head that I'm his girl back home. Everybody will be watching. His parents will be delighted that someone has finally taken an interest in their drippy son. I just know it. And they'll gang up with my parents. They'll be matchmaking. I'm too young to die. I haven't yet begun to live. Help me, Emily. Help me." For all Mary D.'s eye-rolling and head tossing, pleading and despairing and self-dramatization, Emily could see she was genuinely upset.

"What do you want me to do? What can I do?"

"You and I have to be inseparable. If anyone's nice to him, we both are. Get it? No cozy twosomes, no tennis, pingpong, walks in the woods. The three of us together at all times. Don't leave me alone with him for a second."

"What are you afraid of? He's harmless. He's just a bit loony."

"I'm not afraid of Him. I could handle Tommy Van Vorst with one hand tied behind my back. It's the parents. Both sets. Watching us. My parents are throwing me to the wolves. If anyone would dream of calling Tommy Van Vorst a wolf!"

"You're exaggerating."

"Oh no, I'm not. You know my father. The problem solver. What's the problem? I have a solution." She imitated a gruff voice. "Mary D. is the problem. Tommy Van Vorst is the solution. I won't be eighteen until next week and already they have me paired off with the only guy whose parents they know who's still around. And if you think I'm exaggerating, why do you think you're here? You don't think you're here to keep me company, do you? You don't think you're here because my parents never see enough of your parents, do you? You're here so my mother can talk to you about Peter. She just hasn't gotten you alone yet. Now do you see the virtue of clinging to my side? If not for my sake, for your own. Now, do you promise?"

"Do I get to go to the bathroom alone?"

"I mean it, Emily. Do you swear?"

"I'll do the best I can."

"That's not good enough."

"I swear."

"Okay. Now you can have your breakfast. And I'm going to sit with you and watch you eat. I ate an hour ago. Gobble, gobble, gobble, so I'd be out of the dining room before he got there. I haven't seen him yet. He's probably sleeping late."

Emily ate her breakfast without interruption. Mary D. sat with her, alternating watching the food Emily was eating and the entrance door. The Sanfords came in, Beatrice came in and joined the girls. There was no sign of Tommy Van Vorst.

It was too chilly to swim so the girls spent the morning walking around the lake on the trails through the woods, around the stables, uninhabited since the beginning of the war, past the foundation of the cottage the Harris boy had started to build before he joined the navy. By lunch time, they were both quite weary, and Mary D. as usual was famished.

"Thank God you're eating at our table," she said. "I want my

parents to realize how inseparable we are. Bosom pals and all that."
She patted her breasts. "And you're Peter's girl . . ."

"Hey, wait a minute," Emily came back. "This is the second
time you've brought that up. I don't like anybody's parents, yours
or mine, treating me as if I were Peter's girl any more than you
want your parents palming you off on Tommy Van Vorst. I like
Peter, but that's all there is to it."

"It's not the same thing. You like Peter. You just said so. I
loathe Tommy Van Vorst. Besides, Pete is far away; they can't force
you together. Come on, Emily, be a pal. I'll do something for you
some day. 'If you're ever down a well, ring my bell. If you're ever
up a tree, call for me.' I won't tell my mother or your mother that
I saw you going into the Antlers with Mike Mancuso."

Emily was taken aback. "I didn't see you."

"Nope. I was in the car. We thought of going in for a dance or
two when I saw you. I suggested to my date, ahem, who shall
remain nameless so that you can't blackmail me, that we go
elsewhere. So, I know your secrets but you don't know mine."

"It's no secret. The Antlers is a public place. I didn't expect
not to be seen."

"What were you doing with Mikey, anyway?"

"It was a last minute thing. He asked me out in such a way
that I couldn't think of a way out." Mary D. evidently still didn't
know of two other dates with "Mikey."

"Aha. I'll bet that's what they all say. Mikey is very persuasive.
Well, I won't tell if you keep your promise."

As they entered the dining room, Mary D. gasped. "Look,
there he is. With my parents. At our table. Come on. And remember
your promise."

The monster, the horror, at the Van Leuven table was tall,
lanky, beak-nosed, bespectacled (GI steel-rimmed issue), and quite
ordinary-looking. He sat quietly over his creamed chicken on toast
and answered the occasional questions put to him by his elders.

Isobel presided beamingly over the family table. Peter's girl,
an attractive young woman, well-mannered and gracious. Isobel
noticed how she drew Tommy out, got him to talk about life in

the army and kept the conversation from flagging. Mary D., however, rudely and distractedly, concentrated on her food.

Later, in the ladies' room, Emily commented, "He's not as goofy as he used to be, you know. In fact, he's sort of nice."

Mary D. applied lipstick with careful strokes to the mouth she had stretched into an O. "He doesn't guffaw every time he says something he thinks is funny, if that's what you mean. And he doesn't wave his hands and arms like a picked chicken."

"You may have noticed his chin is firmer. I thought people were stuck with chins like his for life."

"I'll bet he had to learn new habits in the army."

"You think he would have learned them at prep school."

"He's a Van Vorst. The Van Vorsts think they can do as they please. They think their lineage is more ancient than any one else's. Mrs. Van Vorst is a descendant of one of the original patentees. Her family pedigree is beyond reproach. Nobody tells a Van Vorst how to behave. The Van Vorsts tell everybody else how to behave."

"That might work in Westerveldt," Emily puzzled it out. "I guess it does. And his family history might have protected him at Andover or the university, but I'm sure it didn't in the army."

Tommy was waiting for them when they re-entered the lounge. He seemed to be glad there were two of them and not just one, that is, if his previous reputation for lack of gallantry, his fumbling inability to turn a compliment, reflected his true nature, then the enthusiasm with which he formed a triangle with the two girls was genuine. Emily tried to look at him afresh, without prejudice. Okay, so he was tall and slim, but his shoulders were narrow and he moved without much athletic assurance. The army crewcut did not become him, but then his civilian fine straight hair always revolving around a double cowlick hadn't been a crowning glory. He had a large head, long ears, a generous nose, and somewhat protuberant eyes, but, it was true, his chin no longer fell off at a oblique angle from his lower lip but miraculously formed an almost straight line perpendicular to the ground.

The blue waters of the lake beckoned, but it was still too cool for swimming, so the trio agreed to take out a rowboat. Tommy didn't have much to say for himself as he rowed them around nor afterwards as they walked back through the woods from the boathouse—no guffaws, no disconcerting adolescent male remarks. He could have been anybody, except, incredibly, the dreadful Tommy Van Vorst.

"You know," he said to the girls, "I always took the woods for granted. I never paid any attention to the trees except to notice when the leaves turned in the fall. I never noticed much in Virginia, either, when I was in school, but all I had to do was see what Georgia was like, and I began to appreciate what I'd always had."

"What is Georgia like?" Emily asked. Mary D. had not yet directed a friendly conversational question his way.

"I suppose parts of it are just as nice to look at as anywhere else. At least that's what they say. I sure never saw any of the pretty parts. Flat wastes, scrub pines, red dirt, ugly, ugly, ugly, and in the summer, it was hell. "Now," he pointed, "look at that oak tree, those maples over there, and that stand of hickory. You can't beat them. And the mosses and the ferns. The woods even smell good. I never thought I'd get homesick, and I certainly never believed I could be homesick for the woods, but I thought about them a lot."

Emily smiled, appreciating his sentiments. If she had not yet had occasion to feel nostalgic for her native landscape, having never been unwillingly separated from it, she nonetheless warmed to Tommy as so he artlessly spoke his mind. Mary D., however, sniffed and arched her eyebrows over her spectacles, interested more in feelings that impelled one to kick over traces, to burst out, to flout, to flee, and not in any that conducted one back into local bondage.

"I think that I shall never see a poem lovely as a tree," she sneered as they passed several fine shining white birches. "A tree who will in summer wear a nest of robins in her hair."

Emily giggled.

"A tree whose hungry mouth is pressed," Mary D. continued, "against the earth's sweet-flowing breast."

Tommy guffawed for the first time. "I was bottlefed myself. I didn't know breasts had that function until I was sixteen. I always thought . . ."

"Trees are a natural resource," Mary D. interrupted him quickly. "What do I plant when I plant a tree? I plant a ship that will cross the sea."

"Arbor Day," Emily giggled again. "Now if we weren't in the woods, we could plant a tree."

"I'm beginning to take an interest in which ones we should cut down," Mary D. said tartly. "I walk around the yard on my break just to get out of the office, but, God forbid my father should find out, I'm beginning to care how the lumber business works. Now I know where the money comes from." She slapped the corrugated bark of a stately ash. "You can really cash in on an ash. Furniture. Unfortunately, we don't handle it any more."

"I don't believe it," Emily said. "You're actually taking an interest in your job."

"Hell, no," Mary D. answered in disgust. "All I do is sort and file and transfer information from one dumb form to another. The only fun is the phone. I'm taking an interest in the business, though. Now I see how my father is the way he is. He has to be tough. The people who work for him are tough. It's a tough business. But you wouldn't believe the files. If I didn't hate it so, I'd do the whole system over. He's using the same system his father used and I'll bet his father, if he bothered to keep files. They don't believe in carbon paper, for one thing. Everything is itemized down to two penny nails, but the girls in the office get so bored they forget to run some items through the inventory forms and at the end of the month there's a foul up. Now he could inventory once every three months if he listened to me."

"Did you tell him? What did he say?" Emily could not picture Gus Van Leuven listening patiently to Mary D.'s prescription for improving his record-keeping.

"Not in a million years would I tell him. I keep my eyes and ears open. That I do. But I know better than to tangle with my father. He likes things the way they were yesterday."

"There's always tomorrow," Tommy said. "My guess is that this is no time for change. Better to keep on an even keel until the war's over—or nearly over. Then full speed ahead into the brave new world."

"Do you have postwar plans?" Emily asked.

"I'm not sure. The pater wants me to go to law school so I can join his office, but it doesn't look like a very exciting life to me. Law. At least the way he practices it. Too much like school. He's always studying books and writing briefs. God knows he cleans up, but he gets his kicks out of fine points. I don't want to be stuck at a desk. I'd like something that lets me run around more."

"Will you come back to Westerveldt?" Emily asked.

"Well, yeah, sure, why not? Unless something better turns up. I like the old burg, and I like it even more now that I'm away from it. Life's pretty much the same all over. Might as well be where I know who the people are and they know who I am. Why start all over in some strange place?"

"Westerveldt is Boring!" Mary D. exclaimed. "It's the most Boring place in the whole world."

"You haven't seen Georgia," Tommy said hotly. "It's the same all over. I'm telling you. So they talk with accents in the South. But the towns are the same as ours—even worse. They're poorer."

"You're not going to tell me that the whole world is as boring as Westerveldt!"

"You mean you didn't know that?" Tommy blocked Mary D.'s path to face her down. "You've been away at school. Where did you find any excitement?"

"School! You can't have any excitement at school if you can't do as you please."

"Right. But once you can do as you please, you can make your own excitement, and for that one place is just as good as any other."

"That depends on what you mean by excitement," Mary D.'s exasperation was mounting. "My mother says all the Sloanes do now that they're married is sit in the living room night after night and play backgammon or Parcheesi when they aren't eating dinner with one or the other set of parents. That you can do anywhere. I agree."

"You're forgetting something," Tommy said. "They have their excitement to look forward to. Backgammon may not seem like the greatest pastime in the world, but it passes the time until they go upstairs and then the fun begins. They don't have to leave the house to have a good time. They're married."

Emily and Mary D. stared hard at Tommy Van Vorst and couldn't think of a single thing to say in answer. Never had anyone seen behind the dull, repetitious, day by day tedium of married life and explained its joys and compensations so succinctly. And the secret had been there all the time, hidden only by a conspiracy of silence.

3

Dinner

"When was it you said you last heard from Peter?" Isobel asked Emily at dinner. She had asked the question several times before—once in the car coming up to the Lodge and once at each meal thereafter—but she still couldn't bring herself to ask the followup questions that would give her the answers she was looking for.

Emily glanced wistfully at the table where her grandparents and parents were sitting with Beatrice.

"About a week, no ten days ago. He didn't have too much to say." Maybe that would put a stop to it.

A week, ten days, was that before or after the Jonah letter?

"Did you get any idea of where he might be?"

"Not really. He described the ocean, so I guess he's at sea."

"My last letter was written aboard ship, too." Not en route from Tarsish to Joppa. Isobel looked hard at Emily. "How did his spirits seem?" she ventured. She had to know.

Emily bravely returned the stare. "He seemed fine, Mrs. Van Leuven."

Not good enough. "Fine" told her nothing. "Calmer?" Isobel asked.

"Yes," Emily assented. "Calmer. Not quite so . . . troubled . . . or mad . . . or whatever he was."

"Pete having trouble?" Tommy asked as he sliced his roast beef. "War nerves?"

"I would certainly not call it that," Isobel drew herself up. "Peter is very brave and stalwart. But he's been in a mood. I don't know how to describe it. Low. Depressed."

194

"Mad at the world," Emily added helpfully. Isobel watched her. Did she know something about Peter his mother didn't?

Tommy looked from one of them to the other. "He can't take it, huh?"

"That's not true at all," Isobel said hotly. "He bears up very well. He just hates the war, but he's more than willing to do his duty and do it well. He worries about the moral part of it all."

"Pete always was a thinker," Tommy said thoughtfully. "That what his trouble is? Thinking too much?"

This time Emily answered him without realizing she sounded like an authority on Peter. "Yes, he thinks too much."

"Right," Gus Van Leuven broke in. The Osterhoudt girl seemed a sensible little thing. "That's what I've been saying all along. He thinks too much. There ought to be some way to keep people from thinking more than's good for them."

"If there were, Daddy," Mary D. said pertly, "I'm sure you'd find it."

Gus took her remark as a compliment instead of her usual sass. He could always get even at the yard and bark at her if she took an incomplete phone message.

"Thinking's not good these days. Not good at all," Tommy said. "But it's hard not to. It's so boring there isn't much else to do but think."

"What!" Isobel was surprised. "How can that be? I thought you were all so busy, training, getting ready to," she hesitated, "go overseas."

"Oh we train. They try to keep us busy, but they can't fill up all our hours. There's training and chow and movies, usually bad ones, and the rest of the time it's sitting around with the guys. All they do is complain."

"Complain!" Isobel was even more surprised. "You mean because they're in the army? Peter never complained about that. He wants to serve his country. He knows it's his duty. What good does it do to complain? Do they complain about the war all the time? No wonder Peter was upset—to be reminded all day long."

"And all night," Tommy added. "But they don't complain about the war as much as they complain about how the war is being run."

"Amateur strategists," Gus said contemptuously. "Think they know more than the generals."

"Not that, Mr. Van Leuven. They complain about conditions. The food, the bunks, the inefficiency, the cra . . ., I mean junk that gets issued to us, like those dumb helmet liners. And the boredom. Mostly the boredom. Complaining is one way of forgetting the boredom, except complaining gets boring after a while. If anything changes, it's usually not for the better, so what's the sense?"

"Poor Peter," his mother sighed. "He never did like whiners. If he has to listen to whining all day . . ."

"You learn not to listen. These guys can't help themselves. Nobody likes being there, but, as you say, we all have to go. Learning to be bored without going crazy is the big challenge. Waiting, waiting, waiting. You find a buddy or two you can talk to. You learn to be invisible."

"I just don't understand," Isobel said. "How can a large number of soldiers together all the time learn to be invisible? The men won't obey you if you're invisible."

Tommy laughed. "Mrs. Van Leuven, I'm not an officer like Pete. I'm just a corporal, an enlisted man. My buddies are hillbillies or guys from the Chicago streets. Most of them didn't finish high school, if they got that far."

"And just why didn't you try for a commission?" Gus asked him. "You're a college man. I'm sure your father could have made some sort of arrangement. Didn't they try to recruit you at the university for Officers' Candidates? Why did you end up like this?"

Tommy was unperturbed. "Too lazy. I didn't bother. I didn't listen. I didn't pay attention. I didn't think ahead. Maybe I thought they wouldn't take me after the mastoid operation. I don't know. Maybe I didn't care."

"How could you not care?" Gus asked. "You could have been an officer and had at least some of whatever comforts military life offers. You would have been with people of your own kind, more or less. I hope you've learned a lesson," he added in the paternal accents his own family tried so hard to avoid evoking.

"Lesson?" Tommy mused aloud. "What lesson? Never get drafted?"

"You heard me. If you're going to be in a situation you can't avoid, at least get the best possible deal for yourself."

"You consider being an officer a good deal?"

"It's better than being a corporal in the infantry."

"Why is that? I don't intend to stay in the army, so what difference does it make whether I'm a corporal or a lieutenant?"

"Self-respect, young man, self-respect."

"You mean I should be ashamed to be a corporal when I could have been a lieutenant if my father had pulled some strings?"

"You should be ashamed to be a corporal if you didn't have to be one."

"I'd be more ashamed to be a lieutenant. You should see the officers we have. Except for the old army men. There's nothing remarkable about them at all. They don't know what they're doing or why they're there except that they'd rather be officers."

"That's reason enough," Gus said, as if that put an end to it.

"You wouldn't think so if you could hear the men. They can spot a good officer or a phony in five minutes. When they don't respect a man, they don't hop to. And behind his back . . ."

"Never worry about what people say behind your back. You should know that by now. The lower orders will always complain. That's our safety valve. Just so long as they know their place."

"You never know if they know their place, Mr. Van Leuven," Tommy explained deferentially. "It's one thing here in Westerveldt where everybody knows who you are and the people who work for you know their livelihood depends on you. It's another thing out there in the big world where guys come from all over. Those hillbillies and street kids are tough hombres. You can't lead 'em just because you've got bars on your shoulders. They have to know that you're just as brave and capable as they are. They may not be able to spell, but they can shoot. And they're plenty quick with their fists."

"You make it sound as if the officers were afraid of the men," Isobel said, thinking of Peter. She wanted to assume that discipline was easier on a self-contained naval vessel.

"They'd be fools not to have a healthy respect," Tommy tried to inform her gently. His own mother didn't seem to understand the world of men and soldiering either. His anecdotes alarmed her. She worried that he might be set upon by what she termed "rowdies" and then she worried about the social order she had never had to question. There were so many of "them" and not nearly so many of "us."

"Oh dear," Isobel clucked. "I suppose that's true in the navy as well."

"Don't fret, Isobel. I know what you're thinking," Augusta said. "Remember, my boys had to go off to war too. Officers are taught to protect themselves. They stick together, and they put troublemakers in jail, even in wartime."

"There's nothing to worry about, Mrs. Van Leuven." Tommy tried to think of some way of calming her fears (Mothers should never suffer needlessly) without letting his other listeners conclude that life in the army was easy. "It's good for us. When did we ever get a chance when we were growing up to see how the other half lives? I'm glad I can hold my own. I feel I grew up in basic training. I know a lot more about the world than I ever learned in school. Good manners may be okay in Westerveldt parlors, but they get you nowhere in a barracks. If anything, they're a liability. I had to forget to say please and thank you if I didn't want to get razzed."

"You mean soldiers don't say please and thank you even to officers?"

"We say sir to officers. Yes sir. No sir. Please sir. Thank you sir. Anything you say sir. But to our buddies we say give me the salt."

Isobel guessed she'd understood. She'd been to the movies. After a minute's thought, she turned to Emily. "Does Peter write about the men on his boat in his letters to you, dear?"

"Ship!" Mary D. and Tommy corrected her simultaneously.

"No, not really, Mrs. Van Leuven. Mostly he writes about general things."

"Such as Jonah and the whale?" Augusta asked her pointblank. Why not? If he wrote sermons to his family, maybe he also wrote them to his lady friend.

"Jonah? I don't know anything about Jonah." Emily frowned and tried to remember. "Does that have something to do with his being at sea?"

Augusta was somewhat disappointed; her first shot had failed. "I don't think so," she said. "No, I'm sure his writing about Jonah had nothing to do with his being at sea. But it did have to do with the war. He was telling us that we should let God do his own punishing. You know, don't you, that he intends to study for the priesthood?"

Before Emily could decide what to answer—yes would mean his decision meant nothing to her and no would mean she wasn't privy to Peter's secrets—Isobel put in quickly, "It was a lovely letter. He analyzed the story of Jonah."

"I guess it was his first sermon. But it was a little too long." Augusta pressed. "You know about his plans, don't you?"

As Emily let out a flat non-committal little yes (Mary D., after all, was sitting right there), Gus rescued the family honor from the malice of his own mother by scraping the legs of his chair against the varnished floor as he rose.

"Let's see what's going on in the lounge."

*   *   *

In no time, it had grown dark. There was no longer a sunset to be watched from the verandah—just faraway shadows of trees against the darkening sky. Too chilly to sit outside without wraps or sweaters, anyway. All three generations gathered in the lounge, the eldest in one corner near the fireplace—Augusta (temporarily declawed), Alida Van Vorst, Tommy's grandmother, Harriet Pearson, his other grandmother, Nelly, and Ted, Sr. the only surviving husband among all those widows. He had turned off his hearing aid, apparently, since he didn't seem to hear any of the remarks his little harem coquettishly addressed to him. "Did you enjoy the custard pie, Teddie" from Alida and "I understand you've taken an interest in baseball," from Augusta. He sat in an overstuffed chair from which he could keep an eye on everyone in the room, a willing prisoner of his own thoughts, above criticism because of his age and infirmity. The women discussed the custard pie among themselves, Nelly surmising that the crust had been made from oleomargarine rather than lard, as least as far as she could tell, although the custard filling had been very tasty. Alida said it was hard to get the things you were used to "these days", and they compared notes on shortages, their aging servants, and the general privations of wartime.

The middle generation made up two tables of bridge. Mabel Van Vorst said she was tired and wanted to go to sleep; Tommy walked her back to the cottage. Horace Callendar decided to take a walk by himself "not a midnight stroll, heh, heh, it's only nine o'clock"—and his wife told him to look out for bears in the woods. Katherine found herself odd woman out, so she picked up a magazine and pretended to become absorbed in its contents.

The youngest generation sat bleakly at the end of the room around the big table until Marianne Callendar suggested a game of Monopoly in which her sister, Beatrice, and Mary D. joined, leaving Emily to watch or wander across the room to talk to her own mother or her grandfather. Everyone, then was occupied in some activity to pass the dull hours before bedtime.

When Tommy Van Vorst returned from escorting his mother down the wooded path to the family cottage, he took one appraising look at the scene in the lounge and went immediately to the record player. The records available were out-of-date and much scratched, but any music is better than no music at all. "I'm dancing with my shadow and making believe it's you," he said as he approached Emily and pulled her out onto that part of the huge floor that was not covered with rugs. Isobel Van Leuven looked up from a poor hand, only two trumps and the Ace of Hearts; she was sure Gus had not understood her answering bid. He never did, but he would blame her when they went down. Emily shouldn't be dancing with Tommy. Where was Mary D.? Katherine looked up from her magazine and instinctively glanced in Isobel's direction in time to see the expression of questioning pain on her face. She heard Augusta say in a very loud whisper to Nelly, "Peter is Emily's beau."

When the song ended, Tommy and Emily went to put on another record and were joined in a trice by Mary D.

"Let's have something peppier," she said as she pawed through the record pile. "Here. This is more like it. Let's have a barrel of fun. Can you polka, Tommy? Emily, you take my turn. I just landed in Jail," and she pranced off with Tommy who didn't seem to mind with whom he danced as long as there was something to do.

The evening passed. The old ladies found things to talk about; Ted Sr. watched them, the bridge players, and the dancers without uttering more than occasional loud throat-clearing noises. The bridge players played on. Katherine learned two new recipes for chopped meat, one for tuna fish, how to plant a victory garden, and what jobs active women in the Midwest had found before she decided to take the plunge and read the full-length novella about the wounded pilot who came home to find that his wife . . .

The Monopoly game was disrupted when Tommy, after five dances with Mary D., asked Marianne Callendar to dance with him, then her sister, and then Beatrice, and then Emily again. After her turn Emily concluded it was too silly to sit at the table and wait for poor Tommy to give them each a fling at this masculine presence, so she persuaded Beatrice to dance with her. The Callendar girls followed their example, leaving Tommy and Mary D. to dance together as long as they wished.

At eleven it was considered permissible to retire for the night, or at least to leave the communal lounge.

"You know," Katherine said in a very low voice to Ted once they were in Wigwam and undressing for bed, "we used to feel a bit déclassé because we could never afford to own a cottage and come up every weekend to get away from the heat in town. We used to justify ourselves by saying we had more important uses for our money. We used to comfort ourselves when we took our little vacations to the shore by saying we were having adventures, discovering new places instead of spending time in the same place with the same people. Remember how we felt?"

"What are you getting at?" Ted asked sharply.

"I'm not trying to remind you that we don't have as much money as the Van Leuvens or the Sanfords, if that's what you think," Katherine shushed him. "That's the farthest thing from my mind. What I'm thinking is that we should roll back the clock and beat ourselves with a stick for every time we wished we had enough money to build one of these cottages."

"What's wrong with them? They're just the same as they always were. They're very comfortable. You're not complaining because there aren't as many servants, are you? You know there's a war on."

"Of course not, silly. I was thinking what fun we had when we drove down to New Jersey and found that shabby little inn at the shore. We went biking on the sand, picked up sea shells, ate clams, and lolled for a week. We had a wonderful time."

"Yes, that we did, but what's your point?"

"When evening came and there wasn't much to do, we played four-handed solitaire, all four of us, sitting on the floor. We laughed a lot. We weren't bored. No matter what happened, even when it rained, we weren't bored."

"Was all this leading up to telling me you were bored tonight? Oh, you were reading that magazine. No wonder you were bored."

"The magazine wasn't that boring. Reading gave me something to do, something to put my mind on. It was the evening that was boring. A group of people, all of whom know each other intimately, get together in a big comfortable room and try to amuse themselves. With that many people there should have been some spark, some electricity, something to talk about, some excitement."

"Well, it you weren't bored, what are you complaining about? Nobody else was bored."

"Everybody was bored. The old people were bored. The children were bored. Even the bridge players were bored. The only excitement all evening was when Gus tried for a grand slam and didn't make it. I've never seen such boredom in my whole life."

"What did you expect to find? You knew who was going to be here. It's a big family. There aren't any surprises."

"I guess not. Maybe it's me. There's a war on. The whole world is on fire. People are dying every minute. The world is changing under our feet, and nobody has anything to say about it. They go on as if nothing were happening, as long as they get their custard pie and a fourth at bridge. As long as it doesn't rain and spoil their fun."

"You don't expect them to talk politics, do you? Or business? You know better than that. Never in mixed company, and certainly not in front of the children."

4

Back Home

As Katherine was about to insert the key in the front door lock, she heard the phone ringing. Who could it be at that hour—dusk? Beatrice had been dispatched to walk her grandparents to their door, to turn on the hall lights inside, to find Martha and tell her they were home, and then to go back for the suitcases. Ted was parking the car in the garage, to shut the door and lock it, instead of leaving the vehicle outside in the driveway on a pleasant summer night as he would have done ordinarily. Two cars had been stolen from neighborhood driveways within the month.

The front door was already unlocked; Emily must have preceded them. Yes, the phone had stopped ringing. Katherine moved toward the alcove to take the call, but Emily put up a hand. "It's for me, Mother."

Katherine went upstairs to change into a housedress, and by the time she had come back downstairs, Ted was settled in the living room with the Sunday *Trib*. Beatrice was reading the funny papers.

"We don't need a big dinner," she said to them. "We've been overeating for three days. Omelet and salad will be enough. Beatrice, would you pick me some lettuce before it gets dark and two or three large tomatoes?"

"Have Emily do it," Ted put down the paper. "Beatrice breaks off the stems."

"I do not," Beatrice protested.

"Have Emily do what?" Emily asked from the doorway.

"Pick me a couple of tomatoes and some lettuce, dear. I thought

204

we'd have a light supper. Just an omelet and salad. We've been overeating for three days."

"I'll pick the salad, but don't count on me for supper. I'll be eating out." She turned to go.

"Just a minute, young lady. What do you mean, eating out?" Her father asked. "We've been eating out for three days. What do you want to eat out for?"

"I have a date," she called from the terrace.

"That must have been the phone call," Katherine said. "The phone was ringing when I came in the house."

"Who's the date with?" Ted asked.

"How should I know, dear? I just got home myself."

"You know very well who it's with," Beatrice said. "It's with Mike Mancuso. Who else?"

Ted looked at Katherine who composed her features efficiently and tried to look non-committal.

"I don't understand that girl," her father said. "We have a wonderful weekend in the mountains with people of our own kind, and she no sooner sets foot back in the house then she's ready to tear off into the night with the likes of Mike Mancuso."

"You don't know who it is," Katherine said by way of feeble defense.

"You wanna bet?" Beatrice said. "There isn't anybody else around."

When Emily walked through the room after leaving the salad in the kitchen, her father asked, "Who are you eating dinner with?"

"Mike." Emily continued on her way. "He'll be here at seven. I'll have to hurry."

"Hold on." Ted stood up. "Do you mean to tell me that after our vacation in the mountains you can't wait to run around Westerveldt on some sort of joyride? Haven't you had enough fun for one weekend?"

"Really, Ted," Katherine said.

"Well, Dad," Emily said slowly, "I'm just going out for dinner, scarcely a joyride, and if anything to forget about the weekend and get back into the real world."

"Real world! You call going out with Mike Mancuso in that jalopy the real world! The real world isn't kiting around the country eating greasy food. The real world is being with your family and friends."

"It may be your real world, but it's not mine. Sitting around, faraway in the woods, as if there wasn't a war on, all snug, rich and cozy."

"Where are you going for dinner?" her mother asked to change the subject.

"I don't know."

"You'd better pick some place where no one will see you," Ted said sternly. "What would Isobel and Gus Van Leuven think if they saw you with that boy after they had entertained you for a holiday weekend as their son's girl? You even rode in their car."

"Only because you arranged it. I can't help what the Van Leuvens think. I never claimed to be Peter's girl, and I'm not going to spend the war sitting at home alone because Peter's parents want me to be his girl."

"Have you no respect for their feelings? He's their only son. Away at war, God knows where."

"Are you trying to say that if I spend the war Not going out, the Van Leuvens are going to feel better about Peter being in the Navy?"

"Don't be fresh. I'm not saying that at all. They wouldn't know what you did at college in the first place. I'm talking about tonight. You spend the weekend as their guest, and no sooner are you home then you can't wait to go tearing out with the boy who delivers the groceries. It doesn't look right, that's all. The more I think about how it looks, the more I want you to stay home where you belong, with your family." Ted looked almost threatening as he prepared to exert his authority.

Emily hesitated. The summer had been an agreeable one—no confrontations, no very serious differences of opinion, no restrictions on her freedom. No one had ever asked her how much she had had to drink when she went out with either Peter or Mike. No one had asked what time she had gotten home or, very often, where she had gone. She had had to endure no more than a few critical remarks which she had, she thought, prudently not answered.

"There's no way I can get out of seeing Mike tonight," she said at last. "I told him I was free and willing to go out with him. I can't tell him my father won't let me. I'm eighteen, remember?"

"You can tell him your family had other plans you didn't know about at the time."

"He'd never believe me. He has feelings, too, you know. It's not just the Van Leuvens who have feelings. He knows very well that he's lower class than we are. I can't offend him."

"You got yourself into this mess, young lady, you'll have to get yourself out of it. Why in God's name did you ever start going out with that boy in the first place?"

"To have a good time. To have some fun. To dance. Why do you think?"

"I don't understand. I just don't understand you. We bring you up carefully—to be a lady. We see to it that you know the right people. We give you a good education. Is this how you respond? You want Fun! You want to Dance! With all the suffering and misery in the world today, you want to have a *good time!*" Ted's color had changed to a red visible even in the lamplight of the living room. He continued to stand by the mantel, relentless, daring anyone to challenge him. Emily stood still in the doorway, leaning against the jamb for moral support, convinced she was in the right, but with no idea of how to get her own way. Neither of them spoke, Ted waited. And waited. Finally he said as firmly and acidly as he knew how,

"What have you got to say for yourself?"

Katherine had been watching them both, alert as a cat. She broke in with, "What can she say, Ted? You are as good as commanding her to do something she can't possibly do. She can't tell Mike she won't go out with him without hurting his feelings, for no good reason at all. If you feel so strongly about it, if you don't want her to go, then the only thing you can do is answer the door yourself and tell Mike what you think."

"WHAT." Ted turned a shade of darker red. "Now what are

you suggesting? That I send him away? I didn't accept the invitation."

"No, but you're the one who doesn't want her to go."

"You're against me, too. You don't care who she goes out with. You don't care what people think. You don't care what the Van Leuvens will be saying about her—your own daughter. Very well. You both know how I feel. You know where I stand. You refuse to do as I ask. I leave you to handle it. I'm going next door to see if Mother and Dad are settled in."

As he started to stride from the room, Emily moved swiftly out of his path and Katherine rose from her chair to stop him.

"Ted, come back here. I was just about to make supper. Don't go out."

"Forget about supper. I don't want any supper. I'm too upset to eat." The front door slammed.

"Christ," said Emily as she slumped into a chair. "I don't believe it. Now your whole evening is ruined. He's mad at you because of me. What can I do?"

Katherine shook her head. "What can you do? What can any of us do? It's too late now, but I wish you could have told Mike you were tired after the long weekend. But that's water under the bridge. Go get dressed. Go out. Try to have a good time, although I doubt you'll be able to."

"But what are you going to do about Daddy? It's not your fault, but he's taking it out on you."

"At least for the time being he's not taking it out on me," Beatrice commented. "For once you're getting your share of his rages."

"This is worse than I ever remembered. What's wrong with him?"

"It's the war. Everything comes down to the war. He has to work too hard. Everything's changing. Everything we ever worked for is threatened by the changes. He sees his whole world crumbling. I tell him Westerveldt isn't the world, that we'll survive and adjust, but these days it's all too much for him. He sees his parents getting old. He worries about money and keeping his head above water while the Van Leuvens are making money hand over fist. He worries about you girls. He's afraid you'll grow away from us, that maybe after college you won't want to come back to Westerveldt to live. That you'll marry somebody we don't know or somebody who's not good enough for you. Then it will all have been for nothing. Well," Katherine changed her tone to put Ted's flareup in the past, "we must be patient. And you'll be back in school in a few weeks."

"I won't," Beatrice said. "I have to stay here and listen to it all. I wish I was back in Pennsylvania with Granma."

"School starts for you next week," Katherine reminded her. "And I don't want to hear any more complaining."

"I'll get dressed," Emily said. "If I'm not ready, you'll have to entertain Mike, and I'm sure that would be the last straw."

*   *   *

It was hard to "have a good time." Emily had tried to put from her mind the scenes she had left at home, but they drifted back. All so unfair. Here she was at the Sea Rover, sitting under a seascape of garish blue water and white waves, eating shrimp cocktail while her mother and her sister were spending the evening at home, cooped up with the smoke her father's rage had left behind when he thrashed out of the house. They had done nothing wrong, but then neither had she. So what she was out with Mike? Why did her father care so much, or why did he let himself care so much, get so worked up? Harmless, harmless, harmless, eating shrimp cocktail with Mike. Her father might have enjoyed the weekend in the mountains enough to be content to sit home in the glow of its memories, but didn't he realize that young people craved a different kind of excitement? Not fair, not fair. And she'd been the cause of family dissension, the nastiest fight she'd fallen into in several years. (The summer after she graduated from boarding school her father had caught her smoking in the garage.) She hadn't disobeyed any rules; she hadn't been careless or thoughtless. If Mike hadn't called, she would have read the paper, listened to the radio, and gone to bed early, but when asked to go out—why not? Why the hell not?

There was no way she could make amends. She could try to atone for the pain caused her mother and her sister by being considerate in some unexpected way, but what could she do about her father? She had defied him, and he would never forgive her. Maybe he'll forget instead. Maybe it would blow over.

"So I told the foreman the end of the week. Four more days and then out. They can see my dust. Over and Out. A week from today, I'm on my way." Mike repeated the last sentence since it rhymed. "Should I ask you to spend my last glorious weekend with me?"

"Up to you, Mike." Emily could think only of her father's reaction to such news and her mother's dismay.

"Such enthusiasm. Where were you all weekend that you aren't rarin' to go? I called your house several times, if you must know."

"With my family, up in the mountains. Since Saturday morning."

"Big old time, huh?"

"Not really." Emily decided to tell the truth; maybe it would help explain her mood. "It was boring most of the time. We could only swim once because it was so chilly up there. The food tasted like the Westerveldt Arms, and there wasn't much of a crowd."

"That means no guys. Right?"

"Not only no guys. Mary D. Some other girls. My sister. One soldier home on leave. The rest were parents and grandparents."

"And you were there for three days? You didn't try to escape? Hitchhike home. La-di-dah is bad enough for an evening, but three whole days!"

Emily smiled at what Mike must be picturing—the stuffiness of the upper classes. "It wasn't that bad," she defended them, but even as she tried to remind herself of their virtues in that well-run, safe, enclosed little world, she began to agree with Mike. Noise, strangers, surprises, unexpected minor perils made New York an interesting city. "Why did you let Emily go to Barnard?" Cora Callendar had asked Katherine Sunday afternoon. "New York is dangerous enough in peace time. I should have thought you'd want her safe at Smith or Mount Holyoke, out in the country, where it's peaceful and quiet for studying." Katherine had answered lightly, "There are so many cultural advantages in the city she wouldn't find elsewhere, except perhaps in Boston—the museums, the galleries, the concerts, the plays." "Do they let her go to those places alone?" "Oh, I'm sure they go in groups," Katherine had lied. When she repeated the conversation to Emily on the qt. and warned against a possible inquisition, they had shared a conspiratorial laugh at Cora. Where had she been hiding?

"You can't fool me," Mike peered into her face. "Something's eating you. If you weren't bored out of your pants, pardon the expression, then something happened."

Emily skated as close to the truth as she dared. "My father had a fit after we got home. He thought we'd had all the fun we needed for the weekend. He wanted me to stay home for a quiet family evening."

"You mean he believes in rationing fun like meat and sugar?" Mike puzzled at this form of puritanism. "A holiday is a holiday until it's over. So tomorrow we suffer."

"Right." Emily agreed, glad he hadn't probed deeper. "Give me shrimp and music instead of omelet and Jack Benny's summer replacement."

"And what about the pleasure of my company? After being with your family for three days, I should be a sight for sore eyes."

Emily laughed as she re-assured him. "You are."

"So I return to my question. What about next weekend? Saturday night. Unfortunately for me, I also have a family, and my mother has laid down the law. Sunday is my farewell party with every aunt, niece, cousin and second cousin they can dig up from the neighboring hills. The wine will flow and the macaronis will be coming out of our ears. But I promised. What can I do? Saturday, I'm on my own. I'd take you to the Villa Florentina, but I can't eat all that guinea food two days in a row."

"Anywhere is okay." Emily was relieved she was not going to spend another farewell evening at the Villa Florentina and risk being serenaded again. "That is, except the Westerveldt Arms."

"No fear. I ate there once to see what it was like. Once was enough. I don't suppose you'd like to come to my farewell party. Ma said I could bring somebody, and I guess she figures that would be you."

"I wouldn't want to intrude," Emily murmured politely. Saturday, his last night out, she could get away with; Sunday with his parents, never. His grandmother might feel the need to tell her grandmother when Nelly walked overtown to choose fruit. Somebody would be sure to tell somebody. Then she'd be Mike's girl as well as Peter's girl. God. At college the girls went out with servicemen all the time, to show them New York and a good time, but not many permanent attachments were formed and nothing serious happened. "Good time" meant a fancy dinner, a movie at the Paramount, dancing at a night club, and a kiss or two in the taxi.

"I see what you mean." Mike had his own reasons for not wanting to formalize their relationship with a family dinner. "I just thought I'd ask." Now he could tell his mother, "no," let her wonder why, blame Emily and the snobs, and it wouldn't be his fault if something better came along in the years ahead. However, he calculated as he watched Emily across the table, if something better took a while, there was no harm nailing down what he had. Of only one thing was he certain. He did not want the sort of "nice Italian girl" his mother kept suggesting he find. He didn't want a nice girl of any origin, most of the time. He preferred girls who were not nice. There was the problem of being seen in public, in good restaurants and bars, with girls who were not nice, and Mike knew he had to get used to the company of nice girls if he wanted to marry properly. He was trying, experimenting, stifling his impulse to transform a nice girl into a girl who was not so nice. When he was with Emily, the temptation to try and the ambition to learn how to behave warred in his mind. Not only were bad habits hard to break, especially pleasurable bad habits, but he had delivered groceries once too often to Mrs. Osterhoudt and been treated graciously, if condescendingly, like hired help. Even if old lady Osterhoudt never found out, he would know. Did he like Emily? Sure, why not? But she was still something between high-class quarry and a stepping stone to a better life.

Did Emily like Mike? She didn't date anyone more than once unless she liked him. That wasn't true. She'd gone to the Rainbow Room to hear Tito Guizar with an arrogant marine lieutenant she didn't like at all, and she'd crossed the river to Palisades Amusement Park with an engineering student she felt sorry for. But yes, she liked Mike. In spite of his cracks, his occasional nastiness, and (it had to be admitted) his taste in clothes. She liked his looks, swarthy handsomeness, dark wavy hair, authoritative muscular build. Even his braggadocio gave him an air of self-assurance she liked. People might see through it as defensive, but with Mike there was always the possibility that he meant it. He wasn't just putting on an act. He'd stand up to anyone who threatened him.

They didn't have much conversation, although they always found something to say to each other—fencing, parrying, wise-cracking, or telling each other anecdotes, rarely personal. He didn't reveal himself. Emily suspected this was just as well. If she knew what was on his mind, she had a feeling she might like him less. Whatever it was between them was not based on affinity, for sure. All they shared was a difference in gender and the fact that each was a form of forbidden fruit to the other. Not too dangerous, but not entirely safe.

"So—it's a date for Saturday night? My last night as a free man? My farewell to civvies and the bright lights of good old Westerveldt," Mike asked as he parked the car in front of Emily's house. "Deal?"

"Yeah, sure. Fine," and after a pause, "I'd love to." The habit of courteous platitude died hard even when it was not in her own best interest. Why was she accepting when she knew she would have to face her father's temper? She could explain, "It's his last night in town. It's the least I can do," but "last night in town" held resonances in meaning all of itself. It would be assumed that she was important to Mike if he spent his last night in town with her. No one would ask what else he could be doing. He hadn't dated another girl in over a month. None of his pals were left to get drunk with. If he spent Saturday night barhopping by himself, no matter how devil-may-care a face he put on, sooner or later someone would feel sorry for him. "Your last night in town and you're out by yourself?" Ted Osterhoudt didn't care what Mike did on his last night in town, as long as he didn't spend it with Emily. But Ted was a decent sort. If he ran into him (highly unlikely), he'd buy Mrs. Mancuso's grandson a farewell drink.

5

Charley Sloane

Charley Sloane's old Ford was not as polished and sparkling as it had been the day he drove the newlyweds to the train for Montreal. Neither was Charley; the sparks he was giving off were invisible. As he was driving down to the Old Dutch Yard to price lumber and put in an order, he went over the incidents of the summer one by one, skipping over the more cheerful and dwelling, with sullen stubbornness, on the those events of the past week which had fouled his mood. The Labor Day picnic with the clan, two dozen mouths to feed, not counting the children, in his backyard, not Rich's, although it was Rich's turn. Molly had said no: they had to have it at their place even though they'd had it last year since it would be the first time they would be presenting Bill's wife at a family gathering. It wouldn't be right, she said, neither right not proper. She was their daughter-in-law; they had to give her a party. And (always an "and" with Molly, one reason was never enough). Genevieve would feel more at ease if she had something to do like helping Molly in the kitchen and setting the patio table. The arrangement suited Rich fine—he'd be off the hook till Memorial Day—but his wife wanted to make sure everybody understood that she had been ready to do her duty, that the change hadn't been her doing. It was not okay with Charley. It was one thing to go to Rich's, eat and go home, another to have to grill all that meat, play host, and then clean up. All because the young folks had decided not to go to the mountains with Genevieve's parents. As soon as Molly found out they were staying in town, she started dickering with Rich and his wife to have the picnic in her backyard.

The affair had gone off as usual, plenty of food, everybody in a
holiday mood. Genevieve looked very pretty, and all the relatives
made a fuss over her. She hadn't dressed for helping out in the
kitchen—some sort of stiff white skirt that spread all around her
when she sat down—so all she'd done to help Molly was carry two
bowls of potato salad out to the table. Most of the afternoon Charley
forgot she was there he was so busy turning hamburgers, hot dogs,
and chicken parts on his brick and concrete grill, but ever so often
Rich or one of the other guys asked him how his plans for
Terpenning house were coming along. Then he'd remember that
Jack Sanford, Her father, wouldn't authorize his loan, and he'd
look over at Genevieve nibbling daintily on her hamburger as if
she thought it would bite back.

No sense blaming the girl; it wasn't her fault. But that was
only half of it by far. One thing after another—no wonder he was
mad at the world. After dark, when they'd all gone home, he'd
tried to relax over a last beer at the kitchen table while Bill was
drying the dishes for his mother. Genevieve was in the bathroom
throwing up, he found out later, all that good food, including
Molly's peach shortcake. Bill told them, probably because he didn't
want his mother to think it was an insult to her food, that "Genevieve
is going to have a baby." Charley controlled his fury and went
through the motions. He shook Bill's hand. He put an arm around
Molly and called her Grandma, and, when Genevieve joined them,
he told her he was glad to hear the news. Then he asked Bill to
come outside with him and check the clutch.

"What in God's name went wrong?" he asked him in the garage.
"You just got married. You're in debt up to your ears. Didn't you
do what I told you?"

Bill was embarrassed. "I couldn't," he tried to explain.
"Genevieve said she'd been to the doctor and he'd fixed her up so
everything would be safe. What was I supposed to do? Tell her I
didn't trust her doctor? She said her mother went with her. She
acted as if she knew what they were talking about."

"Yeah. I'll bet. With a book of instructions. If You don't want
a baby, You have to make sure you don't have a baby. You take the
precautions. Then you know. It's the only way."

"It's too late now," Bill was miserable. There was no doubt about that. If Charley hadn't been so mad, he'd have felt sorry for him

"Did the doctor say what went wrong? What does he say when his advice doesn't work? Or is he just waiting to make a pretty penny when he delivers the baby?"

Bill didn't have a clear answer; the kid didn't know. That was for sure. So this was where a fancy education and doing the latest thing got you. You stick with what you know and you don't get into trouble. You experiment and you'd better know what you're doing. It was okay for the Sanfords to take chances. They had the money to pay for their mistakes. For the likes of the Sloanes there was no playing with fate. The rich always acted as if they knew better. Here was proof that they just acted as if they knew better. What a mess! They'd better not blame Bill. (So he should have insisted.)

Add to the surprise pregnancy Sanford's turning down the loan for the Terpenning house. All he offered, by way of amends, was first crack at any remodeling jobs he heard about. Charley didn't need Sanford to find work for him. He could find his own work. What he wanted was a crack at an investment. Somebody was going to do it some day—fix up those empty old houses and rent them out as apartments. The banks were hanging on to them so they could the same thing their own way and make the money themselves. Keep the Charleys of the town out of the running. Keep everything for themselves, the houses, the money, the opportunities to make more money. A chance. That was all Charley wanted. There it was, sitting there, and he couldn't get his hands on it.

Sanford must have known about the baby when he turned down the loan the second time. An added injustice in here somewhere. They get his boy in a mess with their newfangled ideas, and then they make it impossible for Charley to help out his own boy. Well, if that was the way they wanted to play it, they could foot the bill.

Molly was upset; Charley was merely mad. Molly was worried, as well she might be. Genevieve was a nice girl. They said so every time they saw her. But she was no housekeeper. When Molly said she'd go over and help out with the baby when the time came, Charley blew up. Let the Sanfords help out. Why should you play nursemaid, cook, and cleaning woman for them? Let the girl learn for herself or let her mother teach her. Nobody ever helped you. Is Bill's wife any better than you just because she has a college education? She eats, let her cook. She has a baby, let her take care of it. She can't help herself, Molly said. I watch her. She's not lazy, She's not selfish. She means well. She just doesn't know how. It thought maybe she was lazy or that she didn't care, but she does. There's not a mean bone in her body. If there was, I'd know it by now. She never had to do anything so she doesn't know how. She makes nice fudge and sugar cookies, but she can't fricassee a chicken. Charley had never known a woman who didn't know how to cook. Never. He couldn't imagine that such a creature existed.

He tooled into the Old Dutch Yard still mad, slammed on the brakes, slammed the car door, and clomped up to the office.

"Good morning, Mr. Sloane." A young woman he didn't recognize left her desk near the door and came over the greet him before he could approach the counter.

"Morning," he said, still on his way.

"You don't remember me," she smiled at him. "From the wedding. I'm Mary Van Leuven. I'm helping out here for the summer."

"Nice to see you." Charley tried to picture his daughter-in-law helping out in a lumber yard. "How's your father these days?"

"Here he is now, Mr. Sloane." Mary D. pointed as her father came out of the inner office.

"Charley," Gus boomed. "What can we do you for? Where you working these days?"

"Kitchen over on DeWitt Place. All new cabinets, closets, windows, the works. They're modernizing. I'll need all this by Monday." He put down on the counter his list. "What kind of deal can you give me on this?"

"Rumor has it you have a big remodeling job in the works. When does that start?"

"It doesn't." Charley decided to cut off all conversation before it got started and before his annoyance with Sanford extended itself to Van Leuven and any others of his ilk who might cross his path.

"The word in the yard is you've been looking at paneling. Bob Crane told me you'd be doing a dining room with some of that hard pine."

"I looked at it," Charley acknowledged, "but the deal is off." He hesitated, but then he blurted, "the Westerveldt Bank doesn't want the Terpenning house remodeled. They'd rather watch it fall down little by little."

"That so?" Gus guessed unerringly that it was to Jack Sanford that Charley had taken his request. Why would he take it to anyone else? "The Terpenning house, eh? You're better off. The plumbing is worse than it looks."

"We would of fixed it up brand new." Charley was not ready to make light of his disappointment. "It's a good old house. Foundation, roof, walls. Would of made a nice three-family."

"You're on the wrong track, Charley." Gus told him how to go about his business. "We can't have apartments in that neighborhood, you know. Babies, dogs. Now, why don't you take a look at the Vinson house over on Maple? That's a good old house and the neighborhood's already turned," Gus shamelessly let on. "Vinson wants to sell. He's got a new job in Connecticut or some such place, and he's moving his family out. That'd make nice apartments."

"Wouldn't much matter. I'd still need a mortgage and a loan to get started." This time Charley didn't mention the bank or the banker who stood in his way.

"The Vinson house shouldn't be a problem." Gus was also quick to tell Jack Sanford how to manage the bank's affairs, especially since his advice to an old friend would yield him large sales of lumber and roofing material to an old client. The Vinson house was in bad need of a roof job. "Why don't I give the bank a call right now and see how they feel about it?"

"No need to bother, Mr. Van Leuven." Charley felt himself

waver. This was a good offer, but his anger wouldn't let him take any favors.

"No bother, Charley, no bother at all. Let's face it," Gus was prepared to tell some of the truth, "any job you do brings you down here to us, right? You do a big job like the Vinson house, we go up with the truck full. Makes sense, right?"

"Look, Mr. Van Leuven, I'll have to think about it. Thanks anyway." The blood vessel in Charley's temple began to pulse. "I'll be back tomorrow, day after, to see about these prices here." He turned to go, as if his turning put an end to it. He couldn't say "mind you own business" or "I'll manage myself. You stay out of it."

"Strike while the iron is hot, Charley. Don't beat about the bush." Gus wouldn't have noticed Charley's annoyance even if it had been more obvious.

"Get Mr. Sanford on the phone," he barked at his daughter, the office help.

"Yes, Mr. Van Leuven," Mary D. said efficiently, but as soon as her father had returned to his office to take the call, she started to giggle. Charley Sloane looked at her in disgust. She probably couldn't cook either.

"Never mind, Miss," he said pointedly. "No need to bother Mr. Sanford. When the time comes, I'll speak to my son." Out he went, back to his car and back uptown to De Witt Place.'

Behind his back, the wheels kept turning. Once he got Jack Sanford on the phone, Gus wasted no time. "Jack, Gus here. Look, Charley Sloane just left here. He tells me you won't lend him money on the Terpenning house." And Jack said, "that's right, I won't." And Gus said, "Well, you're right. No apartments on Brunswick. I'm with you one hundred percent. But what about the Vinson house on Maple? Maple isn't much of a neighborhood since the Constable house burned down, so whaddya say? Apartments on Maple wouldn't hurt. Give Charley a break." And Jack had said, "slow down, Gus. You're looking to move your own inventory." And Gus had said, "sure why not? Come on, Jack, is it yes or not?" And Jack had said, "don't rush me, Gus." And Gus had said, "tell you what. You and Jackie join us for bridge tomorrow night, and we'll talk about it. You give me ten minutes and I'll convince you. And Isobel and I will take you to the cleaners if she gets her bidding straight."

*   *   *

"It's nice to eat out for a change," Genevieve said to Bill as she studied the Riverboat menu. "I get so tired of cooking day after day. Or I get tired of trying to think up what to make for dinner."

Bill was still so much in love that anything Genevieve prepared, with or without her mother's help, tasted like food set before the gods, especially when accompanied by his mother's corncake or blueberry muffins.

"It's like the old days before we were married," he smiled over the menu card and the ship's lantern that served as a table lamp. "We used to eat out all the time when I was still living with my folks."

Genevieve was still so much in love that she accepted Bill's locutions as lovable parts of his very lovable self. Even if she didn't adopt them (imagine Jack and Jackie being referred to as "my folks"), she didn't correct them.

"When you lived with your parents, we didn't have to watch the money. But I'd rather be with you scrimping and saving than eating out every week." Genevieve beamed with tenderness. "This is nice, though. What are you going to have?"

"I can't make up my mind." Bill began to read the menu very carefully, working from right to left, from price to item. Nothing too cheap or Genevieve would notice and feel poor, but nothing too expensive either or he knew in advance he wouldn't be able to enjoy it. Working at the bank had begun to affect his feelings about money although he was not quite sure how. He had been brought up to think of money as the reward for the "hard work" a man was supposed to do "to provide for his family." An equation. "Hard work" equals "money" equals "providing for the family." As a car salesman he hadn't stopped to think just how much money his customers paid for their cars, what percentage of their income. He knew by rote the slogan that a car was a major expenditure, but living at home (contributing, of course, part of his salary to his parents for room and board) the reality, the daily lived-through, thought-about, worried-about facts of money had not yet occurred to him. Now he was a married man (with a "family on the way"), a salary coming in and expenses flowing out, but he was also a teller who handled pieces of money all day long, sometimes in large amounts.

His salary was twenty-five dollars a week, considered very good pay for a young man at that time, in that place. Horace Callendar had cashed a personal check for twice that amount on a Monday and come back on Thursday to cash another. What did he do with a hundred dollars in one week? Some of Bill's customers counted out twenty-five pennies to purchase a stamp to stick in a defense bond savings book. Not everybody made money by hard work like his father. Some made money by signing the back of a dividend check, like Augusta Van Leuven. Some made money by talking on the phone, like his father-in-law, not that talking on the phone wasn't work, but it wasn't the sort of "hard work" you could stand back and admire like his father's kitchen cabinets. "Make money work for you" was a saying at the bank, money being a wageless servant who toiled on your behalf; send money out to work, don't spend it. If you spent it, it was gone, working for somebody else. You could tell how hard money worked by looking at it. The flat, stiff, clean bills fresh from the mint had never done a day's work in their lives—those were the ones he handed to Horace Callendar. Then there were the faded, greasy bills, wrinkled with little tears at their corners, worn-out from traveling from hand to hand to purse to pay envelope.

Money was one thing, prices another. A dollar bill, whether new or old, was worth a dollar (or was it true, as they said at the bank, that it was worth only 57¢?). A dollar stayed the same, but prices changed. The government had frozen prices "for the duration" but the minute the war was over, prices would go up and up, so they said at the bank, through the roof. Would he still be making twenty-five dollars a week? He worked at the bank where money worked for you. "Shrimp," he decided.

"Oh, me too," said Genevieve, "except, dear me, maybe I shouldn't Any time I eat anything strong, I get such indigestion. Filet of sole. That can't hurt me. There's no sense eating something I can't keep down. And ginger ale. Mother says that'll help my digestion."

"Mashed potatoes would be good for you, too," Bill suggested. It pained him to watch her suffer.

"There's Mary D.!" Genevieve cried. "What a coincidence. She's with a soldier! Who could that be? And he's not an officer! Some friend of Peter's? No, it can't be. Peter's in the navy. Oh, I don't believe it! It's Tommy Van Vorst! I didn't recognize him with that haircut and those glasses. I could have passed him on the street and not said hello."

"Do I know him?" Bill asked. "The name sounds familiar."

"I don't think so. He wasn't at the wedding 'cause he's just joined the army. His parents were there. You met them. They gave us the oval silver tray, not the round one. The Wilsons gave us the round one. Is it all right if they join us for a minute of two?"

"Just for a minute," Mary D. said as they sat down in response to Genevieve's handwave. "Tonight I'm entertaining the troops. USO duty, even if Tommy isn't far, far from home. Poor boy."

Tommy told Genevieve he was sorry he'd missed the wedding, but that his mother had described it in detail. Genevieve said she was sorry he hadn't been there; they'd all missed him. Tommy told Genevieve that married life seemed to suit her. Genevieve told Tommy he ought to try it. Tommy asked Genevieve if she remembered his sister's wedding several years back and what they'd had at the reception. Genevieve most certainly remembered.

Mary D. let them get involved in reminiscence, turned to Bill, and said in a low, falsely-conversational tone, "I've got news you should know about so you'll be prepared."

Bill scarcely knew Mary D. How could she have news for him?

"My father wants your father to remodel the Vinson house instead of the Terpenning house." Bill was bewildered.

"I work at the Yard. I know everything that goes on. Your father came in today and I heard him say that the Bank wouldn't give him a loan on the Terpenning house. Then I heard my father say the Bank would never give him a loan on that house. They don't want it remodeled. But the Vinson house, over on Maple, is on the market. My father told your father he should try to get a loan for that house because they don't mind it that's remodeled."

"And what did my father say?" Up to now, Bill had kept the two halves of his life separate. He had asked Jack Sanford about a loan for his father. When Jack had refused, he had discussed the matter with his father, feeling in the middle but only as a go-between delivering messages as befits a young man on his way up. As he pictured his father in conversation in a public place with Gus Van Leuven, and as he realized that Mary D. was reporting back to him as an interested party, he felt himself being dragged closer and closer to the center of the arena. He was scared, scared of his father, scared of his father-in-law, and more than scared of Gus Van Leuven who never stopped to listen to anyone.

"I got the impression he wasn't too keen on the idea. But my father said it was a great opportunity and he said he was going to call Uncle Jack—Genevieve's father—and tell him to do it. And your father said not to bother, he'd talk to you. But my father made me call anyway."

"And what happened?"

"How do I know?" Mary D. said primly. "I didn't listen in."

"When did you two start dating?" Genevieve asked.

Mary D. and Tommy blushed a little as Mary D. answered, "This week. Tommy was up at the Lodge for the weekend. How come you two weren't there?"

Now Genevieve and Bill blushed. "We went to a picnic at Bill's parents. Sorry we missed the fun."

"Great fun," said Tommy. "Fun-packed from dawn to dusk and beyond. Not like the good old days when we were all little and swimming and running around was all that mattered. Mary D.'s father went down on a grand slam and we had a tense moment. He was sure Mary D.'s mother had the Ace of Clubs. Old Ted

Osterhoudt turned off his hearing aid and wouldn't go to bed when his wife told him to. Marianne Callendar put the knives on the tables the wrong way and her mother apologized publicly about it and said it would never happen again. What else? There was a rumor Mary D.'s grandmother saw a bat the cottage. Your parents, Genevieve, danced one slow dance to the victrola, and I think Horace Callendar was nipping on the side. He got jovial all of a sudden and said the war would be over next year."

"I hope he's right," Genevieve said. "It's so awful. It goes on and on, but it can't last forever."

"It'll last a lot longer than Horace Callendar thinks," Tommy said. "Unfortunately, Europe's still overrun and so is the Pacific. We've got to begin to beat them back before we can see the beginning of the end."

"Peter's in the Pacific, isn't he?" Genevieve asked Mary D. "What do you hear from him?"

"He's okay. He writes regularly. There isn't much else to do aboard ship, I guess. He writes my parents. I get a letter occasionally and he also writes Em . . ." Mary D. stopped short and her eyebrows rose over her spectacles as she saw Emily Osterhoudt enter the Riverboat followed by Mike Mancuso. "Speak of the," she breathed. The others turned to see.

"I don't understand," Genevieve said. "I thought Emily was Peter's girl."

Mary D. riffled through her emotions as if they were invoices out of order. She had felt a spasm of vicarious jealousy on Peter's behalf. But she certainly knew that Emily was seeing Mike. There was no formal understanding between Emily and Peter. She herself, she knew, would take all the fun she could, plighted or unplighted. It was the noticing and commenting that caused all the trouble. Her filing complete, she decided to defend Emily.

"Oh, I don't think Peter and Emily are that serious about each other. Just good friends, as they say in Hollywood."

"But how," Genevieve asked, remembering how fond Peter had been of her, "would Peter feel if he knew?" She gave the "knew" a faint melodramatic emphasis.

"How is he to know unless somebody takes the trouble to tell him?" Mary D. sounded as sharp as her grandmother. "Besides, Mike's on his way into the service too. Hi, Emily, Hi, Mikey," she greeted as they passed. Luckily there was no question of asking them to sit down; all four chairs were taken. After hellos and how-are-yous, Emily and Mike had retreated to a table as far away from them as possible, Genevieve asked, "What did you say his name was? Emily's date? Do I know him? He looks familiar."

Mary D. couldn't decide if Genevieve was being innocent or snobbish, but assuming that even her Westerveldt society wedding hadn't altered Genevieve's sweet nature gave her the benefit of the doubt. "That's Mike Mancuso."

"From the grocery!" Genevieve exclaimed. "Of course. Do you know him, darling? Was he in school with you?"

"Year or two behind," Bill answered. Any reservations he had about Mike were not based on standards shared by the elder Westerveldtians but on a mild Anglo-Saxon Methodist aversion to Italian Catholics and to Mike's success, totally of the wrong sort, with girls. Among his kind, male chastity was almost as well guarded as female.

"I wonder what her parents think of this romance," Genevieve commented, remembering with quiet perplexity the reservation with which her parents had viewed her own courtship. Bill was several cuts above Mike.

For reasons of her own having nothing to do with Emily, Mike or Peter, Mary D. snapped, "It's not a romance, for Christ's sake. They're just keeping each other company now and then. Jesus, can't you eat dinner with a guy without announcing your engagement?" She didn't look at Tommy as she spoke, but he gave her his full attention.

6

Mike

"Who's the plucked chicken with Mary D.? Mike asked. Emily had taken the seat that put her back to the foursome so she could try to forget they were there.

"Tommy Van Vorst. He's home on leave."

"Local boy, huh? I've delivered Van Vorst. He must be the same kid I used to see around there. A mighty warrior, that one, but not quite Mary D.'s style, I'd say."

"She's just keeping him company while he's home." Emily was almost as testy explaining Mary D.'s behavior as Mary D. had been explaining hers. "There's nothing to do." (How could there be?)

"So she's dumped Hank, er Willard, for one of her own kind."

"Why do you say she's dumped Willard?"

"She's out with Van Vorst."

"I give up," Emily slammed her menu down on the table in exasperation. "You date one girl, you date another. Does anyone accuse you of being permanently attached?"

"It's different. I have a reputation to maintain. If any of my girls—and you notice I say girls plural—want to step out with someone else, there are plenty more where they came from, although I must say I'd sure want to know why she couldn't wait until her next turn with me came up."

His remark was so ridiculous that Emily had to laugh. "I'm glad you're willing to let us have some small measure of freedom."

"I am, but I'm not sure about other guys—these days. Think of the investment. You take a girl out, spend money on her, whisper

227

sweet nothings, what for? So some other joker can reap the harvest? Get her warmed up for somebody else? A guy goes off to war, he wants to think she's sitting home waiting for him, remembering all those nice meals and cheeks-to-cheeks and sweet nothings. He has a picture of her pining as she looks out the window waiting for the mailman."

"Some picture. What about what the guys do when they're in the service and far away?"

"Hazards of war and all that. He's far away, who's to know? Take your fun where you can find it."

"A rule for you and a rule for us. So that's the way it is." Emily found herself irritated again.

"Sauce for the gander but not the goose? Right. That's the way it is. It's all a matter of who's to know. We can carry it further. Say a guy meets a nice English girl and falls in love. Or a gorgeous Polynesian in a grass skirt—didja ever think your admiral might have run across a couple of those? (With a lawn mower, hahaha). The girl back home pining away at the window loses out. I tell you it's the hazards of war. But we gotta have something to fight for—mom, apple pie, and the girl back home, waiting, waiting, waiting."

"Yep," Emily said at last. The hell with it. He was probably kidding. She didn't intend to be anybody's girl pining at the window, but there was no sense being direct about it and destroying the war effort. The war effort had already been seriously undermined on the home front, in her own home. Her father was speaking to her only when necessary and then, formally. His temper no longer flashed and exploded. He had settled for being "displeased", "disappointed" and occasionally "disgusted," one mood or act (as Emily called it to herself) after another. He called Beatrice "Bice" every time he addressed her; she was the only apple of his eye left. Her mother said nothing. When Emily had apologized for ruining their Labor Day evening, she had accepted the apology and made no excuse for her husband's outburst. Emily was, evidently, to have her freedom, after all what were we fighting for, but nobody had to like it.

"Be discreet," her mother had warned when Emily announced she was going out with Mike for his farewell-on-the-town. Being discreet probably meant not picking the same restaurant as the Sloanes, Mary D., and Tommy Van Vorst. It certainly meant not running into Grandmamma or the senior Van Leuvens. Emily had spent the week avoiding prolonged conversations with either of her parents about any subject at all, since sooner or later every subject came around either to the war or to family. War and family soon led one to another. War meant servicemen meant Peter. Family meant Osterhoudt values meant Grandmamma meant Mike Mancuso. Emily couldn't decide whether to go ahead and take Soc 22, *The Family,* so she could understand her predicament better or to switch to *Political Theory from Machiavelli to the Present* and try to forget it.

"Like Cary Grant?" Mike asked.

"Sure. Why? Is he your idea . . ."

"At the Colonial. With Larraine Day. *Mr. Lucky.* You got a choice. We can go dancing or we can take in the movie. Which'll it be?"

Emily opted for the movie without hesitating. At the movie at worst he'd hold her hand. Dancing, he would holding a great deal more of her and the goodbyes, the farewells, in the car might be more entangling than she might wish.

Cary Grant was Joe, a gambler and a con man, who avoided the draft by taking on the identity of a recently-dead colleague, a Greek, who had a prison record. Larraine Day was a strong-minded society girl who ran a war relief office in New York and was trying to raise money for medical supplies for refugees. Cary Grant, unscrupulous, amoral, debonair, was above nothing. He offered to help the society ladies raise tons of money by holding a gambling gala with the equipment from his gambling ship. He intended to make off with most of what they took in. Larraine Day spotted him for an operator the minute she laid eyes on him, and the two of them sparred with each other until Larraine Day's grandfather intervened and told her she should have nothing to do with him. He even called Cary Grant a "dirty, greasy" something to his face.

That did it. Sparks of repulsion turned to tugs of attraction. Emily squirmed in her seat. Mike chortled but the hand that was holding Emily's became clammy as it gave hers an added rough squeeze.

Then that dreadful scene in the deserted Maryland family mansion where Cary Grant and Larraine Day had taken refuge after Grandfather had dug up the Greek's police record and tried to have Cary Grant arrested. Larraine Day called Grandfather and told him, right in front of Cary Grant that, unless he called off the police, she would marry Cary Grant right there in Maryland. Grandfather agreed. Cary Grant was, for the first time, on a furious offensive. He stood in front of the family portraits and told her off—so she thought that she and her family were too good for him, huh? That the blackmail she could use against her grandfather was the threat of marrying him! "I should have slapped your face," she said. "Why didn't you?" he asked. "Because I was afraid you'd slap me back," she said as they stood all alone in the empty house next to the draped furniture. "Ha," cried Mike in triumph. His wasn't the only cheer in the audience, thank God. It was worked out. Cary Grant decided to go straight, for love, got shot in the process, gave Larraine Day all the money, and joined the Merchant Marine to serve his country. Larraine Day waited and pined. Finally they were reunited on the wharf in the fog and the dark. "Oh give me something to remember you by/when you are far away from me." That was what Cary Grant whistled as he came toward her for the final clinch.

"It was a good movie," Emily said to herself as they walked out onto Main Street. "Why did I have to see it with Mike?"

"Some movie!" Mike kept chuckling. He didn't bother to say anything else. Cary Grant had made all his points for him and he was vindicated even if he hadn't been shot and returned the money. He hadn't committed any crime other than being born greasy and he was on his way to serve his country. *Mr. Lucky.* He was Mr. Lucky.

"How about a nightcap?" he offered, wanting his mood to continue as he liquored up Emily.

"Fine," said Emily. Anything to break the spell of the movie before they got back in the car.

There was no one either of them knew at O'Toole's. When Mike told the waiter this was to be his last Scotch as a civilian, the bartender put the drinks on the house. Two customers at the bar raised their glasses in Mike's direction and one said, "Good luck, fella." In the darkness of the tavern, the cigarette smoke wafted upward and whirled in lazy patterns wherever the dim lights gave it substance, the juke box played the songs everyone had been listening to all summer long, and soon Mike and Emily were back in Westerveldt, the war no longer an immediate reality but something out "there" that was happening and affecting their lives only because Mike was soon to join it. Otherwise, just another Saturday night in the old home town.

"So this is it," Mike said as he turned off the ignition. He had parked his father's car (willingly lent for the last date) a good fifty feet away from the entrance to the Osterhoudt house to avoid the glare of the porch light. In his head he had been trying out one line after another. Which would capture the mood? Make him look brave but in need of sympathy? Make Emily remember him? "We who about to die salute you!"

"Stop it!" Emily was searching for sentiments that defined a midpath between polite good wishes and affection, that is, comradely farewells, sincere by lowkeyed. "Don't you dare talk like that?"

She cares, Mike said to himself, but he fished for proof. "It would upset you if anything happened to me?"

"Of course it would upset me." Emily was indignant.

"How much would it upset you?" He spoke in a low voice and waited a second for an answer. He didn't wait long enough before he repeated the question and the mocking tone crept into his voice.

Damn. Emily felt tears of rage welling up into her eyes. We're supposed to love them because they're going away and might get killed, not because we might love them anyway, not because they love us. "I won't know until it happens," she said cruelly.

"Okay, okay." There was no time left to fight. "I asked for it. But tell the truth, will you miss me a little?"

"Yes, I'll miss you. We've had fun together," Emily allowed.

"And will you write to me?"

"Of course I'll write to you."

"And you'll think of me?"

"I'll think of you." They were almost tender with each other.

"And will you give me something to remember you by when you are far away from me?"

Before she could think of any answer at all, sincere or flippant, he had pulled her close and kissed her roughly, and, for the first time, open-mouthed. Emily submitted, not totally without pleasure herself, but when she felt his hand sliding the off-shoulder sleeve of her peasant blouse further off-shoulder, she pulled away. In a second she had found her pocketbook. Goodby, good luck, please write, and several other platitudes tumbled from her lips as she patted Mike's shoulder (fully clothed) and let herself out of the car. Safe outside, her blouse still askew, she poked her head in and said once more, "Goodby. Good luck." As she walked toward her house, righting her blouse, smoothing her skirt, and pressing down her hair, Mike started the engine and moved slowly behind her.

"Whew-whoo," he whistled. "Great legs. Something to remember you by," he sang.

PART V

The Bus Trip

Christmas fell on a Saturday in 1943, Christmas Eve thus on a Friday night. Classes had ended on the 22nd to be resumed on the 5th of January in the new year. Instead of leaving Wednesday evening or early Thursday morning for Westerveldt, Emily stayed in the dorms. Nearly all the girls had left, except for those poor souls who couldn't get home to Vancouver or San Francisco by train and back in any reasonable time. Those waifs stranded during the holidays flocked together on one floor to keep each other company and invent ways to enjoy the city. Some would eat Christmas dinner with "day girls" whose mothers had taken pity on them.

The days were short and dark, the palatial old dorms without the noise and the foot traffic were like ruins abandoned since ancient times, but Emily savored her solitude knowing she could break it at any time. She wanted to go home and spend the holidays with her family, Mary D., and other old friends; she wanted to be where she was safe and loved, where she knew every building, street, and tree, but she felt herself held back by a sense of increasing involvement in something that wasn't home in Westerveldt. It wasn't a person. She still hadn't met a young man she liked all that much although she'd met several she liked well enough. It wasn't college although she had more studying and paper-writing than she had time for. Maybe it was New York where so much happened all the time, even on upper Broadway, the street below her dorm window. New York wasn't suffering like London, Paris, or Berlin. It wasn't at the center of the war in a military sense; it was like a big sister city, organizing backstage, collecting and sending supplies, men, and messages on the ships that left every day.

If in Westerveldt everyone went about his daily affairs and thought about the war a little, in New York the war was always in the air no matter how much its inhabitants kept on making money or love or giving parties or shopping or studying. Emily shared its intense atmosphere, heady and wearying as it was. The pace was exhilarating; there was ever something new to do or think about. It was a challenge when she had to concentrate on her studies amid the distractions. She felt real and alive, a part of what was going on in the world and would be going on. She was afraid that as soon as she stepped off the bus she would find Westerveldt too quaintly quiet for the New York mood she was carrying with her. She gave herself a day off in silence to make the transition.

It had snowed Thursday night. Emily looked out of the window as the bus followed the familiar route upstate—dry autumn grasses spouting up incongruously through the white cover that still had not melted in the 25° daytime temperature. The branches of the black leafless trees were lined in white even to their twigs and tendrils, frozen in time and space under pewter skies. The roads were clear, the snow had melted quickly under the tires—a long asphalt ribbon cutting through the whiteness to trace the path home.

The bus driver was a paunchy man in his fifties, jovial as he collected the tickets, later morose, if Emily could judge from the expression reflected in his driver's mirror. Only six of her fellow passengers were male: four elderly men and two servicemen, a sailor up front behind the driver and a soldier back to the right over the wheel. Two women in front of Emily were chatting.

"So I told Maureen I'd come early to give her a hand with the children and the dinner. Clarence has to work until ten o'clock. I wasn't going to wait around until the last minute and then hop in the car and get there at two o'clock in the morning. What if it snowed again? I said, Clarence, I'm going up early on the bus. You come home, you get a good night's sleep and you take the bus yourself early Christmas morning or you drive. You suit yourself, but I want Christmas to be a real holiday for Maureen and the children with Ollie so far away. A little joy, I say it, we need it this year."

"My daughter didn't want me to make the trip," the other woman answered. "She said it was too much for me, traveling in war time. You never know when they'll cancel the buses or something will go wrong. She wished she could come to me, but she's in the seventh month. If she'd come home to stay, that would be one thing, but she wants to be near the base where her husband's stationed. I can't say I blame her even if she doesn't see him very often. I said I'd come back when the time comes. I'm not good for much any more, what with my pressure, but I can try to be a comfort to her."

"It's hard. Everyone's so far away and you never know from one minute to the next. My nephew, my brother's boy, thought he'd get Christmas home but he got his orders last week. He's in the navy and he's shipping out god knows where in the middle of winter."

Emily thought of Peter, at sea, somewhere, in a warmer climate at any rate. In his last letter he had mentioned Thanksgiving, not Christmas.

"I never thought," he had written, "that I would get sentimental about my father. Don't get me wrong. I love my father, but what I mean is I never thought that the image of him carving a turkey and going through the same old dialogue year after year about white meat and dark meat and how much stuffing could bring tears to my eyes. I even wish I could hear him sparring with Mary D. and scolding my mother for always seeing the good in people, much as it used to pain me when he was harsh to her. I can't believe myself some times. I spent most of my formative years, as they call them, steeling myself for those confrontations that took place once at every meal. I knew I'd miss my mother. I wasn't surprised to find myself missing Mary D., but I was amazed when I began to miss my father. Is life full of these surprises in self-discovery . . . ?"

Gus Van Leuven carving the turkey. He was head of his family.

Emily's grandfather carved the turkey. Christmas dinner was traditionally held next door at Granddaddy's and Grandmamma's with the Catsbys. Once upon a time greataunt Hattie, Granddaddy's sister, and greatuncle Aartsen had been regulars at Christmas dinner, but greataunt Hattie had died in 1938. Greatuncle Aartsen had come by himself but in 1940 he had argued so ferociously with Granddaddy (fault to be found on both sides, everybody agreed) over conflicting versions of some political events of the bygone 1890s that greatuncle Aartsen never attended again. Emily had forgotten to ask where he did go. So, without greatuncle Aartsen, the eight of them would sit around Grandmamma's massive mahogany table, leaves inserted, over-life-size lions' legs visible, the prismed chandelier with its hundred miniature bulbs lighting up the damask tablecloth and Grandmamma's best china and silverware. As soon as they had finished their turkey broth which Grandmamma herself prepared from the neckbone and giblets and assorted savories, Grandmamma would stretch out her foot to press the buzzer under the rug. The buzzer would ring in the basement kitchen, and maybe Martha would hear and maybe she wouldn't. If they didn't hear the dumbwaiter move within a minute, Katherine would signal to one of her daughters to sidle out of the room and tell Martha in person it was time for the next course.

The bird would be magnificent, from a farm just outside of town where turkeys had the run of the place and could eat all the succulent bugs and seeds they could find before they were slaughtered on Wednesday and brought into Mr. Slattery's butcher shop. Two kinds of potatoes, candied sweets, lovingly turned over and over in their glaze no matter how much else Martha had to do, and mashed white to be served with giblet gravy. Grandmamma made wonderful gravy. And white onions in cream sauce. And "dressed celery" chopped in a rich mayonnaise sauce that was Grandmamma's secret recipe. And cranberries, not too tart and not too sweet (another secret recipe), just right with the mixed flavors on the plate.

And then a rest while Martha cleared and crumbed the table and everyone had a little more wine. "Not too much for me. I don't want to get tiddly," Grandmamma would say. Aunt Sarah could, in Ted Jr.'s words, drink them all under the table, so he kept her glass full. "Will I get to drink wine this year?" Emily wondered. "I know I won't get a cocktail. Daddy, Granddaddy, and Uncle Jeff will have two, Mother will have one, Grandmamma will have half a one and say it's too strong, and Aunt Sarah will have three. I'll have to have wine or something to get all that food down."

The pies. Pumpkin, the custard faintly browned where its skin had risen in the oven, and mince with a latticed topcrust, both made by Grandmamma the day before with help and hindrance from Martha. And, of course, ice cream from the creamery, vanilla so it's not too rich, to top the slices of pie. And then coffee and dinner mints. And there can't be anything else, Emily thought, as she remembered and rehearsed. I'm full just thinking about it. And then, what would they do? Martha would be downstairs washing mounds of dishes until the kitchen was clean and she was free to visit her sister since no one would want any dinner that evening. The family would gather in the back parlor and . . . No, *that* didn't bear thinking about.

The soldier sitting up in front asked his neighbor for a match so he could smoke. He looked so young, not like the hardened mature GIs in war movies portrayed by actors in their thirties. Was it the crewcut that made him look so very vulnerable, or was he still a boy? How did Mike look with a crewcut, that mass of black hair, a strong wave teased over one eye, shorn away? Did he look like a kid too? The last two letters from Mike had an APO return address, and he said he was somewhere where they spoke English, but that joke told her nothing. He could be still in the States or he could be in the British Isles. Wherever, she pictured him sauntering out on the streets of the nearest town looking for girls he could pester or seduce. "I hope he's stationed in the country surrounded by cows. Serve him right."

His letters were not like Peter's and not only because he hadn't gone to college. He didn't ruminate on the meaning of existence or worry about how he was expressing himself for rhetorical effect.

letters sounded just like him—quick, racy, wise-cracking, sometimes with unexplained references either he thought he'd told her about (must have been some other girl) or assumed she would know by a pre-cognitive force. "Chuck," for example. Who the hell was Chuck? A buddy, evidently. A friendly buddy? Until further notice. (Peter would say, "my pal, Bob Wilberforce from Texas, is an engineer.") Rarely was Mike personal, although several times her legs were mentioned as if her appendages stood for the whole of her. "Thinking of you," he'd write. The last letter, more wistful in tone, had ended "love ya" whatever that meant. Christmas is coming, Emily surmised.

She was also corresponding with half a dozen other servicemen, maybe even a dozen. Not every one wrote because he had something to say or because he liked to write letters. All of them liked to receive letters; that was for sure. A Columbia boy she'd dated her freshman year started off with short notes begging for long replies about "the doings on good old Morningside Heights" and then suddenly informed her she didn't have to bother any more. He was engaged. She answered with congratulations and the observation that she was glad she'd served her purpose. Emily the virgin whore, a college friend called her, a pen pal on every base in the U.S. of A.

*   *   *

Christmas spirit is catching, just as a cold is catching. You can be busy doing something without a thought of germs, and, all of a sudden, with no warning, you sneeze and sneeze and sneeze and soon you know you have a cold and that you probably caught it from X. With Christmas spirit the symptoms aren't physical, but they appear just as mysteriously. You can be wrapping Christmas presents or writing Christmas cards or making a list of last-minute things to buy before the stores close or be tidying up the hall closet to make room for the guests to put their coats, and, all of sudden, instead of a sneeze, there comes an invisible rush of sentiment that transcends the hundreds of "Merry Christmases" you may have uttered during the day. You find you truly mean it, not because you should mean it or you always more or less meant it (we all wish each other well, most of the time, in theory, when we talk to ourselves). When Christmas spirit takes hold, its symptoms spread; we want to share the tenderness that is its most salient sign, to embrace those irritating, not quite friendly, creatures out there because they are our fellows. Thus the spirit passes from one to another to last a little while until the decorations are put away, the parties are over, and the animosities of yesterday are evoked in careless remarks, and we go back to being ourselves. The magic has disappeared as abruptly as it touched us, leaving behind the regret that it can't last forever and keep us a bit better than we are.

For Isobel Van Leuven Christmas spirit came easily. It was never far from her at other times of the year. Mostly it meant not noticing her mother-in-law's gibes, which when unnoticed stopped proliferating. In this way Augusta caught Christmas spirit without even knowing she had it. She and Isobel passed it on to Gus who couldn't find anyone to contend with. Mary D. was home from Wellesley, and the family talked of Peter, not so often as to feel sad, but often enough so that his place left empty at table was occupied by their thoughts of him.

For the Sanfords Christmas spirit had to wait to enter their hearts until they had concluded a complex series of negotiations on the location to be designated as the site of Christmas dinner. Labor Day had been easy—the young couple went to the Sloanes' and Genevieve's parents went to the Lodge. The Thanksgiving compromise, based on the Labor Day Settlement, had sent the young couple to the Sanfords for dinner and to the Sloanes for dessert and coffee at five o'clock. Both sides were now even. Who would get the young Sloanes for Christmas?

The objections to the marriage, those openly acknowledged at the time as well as those unspoken in uneasy hurts, began to surface no matter how carefully Jacqueline expressed herself to Genevieve or to Mrs. Sloane, no matter how considerate Molly herself was prepared to be, no matter how much Genevieve wanted to please

ANNE DE LA VERGNE WEISS

both sets of parents. There was no reasonable solution except the unthinkable—communal midday Christmas Day dinner at Genevieve's after Christmas Eve with her family and before Christmas night calls on Bill's relatives, since she and the unborn baby were at the center of everyone's concern, the bond they all shared in common.

Aside from the strain on good will that eating (and not drinking) together might put on the parents, there was the subtle change in the relationship between the two fathers in which Bill was implicated, however diffidently. Way back in the fall he had spoken to his father on Mary D.'s advice and found him irascible beyond the reach of reason and self-interest. *Nobody* was going to tell him what to do, nobody was going to tell him how to run his business. It looked for a while as if he wouldn't take the Vinson house from the Westerveldt Savings Bank as a gift. What he wanted was to choose his own house to remodel, for his own reasons, a carpenter's reasons, and apply, as any other entrepreneur might do, for a loan to be decided on its merits. That was the way the system was supposed to work.

"They decide." He slapped the fender of his car. He and Bill were in the garage so their wives couldn't hear and he could yell as loud as he liked. "Which house, which neighborhood, then they decide whether to mortgage or not to mortgage and they decide who gets the mortgage and how much. They don't care if they lose money, and they call themselves bankers. It's control they want— control over the whole town. They decide who gets a break and who doesn't. If they could keep all of us down, they would. They want to own everything and hang on to it."

How could Bill answer his father when he was in such a rage?

"They need us. That's what they forget," Charley went on. "They need us bad. Their fancy houses would fall down if we weren't around to do their dirty work for them. Frank got a call from old lady Van Leuven the other day. Emergency. Lights not working. He drops what he's doing and rushes over. What for? A fuse is blown. Nobody out there can change a fuse? They need us. But we're not their slaves. We do things they can't."

"No handouts." Luckily the fender could take it. "No charity. No favors. I deserve a chance. I've earned it. And nobody's going to dictate to me."

"Vinson house. Phooey."

Bill was worse than caught in the middle. He didn't, at that moment, know if his father-in-law had agreed to Gus Van Leuven's suggestion. He didn't dare ask, certainly not when his own father was ready to refuse. He suggested a ride to cool off. A master stroke of diplomacy. Charley behind the wheel transformed his rage into elegant maneuvers with gears and brakes and the steering wheel, gliding around curves, stopping on dimes, squaring off right turns and slowly calming himself down. Bill suggested, once they had left their own neighborhood, that they turn up Maple, and then he suggested they park in front of the Vinson house and just sit and look at it.

Bill spoke sincerely from his own limited experience. "You can't expect them to change all at once. They give a little here, they give a little there. We get a little here, we get a little there. Half a loaf," he quoted his mother, "is better than none."

Charley looked up at the half-loaf of the Vinson house, all sixteen rooms of it, and began to put his carpenter's eye on it for the first time. Roof, for sure. Some new windows. Entrances, several of them, an advantage. Hmm. He looked around the neighborhood and saw children playing on the sidewalks and riding their bikes in the street. Room for dogs and babies. He told Bill he'd think about it.

Then Jack Sanford made what turned out to be a tactical error. He approached Bill and asked if his father would be interested in the Vinson house. He could have waited until Bill or Charley mentioned it to him, but he was alarmed that Gus Van Leuven might keep pursuing the issue on his own. Also, once he'd decided in Charley's favor, his sense of decency overrode his bankerly habit of keeping the Westerveldt pursestrings tightly grasped until the last minute. He lost the upper hand.

Charley knew better than even to think about gloating. He managed to act grateful when he met Jack at the bank to discuss terms, but his attitude had changed. He was no longer a suppliant. He had been offered the loan and the opportunity to invest in real estate, to own a part of Westerveldt he didn't live in himself— income property. He was now a businessman on his way up. He would be making his own decisions—how to divide up the interior of the Vinson house most efficiently, for example. He would choose the wallpaper and the paint and the fixtures suitable for tenants who might come and go and not according to a color scheme from a fashionable magazine. (There would be no mixing of paint over and over again to achieve the exact pale blue tone that would highlight the cornflowers in the wallpaper of the downstairs powder room in the Lizzie Van Slyke house.) He would, and this thought gave him the most pleasure, choose his tenants. He would decide who would live in his house and under what terms and how much rent they would pay. Clean, responsible hard-working couples who paid on time, swept or shoveled the walks and took out the garbage. Neat, tidy, spick and span, and, above all, new. They had said (they being Gus Van Leuven and Jack Sanford) that the neighborhood was on the turn. He'd turn it around, house by house. He'd show them what hard work and a chance could do.

Jack preferred dealing with Charley when he was still only a carpenter and not an entrepreneur. As in movie houses there are magenta-colored ropes that keep the patrons in line as they wait to file in, so between the Sanfords and the Sloanes of Westerveldt a thick, firm, well-braided invisible class rope separated them; they could see each other, even touch each other, but not step over. That divider now had several fraying strands. Jack could reason that Charley's eventual success could only make life easier for the grandchildren, the barrier dissolved by their joint progeny, but, but, how much more appropriate is the largesse were to come from the Sanford side.

If Charley mentally rubbed his hands with glee, Jack wrung his in self-disgust. As Christmas drew near and Jacqueline endlessly discussed where they should celebrate Christmas and how so that all families could be accommodated, he wondered how he could through it with an amused smile on his face.

"It's going to be too much for her," Jacqueline went over one set of objections. "She's never put together a really large dinner before. Even if I were to bring part of the meal or go over early in the morning to help her. Even if we made the whole meal here and took it over."

"If you're going to make the whole meal here, we might just as well have it here." Jack tried to hold out till the last minute.

"We can't. I've told you time and time again we can't. Mrs. Sloane has invited us to have dinner at their house. We can't offend her by issuing a counter-invitation. Christmas means just as much to her as it does to us."

"There's another very good reason why Genevieve shouldn't cook the dinner," Jack said sadly, "but nobody brings it up."

Not even Molly Sloane.

The women, the two mothers, Genevieve acquiescing, pressed ahead to work through the plans. (Jacqueline would serve an "intimate"—Sanford, Swinton, young Sloane—supper on Christmas Eve before midnight mass.) Christmas morning she and Molly would meet in Genevieve's kitchen and put together the Christmas meal, some specialties from each household chosen with tact (no frozen peas, no turnip casserole), and Genevieve would set the table, pour the wine into decanters ("Yes," Molly had said, "wine. It's Christmas. I won't have any, but I don't want you and Mr. Sanford to do without.") make sure the silver serviceware was beautifully polished and the linen napkins crisply folded. By the time Christmas Eve arrived, speculating, anticipating, imagining had given way to doing. Awkwardness began to disappear, and there was reason to assume that the young couple's first Christmas dinner at home would be success.

*   *   *

Have you heard from Peter? When did you hear from Peter last? What do you hear from Peter? Emily's mother asked her first, her father asked her; Beatrice asked her. At dinner, Ted mentioned Peter again. Christmas so far from home. He'd spent a Christmas in England during World War I, faraway, it was true, but at least in an English-speaking country that celebrated the holiday with recognizable carols, themes, and decorations, and, oddly enough, the same religious service, but the poor Van Leuven boy was in the Far East where there were no pine trees, no snow, no tinsel, no family or loved ones. Did Emily know that the Winton boy's plane had been shot down over the continent? That the Randolph boy had been missing in action since Thanksgiving? That no one had heard from Jim Higgins after the letters everyone assumed had been written in Northern Africa? That Bobby Gorton had no sooner announced he was going to join the Merchant Marine than his mother had had a seizure and was still in the hospital?

"But we've got them on the run," Ted said after he'd finished the list.

"It will still be a long hard fight, but the tide has turned. The Italians have been knocked out of the war. They're on our side now. What we have to do is dislodge the Nazis as we go up the peninsula."

"Until we get to the Alps," Emily said acidly. She had forgotten she was home. To have followed up with a crack about Hannibal and the elephants would have been the sort of bitter irony her collegiate friends used for sparring.

"It has to be done," Ted defended the Italian campaign. "We can't leave the Nazis in control of the peninsula, sticking out into the Mediterranean, threatening our shipping. We need a second front, I'm not denying that, but not yet. We won't be ready to invade until spring. You know, I can't make sense of people any more. Gus Van Leuven says we should never have invaded Italy in the first place. Just keep on bombing and let the Russians do the land fighting. No sense wasting our boys over every inch. Then there's Clifford Balt—he always was a bit of a pinko—he wants us to throw all we've got in right now to take the pressure off the eastern front. I tried to remind him that Stalin signed that pact with Hitler, that there are two different wars going on, but he says it's all the same war and that crushing Hitler is all that matters. Not that in a way I don't agree, but . . ."

Katherine had heard Ted thread his way through these conflicting points of view several times so she interrupted, "I think it would be nice if you called Mrs. Van Leuven after dinner and asked her if she's heard from Peter. It's going to be a lonely Christmas for her. I know she worries about him."

"Speaking of Peter Van Leuven," Beatrice said slyly, "guess what? Grandmamma found out you were dating Mike Mancuso. Don't ask me how she found out. We didn't tell her. Now she won't shop there any more. She goes to Walther's even though she knows the fruits and vegetables aren't as good and it's a good block and a half out of her way. She says she'll never set foot in Mancuso's again."

"I don't believe it." Emily looked at her parents' faces and ascertained that it was only too true. They both looked stern, although Katherine looked a little embarrassed.

"Your father tried to talk her out of it," Katherine said finally. "He tried to explain that your friendship wasn't serious and that Grandmamma was inconveniencing herself and hurting Mrs. Mancuso's feelings at the same time, but she couldn't understand."

"No," said Ted sharply, "she did not understand."

"I think," Katherine chose her words carefully, "that she's remembering the last war more now that we're beginning to hear of so many casualties. She remembers your uncle and she remembers young Roger Van Leuven. He and your uncle were very close friends, and then she thinks of Peter, and . . ."

"And I'm still Peter's girl," Emily cut in in disgust. "I should reinforce that false impression by calling up Mrs. Van Leuven and asking her if she's heard from Peter. Right?" Before anyone could say, "Right," she continued, "I'll call up Mary D. and ask her if she's heard from Peter and I'll tell her to give my regards to her mother. That I will do. Nothing more."

"Two whole weeks," Mary D. moaned. "I'm dying of boredom already. Westerveldt is worse than boarding school. Wellesley is freedom. I can't wait to get back. What are we going to do to liven up the old joint while we're here?"

"We can walk and we can talk. Let's hope it doesn't snow too much."

"In the winter we can build a snowman," Mary D. sang. "Why the hell not? We can't skate on the parking lot. The movies they're showing are cheerful holiday fare for the whole goddamned family. There isn't a man in town. Willard got transferred to a hick sister station upstate, and there's no more where that came from"

"What do hear from Peter?" Emily asked quickly to get it over with.

"Same old stuff. He's okay. I guess he wasn't involved in the recent mess in Tarawa. The last letter was written after that. What did he write you?"

"He missed all of you at Thanksgiving, he said, even the arguments at table."

"He can say that now that I have to fend for both of us. What do you hear from Mikey? I assume he writes you, if he knows how to write."

"He's okay. What do you hear from Tommy Van Vorst?" One bitchy remark deserves another.

Mary D. didn't notice. "I don't. He doesn't write. He doesn't have to. He's stationed near Boston, for the nonce."

"Hmm. We must get together."

"As soon as we survive Christmas dinner, it's a date. Or, I could, with no difficulty, wangle you an invitation to our family spread so you don't have to live through your own."

"Thanks too awfully much. Sunday will be fine. We can walk off the pies. Oh, and please give my regards to your parents."

"To be sure, to be sure. And give mine to yours, even if you don't have a big brother. You going to midnight mass? I'll catch a glimpse of you there."

Grim. It was grim. Grandmamma never missed midnight mass no matter how busy she'd been in the kitchen, and Ted. Jr. always drove her. Ted Sr. never went to church if he could help it, as he said. Weddings, funerals he couldn't help, services he could. Nelly coaxed a little, but remembering how loudly he sang hymns she let him be. Katherine, as usual, begged off, her public reason pre-Christmas fatigue, her private reason free-thinking non-denominationalism with only intermittent flashes of deism which it didn't pay to discuss or explain. So Grandmamma, Ted Jr., Emily, and Beatrice rode over in the darkness to St. Andrew's where everything had been done to create a joyous Christmas spirit. Seasonal decorations exuded pine odors, candles blazed, and the organ blared praise. The congregation faced the war as Mr. Giles recited the names of the dead (several of her age-mates Emily was hearing about for the first time) and then preached a gloomy sermon on the need to be cheerful. Nothing could shake the oppression, not even "Silent Night" sung beautifully, solo, by a boy soprano. We have to *live* through it. We *have* to live through it. We have to live *through* it. *We* have to live through it. No way out. More of the same and no end in sight, only more deaths, more bad news, more waiting, trying to keep life on a leash as it pulled in all directions and then broke loose and chased off over the hills.

Genevieve Sloane had plumped out, everyone noticed as she removed her coat and stood up to sing the processional hymn. Horace Callendar had had more than his share of Christmas cheer; he couldn't sing straight. Augusta Van Leuven had a new fur piece and Mary D. was proudly wearing the "old" fox pelt with claws and head still attached. Everybody the same, only different. "Peace on Earth, Good Will toward Men" and out there, all over the world, people were dying. "I think about the war more when I'm home than I do at school," Emily mused "In New York I guess I think I'm doing something just by being there. Here I wait and brood and there's no relief."

There was no relief the next day either. Christmas dinner lived up to almost all its traditional standards. Granddaddy, Daddy, and Uncle Jeff, however, had three cocktails. Aunt Sarah had four. Emily was offered none. Martha had to be summoned when she failed to hear the buzzer. The cranberries were too tart—not enough sugar which had to be saved for pies. Grandmamma would not borrow a cup of sugar even for a communal dessert. The ice cream didn't have the same velvety texture and deep taste. "Powdered milk, I know for sure," Grandmamma judged. "It's war time," said Katherine.

"That man," began Uncle Jeff. "It's Christmas," said Aunt Sarah. "Did you hear the Phillips boy was killed?" Ted asked, to cheer everybody up.

Mary D. was a pleasure to see the next day. They spent the afternoon together and then declared themselves sufficiently independent to plan a light supper at a restaurant where they could have drinks since Mary D. was now over eighteen. They chose O'Toole's for club sandwiches. ("We don't have to tell anyone where we went. We can say we went to the Arms. How will they know?") The only two women in the pub.

"Let's try to imagine what New Year's Eve is going to be like," Mary D. suggested. "My parents are going to a party at the Swintons' who don't know there's a war on. I'm not invited so I'm going to celebrate in my room listening to Guy Lombardo and shooting paper airplanes. What are you going to do?"

"Same thing. What else? My parents are also going to the Swintons', war or no war. You could come over and spend the night at my house and we can play three-handed solitaire with Beatrice. No, that's out, I forgot. She's going to a party at Marianne Callender's. The boys she knows are too young to fight. We'll play double sol and keep up our morale."

"Why not? Misery loves company. But I'll miss Tommy's call. Wait! I'll write him tomorrow and tell him to call me at your place."

Emily studied her friend, wondering whether or not to pry. She probed. "So you don't hate Tommy Van Vorst any more. Is that it?"

"The grub has turned into a butterfly," Mary D. giggled. "That's a good one. He's okay. He's not the cat's meow and I certainly wouldn't write home about him, but he wouldn't write home about me either. We made an agreement. His mother told him to look me up since I was nearby. My mother told me to be nice to him, so we told our respective mammas that we had done as we were told. The rest is classified information. Our seeing each other is nobody's business but our own. I think it's a great idea. Our parents would love nothing more than our getting together—

a reverse Romeo and Juliet—so we won't give them the satisfaction. Instead we get our kicks not out of doing something they would disapprove of but of doing something they would approve of, if they knew. But we don't tell them. Thus," Mary D. grinned maliciously, "we'll feel terribly wicked, and there's the spice to life."

"Sounds like you see a lot of him."

"Yep. There are one or two other guys around. I'm not putting all my eggs in one basket, but I have fun with Tommy."

"What's he like now that he's grown up?"

"He's a gas. We walk through Boston Common singing at the top of our lungs. We have snow fights. We giggle. We drink gallons of beer. He does imitations of his officers."

"Like two puppy dogs."

"Don't knock it. It's not all fun and games. He has his serious side, but he knows how to have a good time. He's not going to let the war get him down. He takes whatever he has to take, and on the chin. He looks ahead to better days to come. He's got guts. That I would never have thought. You sure can never tell. I always thought he was a namby-pamby Mommy's boy type, but he isn't."

"So this is it?" Emily wondered.

"Who knows? It's too soon to tell. Hell, I'm barely eighteen. If something better comes along, I'm not averse . . .'"

"Do you love him?"

"Sure. Why not?"

"Most interesting news I've heard since I've been home. Even more interesting than the Sloane baby to be."

"Genevieve doesn't look bad preggers, but, ah, poor thing, so soon, so soon. You should hear my dear pater on the subject. I think he hoped they'd never breed and contaminate Westerveldt's finest. He also goes on about their not having live-in help. Mummy has to shut him up. She's afraid Essie will decide she'd rather work for Genevieve Sloane and take care of a baby than listen to Daddy carry on. And, speaking of Genevieve, did you know her father-in-law bought Flossy Vinson's old house?"

"I think I heard. So what? Now that she's moved to

Connecticut, Flossy writes she's going to join the WAVES as soon as she's old enough. That whole family is gung-ho navy."

"So what you say. I had a small hand in that deal. Mr. Sloane wanted the Terpenning house, but Genevieve's father wouldn't give him a mortgage. My papa suggested the Vinson house. I was at the Yard that day last summer when they talked about it. And I alerted Bill the night we ran into them at the Riverboat. Pure luck. I don't think I would have dared call him on the phone. I told him I thought he could bring the two daddies together. It seems to have worked out. Mr. Sloane got the roof fixed before the bad weather set in, and now he's slicing up the insides to make apartments. He's got the right idea about those big old houses. Maybe we can walk over to Maple next week, and maybe if we're real smart and sweet and ask nicely, he'll let us look in."

"What on earth for?" Emily could think of nothing less amusing than inspecting the remodeling of a house she'd known all her life.

"I want to see how he does it." Mary D. was almost serious. "Remember, I was in the lumber business all summer. I take what you might call a professional interest. Okay?"

"Something to do. Okay. But why do you think you had a hand in the deal?"

"I knew Mr. Sloane was mad. He was mad at Uncle Jack, real mad. He wasn't ready to listen to reason. I figured if I got Bill to him on time, he might be able to calm him down. I don't know if my interference worked, but I enjoyed trying. You remember the night. You walked in as I was talking to Bill. You were with Mikey."

"Oh, that night. That was his last night in town."

"Last night! How many last nights have we been through, we poor suffering girls? So are you his girl back home too?" Too meant Peter.

"I'm nobody's girl back home," Emily said firmly. "Is there no peace? I thought you were my friend."

"I am. I am. I must say I'd like to have you for a sister-in-law. Once we're both married we can get into all kinds of trouble together and nobody will care. But—and it's a big but—it would be no good if you didn't love Peter and he didn't love you. So what's with Mikey?"

"He's off somewhere. He writes. I answer. There isn't much to say. He's not likely to be interested in college or life in New York City, so it's hard to think up things to say. I try to keep up morale; that's all there is to it."

"He's a sexpot, that one. I always thought so even when I was too young to know about sex. And he's damned cute. If they polished him up, do you think he'd lose his charm?"

Emily laughed at the thought of Mike polished. "Probably," she guessed. "Half of his appeal is his uncouthness. I never know what he'll do or say next. If he learned manners, he'd be predictable. He might turn out to be like everybody else."

"You never know," Mary D. wondered aloud. "I'm thinking of Tommy. Who would have thought he could be a romp?"

"This is some holiday," Emily said as they were about to leave O'Toole's. "Here we've been sitting, at night, in a bar, talking about the men we know."

"Talking." Mary D. said the word with disgust. "And that's the way it's going to be. Talking."

And so it was. The vacation passed slowly, day by day, evening by evening. It snowed twice, and Emily volunteered to shovel the walk just for something to do. Her father was so busy with the H & B building he might not have been able to find the time. She visited her grandparents every day. She wrote her term papers. She did her nails. She played cards with Beatrice. She saw Mary D. several times, and New Year's Eve was somewhat exciting because Tommy called, from a phone booth on the base, and Mary D. called him back on the Osterhoudt phone as he began to run out of change.

"Here's the money for your parents," she said after an hour and a half of giggling into the receiver. "Now to cook up the explanation. You don't know who it was I was talking to. I refused to tell you. Let them think it was some creep I met at college and I'm being my usual sneaky self."

Katherine was too busy to pay much attention when Emily handed her the money. Soon it was all over, the holiday, and Emily walked to the bus station and went back to college to find in her mailbox ten letters from her servicemen correspondents wishing her Merry Christmas and pleading for long answers describing her holiday so they wouldn't feel so far from home. And the war went on.

PART VI

1

Emily

"Cripes. Here we go again." It was early June. Another school year had ended. Emily was again back home in Westerveldt for another dull summer, another stint at the sweater factory, and no sooner did she set foot in the house than her mother announced that Augusta Van Leuven was dead. The funeral would be on Monday.

"Since you're home, you should go. If you were still in New York, if it were, say, exam week, I could have called you and told you to write a nice note. Under the circumstances, that would have been enough. But you're home and you should go. You're old enough. I used to shield you when you were young," Katherine reminded her. "I didn't want you to have to deal with unpleasant things too soon, but now it's high time you learned how to handle these occasions. You'll wear your black sheer, and I think I have an extra hat that will suit you."

"Cripes. And I suppose Bice doesn't have to go!" Emily felt twelve again in the familiar kitchen having a familiar contest of wills with her mother, but this time there was no contest.

"Bice's turn will come. Mrs. Van Leuven is Peter's grandmother, and in view of your relationship with Peter and the kindnesses his parents have shown you, it's your duty to go." Katherine was at her stuffiest, enforcing the unwritten code of behavior which, at this moment, was more important than any behind-the-scene intimacy she might share with her daughter. No jokes, no light remarks to soften the obligation.

Emily still didn't realize there was to be no discussion. "You mean," she said sarcastically, "that to repay them for that grizzly weekend at Lodge, I have to go to that damned funeral? I'm supposed to start work Monday."

"You'll call Monday and explain. Your boss will know that Mrs. Van Leuven is dead. Everybody in town knows. He shouldn't be surprised that you have to go to the funeral. He knows your background, even if to him you're just a summer file clerk. *And* you'll stop talking like that right away. You can put away all those collegiate damns and cripses while you're home. Certainly in front of your father."

"This is the last summer I come home," Emily muttered to herself. "I don't care if I have to wipe counters at Chock Full O' Nuts."

"When you go next door," her mother continued, "to say hello to Grandmamma and Granddaddy, you'll tell them how sorry you are to hear about Mrs. Van Leuven, and you'll tell them you're going to the funeral."

"Why do I feel this way?" Emily asked herself. "Why do I say this will be my last summer home? Why don't I want to be here?" So many opinions, prejudices, habits of thought, and turns of language usually seemed amusing, bizarre, or, if they interfered with her activities, irritating. Now they were weaving a web that would capture her, arms, legs, and spirit, in their domain. She could struggle no more successfully than a fly. At least this summer there would be no fuss about Mike Mancuso. He was far away, and so was Peter, and there would be no warnings about her seeing too much of either of them. Not much of a consolation. Every reference to either of them annoyed her. Especially every reference to Peter. She knew she was free not to marry him if she didn't want to and she knew he might not want to marry her if he still intended to become a priest, but the public bond between them involved their families beyond her friendship for Peter or Mary D., beyond the respect she had always felt for the Van Leuvens. She would be attending the funeral as Peter's girl. She could not go just as an Osterhoudt. Peter was far away, but Emily was back home, presumably thinking of him.

Grandmamma was pleased to see her, and, after a minute, so was Granddaddy. His watery blue eyes behind his glasses blinked as he said querulously, "Thank you for coming to see an old man."

Emily started to tell him he wasn't an old man, but her grandmother interrupted with a whisper, "He can't hear you if you don't shout." Then she shouted to her husband, "Emily says you're not an old man." The old man grunted.

"I was sorry," Emily said, midway between a shout and a whisper, "to hear about Mrs. Van Leuven."

Granddaddy lapsed into his private silence as Grandmamma answered for both of them.

"I still can't believe Augusta is gone. She was always as strong as an ox. I saw her at the Garden Club meeting last Wednesday. There was nothing wrong with her then. Friday morning she didn't wake up. The maid found her cold in her bed. They say it was her heart. It just gave out." Grandmamma sighed a long, long sigh. "Jen Waverly, Bess Lyon, now Augusta, all in one year. Soon there won't be anyone left to talk to, to play bridge with."

"The Catsbys are all right, aren't they, Grandmamma? And they're nearby."

"Sarah had a bad winter with her hip, but they're all right. Getting on, like the rest of us. They were going to come over tonight for a hand of bridge, but Sarah has a headache. She says she's in no mood to listen to the men carry on about Roosevelt. Neither am I, but I would like a hand of bridge. I think she got the headache sitting in that dark movie house all afternoon."

Granddaddy blinked at both of them and then threw back his head and intoned in a double bass voice that had once bellowed over the boy sopranos and altos in St. Andrew's choir, "Rocked in the Cradle of the Deep."

"Teddie!" Grandmamma cried. "Stop that! You'll wake up the neighborhood." To Emily she said as the old man stopped singing, "Do you have something to wear to the funeral? If you don't have a black frock, then something in navy blue ought to be all right."

"I have a black sheer, like Mother's," Emily answered. "You need one in New York."

"You're getting to be such a big girl," Grandmamma sighed again. "And Bice too. Soon she'll be off the school, and I won't have either of my girls around."

"You'll still see us, Grandmamma. We'll still be coming home." Only two hours earlier she had sworn she would never again come home for the summer and, by implication, never come home to stay after she had finished college.

"It will be a long time," Grandmamma said. "I may not be here when you come back home to live. What," she added after a pause, "do you hear from Peter Van Leuven?"

Emily expected to be asked that question regularly, but its juxtaposition to her grandmother's remark about coming home to live made it more threatening.

"I haven't heard from him in about a month," she answered. His grandmother had just died; how could she burst out, "I'm not coming home to live, Peter or no Peter."

"I wonder if he's heard about his grandmother. So far away. I don't suppose they'd let him come home for a while to be with his family. This awful war. It goes on and on. Worse than the last one."

Grandmamma droned on—the shortages, the inconveniences, the changes. Nobody delivered from the shops any more. Walther's customers served themselves from the bins and the shelves and brought everything to Mr. Walther to be toted up. Then they had to carry the packages home. At least Bice was still nearby to help out her poor Grandmamma by picking up a few things now and then. Whatever would she do when Bice left? Teddie was too busy with his new contracts. He barely had time to drop in once a day to say hello to his parents. Katherine was busy, too. Grandmamma wasn't sure doing quite what, but she was in and out of the house all day long, and her phone was always busy. Volunteer work, she'd said, but Grandmamma didn't understand what kind. There were no teas or luncheons to go to any more, except for the Garden Club once a month in good weather. Many people had to make do with parttime help and cleaning women. No dinner parties—everybody went to bed early.

"I have my crocheting." Grandmamma produced a square of ecru cotton and inserted the hook in a stitch as she spoke. "They still make beautiful yarn. I'm half done. I've finished one hundred and fifty-two squares and I have a hundred and thirty-six more to go. This will be for you, when you get married, to remember your old Grandmamma by."

"It's beautiful, Grandmamma." Emily admired the tiny stitchery.

"If I live long enough, Bice will have one too. Or she can have the one I made for the guest room thirty years ago. It's still in good condition. These last forever."

The next day, Sunday, was as dreary as Saturday had been. Emily couldn't call Mary D. while the family was in mourning. "Wait at least until the funeral is over," her mother advised. No one to talk to except Beatrice who was grumpier than ever, her junior year almost finished. Her parents had decided, now that Ted was doing better, to "make the sacrifice" necessary to send her off to boarding school, the same one Emily had attended, for her last high school year.

"Stockings for dinner, every day. A bunch of girls locked up a dorm far out in the country for a whole year. No boys, nothing to do. Are you ever lucky, living in New York City. I'll bet you don't get bored."

The other changes at home, such as they were, were none of them pleasant. Ted's new contracts gave the family more financial security but also kept him busier than he had ever been in his life. He went back to the office nearly every night to catch up on the paperwork. Katherine's volunteer work—Bundles for Britain, Russian War Relief, and plans for a gala to celebrate Bastille Day and give the proceeds to the Free French—didn't keep her from managing her home with great efficiency, even greater efficiency, but her patience was tauter. She delivered instructions as if there were no room for negotiation or discussion, or, if no room, no time. If her husband seemed overtired, she went to the office with him at night to help him clean up his desk and to keep the bookkeeping up-to-date. She seemed to manufacture energy the more she used.

"It's war time," she said more than once to explain herself. "We must do all we can. Keep busy. No time to sit around brooding and feeling sorry for yourself. Do you hear me, Bice? Now set that table in jig time. Emily, you'll do the dishes tonight, and I want my kitchen left Clean. I'm going to the office to help your father."

The only cheerful news Emily heard during that first weekend was that Genevieve Sloane's baby was adorable, Born just after Easter, a little girl named Jacqueline Margaret after her two grandmothers. Katherine, however, couldn't make the announcement without drawing more lessons for living.

"Genevieve still hasn't learned how to do housework. If either of my girls started off married life as helpless and incompetent as Genevieve Sloane, I'd die of shame." As she spoke, Katherine bustled about the kitchen preparing dinner, opening and shutting cabinets, assembling ingredients. Bang, zip, slam, presto. "Either her mother comes over, or her aunt, or both of them together, or Bill's mother. Somehow they get the house clean and the baby clean and the dinner on the table for Bill when he comes home. All Genevieve has to do is look pretty and make googoos at the baby." Whisk, chop, bang, setting an example her daughters knew they could never follow. "I tell you right now, I'm not playing grandmother the way Jacqueline does. If my children want to have children, they're going to have to learn to manage the way I did."

2

The Sloanes

Baby Jacqueline was taking a nap. So was Genevieve. Her mother had promised to awaken her at four-thirty so she would have time to freshen up before Bill got home around five-thirty. He was over on Maple Street with his father, giving up his Saturdays in partial repayment for the remodeling that had been done the year before on his own house. The arrangement had been Charley's idea, but so far no one had objected. Not even Jack Sanford who was home alone. The others were doing what they did every Saturday. Molly Sloane was in the newlyweds' kitchen where she had just slipped a roasting chicken into the oven. By the time Bill opened the front door, the familiar odor would be there to greet him. Jacqueline Sr., as everyone now called her, plumped up the cushions on the sofa, tidied up the magazines, raised the window shades to let in the late afternoon sun, and proceeded from corner to corner of the room to neaten.

"Mrs. Sanford," Molly said from the doorway, "since Genevieve is lying down, could we have a little chat?"

"Of course, Mrs. Sloane. Let's sit here on the sofa. What's on your mind?"

"I don't know how to bring this up. I can't talk to Bill about it, and my husband refuses. I'm embarrassed to mention it to Genevieve. But you're her mother. Perhaps you . . ."

Jacqueline felt a little alarmed. "What is it, Mrs. Sloane?" she asked calmly, letting nothing seem to perturb her.

"The baby is very sweet. I'm glad to be a grandmother. I always wanted Bill to settle down nearby and have a family. And don't think I mind helping out. I like to come over and give Genevieve a hand in the kitchen. It's what I do best. You understand the other things better than I do." The other things being possessions which Jacqueline knew by instinct and training how to arrange and maintain to create an air of genteel elegance no matter how often Bill plopped in a chair. The living room looked much as it had after the honeymoon, undamaged by daily life, no stains, no evidence of ordinary human sloppiness.

Jacqueline accepted the compliment with a polite smile. Yes, Mrs. Sloane, she thought to herself, you certainly are a good cook, if a robust one. Stuffing in the chicken *and* mashed potatoes are not going to help Genevieve get her figure back.

"And I know Bill is doing well at the bank, so I'm not worried about money."

Jacqueline was patient.

"I think. I don't know how to put this. I wish. I hope. If it's possible, if there were some way." Jacqueline waited. Molly drew a deep breath and said it. "I hope Genevieve won't have another baby too soon after little Jacqueline." She didn't give Jacqueline time to answer before she clarified her remark. "It would be nice if they had time to get used to this baby."

Jacqueline was pleasantly surprised at Molly Sloane's delicacy and tact. Even she herself would have broached the subject a little less generously.

"I agree, Mrs. Sloane." In all justice, if anyone were to make sure Genevieve understood birth control, it was her duty and no one else's. "I've spoken to Dr. Hanson, privately. I have also spoken to Genevieve. Tuesday she will be going in for a checkup. We had an appointment for Monday, but we had to cancel it because of the Van Leuven funeral. But Tuesday we go for sure."

"I'll be here, Mrs. Sanford," Molly answered quickly, "to watch little Jacqueline while you go to the funeral. If you'll tell me what time the appointment is on Tuesday, I'll come over then too so you can go with Genevieve to the doctor."

"You're very kind, Mrs. Sloane."

"I'm only doing my duty, Mrs. Sanford."

"And I shall do mine," Jacqueline answered, accepting the idiom. "We shall make sure that at least a year goes by before Genevieve thinks about a brother or sister for little Jacqueline. You know," she added, sensing that she owed Molly something more than gratitude if not quite so much as an explanation, "Genevieve is only just learning to be practical. She never thought she would have to do her own housework so she never prepared herself. I used to tell her to pay attention to the details of running a house. Even if she didn't have to do any of the work herself, she should know how it is done so she could supervise and manage everything smoothly. My sister and I were brought up to be able to do everything, but once Genevieve went off to college, I'm afraid I let her be spoiled. Who could have predicted this awful war?"

Molly Sloane had been cooking, scrubbing, mending, and sewing new slip covers since she was fourteen, long before she married Charley. Energetic domestic activity without help of any kind had been her life. Although she had developed rigid moral attitudes toward work, cleanliness, and other domestic virtues, under these new circumstances, she stretched her imagination to understand and appreciate what must happen in a house where there is always someone hired to do chores.

"Genevieve tries hard, she does." Molly gave what praise she honestly could. In a way, she was right. Genevieve did try, in her dreamy style. Above all to please her husband. As he tried to please her. They were still a honeymoon couple, in spite of pregnancy and the demanding baby now sleeping peacefully upstairs. Molly remembered the first years of her own marriage and sighed an envious sigh. Not that Charley wasn't a good husband, but romance had faded fast, especially after his aged mother had moved into the spare room when none of her other children would have her. Never, Molly swore to herself, would she torture Genevieve as that arthritic old battleax had tortured her for fifteen years. Still, a little less dreaming perhaps. A little more . . . what? Pep? Ambition? Sense of duty? Bill, too, for that matter. Good that he was putting in time helping his father. Only right and proper.

"I promise you, Mrs. Sloane," Jacqueline said, "I'll do the very best I can. And I shall speak to Genevieve again very frankly. I shall make sure she understands." As an afterthought which she hadn't really let simmer in her mind before she brought it out, she added, "Do you think we're spoiling them, Mrs. Sloane?"

Molly thought carefully. Her first impulse was to answer an unqualified "yes," even if it meant an obvious criticism of Genevieve and her upbringing. But she herself was part of the conspiracy to keep the young couple comfortable—how many roasts, how many casseroles, how many cakes and pies, homemade biscuits, jams, had she concocted in the past year in that very kitchen (and cleaned up after, she might add)? So, she laughed, a rare thing for her to do. She was a downright woman, not much given to mirth.

"Yes. Yes, we do. But I can't seem to help myself any more than you. But, perhaps, if there isn't another baby right away, we can begin to . . ."

She didn't finish her sentence. From the nursery upstairs came the sound of a waking, hungry baby. Jacqueline was on her feet in an instant. Then she looked at Molly Sloane's face and remembered the unfinished sentence.

"You're right, Mrs. Sloane. Let Genevieve take care of the baby. It's time she was up anyway. All I'll do is put the baby's bottle on to warm so we won't have to listen to her cry for too long."

3

The Van Leuvens

It was Essie's night out. Sunday. Isobel had seen no reason to ask her to stay; she could certainly serve a light supper herself without any help.

Gus didn't think so. As he poured himself a second martini from the cocktail shaker, he asked for the third time, "When is dinner going to be ready?"

Still patient, even more so during this doleful period, Isobel answered for the third time, "Whenever you want it. Now if you like."

"But you're in here."

"It's cold supper, Gus. Some roast beef from dinner, a little potato salad, and the rest of the lemon pie. There's nothing for me to do. The table is set and ready any time you are."

"Well, it'll have to wait until I finish my drink. Why did you give her the night off anyway?"

"It's her usual night off, Gus. You know that. I saw no reason to ask her to stay."

"With my mother just dead and the funeral tomorrow? That's not reason enough? What if we wanted something?"

"There'll be extra work for her tomorrow with people coming back to the house after the service."

"I'm not thinking about work. She should be here as part of the family."

"Maybe Essie needs her night out from being part of the family," Mary D. put in.

"Mr. Giles is going to deliver the eulogy." Gus ignored his daughter. "There aren't any of mother's contemporaries left who could do a proper job, and it wouldn't be right for me to do it." He shook his head as the thoughts marched through. "I still can't believe she's gone. Thursday night she was here for dinner. Friday morning they couldn't wake her up. What did she have for dinner that night anyway?"

Isobel tried to remember, her anxiety increasing; some dish or ingredient might, in retrospect, be deemed too rich, too heavy, or too exotic and citing it might trigger an explosion. Luckily Mary D. answered for her.

"You're not suggesting it was something she ate here! We all ate the same food."

"Maybe something didn't agree with her." Gus wanted to get to the bottom of it.

"It was her heart, Gus," Isobel said imploringly. "Dr. McCullough said so. It gave out on her. It stopped beating."

"That's what he said. He had to say something. He has to write something down."

"If you wanted to know exactly what made her die, Daddy," Mary D. said, "you should have let them perform the autopsy." The implications of her father's remarks were too sinister to go unchallenged.

"On my mother!" Gus stared at her, shocked. "Never! We'll have to be content with heart failure, I guess. But I'll never believe it. She was as strong as an ox. Heart failure! First my father has a stroke and then my mother dies of heart failure. Both of them! Do you know what that means? Both sides of the family. We'll never know about Roger—he was killed in the war. Let's see. My father's mother died in childbirth, and his father was hit by a streetcar so we don't know about them. My mother's mother died, she was seventy-five, of influenza, during the epidemic. And my mother's father, he had a stroke too. How long do I have? My grandfather was eighty-two, my father was only sixty-three. Mother was eighty-four. I'm forty-seven. I have twenty, maybe thirty, maybe forty years left."

Nobody said anything. Gus continued, "It won't be the same without Mother. I looked out my window this morning, out over the duckpond, and all I could think of was that I'll never see her again. All these years, every day or every other day, I saw her. Now no more. Never again. It's a terrible thing to lose your parents." He looked at Isobel. Both of her parents were dead, over five years now, but she said nothing. He looked at Mary D. "It's a terrible thing. Remember that."

"You're going to live forever," Mary D. laughed.

"Don't be too sure," Gus sipped morosely on his martini until a new thought occurred to him. "Damn. I forgot about Mother's jewelry. It's sitting over there in the house with those dimwit servants. I'd better . . ." He rose from the chair.

"It's all right, Gus, Sit down," Isobel said. "Mary D. and I stayed after Mr. Phitts came for the body, and we went through everything. We brought all her jewelry back here; it's upstairs in the rosewood casket she kept on her dresser. We also checked everything else in the house—the silverware, everything of value. As soon as the funeral's over, we'll make an inventory."

Gus looked surprised, then relieved. "Just as well," he muttered. "I couldn't have gone through her things. Not yet anyway. Time enough for that." He was briefly quiet, but his mind was running down a list. "I wonder what sort of will she left," he said aloud. "We ought to have the reading after the funeral or Tuesday at the latest. She didn't have many people to leave anything to. Most of it will go to me, I assume. Some small bequests to the servants. Then there's the jewelry, the silverware, the household effects. There's no reason Peter shouldn't have her engagement ring to give to the girl he marries. If he straightens out and decides to marry. The silverware can be divided, half and half, half to Mary D. and half to Peter and his wife. We have our own. We don't need any of it except a piece here and there. And the furniture. Christ! What are we going to do with all that furniture? The house I grew up in! Eighteen rooms!"

"Don't think about those things now, Gus," Isobel pleaded. He was getting red in the face. "Wait until after the funeral and until after the will is read. We'll take our time. We'll find a way."

"Damn it," said Gus. "When is dinner going to be ready?"
Then, as he finished the rest of his drink in one gulp, he turned to
Mary D. "Is your friend Emily going to be at the funeral?"

Mary D. had been listening, not ready to say very much. She
was surprised at herself. She had been home a week, been there the
morning her grandmother had been discovered dead in her bed,
and so far she hadn't felt the rebellious streak as her major propelling
force. "Am I growing up?" she asked herself. She had viewed the
white-maned head on the pillow with mixed affection and distaste,
glad to be excused from more than a second of looking. She had
helped her mother attend to practical matters—choosing burial
garments, finding jewelry, shutting windows. She had observed
her father with interest; never had she seen him vulnerable before.
He hadn't cried, as far as she knew, not in front of her anyway. He
was, however, no mellower. He hadn't been kinder. He hadn't acted
as if he needed emotional support. He had been the same, only
more so. Quieter, or less inclined to discuss anything, gruffer, or
more impatient, most of the time lost in thoughts of his own which
he only occasionally shared, such as wondering about his mother's
will.

It was the thoughtful withdrawal that made Gus seem
vulnerable to his daughter. Was he thinking he no longer had a
parent? Was he conscious of his own mortality, thinking that some
day he would die too? For herself, Mary D. was sad that her
grandmother was dead. Now that she would rarely be home, she
had little to fear from the old lady's interfering ways and critical
remarks. She wouldn't miss the subtle and sometimes not so subtle
ways her grandmother had tormented her mother. Much as Mary
D. had frequently wanted to shake her mother and tell her not to
put up with the sly abuse she took from her mother-in-law, she
loved her and felt sorry for her. She knew her mother had not had
a happy life (perhaps she had only herself to blame), and Mary D.
was determined not to emulate her mother by choosing or being
forced into a situation that could ever demand of her such tolerance,
such patience, such self-containment. Her father knew better how
to enjoy life, even if he took some of his pleasure from careless

rudeness. As she grew older, Mary D. was feeling herself less a tile in some elaborate board game her parents kept playing with each other, but more alone, and glad, she guessed, of it. Better to feel alone than in the middle, she told herself. She listened less to their plans for her, or, for that matter, to anything they said at all.

"I said," Gus snapped, "is your friend Emily going to be at the funeral?"

"How should I know?" Mary D. omitted "the hell" from between "how" and "should." "How should I know" was rude enough for this occasion. "I haven't made one phone call. I answer the phone and accept condolences and give out funeral information," and before her father could interrupt, "I take full and complete messages."

"She should be there," Gus said, as if Mary D. had said she might not be. "In view of her relationship with Peter and our kindnesses to her, apart from our friendship with her parents."

"I'm sure she knows that, Gus." Isobel wanted a peaceful, affectionate relationship with her prospective daughter-in-law. She did not intend to behave like Augusta.

"She hasn't called here?" Gus wanted to know.

"Of course not," Isobel said. "It would be improper for her to call to chat with Mary D. until after the funeral."

"To pay her respects," Gus said, exasperated.

"Her mother did that—for the family. You don't want each of them to call separately. The phone is busy enough as it is. The Osterhoudts sent a beautiful flower arrangement. I thought you'd seen it."

"Too many flowers," Gus said. "You know, the Jews have the right idea, about one thing, anyway. No flowers and bury 'em the next day and get it over with. We have to get on with it. This waiting around is getting on my nerves."

After dinner, without saying a word, he walked out of the house, and they heard his car drive away.

"Wherever is he going?" Isobel wondered to Mary D. "Is he going to see someone who can comfort him properly? God knows I've tried. Everything I say rubs him the wrong way. It's a sad thing to lose your parents, I know."

"There isn't anyone who can comfort Daddy," Mary D. said. "I'll bet he's driving as far out of town as he can on the gas he has, and he'll find some tavern where nobody knows him, and he'll sit and drink and forget anything that's on his mind."

"He could have done that here." Isobel was dismayed. "I wouldn't mind. I understand if he needs an extra drink or two in order to forget."

For a second Mary D. understood her father's irritation with his wife. "He wants bright lights and a juke box and people dancing and making noise."

Isobel was truly puzzled. "But his mother hasn't even been buried yet. Do you really think he's gone off to some road house?"

"I can only guess," Mary D. answered, "but that's where I'd go. If I know Daddy's sense of propriety, he'd go somewhere where nobody would recognize him. If he went somewhere in town, people would say what you just said—that his mother isn't even buried yet."

"I'll never understand him, Mary D., not matter how hard I try. Sometimes I think you understand him better than I do."

"Only sometimes," Mary D. said tactfully, and she gave her mother an affectionate kiss which Isobel gratefully returned. Yes, children could be a blessing.

4

The Funeral

The Episcopal heavens are self-regulating. If the sun had shone in splendor on the Sloane-Sanford nuptials, it retired behind thick grey clouds to provide a properly somber background for Augusta Van Leuven's funeral. It was not quite chilly enough for wraps but not quite warm enough for black sheers. Katherine and Emily decided to shiver rather than carry extra garments, except for raincoats which they left in the car.

The church filled slowly, as if no one were eager for the services to begin. The organist played an assortment of doleful passages, some slow and plaintive, some dramatic and weighty, others saturnine, as the mourners drifted in. Every sense was assaulted. The flowers, piled high around the coffin, sent out a strong nauseating odor which only reminded everyone of the less pleasant aroma they would, in a more remote era, be covering. The light that filtered through the stained-glass windows seemed dark blue or grey, the reds and blues subdued. Worst of all was the music— oppressive, demanding that everyone's consciousness be concentrated on its subject matter. Death. "No," Emily said her herself, "worse. Not death, dying. We must all die. Then when we die, those we leave behind come here to listen to this music and remember that they will die too." A complete depression of the spirit against which even the most light-hearted disposition could not struggle.

The mourners sat straight-backed and motionless in their pews; few whispered comments were exchanged, no head turned. Perhaps Jack Sanford and Ted Osterhoudt, acting as ushers, did run their eyes over the assemblage to see who was present and who could not be accounted for. Not taking attendance, actually, just making mental notes. Unless they were to hear during the next few days that someone had been heartily enjoying himself at eleven o'clock on a Monday morning, his absence (court case in New York, bank examiner's meeting) need not make him remiss or thoughtless.

The Van Leuvens sat up front, Mary D. between her parents, the women in black dresses, black hats with short veils, Gus in a dark suit. Wherever he had been the night before, there was no telltale sign in his stern composed features or stalwart posture. Not far behind them in the pew Nelly occupied every Sunday alone, unless one of her granddaughters joined her, the Osterhoudts sat en famille, no one thinking, not even Ted Sr., whether or not there truly was a deity or did it matter if there were one. Jacqueline Sanford with Genevieve and Bill sat two pews behind with the Swintons, all in black, in those dresses and suits they kept in their closets for such rare occasions. Anyone in the crowd attired in a lighter color had to be described as an outsider—a tradesperson, a distant acquaintance, a neighbor—who was paying respects but did not know the rules of the game.

"I am the Resurrection and the Life . . ." intoned Mr. Giles. The words of the service were familiar enough to all but the younger members of the congregation, such as Emily and Mary D., who would have the next half century to learn them letter-perfect.

"I know that my Redeemer liveth . . ."

"We brought nothing into this world, and it is certain we can carry nothing out. The LORD gave and the LORD hath taken away."

It was hard for anyone not to think immediately of Augusta's will. She was carrying away with her, more or less, an expensive mahogany casket, pearl-grey-satin lined, but she was leaving behind an eighteen-room house on a two acre lot in the most exclusive section of Westerveldt, her jewelry, not extraordinary by Gilded Age standards but more valuable than any other collection in town, and who knew what investments and stocks and bonds. It would all go to Gus, people assumed. So did Gus—to whom else could it possibly go? A successful businessman who already had stocks and bonds of his own would have more stocks and bonds from which to draw income.

"Taxes," thought Horace Callendar with some triumph, remembering how the government had eaten into his father's estate before it was set before him.

"Taxes," thought Gus. "God knows what'll be left by the time the government gets through with me."

"Daddy won't change no matter how much money he has," Mary D. thought. "I won't get a larger allowance. I won't get paid any more for my work at the Yard. Someday I'll get a car, but I would have had that anyway."

"I hope the money doesn't go to Gus' head," thought Isobel. "There isn't anything he really needs that he doesn't already have. But he may feel more powerful. It may make him worse. The money never made his poor mother a happier or a better person. She never used it to help those less fortunate than herself. She gave to the church. She gave to the symphony. Nothing else."

"The days of our age are threescore and ten: and though man be so strong that they come to fourscore, yet is their strength but labour and sorrow; so soon passeth it away and we are gone."

"Mother was eighty-four," Gus thought. "Fourteen more than threescore and ten. She had a good life, not much labour and sorrow. She missed Father, but she had us nearby. She died peacefully."

"So teach us to number our days that we may apply our hearts unto wisdom."

"Number our days," Isobel thought. "Don't expect more than seventy years and try to make the most of life before they've passed. Mother was lucky to have those extra fourteen years. Oh, dear God, please keep Peter safe."

"I will lift up mine eyes unto the hills*from when cometh my help?"

Eyes lifted up to Mr. Giles as he himself, God's vicar, gazed out at the congregation, reciting from memory without need of prayerbook.

"THE LORD shall preserve thy coming out, and thy coming in,* from this time forth for evermore."

All eyes still on Mr. Giles, he closed his own, threw back his head and, raising his voice somewhat, in an Episcopalian toned-down version of an old-fashioned fire-and-brimstone preacher, appealed:

"Out of the deep have I called unto thee, O LORD* Lord, hear my voice . . . My soul fleeth until the Lord before the morning watch* I say before the morning watch," he repeated slowly and threateningly.

Emily was following the service in the small red prayerbook Grandmamma had given her at her confirmation. Whatever does it mean? Morning watch? And why twice? How did anyone ever understand the Bible?

"In my Father's house are many mansions: if it were not so, I would have told you." Mr. Giles had switched to the New Testament (John xiv, l). So that's where that comes from. Okay. So maybe a mansion wasn't a big house, and even if it were, God's house was big enough for all houses, great and small. And if it were not so, He would have told them. Like a parent. Believe me, trust me. I would not lie to you.

"And whither I go ye know. Thomas saith unto him, Lord, we know not whither thou goest; and how can we know the way?"

Doubting Thomas. So that's where That comes from. He wants proof. He wants to know for sure, to be able to see with his own eyes.

"Jesus saith unto him. I am the way, the truth and the life; No man cometh unto the Father but by me."

Emily's mind buzzed. "That seems to narrow it down." She shook her head. "How can that be?"

Mr. Giles raised his right hand, several fingers folded, and pronounced the blessing. "Unto God's gracious mercy and protection, we commit you. The LORD bless you and keep you. The LORD make his face to shine upon you, and be gracious unto you. The LORD lift up his countenance upon you, and give you peace, both now and evermore. Amen."

The organist struck a series of chords to signal that the congregation should rise. Together they sang the words most of them knew by heart but which in the shadows of the church in front of Augusta's casket took on a new meaning. "Abide with me, fast falls the eventide/ The darkness deepens, Lord with me abide . . . Change and decay in all around I see; O thou who changest not, abide with me . . . Where is death's sting? Where, grave, thy victory?/ I triumph still, if thou abide with me . . . Ah, ah, ah men."

The casket was carried down the aisle. Jack and Ted at the back of the church opened the portals to permit the pallbearers and their burden to pass on out to the hearse. As people left, in the name of the family, they thanked them for coming.

Dr. Hansen acknowledged Jack with the question, "And how's that grandson of yours coming along?"

Jack was momentarily startled, wondering if there was perhaps something he had not been told. He corrected the mistake. "Granddaughter, you mean? Jacqueline, after my wife."

"Yes." Dr. Hansen shook his head ruefully. "I remember now. Well, those things happen. Perhaps next year."

As soon as the Osterhoudts had compressed themselves into the Buick for the ride to the cemetery, it began to rain.

"I'm glad we brought our raincoats," Katherine said to Emily.

"Oh, dear," said Nelly. "I didn't think. I brought an umbrella."

The skies thundered and the rain began in earnest, whipped by a wind so that Ted could barely see to drive.

"An umbrella won't do you much good in this weather, Mother," he said. "I'm going to take you and Dad home. We can pick up the funeral procession later."

"Oh, no, Teddie, I couldn't do that," Nelly protested. "I have to pay my final respects to Augusta at the cemetery. It wouldn't be right."

"It's getting cold," Beatrice said. "I'm freezing," although she was sitting up front squeezed in between her father and her grandfather.

"You're right," Ted said. "The rain and the wind must have dropped the temperature a good ten degrees. No more discussion, Mother. I'm taking you and Dad home. I don't want either of you catching cold."

"I don't like it," Nelly answered, "but perhaps you'd better. However much I'm going to miss Augusta, I don't want to be in too great a hurry to see her again."

Since no one knew if the remark was to be taken as witty or as truly serious, no one said anything.

5

Mary D.

"We can't go to the movies. We can't go to the Sweet Shoppe, but it's okay if we walk around in a nice neighborhood or better yet if we go back to your house and sit on the terrace. Can you beat that?" Mary D. was laying down the law to Emily as it had been laid down to her. "Not all summer. For a while. A while has not yet been defined. I can go to the movies with them after some sort of while. Maybe, maybe I can go to the Sweet Shoppe in August. Next week I can walk around where I please. But 'appearances' must be thought of At All Times. So—I can't look as if I'm enjoying myself or or forgetting for one minute that I'm in mourning. Every time we pass someone, make sure you don't giggle but talk very somberly as if we were thinking about death."

"What about work? Can you go to work?"

"Oh yes. Life must go on, so work is fine. Just no pleasure. I start Monday, and I assure you I can't wait for the relief. It will be heaven to answer the phone and be able to sound cheerful to customers and maybe even sneak a laugh with one of the stockboys. Where did they get the idea that people had to go around mourning constantly when there's a death in the family?"

"Is it really that bad? We haven't had a death in the family since Greataunt Hattie died in 1938. That didn't affect us much in the house. My mother's college roommate died a couple of years ago. My mother was very upset, but she wasn't plunged into gloom. We just left her alone, more or less, for a couple of days. Then I discovered that she wanted to reminisce so we talked about her college days, and it made her feel better."

"I don't know if this is the way it is in everybody's house or if it's the way it's supposed to be. You can't tell with my parents. My father can make every whim of his sound like an ironclad social law. My mother only gets rigid about something that usually makes some dim sense, even if it's an old-fashioned way of doing things. This time, however, they are in total agreement, so I'm cooked. I think, but I can't be sure, that Mummy's afraid Daddy's more upset than he's letting on. She doesn't want to give him an excuse for getting, shall we say, 'emotional'? For her own sake as well as mine. But it's gloom street. The curtains are always drawn. No sun anywhere. I expect the food to be served on black plates. Oh, and you can't even get a decent meal. It's as if we have to suffer because Grandmother died. I absolutely do not see the point. Can't we be sorry she's dead and miss her without suffering any more than that?"

"How is your father taking it?"

"With him you can never tell. He seems the same. Once or twice in the evening, I've caught him looking out the living room draperies toward Grandmother's house as if he expected to see a light on. One night at dinner, he said, 'I've moved up a generation. Now I'm the older generation,' but I couldn't tell if he likes the idea or hates it. Actually he's been pretty quiet all week since they read the will." Mary D. was smiling broadly as she spoke although her words came out evenly.

Emily waited. The Misses Bedford, as everyone referred to them, were on the other side of the street and about to cross and come their way. Katherine would salute them, "Good morning, Misses Bedford," and Emily invariably giggled. They were very much alike, the same height, the same frail build, the same white hair rinsed blue under pert woven straw hats. They both carried matching straw pocketbooks in their white-gloved hands and kept pace with each other in sensible shoes. Mary D. drew in the corners of her mouth and tried to look soulfully sad. "Good evening, Misses Bedford," they said at the same time, in imitation of their mothers, as if they too had moved up a generation. The Misses Bedford, who had watched their comings in and their goings out all these years with excellent memories for lapses and shortcomings, answered sternly, "Good evening, girls," as if they were surely up to something.

"Christ," said Mary D. three elm trees later when she thought it was safe. "Some things never change. You forget when you're away at school, college anyway. Not everybody watching you every minute. Those two disapprove of everything, you can be sure. They were never young."

"My mother says Miss Cora Bedford's fiancé died in the Spanish-American War, and she's never gotten over it. Only a couple of thousand men died, but he was one of them. I don't think he was shot. He died of a fever of some kind."

"Why the hell did he go?" Mary D. wondered. "You didn't have to in those days. Maybe he went to get away from her. But," she paused, "I am being unkind. Now," she said importantly, "I have something to tell you, as long as you promise me, faithfully, on your heart, and all that crap, that you will tell no one—ever—no matter what, even if you find out they know. This is a big secret."

"I promise," Emily looked with surprise at her friend. "You're very mysterious."

"I have to be. I've got a first-class grown-up problem. I have to have somebody to talk to, and you've been chosen. Are you sure you can handle it?"

"Mary D.!" Emily exclaimed. "You're not pregnant or anything like that, are you?"

'No, but you're on the right track. More or less. Solemn promise?"

Emily nodded vigorously.

"Okay, Here goes. Grandmother's will was read the day after the funeral. There was a codicil she put in last year that no one knew anything about and no one expected. She left everything to my father, as we knew she would. A thousand here and there to the servants and the church, but everything to him. Except." Mary D. knew how to pause theatrically to prepare her audience. "Except. I get ten thousand dollars as soon as I'm twenty-one. Peter gets his automatically since he's already over twenty-one. Now here's the clincher." Another long deliberate interruption. "Her house, that eighteen-room Victorian monstrosity, goes to the first one of us, Peter or me, who marries someone my father approves of. If neither of us is married within five years, my father gets the house."

"This is a shocker," Emily agreed, not entirely pleased with any possible connection such a codicil might have with her. Rather than let her mind race, she waited for Mary D. to continue.

"Daddy had a fit. He didn't want either of us to have a cent until he died. Too young, too irresponsible. Run through it. Terrible misuse of good hard-earned money. Thought Mother had more sense. Blah, blah, blah."

"Why did she do it, then?" Emily asked. "She was a strict old lady, wasn't she?"

"No, she wasn't, actually. Sharp, critical, but she wasn't strict. She was a holy terror when she was young. I think, but I can't be sure, but I'm guessing she was playing a game with Daddy. She wanted to see if he could control us if we had some money of our own. But if you think Daddy was mad about the money, that's nothing. He's in a cold fury about the house. He says it will sit there and deteriorate for five years and be worth less than it is now."

"What would he have done with it if he's inherited it?"

"I don't know. He won't say. I've asked him several times. It's a perfectly legitimate question under the circumstances. He refuses to discuss it. However," Mary D. drew herself up tall, "I know what I'm going to do with it."

"I don't understand. You said that whoever got married first gets the house. And you said it has to be someone your father approves of."

"Now you're beginning to get my drift."

"Mary D! You're not going to get married! You're only eighteen."

"Not right this minute. The instant the war is over, and if they invade this year, it can't last forever. A year, a year and a half, two years, at the most. No matter what, I'll get married under the five-year limit. I'm going to take my ten thousand dollars and I'm going to redo that old house. I'm going to make apartments out of it. I'll bet I could get four out of it. I'll have income property by the time I'm twenty-two! Yippee!"

Emily couldn't believe her ears. "Do you think you can get away with it? What about your father?"

"He can't stop me. There's nothing in the will that says I have to keep the house the way it is. There's nothing in the will that says I have to live in the house, all eighteen rooms of it anyway. I'm perfectly willing to live in one of the apartments for a while. I've been doing estimates, pricing what I need. It pays to work in a lumber yard, I tell you. I can do it! It's on city water and sewer and the city gas supply. I'll have to worry about the wiring and the plumbing, new fixtures, kitchens, and all that stuff. But, well, I'll show you the floor plans."

It was all going too fast for Emily. She repeated, "Floor plans? You made floor plans?"

"The night after the will was read. I stayed up to the wee hours. I haven't dared to go over to the house to measure or to make sure I've got the plumbing lines laid out properly. That'll have to wait."

"Okay. But you've left out a good part of your plan. You only get the house if you marry someone your father approves of. How are you going to work that out? Your father doesn't approve of any man you've ever said hello to, except Tommy Van Vorst."

"Heheh," cackled Mary D. "So you haven't guessed. Even after Christmas vacation. I'll tell you, but the vow of secrecy is even more sacred in this area. Or is it? No. I think my plans for the house would cause more of a row. Nevertheless, I still want to avoid fuss. I don't want a lot of talking, planning, more talk and more planning. You'll understand when I tell you. I'm engaged to Tommy." Mary D. looked very pleased with herself, but Emily could only half believe what she had just said.

"I know you've been seeing him, but I can't help remembering that a year ago you were begging me, bribing me, to keep you two apart."

"That was then. I judged him by past appearances. You remember how drippy he looked in his prep school clothes. The army's been good for him, I told you. He can hold his own. I'm impressed. In his outfit he's come up against all types and kinds, and he knows how to handle himself. He knows when to be prep school polite and when to be GI tough. And, most important of all, he's crazy about me."

"Why shouldn't he be? You're the biggest catch in town."

"Oh, it's not because I'm so gorgeous and because my father has so much money, if that's what you mean. He's crazy about me because we have the same plans for the future. And you know what? That's why I'm crazy about him"

"Explanation, please." It was Emily's turn to be impressed. She had no firm plans for the future other than finishing college, finding a job and, with luck, someone to marry.

"Look. You know that Peter isn't in the least interested in the business. Right? I don't think he'll change his mind. He doesn't have the temperament for it. So who will the business go to? Me? I'm a GIRL. Okay, now we come to Tommy. He's decided he doesn't want to be a lawyer just because his father wants him to. He wants to go into business, and, as far as he's concerned, he'd just as soon go into a business that's already established and making good money. So, my dear father will get a son-in-law he has to approve of—or risk offending the Van Vorsts and everybody else in Westerveldt. He will also get two young energetic partners in the bargain."

"You mean you?"

"Oh yes. Here's the way it will work out. Daddy will be senior partner and control half. Tommy and I will be junior partners and control the other half. But it's the two of us or no dice."

"How can you make him agree?"

"I'm thinking that out now. I can hear him, objection, objection. He'd be happy to have Tommy, as a lackey, on salary. That I'm sure of. But he'll expect me to stay home and have babies and give dinner parties. I refuse. I absolutely refuse. If I don't get to work at the Yard with reasonable responsibilities befitting my age and experience, then I take my ten thousand dollars and Tommy takes his savings and we go elsewhere and start our own business. Far, far away for ultimate revenge. I can also sell Grandmother's house to someone who will make a terrible neighbor. I've got my father where I want him."

"You'll never bring it off."

"Oh yes I will. I may not even have to threaten. Tommy's parents don't want him to leave Westerveldt, and he really doesn't want to leave. We are, nevertheless, in agreement. We're not going to stay in town if it means being bullied by our parents once we're married. We stay only if we can be independent and busy and do as we please. I mean, Genevieve Sloane is a sweet girl, but she doesn't even run her own house. Can you picture me living like that?"

Emily could not.

"Tommy doesn't know the latest development—about the will. We started making plans before I became an heiress. He knows I'm ready to go into business with him and make a life here, on our own terms. Wait till he hears the news. We've got it made."

"But no babies?"

"Sure babies. One anyway. But not until after we're established. Then I can have all the babies I want, but I can still work and I can afford someone to look after them."

"Your father won't like it."

"My father will have nothing to say about it. I will refuse to have any babies at all if I can't work. Then he won't have any grandchildren. Unless," Mary D. looked at Emily, "you think Peter will change his mind and decide not to become a priest."

"Who knows what Peter wants," Emily answered vaguely.

"I hope you don't think I'm trying to cramp your style," Mary D. said quickly. "You are my best friend and I wish you all the luck in the world, but I promise you, if you and Peter decide to get married, I'll beat you by ten minutes just to get that house."

"I can't say I blame you,' Emily answered. "Don't worry. I won't compete with you for your grandmother's house."

"What about Pete? Have you heard from him lately?"

"Two weeks ago. He seemed in good spirits." That was still how Peter was described—in good spirits or poor spirits.

"Mother got a letter yesterday. He still doesn't know about

Grandmother, of course. Mail takes forever. Daddy sent a telegram or a cable or whatever they send overseas, but we haven't had any answer yet. Does he ever write to you about his postwar plans? Are they still the same?"

"It's had to tell," Emily said. "It sounds as if he were doing whatever he has to do and waiting for the war to end. He isn't thinking ahead. Not like you and Tommy."

"Doesn't he say anything about being with you?"

"He says he wants to see me again. Sometimes he gets what might be called affectionate."

"My brother is a cold fish. Even if he is my brother. Didn't he ever try to . . . you know what I mean?"

"No. But he wouldn't with me. Not with our parents such friends."

"That never stopped Tommy. I guess that's why I fell in love with him. He's a free spirit. He doesn't let his family obligations keep him from being real."

"You mean . . ."

"Of course that's what I mean. You don't think I'd marry someone I hadn't tried out, do you?"

6

Emily

Alone that night in her room with Mary D.'s secrets, Emily tried to sort it all out. She was happy for her friend, she was sure of that, but she began to feel a little envious. Mary D. had it figured out. A husband, a life, even a career, a business. The past didn't weigh on her with all its donts and cants and shouldnts but was ready to serve her opportunities. And it couldn't be called plain luck. Another girl in Mary D.'s position might not have seen the opportunity. Another girl might have married someone she didn't love because her parents wanted to keep the house in the family, or another girl would have given up the house, taken the ten thousand and made a new life elsewhere. Mary D. was going to have her cake and eat it. She was also going to help run the lumberyard. Emily knew she would. Such a plan might never have occurred to someone else. It took Mary D. (perhaps dreaming and scheming with Tommy Van Vorst) to come up with a foolproof blueprint for getting her own way. Gus Van Leuven wouldn't like it at first, but he'd give in sooner or later and be proud of his daughter in the bargain. How could she lose? The biggest tangle would come when Mary D. started to remodel Augusta's house, but Emily didn't doubt that Mary D. would find a way of convincing her father. "She'll make apartments for the widows of Westerveldt or old couples who don't want to live in big houses any more. She'll think of something. She'll have everything, and she won't have to leave Westerveldt to find it."

"I have to give her credit. Why can't I think of some solution to my life?" Emily's mind churned, but no solid substance settled to its bottom. "What's here for me? I don't want to be an architect or a doctor or a lawyer. I don't know what I want to be, and I haven't got anyone to make plans with."

Peter, poor dear Peter. Did she want to be a minister's wife if Peter decided to forego celibacy? In Westerveldt? Living in the drafty old rectory the Gileses had complained about for so many years? That old house was one Mary D. would remodel with a vengeance. Or in some other town wherever Peter was called. A pastor's wife. Poor, except for the interest on the ten thousand. Could she herself work if she were a minister's wife? Or would she have to set a domestic example, have babies like Genevieve Sloane, visit the sick, worry about the altar flowers, type Peter's sermons and be polite and charitable at all times to all persons. Under those conditions, any town would be as confining as Westerveldt now was. But if Peter could decide to go into his father's business . . . that could be as exciting a life for her as for Mary D. No, Peter would probably turn out like his father and want his family and business lives separate. She might then have to entertain and run the house (whichever house), keeping up standards and doing all the things she didn't particularly like doing now.

Poor Peter. Dear Peter. No, it couldn't be. No joyful enthusiastic picture of life together spun itself out of her imagination. Quiet, gentle propriety and more of the same was all she could see. Nothing Peter had ever said or written gave her a hint of any other possibilities. He liked her liveliness, but he didn't have any of his own.

Emily ran down a mental list of other local young men. There wasn't anybody else in Westerveldt she could think of as marriageable. Never could she marry Mike Mancuso and go into the vegetable business. Even if he covered himself with glory on the battlefield and came home a four-star general, even if he learned to behave and speak properly. The future lay elsewhere and there was no way of knowing where or with whom. If, Emily reminded herself bitterly, there would be anyone left to marry.

The city. Of course, New York City. If there were jobs or careers or husbands to be found, a life to be shaped, it would be in the city which she already knew and felt comfortable in. Not so far away that she couldn't come home to visit her family ever so often. These were her first cheerful thoughts in the evening's self-examination, and she put herself to sleep dreaming about the career (newspaper work? graduate school? . . .) she would start studying for in earnest and the unknown man who would appear sooner or later. At the moment he was out in the war and wouldn't be home for a long time.

By one of those coincidental quirks that family life breeds, Katherine broached the same subject to her daughter that weekend. "It's high time you began to give thought to what you're going to do when you get out of college. You're going to have to earn a living somehow. Even if you get married, it might not be for a while. Besides, you don't want to be totally dependent upon your husband. You're too independent a girl. These days a woman has to know how to earn a living, married or not. You never know what can happen. You'll never make a bridge player or a Junior Leaguer. You'd better find something you like doing, something you can fall back on if times get hard. You don't remember the depression, but I do. It could happen again."

This was not the first time that Katherine had wondered aloud what Emily was going to do when she grew up, but it was the first time mother and daughter began to enter into a satisfactory dialogue on the subject. Emily said she was thinking of seeking her fortune in the city.

"That's not a bad idea at all," Katherine said. "There aren't many professional opportunities in Westerveldt. Not for a woman, anyway. Dr. Langley is a woman and Miss Howard is a lawyer, but they've had a long row to hoe to establish themselves. Your father would like it, of course, if one of you girls wanted to be an architect, but . . ."

"You don't have to say it, Mom. I can't draw a straight line, even with a ruler. If anyone's inherited Dad's talent, it's Bice."

"A woman architect would have a hard time facing the world alone. Half the job is getting along with the workmen. I think your father's idea of an assistant is someone who sits in the office and draws blueprints. Especially now that he does industrial buildings. No, I suspect Bice will have to think of other ways of using her talents. It's very irritating the way in which the world is divided up, but there isn't much we can do about it." Katherine seemed to know what she was talking about, even if she didn't say precisely why.

"Did you like working in Philadelphia before you were married?" Emily wanted to know.

Katherine's eyes gleamed. "I loved it. Busy, on the run all the time. That's how I met your father. My boss took me along to help design a living room and your father was there, helping his boss go over the structural changes. You know the story."

"Whenever you used to tell the story, I saw only the romance. The love at first sight."

"Oh, that it was," Katherine said. "He's almost as handsome now as he was then. What I really liked, though, was working with him. I saw us as a team. We worked well together, most of the time anyway, and certainly before your father decided to move back here and open his own practice."

"Then it all changed?"

"You came along. Then Bice. And what can I say? He likes me to help him out, but he doesn't like it when I take charge too much."

"You could have worked on your own, couldn't you?"

"Not here. I got tired of arguing. I've given advice here and there over the years—for nothing I might add. Wives in Westerveldt do not work. You know that."

"Does it have to be that way?"

"Maybe not forever," Katherine sighed, "but certainly for the time being. It doesn't have to be that way for you. Not if you think of a career that will keep you in the city. New York has even more possibilities than Philadelphia. You just have to know where to find them."

"I'll put my mind on it, starting right now," Emily vowed. "Maybe then I can stop being so depressed."

"Good girl." Katherine patted Emily's knee as she had for many years whenever they came to a meeting of minds. "Don't forget. Not only are there more jobs in the city, but there's also much more to do. I get in so rarely, but I get a lift every time I do."

"Why don't you come down more often this fall?" Emily suggested. "We can explore together."

"Why don't I? I'm beginning to like this idea. New York isn't far away at all. We'll always be here if you need us. You can come home whenever you like. We can come to see you. Or I can come in by myself if your father's busy. We could go shopping or take in a play or eat in a French restaurant. After you graduate and get a job, you'll be getting your own apartment. Would there be room for your poor old mother on your sofa? If she gave you the sofa?"

PART VII

1

D-Day

Then it happened. Everyone had been expecting it, predicting where it would take place and exactly when. "It'll have to be soon now," Ted Jr. had said on June first. "There are only a few good fighting months left. They won't want us bogged down in rain and then snow when we've barely started." Bogged down—the war had been bogged down for years. In December of 1943 the war was already four years old, if you counted back to 1938. Most Americans preferred to count back only to December of 1941 and Pearl Harbor, and those two years had been enough for them. Something had to be done to break out of the stalemate. High up in trans-Atlantic political and military circles, the necessary decisions had already been made and the comprehensive preparations begun, but even up to the night of June 5th, many Westerveldtians debated the pros and cons of a second front, an invasion, which would send thousands of men across the English Channel to sweep the continent clean of Hitler and the Nazi war machine, liberate France and all the other countries that had been occupied. America had helped out before in the Great War (now known as World War I since the new war had become the Great War or the Big War). The British and the French had held the lines for three years before the Americans arrived in 1917 and the Allies began a push to make the world safe for democracy in the war to end all wars.

Now, not much more than a quarter of a century later, the first war was no longer the distant past for those who had lived through it but a memory revived as the news reached the home front by radio and daily newspaper, as report followed report.

With the excitement came hope. Sooner or later, now, as before, the Allied armies would advance into the continent, head toward the heart of Germany, and the war would be over. People had been saying all along that it couldn't last forever, but now they had reason to mean it. Finally something was being done, and the terrible waiting had come to an end.

The fighting was being done thousands of miles away. Back in Westerveldt, few people would ever know what it was truly like and then only long afterwards. Paratroops, landing craft, lst U.S. Army, 2nd British Army, Omaha Beach, St. Malo, Caen, Cherbourg—words, names. Omaha Beach not even a real place but a military code name for a part of the Normandy coastline. Some of the French villages were so tiny their names didn't appear in home atlases, and people had to rely on newpaper maps to show them where those little dots were. Reality was suspended between two worlds. American soldiers were halfway around the world moving through lands they'd never seen, hearing languages they couldn't speak, to defend the country they'd left miles and miles away. Back home, even their relatives couldn't imagine what exactly they were doing. They were units in an abstract plan doing whatever it was they'd been trained for—even that reality was hard to visualize. No matter how many newspaper accounts anyone read, how many war movies one saw, he couldn't picture in his mind what was happening. Facts piled upon facts (were all those facts true? only history could set the record straight), numbers upon numbers, descriptions upon eye-witness accounts, but in no way could the reality of the invasion invade an American living room even through the words of commentators on the evening news or the photographs of soldiers packed into jeeps or lying dead on distant beaches.

There were still jobs to go to, dinner to be prepared and served, curtains to be laundered, dogs to be let out, new shoes to be bought (if there were ration coupons available), the chores and concerns of daily life. As the soldiers inched across northern France, Jacqueline

Sanford put the summer slipcovers on her living room furniture. Isobel Van Leuven wrote up a list of all the pieces of furniture, lamps, rugs, and bric-a-brac in her mother-in-law's house. Katherine Osterhoudt tried to streamline a week's menu by planning around seasonal foods. The excitement and the sense of hope made the chores go faster for many, as if getting through the day with the right attitude was a contribution to the war effort.

It was harder for others. Parents who knew where their sons were or could make a good guess that they were probably part of the invasion spent days and nights sleepwalking, afraid to conjecture, waiting for the next letter. They comforted themselves with well-worn phrases ("he's doing his duty for his country" "he was always a sensible boy—he'll know how to protect himself and stay safe"), waiting, deluding themselves that if somehow their son survived the invasion, he could then survive whatever lay ahead. Unreal— to have the scene of action so far away. In *War and Peace* the Russians knew they had been invaded; they suffered the war. The French were suffering this one. The British dodged bombs every night. Americans had to absorb the reality second or third hand, knowing, feeling, worrying, fretting, and then looking outdoors at the familiar reality of their trees unscathed overnight by machine gun or rifle fire, their streets empty of tanks and troops, marveling that anything could be happening if it was not happening before their eyes.

Ted Jr. and Bice drew to scale a large map of northwest Europe and on it Ted could pinpoint the movements of the armies. He'd drawn one of Poland in 1939, assuming the trenches would be dug on its western borders. He'd never expected *blitzkrieg* and Poland's total collapse. "Poland" now hung in his study as a reminder that history never repeats itself. He had no sons, but he could remember being a soldier in the first war, he could remember losing a brother and sharing his parents' grief, but his imagination could not encompass this war as it was being fought—new weapons, different tactics, no trenches. All he could do beyond working on his map was to share in the atmosphere of excitement and hope . . . and fear. This was a job that had to be done—hadn't Winston Churchill used just such an image? For some the job meant dying.

Ted was the first to know. It was considered his prerogative to bring the Westerveldt *Herald* in from the front porch when he came home from the office and he read it as he waited for dinner to be served. Every night he opened the paper, studied the headlines and lead paragraphs of the war news and looked for the casualty list. Ted was not morbid, nor was he obsessed with the war; if anything he felt it his duty to be informed as he doggedly kept absorbing any news there was for him to know about.

That night in the last week in June when he read the name, he was shocked. "Michael Francis Mancuso, son of Mr. and Mrs. Joseph Mancuso, reported missing in action and presumed dead." He'd known the Mancusos since he was a little boy and his mother had sent him "over town" on errands. Old Mrs. Mancuso had frequently pinched his cheek and given him a peach. Her English was heavily accented and he didn't always understand what she said. In the afternoon she usually smelled of garlic, but she was a kindly soul. Ted had never liked Joe, her son, very much, for no reason he could put his finger on, but they always greeted each other. Jeannette, his sister, was friendly, like her mother. Until Nelly had given up shopping at the store, the two families had been in daily contact with each other for fifty years, even before Ted had been born. Dead. Mike Mancuso added to the roll of Westerveldtian young men who had given their lives for their country.

Ted's year-long feeling of annoyance with the Mancusos vanished as soon as he saw the name. Mike had presumed. Emily had let him. She had gone out with him and been seen in public with him, but no social transgression exacted this price. They would probably have forgotten about each other eventually anyway. He got up from his chair and went into the kitchen where Katherine was peeling potatoes and wordlessly handed the paper to her.

"Oh, no," she cried, dropping knife and half-peeled potato into the sink. "Does Emily know? Did you tell her?"

"I think she's upstairs. I just got the paper. You tell her. I can't." And he couldn't. There was no predicting Emily's reactions and moods these days.

Katherine found Emily changing into clam diggers after her day at the sweater factory. "I have some bad news," she tried to begin.

Emily was hot and tired after the bike ride home and feeling sulky besides. "Now what?" she asked. Give it to me. I'm ready for it.

Katherine took her measure and wished she could go back to her potato. "It's Mike Mancuso. He's been reported missing in action and presumed dead." She was ready to comfort Emily, to put her arms around her and let her cry as much as she liked. Emily picked up a box of Kleenex, luckily nearly empty, and flung it across her bedroom, knocking down a lamp. "Goddammit all to hell!" she roared. She sounded just like her grandfather.

Katherine picked up the lamp and the Kleenex box, eyeing her daughter. "Stop it!" she said sharply. "Stop it at once. No tantrums."

At that familiar word out of her second-grade past when she couldn't get her spelling assignment straight, Emily threw herself on the bed and began to scream. Katherine closed the door behind her as she went to warn Ted and Beatrice to leave Emily alone until she came to her senses. The screaming stopped before it got any louder and there was no sound at all from the room.

Her feet on the pillow, her head at the foot of the bed, Emily found one violent emotion after another rising into her consciousness so fast her mind didn't have time to define them. Horror, outrage, sorrow, rage against the world and the war. A hole in the world where Mike had been. Another hole. All that letter writing. Writing couldn't keep her friends alive. How many now? Don't count. You're not the only one. Remember that. Who are you to carry on? You're not his girl or his sister. He was just a friend and for a few weeks you got a little closer. He kissed you. Think of his mother and his grandmother. His grandmother thought he was wonderful. The rage wouldn't go down. Why do they do this to us? Any of us? Not just me. We wait and we wait and then we find out they're dead. We could pray all we wanted but that wouldn't save them. When it's time for them to get killed, they get killed. They leave holes in the world, and now the world is full of holes.

By the time Mary D. called that evening, Emily was calm again. "It's tough," Mary D. said. "I couldn't believe it when I read it. Good old Mikey. I've known him since he used to pull my pigtails. How you holding up?"

"I'm okay, I guess." Emily tried to explain herself. "I'm mad and sad at the same time."

Mancuso's shut for a week. A sign in the window announced the reason. A requiem mass was held in Mike's memory at St. Peter's, and Emily attended, sitting inconspicuously in the back, unable to look at Mike's parents, brothers, sisters, his grandmother, uncles, aunts, and cousins as they came up the aisle after the service. She sent a condolence card to the family. The big surprise came when Mancuso's opened for business on Monday and Grandmamma was an early customer. She held old Mrs. Mancuso's hand in both of hers and told her how sad she was to hear about Michael. He had always been such a sweet, polite boy.

2

Swimming

"Swimming, what else?" Mary D. declared on the phone to Emily. "It's hot as hell and tomorrow is the Fourth of July. We gotta celebrate somehow. The Kill is cleaner over by your place, at least it was the last time I looked. I'll bike over, and we'll go from there."

"Why not? I can escape the ball game and cool off at the same time. The lawn got mowed this morning, and I've already taken a bath and washed my hair, but for you anything. Bice wanted me to go hiking with her, but I begged off so she's gone with Bert and Billy to explore the end of Greene Avenue. You know, where it turns into a meadow. The place where the new golf course is supposed to be if the war ever ends. For all her complaining, she's a busy bee."

"Busy bee Bice," laughed Mary D.

"That's a good one, but we'd better not repeat it. She's very touchy these days."

"How come?"

"I think, Mother thinks, it's because she's going off to boarding school in less than two months. She said 'nothing to do' once too often, although I think they would have sent her anyway. It's a refrain. Nothing to do, nothing to do. Mother piles on the chores, and there's still nothing to do. She goes out with Bert and Billy nearly every day, and there's nothing to do. She went to a movie with them the other night, and there was still nothing to do. I never got to go to a movie with Men while I was home, but my mother has relaxed her high moral standards. Either she trusts

Bice more than she did me (and I can't understand why although I'm sure she'd be glad to tell me) or else she figures there's safety in numbers. With both Bert and Billy how can she get into trouble?"

"We won't go into that," Mary D. giggled, "but two more harmless boys I've never met. Maybe they just seem harmless because they're younger than I am. So we go to let our hair down in the muddy waters of the Wester Kill and spend half of the glorious Saturday night ahead of us scrubbing it out."

They biked over to the same part of the creek bank where Emily had gone swimming with Peter. Mary D. brought up Mike, not Peter.

"He was such a devil, so quick with the sharp crack. Westerveldt isn't going to seem the same without old Mikey to liven it up."

"How can Westerveldt ever seem the same again?" Emily asked petulantly. "When the war's over, we won't recognize it."

"You're in a sour mood," Mary D. appraised her friend. "What's eating you? Mikey?"

"I guess." Emily wasn't sure what it was. "I was doing fairly well until that happened. I was beginning to put my mind on my life. Now I can't."

"No connection as far as I can see. Mikey wasn't part of your life. Really. Was he?"

"No, not really. But you can't see someone as often as I saw him without his becoming more special than someone you don't know very well. We wrote letters. He was part of home."

"Ah yes. That he was. In the broadest sense of the term. I wonder what he would have done after the war. Did he ever say?"

"Some. Not much. Once he mentioned higher education as if it were a duty worse than the army, a necessary evil. That's a good business his family has. Maybe he would have stuck with that."

"We'll never know. We have to deal with what is, not with maybes and what-ifs. As Daddy says, we must keep our eye on the ball."

Emily wanted to come back with, "That's easy for you to say. You've got Tommy and you've got plans and it'll probably work out for you," but her affection for her friend and her sense of justice forced her to admit that no matter what happened, Mary D. would land on her feet. She had her father's drive or whatever it was that made her see success in life as the only road before her. If any of the features of that topography were erased by chance, she would pave new ones, or, if necessary, choose another road altogether if the one she was on became too arduous to travel. For all her tomfoolery and rebelliousness, she was good-natured, thanks to her mother's softening influence (or so Katherine put it). She was no female version of Gus, not vain or arrogant or selfish. She would run roughshod over people only if she had to. So instead Emily said, "I wish I had your optimism."

Then, after a minute, she added, "You know what I think. What's upset me is that Mike had so much life in him. He was strong and tough. But the war got him. Like you can't win. Like it's not worth trying. You can try to make your future, but they'll get you . . ."

"In the end!" Mary D. laughed uproariously at the joke they'd both made a hundred times.

Emily was too morose to laugh.

"Come on, kiddo. I was only horsing around. You know who you remind me of right now?" Mary D. turned serious and stared at Emily when she didn't answer. "My brother, my brother whom I dearly love. Brooding, letting it get to you. Thinking too much about what it all means. It doesn't mean anything, not that I can figure out. It's just happening."

Emily was stung. Tact prevented her from snapping, "I'm not as bad as Peter," and into her mind rushed the memory of that afternoon a year ago when they had sat on the same creek bed, not ten feet away from where she and Mary D. were now lolling, and accused Peter of doing what, she had to admit to herself, she was herself now doing. At that time Emily had jabbed at Peter, trying to awaken a spark of life in him, lending him her energy. Here was Mary D. doing the same thing to her.

"You're right," she said finally. "Let's swim off my rotten mood." It had worked with Peter, why not with her?

They couldn't decide while they were drying off in the sun whether the Kill was getting dirtier or not.

"It starts off clear enough up in the mountains," Mary D. said. "About ten miles from the Lodge it's a crystal-clear brook.

Where does it pick up all this mud as it babbles along? My father says it wasn't this dirty when he used to swim in it."

"Mine too. Now that you mention the Lodge, how come you're not up there this weekend swimming in clean, cold water? It's the Fourth of July. Not like your family to stay in town."

"We haven't been up since I've been home, and I don't know why. I don't ask because I'm no longer eager to go and spend my days thinking of things to say to Marianne Callendar and the rest of the younger set. Mummy hasn't suggested going. It's different since Grandmother died. Maybe toward the end of the summer."

"My grandparents are celebrating their fiftieth wedding anniversary next month. My grandmother's been dreaming for ten years of having a grand party, but since your grandmother died, she hasn't mentioned it. I guess she feels she's losing her friends the way we're losing ours. No time for parties."

"Now that's worse than too bad. Fifty years is a long time. They have every right to whoop it up. They can't help it if other people fell by the wayside."

"That's not quite the way my parents put it, but they agree. They're going to give them a party anyway, but they're plotting in secret with Bice and me. They, what can I say, aren't eager to spend the next six weeks discussing the plans with Grandmamma. She frets so. They're making the arrangements, and then they'll tell her after the first of the month so she'll have enough time to buy a new dress but not enough time to . . . well, you know."

"Is it going to be a three generation party? I mean, will we be called upon to fill the gaps left in the older generation?"

"That's what my mother has in mind. If they stick to the octogenarians, it would be a small gathering."

"The history of Westerveldt. Hey, make it four generations and invite the Sloane baby. Then we can see all the changes in a row."

"The changes upset me. The changes around me and the changes in me." Emily tried to explain herself. "I'm afraid I'm not going to fit in. I don't think I'll even want to try."

"You'll find a way. You're not through school yet. You've got two more years. Something will occur to you."

"I can't think of what I could do here. I know I'm not going to become a school teacher."

"God forbid. If you think all eyes are on you now, can you imagine what teachers go through? I'll bet they think twice before they wear a red blouse. No, pal, you're not thinking right. You have to think ahead. Number One—transportation. Now we have bikes in good weather, or we take buses, or our parents drive us, or we walk. There's a war on. No gas, no place to go. The war ends—we get cars! Then we can go anywhere we want and it won't be so dull. Every place will be more lively. Number Two—a town can't stagnate. Come peace and who knows what will happen. There will be what Daddy calls new enterprises. Maybe even, isn't it possible?, new people."

"I like your positive attitude," Emily began to mull over hopeful rather than hopeless changes. "I've thought, perhaps, that I might stay in the city and find a job there. At least, I was beginning to think until . . ."

Mary D. interrupted her from going backward. "You could do worse. You're not that far away if you want to visit. But you'll be consigned to perdition. You'll be living in your own apartment. And you know what that means. Wait and see. Maybe I could find a place for you at the Yard. It'll boom when the war's over and we can get stuff again. Building will take off."

"Don't you think your father will have his hands full with you and Tommy?" Time out for a chuckle.

"For sure. But that's just an example. You have to keep your ears to the ground."

"I used to think of Westerveldt as familiarity and safety. Now all I see is gloom and loss and sad changes."

"That's life, friend. The old order changeth, yielding place to the new. And God fulfills himself in many ways lest one good custom should corrupt the world."

"Don't tell me college is getting to you?"

"Father Wadsworth, silly. You weren't listening Sunday. He was quoting from *Idylls of the King*. I looked it up when I got home. Good old Bartlett."

3

Peter

What can be said about grief? It's almost rude to try to describe how people feel when they lose someone close to them. There is probably no more private emotion much as people try to relieve their anguish, much as they struggle to find words to release it from their breasts. The very power of grief is unutterable—a cry, a keening consecrates it best. The mouth moves, sounds come out, but not everyday speech too vulgar for what has to be expressed. Keening, however, belongs to those who have not come into the twentieth century, who stick to the old ways that may go back several millennia. We have our platitudes, our pat phrases of condolence—"So sorry to hear the bad news"—which convey not much more than good will toward the bereaved. Those who grieve are no longer permitted to beat their breasts and tear at their hair and garments. As soon as they get out of hand, there are sedatives to make them sleep with the shock, to send it deep inside the soul where it will be buried like a thorn, forever.

Isobel had no sooner said to Gus and Mary D., "I can't imagine the rest of my life without Peter," then she was ushered off to bed and forced to sip two hefty spoonsful of a syrup Dr. McCullough had said should do the trick. Mary D. kissed her mother fondly on the forehead, put her arms around her for a goodnight hug, and went down to the living room. Gus knew he had to say something comforting, but he didn't know what other than, "We'll live through it somehow," before he gave her a quick kiss and joined his daughter. The wicked telegram was still clutched in Isobel's hand, her last physical link to her dead son. Lost at sea when his ship was hit by a Japanese bomber. Soon sleep came, forgetfulness for the time being, the pain to be faced again and again every day for the rest of her life—a life without that wonderful, handsome boy, the one person who had truly understood and loved her.

Gus and Mary D. didn't have much to say to each other. There was little they could say, so they addressed practical matters. They must begin to tell relatives and friends. Mary D. had a suggestion.

"I can't make a lot of calls to tell people. I know I'll break down, but I could call one person and ask that person to help, to make calls for me. It should be someone who doesn't have a son in the service and someone who can be calm. I thought of Mrs. Osterhoudt, but Emily is going to be very upset. What do you think about Mrs. Sanford? Aunt Jacqueline? She's a good friend and she's very nice. She'd do it for us, wouldn't she, Daddy?"

Gus thought for a moment. He didn't like to consider that the Van Leuvens couldn't do their own dirty work, but he usually left social obligations to Isobel. Mary D. was being strong, she hadn't broken down, but if he asked too much of her, she might. She was only eighteen and she had loved her brother very much.

"Why not? It's a good idea. You can tell her that your mother had to be put to bed. Perhaps she and Genevieve, Swinton, not the little mother, can pass the word along. Tell her we'll have a memorial service in a week or so, as soon as your mother is well enough to attend. I'd better get busy on a notice for the paper."

Mary D. called Jacqueline and was much touched by the warmth of her sympathy and her soft gentle voice that somehow said just the right words. Of course she'd telephone; it was the least she could do. "People will ask, dear, whether you want visitors or not. What should I tell them? To wait until the weekend, do you think? Or get it over with?"

"Would it be too much, Aunt Jacqueline, to have them keep in touch with you? Her friends may turn out to be a comfort for Mummy. She may find she needs a little company, but it's too soon to tell if she's up to it. It's hard for all of us, but it's hardest for her. My heart breaks for her."

"I know, dear." Jacqueline began to cry herself. "We must help her through it, but it will take a long time, I'm afraid. There is no worse sorrow than losing a child. We expect our children to outlive us. Remember, she has you, and you will be doubly precious to her now."

Jacqueline had not expected phoning to be easy, but as she repeated her news, first to her sister and then to her daughter and had to share their reactions, the enormity of the truth began to take hold of her. When she called Katherine Osterhoudt, Emily answered the phone.

"Hello, Emily, dear, this is Jacqueline Sanford," she began. Then before she could bring herself to make a statement that might prepare Emily for the shock to come, her courage left her and she prudently asked to speak to Katherine.

Katherine said, "Oh, no. How terrible. Isobel, poor Isobel. She must be devastated. And Gus, so soon after he lost his mother. And Mary D.—that poor family!"

Emily, lingering near the phone, divined instantly what the news was. She did not go into a rage as she had when she'd heard about Mike. Instead she started to weep for Peter, for Mike, for all her dead friends, but especially for Peter, so handsome, tall, brave, and so very vulnerable, as if he were there waiting to be killed.

In the weeks that followed, Mary D. didn't know what to do with her spirit. She had channeled it into mischief and rebellion for so many years that mischief had become an instinct, or at least a reflex action. With her grandmother's death and the possession of a little fortune, she had begun to make plans in which rebellion played only a minor role. She had Tommy on her side, and the two of them together, with financial backing insured, could work their way around their parents. Mary D. knew that sooner or later her father would be pleased with her. Now, as she tried to recover from the shock of Peter's death, her plans seemed selfish to her. How could she write gay conspiratorial letters to Tommy outlining how they could outwit their elders and get what was, in truth, rightfully theirs? How could she envision a happy, busy, productive, and challenging future for herself when her brother would have none at all? She wanted him to come back so she could give him her schemes for his own, so he could plan a future for himself the way he wanted it. She couldn't bear to profit from his death (Grandmother's had been another story). Whenever she started to go back and dream, she would start crying all over again, as if her dreams were being built on Peter's fate. She knew better, but she missed Peter so much that she was afraid to think of any possibility of happiness for herself. The energy was there, and the impulse, but not the will.

Luckily she could still work at the Yard, even if she no longer dared covet it. It cannot be said that she went about her chores with humility, but with new soberness and efficiency, as if the Yard mattered more than she did. Working—filing and answering the phone—kept her out of the house where her poor mother languished, not able to come back from the limbo of the soul where she was joined with Peter.

Isobel couldn't put her mind on dinner menus or redecorating the living room or disposing of her mother-in-law's surplus possessions. She went through the day half awake, half in her private zone where all was still well, where she could talk to Peter in her mind and hear his dear voice answering, telling her to be patient, to be her gentle self, to forgive the world's wickedness. She could talk only to Peter. To Gus, she was polite, affectionate, and matter of fact. She no longer heard his outbursts. As for Mary D., she was grateful for her presence in the house as another familiar emanation, but there was no conversation between them. Mary D. began to suspect that her mother had withdrawn from the everyday world, and she didn't know how to bring her back. The sweet, sad half-smile told her everything she needed to know. Maybe her mother was happier where she was, maybe it was only a temporary vacation from reality that she needed to get over the grotesque blow to her psyche. Maybe, with time. Whenever she was home, Mary D. petted her mother, paid her extra attention, and let her physical presence, reading a book in the living room instead of upstairs alone, stand for everything she couldn't do to share her mother's state of mind.

With her father, life began to return to normal. On the rides down to the Yard and back, Gus discussed business (or those aspects of his business he thought it safe for her to know—he never told anybody everything or he might lose his advantage) or the latest war news, accepting the war as a fact and not as an enemy that had shattered his family. He rarely mentioned Isobel. He was kinder to his wife, for she was still his wife, and in his own way, for better or worse, he cherished her. When he mentioned Peter to Mary D., he would sometimes get churlish. "Damned shame. Out there in the Pacific, in the middle of nowhere" and behind his words would be the unspoken thought that somehow Peter was responsible for having been where he was at the wrong time. If he'd had more get up and go, the Japanese bomber would never have hit his ship.

4

Mary D. and Emily

It was a while before Mary D. could face being with Emily. The closeness between them made it harder rather than easier to talk. With her parents, wordlessness came easy; with her friend, there was no point. They met by accident one Saturday as Mary D. was coming out of Mancuso's with a summer squash her father wanted for supper. They were both delighted—arranging a meeting would have been awkward for both of them. Being thrown together was what they both needed to bridge the new shyness between them.

"Let's have a hot fudge sundae and say the hell with the calories," Mary D. said in her old "Let's because we shouldn't" tone. Not to the Sweet Shoppe where the high school kids would be spending the afternoon in noisy syrup but to the genteel Ice Cream Parlor that serviced all generations and saw a great deal of Sarah Catsby on her way to the movies on hot summer afternoons.

"How are you holding up, old chum?" Mary D. asked. "It sure has been tough."

"Lousy," Emily agreed. "Triple lousy. What can you do? How is everything in your house? My mother talks about you all the time."

"She's been very nice to my mother, your mother has. She drops by every couple of days in the afternoon, just to sit with Mummy. It helps. If anything can. How's work?"

"Something to do until school starts. What else? I read in the evenings. I can't listen to the radio. It hurts."

"Know what you mean. Do you think we'll ever start living again?"

"Sooner or later. Probably later. It'll help to get back to school. Among our own kind. Then we can giggle or be silly and not feel out of place. Work through it all in our own way together. My mother means well, but I've had all the middle-aged wisdom I can take. It may keep her going, but it drives me nuts. To tell you the truth, Mary D., this whole damned war makes me furious."

"You're right." Mary D. gooed the whipped cream and the fudge into a revoltingly tempting rippled mess. "It's a goddamned waste. Why can't they get it over with? They keep killing and killing. You'd think they'd get sick of it."

"What do you hear from Tommy?" Just because Peter and Mike were gone, there was no reason not to let Tommy Van Vorst have his life before him.

"He's in luck. I think, anyway. They've got him doing something at the base. I can't figure out what, but they may keep him stateside and not far from me. And safe, for the time being. I told you, he's no dope. He must have made himself indispensable in some way. He doesn't talk about it, and, under the circumstances, I don't ask. I'm glad he'll be nearby. I need him, and I wouldn't be surprised if he needed me."

"I'm glad." Emily truly was. "Do you have the same old plans?"

"Sure, why not? They're good plans no matter what happened." She couldn't bring herself to mention Peter's name and changed the subject abruptly. "Poor old lady Mancuso looks awful. She's got furrows down her cheeks as if she cried herself to sleep every night. She has six grandsons, but Mike was her pet. Someone told me he looked like her husband when he was young back in the old country."

Emily couldn't bring herself to mention Mike's name or Peter's, but she felt as she were betraying them. "Rotten," she said.

"How about a walk when we finish this glop? I'm supposed to come straight home with the squash. Daddy loves creamed summer squash, can you imagine? And I have to eat a small portion just like I was still six. But maybe if I take my time it will be too late for Essie to make it."

"I'll walk you halfway home, very slow. I'll turn around before we get to St. Andrew's. With what we just put away, you won't have room for squash anyway."

As they passed the Sloane house on Brunswick, they looked toward the backyard and saw a baby carriage swathed in mosquito netting and Genevieve on a chaise longue beside it.

"Why not?" Mary D. asked. "I've never seen the baby up close, and I'm sure Genevieve is dying of boredom on a day like today. There's no sign of Bill."

"Me either. I don't think I've been up close to a baby in five years. But let's be quiet about it. If we wake it up, it'll start to yowl. My mother says it's got the eyes, Genevieve's and her mother's, but that otherwise it looks like Charley Sloane."

"I'll bet Charley was good-looking as a boy," Mary D. speculated. "I take a shrewd look at him when he comes in the Yard. He's kinda weatherbeaten, but you can see the good looks underneath." Both girls chuckled. All was not lost. Mary D. could still spot 'em.

Genevieve was happy to see them. She was indeed very bored. Bill was out for the afternoon helping his handsome father choose fittings for the new kitchenettes in the Vinson house, as if Bill's marriage had given him access to superior taste in hardware. She made them tiptoe over to the carriage and peek silently through the netting at little Jacqueline sleeping behind her closed lovely eyes. Then they moved across the lawn so they could talk without disturbing her.

"It's too hot to make anything elaborate for dinner," Genevieve said, as if the heat explained her absence from the kitchen. "I'm going to throw together a big salad and Bill's bringing cold cuts. His mother brought me over a berry pie for dessert. You wouldn't want a piece now, would you? She's a terrific baker. Better than the Woman's Exchange."

"We just finished hot fudge sundaes," Emily declined. "I think we've sinned enough for one day."

"Sundaes! I haven't had one in years." Genevieve was half wistful at the memory and half superior as a matron who no longer chased youthful indulgences. "At the Sweet Shoppe?"

"The Parlor," Emily and Mary D. said together. They all three understood about the inappropriate noise at the Sweet Shoppe.

"I haven't seen you since the memorial service," Genevieve began, knowing she had to say something about Peter. "How are your parents? My mother says Aunt Isobel is still very sad."

"It'll be a while," Mary D. said non-committally. Had everyone in town observed how much her mother had changed? Did they hold out hope?

"I can't get over it myself," Genevieve said. "There'll never be anyone like Peter. If I hadn't fallen in love with Bill, I know I would have fallen in love with Peter." As if Emily were not there.

"We all miss him," Mary D. said. Genevieve had married Bill and forfeited all rights to proprietary grief.

"How's motherhood treating you?" Emily asked before there was more talk of Peter.

"She's darling. We both love her to shreds. But it's a lot of work taking care of a baby. Sometimes I wonder how I get through the day. My mother has been an angel and so has Bill's mother and Aunt Genny. I don't know how I could have managed without them. So much to do. My mother says I can't have another one for at least a year and a half."

There was an embarrassed silence as Emily and Mary D. wondered exactly what she meant. Being unmarried, they couldn't merely ask.

"Does she cry a lot?" Emily asked.

"Only when she's hungry. She sleeps most of the night now so we can get our beauty rest. We don't have to think just about her all night long."

The three women sat a little longer on the grass and smoked cigarettes until Mary D. remembered the squash. Out on Brunswick, neither would speak first. Finally Mary D. could hold it in no longer and gave Emily her famous old evil sidelong glance.

"Christ! And in spades. Heavens protect me, and you too. Can you imagine ending up like that?"

"Not in a million years. Is that what they teach them at Smith?"

"That's Genevieve. You couldn't ask for a nicer girl. Right? Right. But just looking at her puts me to sleep. I wonder what Peter saw in her."

"She's gorgeous, that's what. Which you and I will never be. We're just pretty." Don't talk about Peter, please.

"A woman ought to be able to get married and have a baby and still have some life in her."

Emily thought of her mother, energetic, alert, and very efficient, but then she thought of Isobel Van Leuven whose spirit Gus could never reach again to crush. There was no answer.

"I'm certainly going to try." Mary D. was thinking of her mother with more sadness than she could bear.

They parted in front of St. Andrew's next to the sign that announced the topic for Sunday's sermon, "Warriors for Christ," averting their eyes from unpleasant reminders of war, both of them pleased that they had made contact with each other and not hurt each other's feelings. Perhaps soon they could begin to chat like old times.

5

Emily and Bice

"I've done the towels and the sheets. Now I suppose you're going to make me do the socks." Emily had folded the last piece of linen onto a neat pile and stood, needle in hand, over her sister.

"Please, sis. You make much smaller stitches than I do. I'm never going to get them done. It isn't worth all the trouble."

"You wouldn't say that if you knew what could happen to your laundry. Sew your name on anything you ever want to see again or you won't."

"Half of me can't wait to get away and the other half is scared to go," Beatrice confessed.

"You'll be glad. You've been saying for two years you couldn't wait to go. Now you're nearly off. It'll be a change."

"I think they want me to go," Beatrice whispered although her parents were both downstairs. "They want to get rid of me."

"They want to get rid of both of us, if I can read the signals," Emily hazarded. "We complain too much. I overheard Mother on the phone the other day with Jacqueline Sanford, Mrs. Too-Long-On-The-Telephone, talking about adolescent turmoil. That is us—turmoil."

"And they want peace and quiet so we can take our turmoil elsewhere." Beatrice tried to reason it out. "So I'll be with other girls in turmoil and we can be in turmoil together."

"Beats arguing. If you stayed home, you wouldn't have much freedom anyway. You'll write, won't you, Bice?"

"That's what I wanted to ask you about. I don't mind being

Bice at home. I'm used to it in the family, but I don't want all those strangers calling me Bice. What do I do?"

"Keep it a deep dark secret. Never let anyone know. When I write, I'll only write Beatrice."

"Will they pronounce it Bee-triss? I hate that."

"Beats being called Em. That was my boarding school nickname. I felt like Aunt Em in the Wizard of Oz. They give everybody nicknames, and sooner or later one sticks. Just pray it's one you can stand. They first tried to ring changes on Osterhoudt, but the only one that worked was Toasty, and then they seemed to prefer Em."

"Will I hate it? Once I'm there I can't come home. Especially with all that sacrifice talk downstairs."

"You won't hate it. I can't guarantee you'll love it, but it isn't that bad and you get used to being on your own. You get used to being alone."

"Alone, with all those girls?"

"You're all alone. But you'll make pals. Some of them might even turn out to be friends. Take your time. Remember that anything you tell anybody will be all over the dorm in no time, so don't tell anybody anything you don't want everybody to know. Watch your mail. If you get letters from Bert or Billy, hide them. It's a goldfish bowl. They capitalize on every little thing. There isn't all that much else to do."

"Now you're scaring me."

"You'll get used to it. College isn't that bad because there's so much more to do, and you can escape the dorms. But girls are girls and they want to know your business whether you like it or not. How many pairs of socks are you taking, anyway?"

They continued to chat and sew name tapes on countless articles, closer in mood and frankness than they had been in years now that they were about to be separated. There would be more to share as Beatrice ventured outside Westerveldt and began her own growing up. Emily gave her all the advice she could think of, cautions to avoid slights and pain, what teachers to watch out for, which rules could be broken without too many repercussions and which were crimes.

"Whatever you do, don't smoke. Ever."

"I don't smoke. You know that."

"Neither did I until I got to school. They taught me how. Then the big game is sneaking a cigarette. I did it a few times to be part of the crowd, but it's not worth it. But it's more popular than putting pancake makeup on your legs and running an eyebrow pencil up your calf so you look like you've put on stockings for dinner. For the stocking game, they just bawl you out. Get caught with a pack of cigarettes, and it's home in disgrace."

"You're kidding."

"Unless it's changed in three years. Smoking is the big crime. Only sneaking out, especially if a boy is involved, is worse."

"You said Mary D. tried it at her school."

"You're not Mary D. and neither am I. She can talk herself out of any mess she gets into. She probably said she was sleepwalking."

"Will Mary D. be at the party? Mary D. and her family?"

"The party for Grandmamma and Granddaddy? I guess so. I know they've been asked. It'll depend on how Mrs. Van Leuven feels, I guess. Why do you ask?"

"Maybe I can pick up some more tips from her."

"Just don't let her corrupt you. She was a holy terror in school."

They heard the doorbell and then their Mother's footsteps. In a minute Katherine called upstairs. "Letter, Emily. On the newelpost."

The handwriting was unfamiliar, round, neat, and strong. The return address frightened her. Michael Mancuso, APO, etc. etc. Oh no, his last letter before . . . She didn't want to open it.

"Let me," Beatrice said. "It won't upset me the way it will you. You can't not open it."

Dear Emily, Beatrice read aloud. Before you flip your lid, let me inform you that this letter is being dictated to a very beautiful nurse since my arm is in a big bandage and can't be used until further notice. She, my beauti-ful nurse, whose name is Barbara, had promised to write down everything I say no matter what I say. I am no longer dead. I'm here in a hospital. I can't tell you where, but everybody speaks English, no frogs or krauts. I got winged and passed out, and they didn't find me for days. Unfortunately, I can't tell you all the gory details without giving aid and comfort to the enemy. When they couldn't find me, they figured I was part of an explosion that blew pieces of soldier all over the map and so they set about informing my family that I had gone to my reward. The world does not get rid of Michael Mancuso that easy. I'm still among the living and intend to stay that way. There are too many mountains to climb and too many lovely ladies to . . .

"Give me that." Emily snatched the letter from Beatrice.

"I was only trying to help." Beatrice was ready to cry.

"I'm sorry. I'm sorry. Honest, I'm sorry." Fear had turned to joy and joy had quickly become another fear—that Mike's helpful, beautiful nurse was about to pen words that Beatrice should never read or the whole family would soon know what Mike was capable of. A year at boarding school would bring more discretion.

Katherine heard the shrieks and came upstairs.

"Are you upset? Don't read it if it upsets you. Throw it out."

Emily laughed as she cried. "He's alive! He's not dead!. They made a mistake. He's in the hospital, but he's not dead and he's going to be all right. I can't believe it. He's not dead!"

"Thank God for that," Katherine prayed. "What does he say?"

"That he has a beautiful nurse named Barbara," said Beatrice.

Katherine laughed. "I guess we should thank God for that too." Even Emily laughed as Beatrice dared, "Does that mean that Grandmamma will stop shopping at Mancuso's again?"

"We'll tell her about Barbara," Emily said. She was too happy to take offense.

She went to her room to finish reading the letter in private. Barbara had kept her promise to write whatever she was told.

. . . lead down the primrose path. They say my arm will take a couple of months to heal, but that I should be as good as new and be able to pull triggers or pinch female flesh as much as I want . . .

"Yuk," Emily groaned.

. . . It's been an adventure, I can tell you. The wound was infected and it was touch and go for a while. But now my mother knows I'm okay so she can stop praying for the repose of my soul. It must have been a rough time for her and Grandma too. How about you? Did you cry for me? Barbara says I shouldn't have asked you that. So I lie here on my bed of pain and wonder what to say next. How is the old home town? Did I have a nice funeral? Write and tell me all about it. Mr. Lucky still has something to remember you by. Keep those gorgeous legs in shape till I return and we'll make up for lost time. I ain't dead, lady, and don't you forget it . . . Love ya' Mike. P.S. Barbara says she's glad it's my right arm.

6

The Party

The party couldn't be a complete surprise or it would be more of a shock. Although Ted and Katherine had planned for several months to give Nelly and Ted Sr. a grand reception for their fiftieth wedding anniversary, they had held back discussing arrangements. The sad news in the Van Leuven household, two deaths so close together, had curbed everyone's enthusiasm for festivities. On August first, however, the time had come to tell the elder Osterhoudts that they were to be honored on the twenty-first. Nelly demurred, but not for long. Her dream would come true, and much as she had pictured herself as the prime organizer, it was with relief that she turned that role over to the younger generation. The family had gathered on Nelly's back porch.

"We thought you'd like to have it here in your garden, Mother . . ." Katherine proceeded slowly, carefully, and with great tact. "But you're not to worry about a thing. Crosby and Ted and the girls will make sure that everything—the lawn, the shrubs, the flowers—is in perfect condition. And we're arranging, if you think it's a good idea, to have a big canopy put up over there near the lilacs. If it rains, the guests can take shelter and still enjoy the outside. That way you won't have all those people trooping through the house. We have help coming in for the day, and they'll make the sandwiches in our kitchen. We'll bring them over here at the last minute. Ted will make the punch in your pantry. You and Dad won't have to do anything but rest in the morning and take your time getting dressed after lunch."

Such a capsule description was not quite slow and careful enough for Nelly and had to be repeated in fragments and details several times. The canopy was a sensible idea—it had worked well at Peggy Van Vorst's reception several years before—in the event of rain or, for that matter, too hot sun. It would be better situated between the pear tree and the ferns even if that location meant more of a trip to take things out. The idea that her kitchen would be used to store food and not prepare it disturbed her at first.

"I think I would like to make some of my little party cakes. The kind I make for the Garden Club parties. I can whip them up the day before and keep them in the larder overnight so they won't dry out."

Katherine and Ted exchanged glances. They had ordered, as a surprise, a wedding cake with gold trimmings, but they knew without having to say so that Nelly had to show her friends that she was still a remarkable cook.

"That would be lovely, Mother," Katherine said, "if you promise not to tire yourself out. Would you like the girls to help you so they can learn at the same time how to make them?"

This was the first of several meetings conducted with forbearance through which Ted Sr. sat, not listening, blinking, but well aware of their importance. The guest list was expanded, the sandwich spreads discussed, fine points reviewed over and over as if they were holding a series of Big Four conferences to shape the postwar world. Would the Van Leuvens come after the tragedies in their lives? Augusta, poor Augusta, she hadn't lived to see the day. They may come or they may not, but they must be invited. It might be too much for Isobel. How was she coming along? Everyone would understand if Gus and Mary D. came without her. The Sanfords would be coming, of course, and the young Sloanes. Why not invite them to bring the baby? An unusual idea, but it would be nice to have a baby in their midst on such a family occasion.

"What sort of punch are you going to make, Teddie?" his mother asked.

"I have Ben Swinton's recipe," Ted answered.

"Not that fruit punch he had for Genevieve's wedding!" Nelly gasped.

"No, Mother, of course not. His champagne punch recipe."

"But, Teddie, the expense. Champagne! Let me pay for it. Both the girls away at school this fall. How can you afford it?"

"I have two new contracts, Mother." Ted puffed himself up a little. "We can afford it and we want to."

And so, on the last Saturday in August under skies that were not too sunny but benignly hazy, not threatening rain, breezes blowing gently enough to cool the guests but not roughly so as to threaten the orderly transport of food and drink, the Osterhoudts' friends assembled in the garden. Ted had rigged up Emily's phonograph on the porch and found a record of the Wedding March. He'd had to buy the whole opera to get it and then had to learn how to cue it up.

It was agreed that the guests of honor would not appear until everyone had arrived. At just the right moment, Ted Jr. went into the house and told his parents it was time. He then preceded them out the back door and ran to his post by the phonograph. He put the needle in the right groove and the strains of the Lohengrin March rose over the babble of conversation. The back door opened, and his mother and father appeared. Ted Sr. had on his white suit and his hearing aid and had promised not to turn it off until the party was over. Nelly was wearing off-white chiffon, ecru, almost the color of bedspread cotton. "White-white" is for brides, she explained, but this is "off-white"—possibly the closest she ever came in her life to an off-color joke. Slowly and carefully, Nelly descended the stairs on Ted Sr.'s arm. When they had cleared the last step and were safe on the ground, the guests applauded and came forward to congratulate them. Ted Jr. let the phonograph finish the March before he turned it off and hurried to the canopy to pour himself a glass of punch. Then he called out.

"Please. A toast. A toast. Everyone, your attention, please. Get yourselves some punch and help me toast my parents."

"I want, first of all, to thank you for coming. We have been looking forward to this day for a long time, and it is important to us that we share it with our friends." He raised his punch glass in salute. "I give you my parents, married for fifty years today. A half century. Fifty long years together, for better for worse, richer or poorer, in sickness and in health."

"Fifty more," Ben Swinton called out.

"Hurrah," Jack Sanford joined in.

Nelly chuckled and looked up at Ted Sr., for a brief second seeing beyond the bald pate and faintly stooping posture to the erect young man with a glorious crown of black hair she had pledged her life to so long ago. "Poppy," she said into the hearing aid, "they want us to stay married for another fifty years. I'm willing if you are."

Ted Sr. beamed at the compliment. Gallantly he put his arm around his bride's waist and kissed her on the cheek. Then he waved to the audience.

"Fifty more. Fifty more years." Cheers and applause from all sides.

Later on, Katherine stepped forward to guide the couple to the canopy and the ceremony of cutting the three-tiered wedding cake; as the two right hands together cut the first slice, there were more cheers and applause.

At just that moment, a boy around fourteen, with curly dark hair, appeared at the back gate with a huge basket tied up in cellophane and decorated with wide gold ribbon. He looked around until he spotted Nelly, and then, without hesitation, walked up to her and bowed low.

"My grandmother said to say congratulations to you and Mr. Osterhoudt," he said in presentation. Fruit. The best and the freshest from Mrs. Mancuso to Mrs. Osterhoudt.

"Please tell your grandmother thank you very much from both of us," Nelly's bow was regal. "I shall walk over town the first thing Monday morning and thank her in person. And thank you for bringing this beautiful basket over. Come, have one of my little party cakes as a reward."

There were hundreds of party cakes, it seemed. With the 'wiches and the wedding cake, the guests at this Westerveldt ʼon reception had almost enough to eat, enough anyway to ʼir appetites for dinner. Little Jacqueline Sloane was brought over to Nelly, once she had sat down on a lawn chair, and placed in her arms.

"What a lovely child," she exclaimed before she handed her back to Jacqueline Sr. "I hope I live to see the day when one of my girls . . ."

Emily and Mary D. fled to the punch bowl to giggle out of earshot.

"No peace," Mary D. said after a hefty swig. "It'll never stop. First they tame us into little ladies who can't climb trees. Then they make us get good grades in school. Then they fuss and fume over us until we get properly married, and then they want us to have babies for them. No peace, no peace at all. How do we stand it?"

"If we act helpless enough," Emily whispered in return, "they won't make us have more than one baby. Did you notice? Aunt Jacqueline has been holding her all afternoon while Genevieve has been enjoying herself. I do not picture my mother doing that."

Then she bit her tongue. Isobel Van Leuven walked past them, evidently looking for Gus. She was smiling, but in such a vague way that no one could be sure why she was smiling or at whom. She wandered toward the edge of the lawn where it met the peony bed and began to pace the periphery of the lawn in slow steps.

"It's too much for her," Mary D. said. "I don't think we'd better stay much longer. I'll find Daddy and get her home."

As the guests began to leave, Ted Sr. relaxed to the point of joining Jeff Catsby in a cigar over near the ferns. Emily declared afterwards that she heard Roosevelt's name mentioned only once, although there were two other references to "that man."

Jacqueline Sanford, Baby Jacqueline still in her arms, took Katherine aside to tell her, "This is just what we needed. A happy day. And you know, my dear, This is what We're all about."

The Osterhoudts sank into chairs after the last guest had gone.

"Where's Mother?" Ted Jr. looked around. The canopy had just been taken down and there was no sign of Nelly anywhere.

"I'm right here, Teddie," she said from the door. "I went to get these," pointing to the small boxes in her hand. "This is the time to give them to you. You'll get the other things after I'm gone, anyway, but I wanted to say thank you."

She handed a box first to Katherine, then another to Emily, and the third to Beatrice. "Please open them now."

Katherine's held the ruby dinner ring Ted Sr. had given his wife on their twenty-fifth anniversary. Emily's a gold and seed pearl brooch and Beatrice's a string of gold beads. As the three women rose to embrace her in thanks, Nelly explained her gesture.

"I wanted you to have something to remember me by. Something I'd given you especially in memory of this lovely day."

———————